GARDEN OF THE DEAD

The grotesque creature rode the current's downwash toward her. Disa swam for the far wall and began to kick her way upward. An opening, there! She ducked in, still trailing her rope, and found herself in a dead-end pocket, floored in fuzzy, lumpy carpeting rather than rock. She started to retreat, but saw the guardian only a few feet outside.

The girl moved deeper into the pocket and turned so that she could examine the floor and watch the entrance all at once. The fuzzy gray lumps were plants, or fungus—a garden. A death field. Something caught her eye. A diving suit. A helmet.

A human body.

By Marti Steussy
Published by Ballantine Books:

FOREST OF THE NIGHT

DREAMS OF DAWN

DREAMS OF DAWN

Marti Steussy

DEL REY

A Del Rey Book

BALLANTINE BOOKS • NEW YORK

A Del Rey Book
Published by Ballantine Books

Library of Congress Catalog Card Number: 88-91973

ISBN 0-345-35233-5

Printed in Canada

First Edition: November 1988

Cover Art by Barclay Shaw

To my best and dearest circlemate

CHAPTER ONE

〜〜〜〜

Trim blond Kelda Nygren glared at the com receiver log. "Damn!"

Her fifteen-year-old daughter, Disa, sat puzzling over a physics assignment at the log cabin's only table, six feet away. Wide green eyes looked up at Kelda. "What's wrong, Mom?"

Kelda slapped her tool belt down beside the com console. "Message from Karg. And if First-In relayed it here by courier capsule, it's not good news." She punched for playback. "Urgent summons to Circle Dawn from Sweetwater Warren on Karg. Frilandet Colony has violated the settlement treaty. Please send a team immediately." That much of the message was in Kelda's own voice; she had recorded it twenty years earlier, before she had left Karg. The Kargans had remembered their transmitter instructions well enough to add a postscript in their own language: "Groundlings dying. Caused by human-gods. Please help."

"What the hell?" Kelda muttered. Sunlight filtering through giant ferns made dappled patterns on the window screen above the console. Kelda frowned and played the message again.

"Groundlings are dying?" Disa asked, her face crumpling. Disa loved Kargans. The girl spent more time with the aliens than she did with humans, Kelda thought. But such attachments weren't unusual for children raised in the multispecies kinship of a First-In circle.

Kelda's husband, Per, entered the cabin behind her. "What's this about groundlings?" he asked, as he wiped his machete and hung it by the stove.

Kelda smiled grimly at him. "You always said you wanted to visit Karg. Here's your chance. It seems Frilandet's broken its settlement treaty."

"What?" Per said, automatically ducking a low rafter as he crossed the room to the console.

Kelda played the message a third time. Per, sweating heavily after a morning clearing trails, mopped his forehead with a shirttail. "I wanted to see Karg—but these weren't the circumstances I had in mind." He took a closer look at the signal board. "What's the other message?"

Rattled by the news from Karg, Kelda hadn't noticed that a second message waited. The familiar voice of Circle Dawn's senior coordinator sounded less relaxed than usual. "To Dawn's Team Three from Dawn Core. You heard Karg's message. Per, Kelda, and Calypso, take our Kargans and the ship and find out what's going on. Stop by Regency on your way and pick up Sulman. Tell the rest of the team to keep working. I think if we push time-correction we can get a ship and some extra personnel to them in about six weeks. Good luck."

"Shit," Kelda said. She had joined First-In because she liked exploration. She loved working with her teammates on solving problems of climate, ecology, safety, and nutrition, clearing the way for a planet's colonization. But the interspecies exploration teams of First-In had developed fluency that brought translation contracts, and after translation followed diplomacy.

"Guess we better talk to Calypso," Per said. "I think she's testing her 'cheese.'"

Kelda nodded affirmation, then glanced at Disa. "Will you tell the Kargans?"

"Sure, Mom." Skinny and serious, Disa switched off her terminal and headed for the synthetic cave that the team's Kargans inhabited.

Kelda herself walked with Per down a fern-shaded path to the First-In team's small lab. Through the open door Kelda spied her teammate Calypso's bright anemone form. Chitin scales covered the alien's four-foot-high, one-and-a-half-foot-thick stalk. Algal symbionts swept in fantastic pink and orange swirls across the chitin. From the stalk's top emerged a compound eye and five deft tentacles, two of which gripped Calypso's supportive crutches, while the other three prepared to assay the riboflavin content of a "cheese" sample. "Greetingss," the alien said, her speech synthesizer adding a faint hiss to the words. Kelda nodded acknowledgment.

Across from Calypso sat Kelda's foster daughter. Yvette was eighteen months older and twenty curvaceous pounds heavier than Disa. The girl looked up from her DNA sequencer. "What's wrong, Aunt Kelda?"

"We have to take a little trip," Kelda answered. "To Karg."

Yvette's lips pursed. "I thought we were going back to Core!"

Kelda grinned. "Karg has boys, too, you know. I've even got a nephew your age."

Yvette frowned, but added no further objections. Calypso took the news less lightly. "What hass happened?" she asked, following First-In custom of addressing teammates in their own tongue.

Per answered in Calypso's Sheppie language. "Kargans say the colony has broken its settlement treaty. They say humans are causing groundlings to die."

"By what meanss?" Calypso asked.

"They did not say!" Kelda answered, frustrated. Why hadn't the Kargans given more information? She supposed the Kargans, primitive as their present civilization was, had done well simply to be able to activate the emergency message system.

"We are to pick up Sulman at Regency," Per added.

"That iss well," Calypso said. Kelda nodded agreement. Sulman and Calypso had helped negotiate the original Karg treaty, back when Kelda was only a bright-eyed recruit. She would enjoy seeing Suli again, now that she had her feet under her.

"When do we leave?" Yvette asked.

"As soon as we're packed," Kelda told her. "Let's get to work."

Disa groped through black dampness. As a toddler, she had been able to walk upright through the tunnel. As a tall, gangly teenager, she traveled it on hands and knees. A claw wrapped playfully around her leg. "Enki?" she asked into the dark.

A click answered Disa's query. She laughed, fumbled in her pocket, then reached toward the source of the click. Her hand met with something its own size, a highly dextrous set of pincers. She placed a cracker in them. "Here's your treat, and if Ea's around I've got one for him, too." Groundlings were sexless, but Disa had never been able to think of one as "it."

Enki made short work of the cracker and groped for more. Disa laughed and gave his pincer-hand an affectionate squeeze. "No. You know if you eat too much of my food you'll get sick. Now please let go of my leg. I need to talk to your mother." Enki clung a moment longer, then released the girl.

Disa crawled a few yards farther and emerged into a chamber the size of a small bedroom, where the elders usually lounged. Disa had brought no crackers for them—elders ate only the "honey" secreted for them by their groundlings. Two voices greeted her. She recognized the voice to her left as that of Enki's mother, Erishkegal. Risky, as she was called, was the younger and more fluent of the First-In team's two Kargan elders. "Welcome, Disa."

Disa nodded acknowledgment. The elder, although blind, would detect the gesture perfectly by sonar.

"Disa unhappy," Risky observed.

Had her voice cued the elder, Disa wondered, or had Risky's keen sense of smell detected the girl's agitation? Disa used a castanetlike instrument to answer. *Yes*. She continued in the rough gutturals of spoken Kargan. "Message came. Sweetwater Warren says groundlings dying. Caused by human-gods. Warren asks help. We go to Karg."

"Good!" said Risky's cavemate Inanna. Inanna seldom complained about the artificial cave, which she inhabited aboard ship or when the team worked in caveless areas, but Disa suspected that Inanna was bitterly homesick for Karg's huge limestone caverns. Inanna, who still had trouble with English, switched to her own language. "In Sweetwater Warren I will mate."

"I rejoice with you," Disa affirmed. Risky and Inanna had left Karg with six groundlings. Four had died, victims of their intense curiosity. If anything happened to Ea or Enki, the remaining groundling would have great difficulty providing enough honey for two elders. Yes, Risky and Inanna both needed to mate. "I rejoice with you also, Risky."

Risky, uncharacteristically, did not respond. Disa frowned and groped leftward. She felt Risky's claw first; it was big and strong enough to sever Disa's wrist. Following the arm back to Risky's cool shelled body, three feet wide and about a foot thick, she laid her hand on Risky's small manipulative claw and felt its tension. "What will Risky do?"

Risky's big claws chittered nervously. "I think of dreamer trial," the elder said.

Disa sucked in her breath. Dreamer trial! What would Risky be like as a male?

Inanna's claw began chittering, too, for in the normal order of things, a junior cavemate such as Risky never attempted metamorphosis to dreamer. "You will not leave me!"

"I will change Enki," Risky promised Inanna in their own language. "I will begin its change now. When I go to dreamer trial, Enki will be elder, be your cavemate."

Enki an elder, female, intelligent, and able to speak? Risky a dreamer, discovering the male Kargans' unknown secrets? Disa's eyes were wide from more than darkness. She rested her head on Risky's shell and listened to her speak of going home.

CHAPTER TWO

❧❧❧❧❧

FROM THE DECK OF A HASTILY COMMANDEERED FERRY-
boat, Skip Nygren stared upward. Sky and water, dark
when the ferry left dock, had brightened to clear blue and
aqua. Bandannas hung as banners from the ferry's railings. Machinery for loading silk bales from boat to space
shuttle had been shoved to the rear of the deck, and in
that space a dozen of Skip's friends tuned musical instruments. Skip winced at the cacophony. His brother, Hal,
might at least have let the colony's official band come!

Hal's son, Leif, stood with arms folded against the
breeze. "They could have picked a civilized time to land,"
the boy grumbled.

Skip found himself defending the expected visitors.
"Circle Dawn holds by its name. I suppose with its mix of
species, no time's more civilized than any other."

Leif's attention was elsewhere. "There it is!"

High above the sunrise, light flared, meteorlike. A
sonic boom followed, then came the screaming roar of at-
mospheric braking. Unlike the silk shuttle, which descended in an efficient, inflexible glide, the strange ship
maneuvered. It banked inland across the Meade River's

fertile valley and the forested hills beyond, then turned to
swoop low over Holmstad's harbor at the river's mouth.
The lander waggled its fins, signaling goodwill and a pilot
sure at his, her, or its controls.

Leif watched wide-eyed.

Skip's stomach tightened. The ship was going to land
inland of the barrier island, in the shallow, reef-filled
waters of Meade Sound. That pilot had damn well better
be good!

The lander skimmed the waves. It slapped once against
them, throwing up a diamond plume of spray. Then the
stubby ellipsoid craft stalled and settled. It floated high in
the water. Skip's nephew sighed. "That thing could land in
a mud puddle, couldn't it?"

"Umm," Skip said. Perhaps he shouldn't have brought
Leif. Hal, reluctant to have anyone at all meet this ship,
would exact payment in blood if his boy fell in love with
First-In.

Water steamed from a glossy white hull. Eastward, Frilandet's sun rose, its rays illuminating a starred circle on
the lander's side. That emblem was older than humankind
and recognized across the galaxy. Skip's borrowed boat
churned closer. As the ferry came within hailing distance,
the lander's hatch dropped to form a platform eight feet
above the waves.

A human woman emerged, blinking at the brightness of
the morning. Dawn light lent a rosy tinge to her white silk
uniform and short-cropped blond hair. Skip's sister,
Kelda, had always been a looker; now she was stunning.
Legs braced apart against sea-motion, she raised both
hands in greeting.

Skip ran to the ferry's railing, waving his arms. "Heg!"
The word, pronounced "hey," meant both hello and good-
bye. "Heg, Kelda! It's me, Skip!"

She shaded her eyes against the sunrise. "Heg, Skip!"
Her hands dropped even farther to form a trumpet.

"We're at firm anchor," she called. "Drift in slowly from this side, and toss us your lines."

Others joined Kelda on the platform, but Skip's eyes stayed on his sister. Ferry and spaceship bumped gently. While Kelda's companions secured mooring lines, she sprang lightly from the platform to the ferry deck six feet below. She seized Skip in an exuberant hug. "Heg, it's good to see you!" Kelda said.

Her boyishly short hair seemed strange to Skip. Women on Frilandet, as on MacKenzie where Skip had done his guild training, wore heavy braids. But the cut suited Kelda's personality and showed to good advantage the gem-decked hoop in her right ear. The gems, red and gold like the stars on the circle above the hatch, said that Kelda had pledged her life to Circle Dawn. Skip wondered where she had been and what she had done in the twenty years since she had left Frilandet. He had not expected to see her again. "Heg, yourself!"

She looked around. "Where's Hal?"

Skip's face shadowed. "He said anyone fool enough to get seasick staring at monsters was welcome to meet you, but he stayed home." Hal had said other things that Skip did not care to repeat.

"He hasn't forgiven me for joining First-In."

Skip hesitated. "You know Hal's feelings about explorers who meddle in the affairs of settled worlds."

"Is that why he refused us passage on the silk shuttle?" Kelda asked.

Skip took a deep breath. "He said there was no reason to subsidize you poking your nose into our business. Speaking of which, why are you here? First-In teams don't show up for social visits."

Kelda stared at him. "You don't know?"

He shook his head, reluctantly, eloquently.

She tipped her face like a small, bright-eyed bird. "The Kargans say you've violated your settlement treaty."

Skip's jaw dropped. "Us? The colony?"

Kelda nodded. "You didn't know?" she asked again. "Don't you *talk* to the Kargans?"

Skip spread his hands. "Since Ingrid vanished, no one's cared to chase crabs in the dark."

Leif winced, still haunted by his mother's long-ago disappearance, but Kelda's tears for her best friend were long since shed. Lost communication was what worried the First Innes now. "For thirteen years you haven't spoken to the Kargans?" she asked.

Stung by her expression, Skip switched to the colony's defense. "Look, don't blame me for the colony's attitudes! What do a bunch of crabs have to say to us, anyway?"

"Not much, if you aren't listening!" Kelda snapped, then stopped and rubbed her forehead. "Shit. You haven't heard anything from them at all?"

Skip shook his head. "Zip. What is it we're supposed to have done?"

"I don't know. The message was vague. Something about their young dying and it being the colony's fault."

Skip frowned. "We use groundling labor in the silk fields, but that's been going on for years. There's no associated mortality that I know of."

Kelda sighed and flashed Skip a conciliatory smile. "I guess we'd better go ashore and talk it over."

"Want a ride?" Skip asked, glancing around the ferry he had so hastily readied to welcome his sister home.

"That'd be nice. Our launch is a bit small for the full team. Is it safe to bring my circlemates?"

"What are you traveling with?"

"Just humans, a Sheppie, and the Kargans."

"You'll be fine for now. But I wouldn't keep Kargans in town overnight."

Kelda's gray eyes narrowed. "Didn't plan to. We'll camp on neutral territory. I don't want the kids exposed to ugliness."

"Kids?" Skip, envious of anyone with family, looked beyond her to the hatch. "You brought Disa?"

Kelda glanced up at the platform and beckoned. "We did. Girls, come meet your Uncle Skip."

Skip recognized Disa instantly from the fifteenth-birthday portrait Kelda had sent. Like her mother, Disa wore white, but her loose-fitting jumpsuit lacked First-In's starred circle insignia, and her ear was bare of jewelry. At five foot six the girl stood taller than her mother, but Disa had yet to grow into her height. She showed the stoop-shouldered, reed-thin gangliness of adolescence, whereas Kelda held her five-foot frame with the firm poise of a trained dancer or fighter. Disa's eyes, bright green in a delicate face beneath short blond hair, dropped shyly as she saw Skip.

Behind her walked a somewhat older girl, a lush dark beauty. Skip saw Leif, beside him, stare entranced. "My foster daughter, Yvette," Kelda explained. "Girls, this is my brother Skip you've heard so much about—and Uncle Hal's son, Leif," she guessed, correctly. Skip realized, belatedly, that he should have introduced his nephew.

A tall blond man pushed between the girls to place a ladder between the platform and the ferry deck below. Kelda caught his hand as he descended. "My husband, Per." She looked like a pixie next to him.

Per smiled. "I'm glad to meet you."

"And you," Skip said. Trust Kelda to find a man who looked like a Nordic god! Per was as handsome in person as in pictures.

"Let's get the formalities done," Kelda suggested. "Then we can talk."

She climbed nimbly up the ladder. Skip cued his volunteer musicians to readiness. Kelda ducked into the hatch and reemerged arm in arm with a pink paisley alien.

The band, distracted by Kelda's unusual companion, gave a distinctly amateur performance. Most colonists had

seen Sheppies twenty years before when First-In negotiated the original Frilandet treaty, but memory faded with
time. There was nothing faded about Kelda's companion.
He—she—looked just like a Sheppie from a child's car-
toon book: a fat, well-decorated squid. Two firmly mus-
cled tentacles curled around crutchlike supports. A third
tentacle embraced Kelda's shoulder, while the final two
waved at the colonists, who missed their notes as they
came under the scrutiny of the Sheppie's compound eye.

Skip frowned at the vibrant pink and orange of the
Sheppie's carapace. As a geneticist, Skip knew something
of what could and could not be accomplished with algal
symbionts. He decided that the Sheppie must have had a
dye job. A tasteless one.

The Sheppie didn't bother with the ladder. It gripped
the platform edge with three tentacles and vaulted over,
crutches swinging wildly until the stalk's suction foot met
the ferry deck in a firm plop. Upright again, the creature
bobbed its tentacles in ludicrous imitation of a bow. One
or two people laughed.

Next from the hatch came two brown, crablike groundlings, the only type of native Kargan most colonists had
seen. From the front of their three-foot-wide shelled
bodies extended arms with highly dextrous graspers
known as "hands," but what caught one's eye were the
next, much larger arms tipped by wickedly sharp, foot-
long pincers. Behind those grew the four pairs of jointed
legs upon which groundlings scuttled. If a mud-colored
groundling were flipped over, the so-called honeytit
through which it fed its elder would be revealed.

At first such nimble nocturnal groundlings had terrified
the Frilandena. Then humans discovered that if a nearly
intelligent groundling understood what was wanted, it
made a useful servant. So groundlings cleaned Holmstad's
streets by night and tended the colony's silk plantations.
As a concession to daylight, the circle's groundlings wore

dark goggles trimmed with First-In's white silk. Skip's companions stirred uncomfortably at such tacit inclusion of groundlings on the team.

Under proper stimulus, a groundling metamorphosed into a blind, amphibious, intelligent, female elder. Twenty years before, spurred by his sister's ungodly interest in First-In, Skip had crawled underground to peek at an elder. Most Frilandena had never seen one. The band's stumbling march halted entirely when two of those near-legendary creatures emerged from the First-In ship. Shaped much like groundlings but with stronger claws and thicker shells, elders weighed about seventy pounds apiece. They were white. Not bright decorative white, nor yet pale pearly white, nor even soft creamy white, but simple, uncaring, splotchy white as if someone had forgotten to color them. Heavy silk veiled the soft parts of their bodies, but Skip imagined that he glimpsed gill slits where cloaks fit loosely between claw arms and frontmost legs.

With eerie economy of motion, the elders crossed the platform and slithered down the ladder, clicking faintly as they sounded for bearings. The elders, like their groundlings, wore starred circles.

Kelda followed the elders down the ladder. Behind her came a man of perhaps forty-five, with curly hair, deeply tanned skin, shining dark eyes, and a dazzling smile. Skip recognized him instantly: Sulman, the First-Inner who had saved the colony from stereochemical poisoning, discovered the Kargans, and scandalized everyone with his flirtations. Skip glanced at the druggist, Erica. Her clarinet dropped from her lips as she stared at the visitor.

The Sheppie, the Kargan elders, and the silk-clad adult humans fanned into a half-circle, arm in tentacle in claw, facing the colonists. Disa and Yvette stood by Kelda on the right-hand side of the semicircle, while the groundlings squatted patiently behind. The musicians hazarded a final fanfare, then set their instruments aside.

Skip straightened his coat. "On behalf of Statsminister Halflek Nygren, greetings to your circle. May peace attend you on Frilandet." Kelda's husband, Per, frowned. Skip wondered what he had said wrong.

Kelda and Sulman took simultaneous half-steps forward and stopped, looking startled at one another. Sulman grinned, shrugged, and waved Kelda on. She moved smoothly to the half-circle's center. She had always had dramatic flair—their father had called it "exhibitionism," but Canute's standards for his only daughter had been strict. "Citizens of Karg," she said. "Circle Dawn gives thanks for your welcome. We come in peace and hope it deepens."

It was Skip's turn to frown. So they wanted to call his world Karg, using an ugly, guttural, crab name instead of the planet's chartered title!

"Allow me to introduce my circlemates," Kelda continued. The Kargan elders' names, assigned by a human mythologist twenty years earlier, were hard to remember, especially since Erishkegal and Inanna looked exactly alike. Many faces mirrored Skip's confusion. He did mark that the pink paisley Sheppie, whose real name was unpronounceable by humans, went by the nickname Calypso. He had heard that name before. Did many Sheppies call themselves that? he wondered.

Calypso shuffled forward to tap Skip's hands with two surprisingly warm, firm, tentacles. "I am pleassed to meet you, Masster Sskip." The voice, slurred but understandable, came from a box strapped around Calypso's stalk. "Pleasse exxcusse me briefly—I musst fetch ssome equipment, before we go to your ccity. Alsso, have you an enclossed sshelter on board? Karganss do not like the open."

"Uh—sure."

Leaving her crutches on the ferry deck, Calypso vaulted into the water. Skip shook his head, then turned toward the Kargans. Disa was kneeling to reassure one of the silk-swathed female elders. Elders ordinarily never left their caves. Skip hadn't thought how sea and sunshine must terrify them. He beckoned to Leif. "Show the Kargans to the pilot's cabin."

Leif, with an apprehensive glance at the elders' claws, nodded.

"I'll go along," Disa volunteered. "He'll need a translator."

"You, too, Yvette," Kelda said briskly. "Leif can answer some of your questions about the planet." Looking much happier, Leif headed away.

Disa spoke in a throat-grindingly alien tongue. Skip guessed it was Kargan, for the weirdly shrouded elders and their groundlings turned to follow Disa as she went with Leif toward the pilothouse.

Kelda smiled up at her brother. "You look wonderful, Skip!"

"So do you." By contrast, Kelda's childhood playmates were worn and graying. Suspicion crossed Skip's mind. "How old are you?"

She laughed. "Thirty-seven, standard subjective. Only about a year of transit loss."

"You look younger. You could be thirty-two, like me."

Kelda shrugged and smiled. "Good health, plain food, hard exercise, a man I love—I'm sorry I didn't get home before Dad died."

"I'm sorry, too. He swore about you more often and loudly than he spoke of Hal and me put together. You were his favorite, Kelda. You broke his heart."

"He understood why I went. He was proud of me."

Ready to change the subject, Skip fingered the fine shimmering fabric of Kelda's full-sleeved blouse. "This is ours, isn't it?"

"Certified Kargan silk—and we were the first circle in the galaxy to wear it. I noticed, when I flew the recon pass, how much land's in plantations now. Silk trade's done well?"

"*You* flew that landing?"

Kelda grinned impishly. "Just call me Pilot. Ship engineer, too. You'd be surprised the things I can do." She reached out to examine Skip's guild ring. "You've changed some yourself, brother. Grown up tall, gone to university, learned yourself to talk like Family—I'm still amazed Dad let you go."

"A boy has to call challenge sometime." Skip half smiled, remembering the fight. "And it was painfully obvious we needed a geneticist. I just didn't know what an outsider the offworld education would make me."

"Sometime while we're here, you should talk shop with Calypso. She's into symbiont microbiology."

"Symbiont microbiology—" Skip stared after the gaudy alien. "Are those colors real?"

Kelda smirked. "From Karg, in fact. It took a whole special procedure to adapt them to her body chemistry."

"The Calypso Twist!" Skip knew of that technique for getting right-handed proteins to interact with a left-handed system. He had used it extensively in his Master's Demonstration and since. "I wondered when you gave her name, but figured it must be common with Sheppies. A First-Inner developed the Twist? I thought it came from the big Institute on Challa."

"Nope," Kelda answered with obvious pride. "It came from First-In. From Circle Dawn, in fact."

Skip said the first thing that came into his head. "Your Circle must be rich, then."

Kelda frowned impatiently. "You know we aren't allowed royalties! The big corporations would quash us in minutes if we started competing on their turf."

"Oh." Skip hesitated, eyeing the crutches the Sheppie

had left on the ferry deck. "What's it like to live with the inventor of the Calypso Twist?"

Kelda laughed. "Drives us nuts. Calypso's a trooper and wonderful to work with. But she *must* have ninety minutes a day to fuss with her carapace!"

Calypso's return interrupted the conversation. The garishly decorated Sheppie spurted through the water pulling a streamlined seven-foot raft. "What's that?" Skip asked, helping the alien secure a tow line.

"Life-ssupport equipment. We Ssheppiess aren't comfortable sspending long periodss in your dry buildingss." Calypso's multilensed eye stared at Skip as she pulled aboard. "I have casst uss loosse from the lander. You may tell your helmssman we are ready to leave."

On the bridge, Skip found Yvette in lively conversation with Leif, while Disa soothed the Kargans who huddled together under a table. By the time Skip returned to the ferry deck, Calypso—evidently an extrovert—was quizzing the musicians about their instruments. Per and Sulman engaged the rest of the hastily assembled welcoming committee in conversation. Kelda remained at the rail, her expression a grim contrast to the merry morning sunshine. "You really didn't know there was a problem?" she asked when Skip rejoined her.

"No. How did you hear?"

"We left the Kargans a transmitter. They broadcast six months ago on Standard Distress Frequency. A little trader called *Blue Shadow,* docked at the silk station, logged the call and relayed it on the First-In courtesy net. Didn't you hear even that much?"

Skip shook his head. "The station's run on franchise— our only contact is loading and unloading the shuttle. Probably no one on Frilandet heard about the call. If anyone did, he didn't care—"

Hal owned controlling stock in the station. They both

knew how he would react to a distress signal from Kargans.

"If it's any comfort to Hal," Kelda said, "I don't like being here in the line of duty any more than he likes having me. This is a First-Inner's nightmare—a mysteriously broken treaty, an uncaring offender, and probably no third parties interested enough to intervene. The colony won't pay us, and the Kargans can't pay us. Ugly."

Skip looked again at her earring—seven jewels on a gold hoop, standing, he had heard, for the seven people of a circle who had died rather than stand aside while the treaty they had negotiated was broken. Surely Kelda, passionate though she might be, would not go to such idealistic extremes?

Kelda set her jaw. "Dammit, I didn't do anything to deserve being front and center in this mess!"

Skip shrugged aside his worries. Tousling Kelda's hair, he set the record straight. "You hacked off your braids, spit in your father's face, and ran away with First-In. You showed more courage than anyone since the Frilandena left Valhalla. But you went yourself one better when you decided to come back. Sister mine, the whole town's turned out to see what happens when you put foot to shore."

CHAPTER THREE

❦❦❦❦

KELDA STOOD AT THE FERRY'S BOW RAILING AND SUR-
veyed the crowd thirty yards away. She had landed on
planets that met her with gala celebration, and others
where military escorts whisked her away under tight security. She had passed through Regency Station where
every third shoulder seemed to bear the starred circle, and
she had splashed down in virgin wilderness where only
sailfish and water birds observed her coming. None of
those arrivals had been as uncomfortable as her arrival on
Karg.

Some three hundred people waited on the quay, an
enormous crowd for so early in the morning. Children
bubbled with curiosity. Here and there an old friend
smiled eagerly. But most adults eyed the ferry with sullen
suspicion. As Skip warned, Kelda's older brother, Halflek, had not come. So be it, thought Kelda. She could
greet a crowd without Hal's help.

With a final whine of its engines, the boat shuddered
against the pier. Homespun-clad longshoremen secured
mooring lines, latched heavy planks in place to serve as
ramp, and stood aside. Disa and Yvette herded the team's

19

Kargans from the pilothouse toward the other First-Inners at the top of the ramp. Curly-haired Sulman grinned at his comrades. "All ashore that's goin' ashore!"

It was late summer, and the still-cool morning promised to turn muggy. Kelda walked abreast of Sulman, her face deliberately relaxed and smiling. The planks bounced under Calypso's crutches. Kelda heard hostile murmurs when the Kargans began to descend, and despite herself her lips tightened.

As if to counteract the crowd's murmurs, Skip's musicians gave their march a final try. Music did not lighten the crowd's mood. The Frilandena fell back from their visitors, leaving open space where the pier touched shore. Kelda faced eastward, morning sun rippling on her white silk uniform and its seven stars. Her teammates once again formed a half-circle around her. Before Sulman could seize initiative, Kelda raised her hands. "Greetings to Karg and the Frilandena from Circle Dawn of the First-In. We come in peace and hope it deepens."

The situation demanded a colony response. The Statsminister was not there. Hal's son, Leif, stood ready to substitute, but he was elbowed aside by a man Kelda's age, moderately tall and solidly built, blond, blue-eyed, and bearded, as were most male Frilandena. He looked familiar to Kelda. A handful of his companions, two of them scarcely older than Disa and Yvette, gathered behind him in a half-circle facing First-In's. "On behalf of the people of Frilandet," the man said, using the colonists' name for their world, "and in the absence of our Statsminister, I note the arrival of Circle Dawn. May we ask why you come?"

Kelda took a deep breath and decided to try informal friendliness. "We thank you for your welcome. Some of us are from this planet, and it's been a long time since we've been home. I'm Kelda Nygren, and this is my husband, Per; my daughter, Disa; my foster daughter,

Yvette." Faces softened—people everywhere identified with family ties. Kelda nodded toward Suli. "Sulman's from Korsabad, but he's been here before." The crowd's hostility returned. Evidently they remembered who had discovered Karg's native population.

Expressions tightened more as Kelda introduced her alien teammates. "Also returning home are the Kargan elders Erishkegal and Inanna, with their groundlings." Kelda did not bother to name Ea and Enki—the colonists would never remember them, and the groundlings themselves would not notice the omission.

Each elder ducked courteously as her name was called. Disa had done a good job coaching, Kelda thought with maternal pride. She finished off her introductions. "Our Sheppie is named Calypso. She was here before, too."

Hoofbeats interrupted the blond man's reply. A uniformed courier rode through the crowd. His handsome gray mare moved in a banner-tailed, stiff-muscled prance that brought flecks of sweat to her shoulders. People stepped hastily aside.

Kelda gasped, glancing at her teammates. Did they understand that profligacy? On frontier planets aplenty, self-repairing, self-reproducing horses provided practical transportation and power. But on Karg, a horse could not graze free. That splendid animal competed for food with the spindly-legged, big-eyed children in the crowd. The horse and the children were southpaw—and Karg was a northpaw planet.

Kelda had had to explain it to Skip when they first arrived on planet. Kelda had been twelve, her brother six, and colony animals were dying horribly all around them. "Your body's made of things called proteins. Proteins are made of amino acids, strung together like snap beads, or hands linked thumb to little finger. Look at your two hands. Are they exactly the same?"

The child set down his porridge and examined grubby

fingers. "This thumb points this way and that thumb points that way."

"Can you turn your hands so they both point the same way?"

"Now one hand's upside down," Skip reported.

"But if you look at your right hand in a mirror, it matches your left." Skip ran inside, then came back nodding. He picked up his bowl.

"Amino acids are the same way," Kelda said.

"What are amino acids?"

"I just told you—the things proteins are made of. You get them from your food. There are two kinds, mirror images of each other. Like right and left hands. Our bodies use only the left-hand kind."

"What about Gerda?" Skip asked, looking at the spotted nanny-goat he had befriended on ship.

"Gerda uses the left-hand kind, too. Everything on Valhalla used the left-hand kind. All our food has the left-hand kind. But everything here uses the right-hand kind."

"Things don't look backward," Skip said, gazing up at the tree they sat under.

"The differences are in molecules. They're too tiny to see."

"If Frilandet is backward, how can our seeds grow?" Skip asked. They had spent the morning planting.

"Because water and soil minerals don't have right or left. They're like balls—they fit either hand."

"Ground's the same?"

"Yes."

"Then how come Valhalla got left hands and Frilandet got right?" Skip asked, interested in biochemistry already.

"You have to have all the same kind, or they don't fit together right. Some planets go one way, and some go another. Nobody knows what decides it. Just chance."

"We should have gone someplace with our kind of molecules." A lot of others said that, too.

"Frilandet was listed in the southpaw registry. Somebody made a mistake." And because they had bypassed First-In's assistance, the colonists were alone on the planet before they discovered the mistake.

"Is Gerda sick because she ate the wrong kind of acids?" Skip asked. His face twisted with concern as the goat nipped weakly at her bloated flank. She reeked of feces that spurted out in small drips and matted the hair on her legs and belly. Her kid was already dead, for under the stress of starvation and dehydration Gerda's teats were dry.

"Yes," Kelda answered.

"I should give her some of my food then."

Kelda, heartsick herself, had to snatch the bowl away. "No, Skip. Save the food for yourself. It has to last until help comes."

Help came as a team from First-In's Circle Dawn. Drawing on the combined expertise of nutritionist Sulman and microbiologist Calypso, the team developed a fermentation process that broke Karg's proteins into amino acids and converted the acids from right- to left-hand form. The gruel tasted awful, but it kept the Frilandena alive until their crops matured. The team pointed out that the situation could have been worse—Karg's sugars, at least, were stereochemically the same as those in humans.

Later, Dawn had used First-In contacts to locate northpaw draft animals, ones that could graze on Karg's vegetation and not compete with humans for precious southpaw grain.

But—a *horse?*

The messenger rode directly to the First-In team, forcing the man who had greeted them to step aside. The mare, wary of Calypso, stood stiff-legged. At fifteen and a half hands, her withers were higher than the top of

Kelda's head. The rider peered about. "Is there a Miz Kelda Nygren here?"

"Heg," Kelda said. The rider could hardly have mistaken her.

He extended a rolled parchment. "A summons from the Statsminister. He will receive you at seven this morning."

Kelda looked automatically at the sun, but its position told her nothing since she had not yet regained her sense of Kargan directions and day length. Her beacon—a navigator, communicator, distress alarm, and timekeeper, preset to local time—said 6:30. She clipped it back onto her belt and handed the offending parchment to Sulman. "Where?"

"The Statsminister's residence—about twenty minutes from here by foot." The messenger departed at a smart trot.

"I'll show you," Leif said in a low voice. Kelda was glad the boy had decency enough to be embarrassed by his father's arrogance.

Calypso swung a pace forward. Glad of support, Kelda yielded the stage. Calypso adjusted her synthesizer to make her voice audible to the crowd. "It appearss we musst depart promptly for the Sstatssminisster'ss ressidencce. But we thank you for greeting uss, and welcome all who wissh to sspeak to uss while we are here. May thiss and all planetss be placcess of freedom and plenty."

Surprised by her use of their own "freedom and plenty" slogan, the Frilandena broke into scattered clapping. Calypso turned toward Skip. "Allow me to recover my life-ssupport equipment from the raft. Then we will depart."

The dirtsiders, won for the moment by Calypso's deft speech, watched fascinated while the Sheppie unpacked and slid into a transparent dome-shaped tank, decorated around the bottom with its user's distinctive swirling pink and orange pattern.

"Sheppies are estuarine creatures," Kelda explained,

knowing that education could defuse hostility and suspicion. "They tolerate salt and fresh water at many different temperatures, and can function in air if they keep their skins wet. But for long periods out of water, they prefer to suit up."

Calypso slid her muscular tentacles into sensor webs that controlled mechanical arms outside the tank. She flexed the artificial appendages, satisfied herself that all was in working order, then activated the tank's air suspension. She floated to the man who had greeted them. With exquisite delicacy, she lifted a surrogate tentacle to his hand. "Pleasse exxcusse our hassty departure. I hope to ssee you again."

"Uh—sure," he said, nonplussed, as the team followed Leif and Skip away from the dock. "Heg, Kelda."

"Heg," she answered. She caught up with her brother. "Who was that, anyway?"

Skip looked surprised, then grinned. "Ole Hanson."

Kelda stared over her shoulder. "You should have told me."

"I thought you'd recognize him," Skip said.

Kelda tossed her head. "It's been a long time."

"Ole's no love-struck boy now," Skip warned. "Don't trust him farther than you can see him—he's made political hay at First-In expense. He wouldn't be here this morning, except he couldn't resist the chance to point up Hal's rudeness."

Kelda lapsed into silence. Leif looked acutely embarrassed. Disa lagged behind, crooning to the elders in their own language. *"Taka, tikagee."* The fans on Calypso's tank buzzed softly. Kelda saw Per stare curiously at a planet he had heard much of but never seen.

Holmstad nestled on the northern edge of the Meade River's delta, between river and plateau. Twenty years before, when Kelda left, the city had been a collection of tiny cabins, erected by colonists with too much to do and too little time to do it. Muddy ruts had wandered helter-skelter in whichever directions people traveled. Since then the main roads had been straightened, and a few even strewn with gravel. The cabins, built as temporary shelter, still stood, but they sagged in settled poverty, surrounded by pottery shards and broken cart wheels. Shabbily dressed children stared at the Kargans and Sheppie with dull hostility.

However bitterly the Frilandena claimed that Valhalla's taxes impoverished its people, Valhalla's back alleys looked nothing like this. Kelda avoided Per's eyes.

The ugliness fell behind as Skip led them uphill through an area that had been forest when Kelda left. Workers had cleared underbrush and small trees, leaving a few graceful giants to shade the broad smooth road. On either side, at a discreet distance from the street, sat well-kept houses with gaily painted shutters and doors. Beside them grew luxuriant vegetable gardens. Spiceberry bushes bowed beneath ripening fruit.

Kelda knew that Hal had done well, but still she stared when they reached his three-story mansion. A wide, neatly trimmed lawn stretched to the very foot of a limestone bluff on the right. Water splashing cheerily from the rock tumbled through a series of sculpted basins and finally into a tiny stream, which watered the paddock where the gray mare grazed. Around the fountain bloomed an exquisite semiformal garden.

The uniformed man who had delivered Hal's summons appeared on the porch—a butler? Ignoring him, Kelda struck across the grass toward the garden. Surrounded by elegant, golden-edged pink blossoms, she stared at the inscription on the fountain: *To Ingrid, Inge, and Borg Nygren from their husband and father Halflek.*

Per, Disa, and Skip had trailed her across the lawn. Disa frowned, puzzling out the unfamiliar script. "Borg and Inge were the twins Aunt Ingrid lost?"

Kelda nodded, troubled by the memorial to a niece and nephew she had never met. "Leif's brother and sister. They were just tots when they found what looked like strawberries, and like all tots, they stuffed what they found into their mouths." Their small bodies, already ravaged by frontier flu, had been too weak to deal with the Kargan berries' unexpectedly high protein content. "For God's sake don't taste any native fruit, Disa."

Disa sounded only a little impatient as she said, "I won't, Mother." Such cautions were second nature to a circling.

"You said Hal avoided everything Valhallan," Per commented as he fingered one of the pink and gold flowers.

"Mama brought the paxflowers," Kelda answered with a wistful smile. Their delicately sweet scent brought powerful memories. "She used her personal cargo allowance for them. Dad was furious." Brynhild, shorter even than Kelda, with lush blond hair in a heavy braid atop her head, had never submitted to Frilandet notions of wifely behavior. Neighbors had looked askance at the Nygren household's bickering, but Kelda was proud to be Brynhild's daughter.

"Is that why you chose them for your pledge crown?" Disa asked, glancing at Leif, who was leading the rest of the team toward the house.

"One among several reasons," Kelda answered, her eyes meeting Per's. Leif's group had reached the steps. "We'd better go inside."

"Heg, I'm Dana Nygren," said a pale but pretty woman in the front hall. Kelda straightened under the woman's curious stare. "The Statsminister will meet you in the reception room," Dana told the visitors.

Obedient to a custom she had nearly forgotten, Kelda pulled off her boots and set them with others by the wall. "Wasn't Dana a playmate of yours?" Kelda asked Skip as they walked, sock-footed, at the rear of the group. She

had never understood how her capable, congenial brother
had remained single. "Why didn't *you* marry her?"

"I was studying genetics on MacKenzie," he said
curtly.

Dana left them in a roomy hall with windows overlook-
ing the memorial garden. On a stand on a table at the far
end lay the colony's symbol of state, a silver hammer rep-
resenting Thor's lightning. A gloomy iron gong provided
thunder. Kelda vividly remembered the day Ole Hanson's
father, the colony's original Statsminister, had surren-
dered the hammer to Kelda's own father, Canute. "Whatever happened to old Einar Hanson?" she asked.

"Sixty-five and still irascible," Skip answered. "Determined to see the hammer in Hanson hands again before he
dies."

Behind the hammer hung a picture of Ingrid and Hal,
flower-crowned, pledge cups in hand. Kelda's eyes
brimmed. A door opened behind her. The butler bowed.
"His excellency, Statsminister Halflek Nygren."

Nygrens ran small. Hal, at five foot eight, was the tal-
lest and most heavily built. He had aged more than Kelda
expected, showing a definite paunch and worry lines in his
face. He stood erect in the door and saluted.

Kelda ignored the salute. She walked toward her
brother with outstretched hands. "I'm home, Hal."

"You're in my home. What are *they* doing here?" He
nodded his head at the elders, who crouched in the room's
darkest corner. The groundlings sat with them, their scent
whiskers lifted attentively toward Hal.

Kelda swallowed anger and disappointment. Hal had
never liked aliens, and losing Ingrid had doubtless height-
ened his antipathy. "You summoned the team. They're on
it."

Hal was not budging an inch. "I'll word the next summons more carefully. What else have you brought?"

Kelda reached for Disa with one hand and Per with the

other, guiding them forward. Yvette followed. "Here are your brother-in-law, Per; your niece, Disa; and her foster sister, Yvette." She would kill Hal, Kelda thought, if he was rude to her family.

Per extended a hand. "You have a fine touch with pax-flowers, sir. I've never seen Freya's Kiss bloom in such hot weather."

Hal stared thoughtfully at him, then took the proffered hand. "Heg. I always wondered what sort of man would marry Kelda." To Disa and Yvette he said, "Have you met my son, Leif? He's about your age."

Disa nodded.

"He's a most impressive young man," Yvette said, sounding ludicrously grown-up. Leif, who had faded into the wall when Hal entered, reddened.

Hal looked back at Kelda. "You brought some others, too."

Calypso, parked by the wall in her tank, bobbed demurely when Kelda introduced her. "Ssir." She knew Hal from her last visit here. So did Sulman, who inclined his head but did not pretend friendship.

"As soon as we finish here we'll pay our respects in the caves," Kelda told Hal.

Hal looked again at the Kargans. "Don't let me delay you."

Kelda, although bitterly disappointed by Hal's gruffness, stood her ground. "Before we go, what do you know about groundlings dying?" She wanted to know as much as she could before she entered the Kargans' subterranean labyrinths. She looked expectantly at Hal.

He sighed. "The station manager said you'd ask. I don't know what's riled the crabs."

Whatever Hal's other faults, he had never been a liar. Kelda turned her attention to more mundane business. "We need a place to stay."

"Not in Holmstad."

"I didn't say in Holmstad. What's happened to our old camp?" Located on a bluff three miles upriver, the site would offer water for Calypso, land for the humans, a cave for the Kargans, and easy but not too-easy access to town.

"We scavenged logs from the buildings. Other than that we haven't bothered it."

Temporaries, then. It stung to sleep under canvas coming home. But after their cold reception, Kelda would have turned down Hal's hospitality if he had offered it. "You can find us there if you need to. We'll tell you when we find out about the complaint." She hesitated, noting how Disa and Yvette watched Leif. They needed to learn to mix with dirtsiders, and they could probably do it better without adult interference. "May we borrow Leif for an hour or two?"

"Huh? Why?"

"I want Disa and Yvette to buy supplies, while our elders go down in the caves and the rest of us fetch equipment and pitch camp. The girls will need someone to show them through town. Leif seems intelligent and well mannered."

Hal rubbed his beard. "I guess there's no harm done. How will they get the goods to camp?"

"Ea and Enki can carry things to the river," Kelda said, indicating the two groundlings. "We'll meet them there with our boat." She turned to her teammates. "Let's go. There's a lot to be done. Heg, Hal."

"Heg, Kelda." A troubled expression on his face, he watched them leave.

CHAPTER FOUR

❧❧❧

DISA SAT ON THE ENTRYWAY'S POLISHED WOODEN FLOOR and tugged at her boots. "Mainly we need supplies for dinner tonight," Kelda said. "Don't forget Calypso. She can't forage here any better than we can." Sheppies were biochemically southpaw, like humans.

"Chocolate?" Yvette asked, with her most winning smile.

Kelda laughed. "What the hell. We deserve a treat! Leif can tell you what prices are fair and which things are local specialties. Uncle Skip says melons are good just now."

Disa wished her mother would quit calling him that. Yvette's father Jack had been an uncle. Kindly old Chan who ran Circle Dawn's training was an uncle. Even lady-loving Sulman, who had teamed with the family only since Regency five weeks ago, was an uncle. But a dirtsider Disa had never seen before? Couldn't Skip be "Morbror," as Per's brother on Valhalla was "Farbror"?

Kelda reached for her belt pouch. "Gold or star credit?" she asked Skip.

He handed his amber-stoned guild ring to his nephew.

"Let Leif credit it to my account. We'll settle later."
Didn't Frilandena use standard currency? Disa wondered.

She eyed her cousin. He stood little taller than Disa,
but he had hard wiry muscles and a deft confidence like
Kelda's. Slightly blemished skin and a fringe of blond
beard bespoke developing manhood. He slipped into well-
worn sandals, then opened the door for Yvette. Disa
scrambled to her feet and followed.

Sun shone hot and bright outside. The groundlings'
whiskers clamped in displeasure. Disa heard a faint clicking from Inanna. She knelt, concerned, for that sound
meant that the elder was near panic. "Caves soon," Disa
said in Kargan.

"Hate sun," Inanna responded. Disa rubbed the base of
Inanna's claw. She hoped Inanna's people greeted their
returning sisters more kindly than Hal had welcomed
Kelda's family.

Skip and Leif led the team toward town. The road split
at the edge of Hal's hillside neighborhood. "Meet us at the
west pier at nine-thirty," Skip told Leif. Disa glanced at
her beacon. Two hours.

Whistling to Ea and Enki, she followed Leif and Yvette
from the shady coolness of the lane between the mansions
onto the hotter, sunnier left-hand fork. Ahead lay shabby
log and clay huts like those Disa had seen on a half-dozen
other frontier planets. The huts seemed ugly and disrup-
tive, a cancer on the hillside. Disa far preferred the leafy
arbors used by biotechnological species. Yet she knew
that such technology could destroy an ecosystem or the
technology's own creators at least as fast as could the inorganic technology favored by humans. All a matter of
taste, Disa supposed. Her taste found the huts ugly.

Leif looked suspiciously at the groundlings following
Disa. "I thought those things didn't like daylight."

Disa reminded herself to be patient—after all, Leif
blamed the Kargans for his mother's death. "They aren't

things, they're people. Sort of. Their names are Ea and Enki. And they don't like daylight, but they like company so much that sometimes they come out in the day anyhow. Don't your groundlings like to be with you?"

"The Nygren family doesn't use groundlings," Leif said, sticking his hands in his pockets. "What do you need to buy?"

"Chocolate," Yvette answered. "And fruit."

Disa understood her friend's cravings. A scout ship, which orbited for months unattended, could produce at best salad greens and fast-maturing vegetables. But the girls had others to think of, as well. "Fish," Disa said.

Leif's freckled nose wrinkled. "Chocolate's easy. And fruit. We'll get that last since it's hard to carry. Fish you can't have."

"Why not?" Yvette asked. Her dark curls bounced as a stray breeze swept the street. All of Yvette bounced. Disa glanced at Leif.

"We don't have fish here," he explained. "Not our kind, I mean. We tried pond culture, but Kargan bugs and algae kept growing in them, and then the fish died. It smelled awful. Ole's store has smoked salmon from Valhalla, but it costs."

Disa had eaten smoked salmon on Valhalla itself. It tasted wonderful—but it was beyond First-In's budget. Besides, Sheppies detested processed food. "Smoked won't do. How about meat?"

"Expensive—it's hard to keep livestock safe from groundlings. But if you're willing to pay, Gunter makes really good jerked rabbit—"

"Don't you have anything raw?" Yvette asked.

Leif looked warily at her. "Don't you believe in cooking?"

Yvette giggled explosively into her hands. Disa giggled, too, at the vision of herself and Yvette wolfing huge chunks of raw dripping flesh. Disa pitied Leif's bewilderment, but each time she tried to explain, fresh laughter interrupted. She sobered when she saw a dirty-faced six-year-old stare at her from a yard of packed mud and scraggly weeds. "It's for Calypso."

"Was that what was so funny?"

Yvette snorted again. "You thought *we* wanted it raw!"

He looked embarrassed. "Who knows what First-Inners want?"

"Have you heard stories? Tell me!" Yvette teased, with bright spots on her cheeks.

Disa looked away. Dirtside voyeurs projected a great many fantasies upon First-In. Why did Yvette encourage it?

"Some other time," Leif said. "How much raw meat does your Sheppie need?"

"Pounds and pounds," Yvette answered, with characteristic exuberance. "She's a carnivore and it takes a high metabolic rate to maintain body temperature underwater. Of course Calypso can ferment nutritious rations from practically anything. But nutritious doesn't mean it tastes good. Calypso's unbearable when she has to eat gruel."

"Uncle Skip designs fermentations," Leif said. "He's a Master Geneticist. I'll 'prentice to him when I finish school. If I do well Dad'll let me finish on MacKenzie."

"I want to be a geneticist, too," Yvette responded, "but I'd rather go to the Institute on Challa."

Leif's eyes widened. "That's a Sheppie planet!"

"So?" Yvette asked carelessly. "I can swim."

The dirtsider looked bewildered. "I suppose you have to be a First-Inner."

"Not at all," Yvette said. "Money couldn't pay me to stay in First-In." Leif raised his eyebrows inquiringly. "You can't specialize," she continued. "With all the languages and learning basics in half a dozen fields, you can't expect to be tops in any one of them."

"Calypso's tops," Disa argued.

"She's a Sheppie," Yvette countered, as always when they had this discussion. "Sheppies live longer than we do and are smarter, and anyway Calypso trained before she joined Dawn."

Huts crowded the road, with narrow three-foot alleyways between. Only an occasional apple tree or staked tomato varied the brown. Adults lowered their voices and averted their eyes as the three human youngsters and the two groundlings passed, but Disa saw the surreptitious stares and heard the whispers. Everyone on Karg seemed to wear multiply patched gray homespun garments. She herself wore Karg's finest silk. Its cut and color marked her as First-In's own, even with no earring or starred circle.

She wanted to hide. Her mother would have chided, "Stand straight, child! Slouching won't make you invisible. Show the world what you're made of!" Easy for beautiful, competent Kelda to say. Disa balled her fists and tipped her chin up.

Yvette, whose rich dark coloring marked her even more a stranger, also walked with shoulders back and head high. Yvette loved to be stared at, Disa thought. The dark-haired girl was talking to Leif. "The real problem with First-In is you get killed. Or someone you love does."

"I thought you took good care of yourselves," he answered.

Yvette's chin trembled ever so lightly. "My father was killed on Tapachula two years ago." Disa flinched at the memory.

"What about your mother?" Leif asked.

"She was kidnapped by a terrorist strike team while she was pregnant with me. I was born in the pirate ship's hold. To let the rescue team in, she improvised a grenade and breached the ship. There was only one suit that worked.

She put me in that one. Vacuum killed her before the rescuers reached us."

Leif gaped, clearly caught between skepticism and his ignorance of circlings. Disa shook her head in mild amusement. Why did Yvette, so quick-minded and articulate, waste her talent on outrageous mother stories?

The road widened again as it approached the center of town. Sunshine danced off puddles in the ruts. Ahead on the left stood a plank building forty feet wide. Two women, knitting on the porch, watched the teenagers approach.

Leif inclined his head politely. "Heg, Miz Erica, Miz Hanson."

"Heg," Erica said. Disa recognized her from the boat. The woman nodded pleasantly at the girls. "Out for a stroll? Looks like a hot one."

"Burr's inside," Miz Hanson said, bobbing her head nervously at Disa and Yvette. "He'll take care of you."

"Miz Erica's our druggist," Leif said in a low voice, as he held the door for Ea and Enki. "Miz Hanson is Ole's wife. This is his store."

"Is he the man we talked to this morning?" Disa asked.

Leif nodded. "Einar's son."

Supplies and equipment of every description jumbled the store's interior. As her eyes adjusted to the dimness, Disa saw edible wares to the left, beyond the bins of nuts and bolts with their faint smell of machine oil. Most of the food was clearly local—rice and flour, fragrantly ripe peaches, and bins of potatoes and beans. Imported fish, pickles, crackers, and candies beckoned from the place of honor, a neat rack hung on the wall above the reach of small children's fingers. "If you want chocolate or fish," Leif said, "this is the place to buy them, but get your staples at the farm market. Ole's prices are too high."

"You criticizing our store, Nygren?"

A lank young man sat beside the produce scale in a

tipped-back chair. His beard was thickening into bushi-ness. Had Disa seen him in the half-circle behind Ole this morning? He looked the girls over. "Heg, Leif, you keep odd company these days!"

Leif lifted his chin. "This is my cousin Disa Nygren—"

"Too skinny," Burr said.

"—and her circlemate Yvette—"

"There's a fox."

"—and this is Burr Hanson."

"Mr. Hanson to you," Burr said.

Leif paled, but stood his ground. Yvette's weight shifted onto the balls of her feet. Enki and Ea, sensing tension, pressed at Disa's calves. Automatically she scanned the distance and direction to the door.

"We don't allow crabs in here," Burr said. "They make a real mess of the food."

Groundlings' curiosity got them into nearly everything, and most of all they loved human food. They would eat until the alien protein sickened them, and sometimes more. But Ea and Enki had been carefully disciplined. "We'll watch them," Disa promised.

"I said leave them outside," Burr growled.

The groundlings had experienced more that day than their limited intelligences could comprehend—transfer from scout ship to lander, splashdown, ferry ride, the strange sounds and smells of Holmstad, and long periods in bright sun. They were frightened and disoriented. Disa wanted the group together. Her throat refused to vocalize any of that.

"They're our porters," Yvette said. "They won't hurt anything, but we'll stand good for it if they do."

Leif twisted Skip's ring around his thumb.

The chair's front legs cracked against the floor. Burr stood. His frayed cutoff sleeves brushed work-hardened muscles. "Get them out or I'll carry them out. You get out, too. Hansons don't cozy to gypsies."

A groundling, no matter what the provocation, never attacked a person who had befriended it. The serrated claws could make short work of other assailants, as Disa had discovered at age four when Enki dismembered a wild doglike creature that attacked the girls. Would the groundlings classify Burr as friend or foe? Disa's right hand hung by her side. She snapped her fingers in the command that meant "back."

Yvette spread her a scornful glance, then looked toward Burr. "Our money's as good on Exchange as yours. You treat all your customers like this?"

Burr's fists tightened. "Move over, Nygren. I want to talk to this lady."

Leif stepped reluctantly but determinedly into Burr's path. "She's a guest, Hanson. You given up on manners?"

"Get out of my way." Burr struck at Leif. Leif dodged and lashed back. Burr, barely wincing at the blow, knocked Leif sideways into a potato bin. Yvette stepped forward. Enki's claw clacked—a threat display.

Disa grabbed Enki's shell in the hollow by his claw arm. "Come!" She hauled him toward the door. Ea followed, agitated.

"I wouldn't," Yvette warned Burr, who was sizing her up. "First-Inners don't start fights, but we defend like hell."

"I'm not gonna hit you," he sneered. "Wouldn't be fair."

"Come on," Leif said, extricating himself from the bin. "These potatoes are rotten anyway."

Disa yanked Enki out the door and gave Ea a reassuring pat. She didn't hear Burr's reply. Yvette walked out seconds later, with a flushed face and an energy in her steps that Disa recognized as fury. Leif followed, lips pressed angrily together.

The women on the porch lowered their knitting. "What's wrong?" Erica asked.

"Burr said he didn't want our business," Leif told her.

Miz Hanson bit her lip. "I'm sorry, Leif. Please apologize to your guests."

"Come on," Leif said. "Farmers' market's that way."

Burr emerged from the store. "Heg, Nygren! Come back some day when you're keeping better company."

Leif hurled a thundercloud look over his shoulder as he led the girls into the bright street. Burr stood insolently in the door, watching them go. Disa's shoulders burned under his gaze. She clenched her hands in her pockets to keep them from shaking.

"You shouldn't have run," Leif told her. "It just encourages him."

Disa had her reasons, but again her voice failed her. She swallowed and looked away.

"You okay?" Yvette asked Leif. "That was a nasty hit you took."

Leif rubbed his shoulder. "It was the potato barrel that got me. I'll be okay."

"Let me see," Yvette said as they rounded a corner. She stopped, blocking Leif, and began unbuttoning his shirt. He stood wide-eyed as a rabbit. Yvette prodded gently at his sunburnt shoulder. "I've had special medical training," she said. "Does this hurt?"

Leif flushed. "Feels fine."

Disa gritted her teeth. Yvette had played that game with at least three circle-cousins, and they had all fallen just as stupidly for it. "Every circling learns basic first aid," Disa told Leif.

"I'm glad," he answered, smiling rakishly at Yvette. Frustration added to the blur in Disa's eyes.

"What was Burr so touchy for?" Yvette asked, rebuttoning Leif's shirt.

He shrugged uncomfortably. "Hansons and Nygrens don't get on too well. Ole's opposition leader now. He encourages folk to blame First-In for every problem we have. That reflects badly on us since everyone knows Aunt Kelda and my mother worked with the team."

"Why didn't Burr's mother do something?" Disa asked. Miz Hanson had clearly disapproved of her son's behavior.

"She couldn't," Leif said. "Burr won his challenge two weeks ago."

"His what?" Yvette asked.

"Challenge," Leif repeated. "You know. When you fight your father. If you win you're an adult."

"What happens if you lose?"

"You fight him again next time you have an argument."

"What if you never win?" Yvette asked.

Leif frowned. "You can't marry without approval. You miss out on the inheritance. Of course some men pull their punches, give the son a break. Ole probably did. My dad won't. He says until I beat him fair and square he gives the orders." Seeing Disa's expression, he added, "Doesn't First-In have a challenge?"

Disa had heard her parents discuss this custom. She answered, like her father, "We're not savages."

Leif's mouth snapped shut and he walked stiffly ahead, not looking at Disa. She could not retrieve her words. Why did the cat take her tongue when she needed it, then give it back for this? She was glad to see a bustling open square ahead, full of people with baskets. Shoppers fingered an array of fruits, vegetables, and grains. "That's the market," Leif said to Yvette.

They encountered no overt bullying here, only a disturbing sequence of stares, whispers, and mothers calling small children to heel. Prices doubled at each stall the girls visited. "Come on," Leif said to a red-bearded farmer. "Dana bought a bushel of those last week at half the price."

The farmer shrugged. "Demand's up. First-In can pay, can't it? They owe us some."

What? The Frilandena owed First-In, Disa thought, for bailing them out of their stupidity and for keeping them alive to build their colony at all. But the demon in her tongue kept mercifully silent.

Shopping seemed to take forever. Holmstad shimmered with moist heat by the time the youngsters turned toward the dock. Enki and Ea dragged their loads of grain and potatoes without complaint. Disa's right sleeve unrolled to her wrist, and she could not roll it back up without setting down the melon balanced on her shoulder. The melon grew heavier each time she had to lift it. Even Yvette's bangs drooped with sweat. With relief Disa spied Kelda standing small and straight beside Skip on the riverbank. Kelda had shed her silk for a trim tan coverall with short sleeves. "Enjoy your tour of Holmstad?" she asked.

Disa didn't want to say, in front of Leif and Uncle Skip, that she hated the planet and its people. She looked at a lavender flower on the riverbank. Yvette kicked a pebble. "It was okay."

Skip frowned. "Find what you needed?"

Leif handed back the guild ring. "Not everyone wanted to sell," he said. "Burr threw us out of Ole's store."

"What?" Kelda exploded. "Goddammit, Skip, you said this place was civilized! Who the hell is Burr?"

"Ole's eldest," Skip told her. "Won his challenge two weeks ago and he's trying his wings now."

"Leif got a bruised shoulder trying to defend us," Yvette announced.

"I fell in a potato bin," Leif muttered.

Ea and Enki waited by Disa, hunching nervously as groundlings did when they felt exposed. Kelda assessed their cargo, the set of her shoulders still showing disapproval. "Anybody else hurt?"

Disa and Yvette shook their heads.

"Then let's load the boat and get out of here."

"You want any more help setting up?" Skip asked.

Kelda tossed her head. "No, thank you. I think we've had all the colony contact we need, for today."

Skip looked irritated and regretful. "All right. But come off your high horse, Kel. We're not the only colony that suffers from prejudice." He looked straight at Disa. "I'm truly sorry. I had no idea Burr was minding the store. Come on, we'll help you get this stuff in the boat."

First-In's launch rocked beside a rough but solid pier. Enki and Ea crawled into a niche beneath the deck. Skip and Kelda stowed groceries in a stern compartment. Disa and Yvette seated themselves on the bench amidships. Disa felt eager to be gone. Kelda, never one to hold a grudge, jumped lightly from the boat up to the dock and hugged Skip. "Thanks, brother."

"I'm sorry again about Burr," he said. "Let me know if you need anything."

She lowered herself into the boat's pilot seat. "Let us talk to the Kargans first. Heg!"

"Heg, Yvette!" Leif called. Skip prodded him. "Heg, Disa!"

"Heg!" they called back. Kelda bumped the throttle, and the small boat swung away from the pier.

The launch's motor, designed for use around Sheppies, ran near silently. Water bubbled softly under the hull. Birds circled overhead. Leftward on the delta Disa saw rice paddies and fields of Valhallan wet-wheat, as well as native rushes.

To the right, beyond a driftwood-littered beach of mud and sand, limestone bluffs rose thirty feet to the more gradual hills of the forested plateau. Shrubs and vines cloaked the bluff faces. Disa wondered which dark recesses opened into caves and which were merely shaded niches.

"Tell me what happened," Kelda ordered.

"We walked into a store to buy chocolate," Yvette said, sounding less cocky than she had on shore, "and a stuck-up bully ordered us out. He said they didn't allow groundlings, but I don't think he liked us, either." Her voice wavered. Disa's resentment softened a little.

"It came to blows?" Kelda asked.

"Leif and Burr swung at each other. Neither of them knows how to hit. Disa ran. I meant to teach Burr a lesson, but it was over before I got a chance."

"Leif didn't seem very surprised," Disa said.

"The colonists have been shut up with themselves too long," Kelda answered curtly. "Don't let their peeves upset you. They're just dirtsiders." She swung the boat northward around a wooded point. Ahead floated the welcome bulk of the First-In lander. Buoys marked Calypso's underwater camp.

With the ease of long practice, Sulman and Per had raised temporary shelter on a stepped bluff above the river, exposed to breeze and protected from flood. Steps cut by the previous team provided access to and from the beach. Disa saw a dark opening in the hillside behind camp—the cave entrance. She shivered in excitement. How soon would Kelda let her go into the cave?

Kelda cut the motor, a courtesy to their water-dwelling circlemate. "Grab a pole, Disa." Disa lifted a long, lightweight shaft from its stowage along the side and helped push the boat toward shore. The river appeared to be at a late-summer low. Disa nearly lost her balance as the boat received an invisible push. Kelda laughed and tapped on the floor, Sheppie code for "thanks."

Per, wearing a farmer's coverall, spotted them from the clifftop. "Heg!" He nimbly descended, reaching shore in time to help Kelda half beach the boat. "Find some dinner?"

"Melon," Yvette said.

Per waded into the shallows. "Heg, kids. Let's keep you dry until you get those clothes off." Yvette demurely wrapped her arms around his neck and let him carry her to shore. He deposited her on dry sand and returned for Disa. "Where's your smile?"

"Leif's friends don't like us," Yvette said.

"The girls met some pushy dirtsiders," Kelda explained.

Disa said nothing.

Sulman helped unload. "Looks wonderful. When do we eat?"

"Get a nosebag," Kelda told him. "No fancy dinner until we've talked to the Kárgans."

Disa, on her feet again, started for the steps. Per's hand restrained her. "Want to talk?"

She managed a smile. "I ought to change."

"Find me when you're done," he said.

The team carried equipment in modular containers that expanded into small huts. Yvette stood in the unit that held personal gear. She was already half undressed, her silk shirt in her hands. "This thing needs washing. I haven't sweated so much since Tarshish."

Disa stripped off her own uniform. "Leave it for tomorrow. We need to talk to the Kargans." From the compartment holding her tumble of camp clothes, she pulled a smoky blue top and shorts.

"You think it's too warm for my green blouse?" Yvette asked.

"Suit yourself," Disa said, transferring her knife from her white dress boots to her favorite sturdy brown footgear. "See you later."

Her father waited unobtrusively outside, examining a glossy green, thick-leaved bush with fist-sized rough-husked fruits. "Silkfruit," he said. "Let's go for a walk."

They went down the steps. Kelda and Sulman were transferring groceries to the kitchen unit, which stood on the beach so that it would not attract animals to the sleeping area. Per and Disa waved, then turned upriver along the broad flat beach. Disa walked near the water where dampness made the sand firm. Per surveyed the smooth round rocks farther up, chose a disk-shaped one four inches across, and sent it skipping across the river's flat brown surface. "What happened?" he asked.

Disa kept her eyes on the wavelets at the water's edge. "A boy told us to get out of his store. Said they didn't cozen to gypsies."

Per walked in silence.

"None of the Frilandena likes us," Disa added.

"What makes you think that?"

"They stare. They whisper. They pretend they don't see us. They raise prices."

"I'm sorry," Per said. "We didn't know it was so bad."

"Why do they hate us?"

Per skipped another flat round stone across the water. "It goes all the way back to the settlement, Disa."

"I thought Circle Dawn saved their lives."

"It did. People don't necessarily thank you for that. According to the Orion treaty, we could have evicted the colonists when we discovered the Kargans. We didn't. The colonists don't remember that. They remember being cooped up for six years while we learned the Kargan language."

At the end of that time, Disa knew, the Kargans had surprised everyone by inviting the colony to stay. The First-In team had had severe misgivings. Humanity's history of cohabitation with aliens made depressing reading. Human xenophobia and aggressiveness had taken their toll on planet after planet. "The Orion treaty gives you control of your own world," Dawn's team counseled the Kargans. "Send the colonists away."

But the Kargans, citing a legend that said that their planet's ancient civilization had fallen through failure of hospitality, persisted in the invitation. The Frilandena, by then self-sufficient and exploring the commercial potential

of Kargan silk-making techniques, accepted. Circle Dawn
had worried about the situation ever since. "The Frilandena know we thought they should leave," Per said.
"They suspect we still think it and they fear we can force
it."

"Can we?" Disa asked.

Per's face was grave. "I don't know, sprite. The Orion
treaty gives us power to issue the order. But whether we
could find a signatory to back the order is another question. I hope it won't come to that."

"Me, too." With anyone else, Disa would have stopped
there. To her father she said, "I wish Leif would like me."

Per sat down on a driftwood bough. "Come here,
elfling." The childhood nickname, an embarrassment
when others heard it, warmed Disa. "I know you do. I
want him to like you, too. But his whole life, Leif's heard
poison about First-In and our family. Maybe he'll come
around. Probably he won't. Try not to worry about it."

Disa leaned against Per's shoulder. Gentle arcs of water
lapped shore. Disa's throat hurt. She wanted Leif's re-
gard. But dirtside and circle mixed poorly. Disa was old
enough to know that.

"The team has something to ask you," Per said, his arm
cradling Disa.

She pulled away to look him in the face. His expression
was serious. "What?"

"We're meeting the native elders as soon as Risky can
get it arranged. You know Kargan better than any of us.
We'd like you to speak for the team."

Disa straightened, startled. "Me? Why? Couldn't Calypso..." Her voice trailed off, her thoughts in turmoil.
Yes, she did speak Kargan better than the adults, better
even than Calypso. Was this why she had been made to
listen to so many lectures on First-In tradition and procedure? To speak for the team, in so delicate a situation!

Per's hand remained lightly on her shoulder, the touch

bespeaking sympathy and concern. He did not push for an answer.

Disa's eyes searched his face, then she nodded. "All right."

Wordlessly he extended his arms. Disa fell into the hug. "I'm proud of you," her father said.

Silently Disa returned his embrace.

CHAPTER FIVE

❧❧❧❧

DISA AND HER FATHER RETURNED TO FIND YVETTE AND Sulman playing whizdisc on the beach. Kelda sat cross-legged in the shade, reviewing records of Dawn's last visit to Karg. She stood when she saw Per and Disa. "About time you got back!"

"Never hurts to explore," Per said. "Time to go underground?"

"Risky said to give her another half hour to arrange things," Kelda answered. "Get yourselves something to eat."

The sun stood a handsbreadth shy of zenith. Disa claimed two of the peaches she had bought in town, and fresh rolls stuffed with spiced boiled egg. Before she finished the meal, excitement overwhelmed appetite. She returned the second peach to its basket, locked the kitchen unit, and hurried up the bluff steps.

The team had set their cache of climbing, diving, and caving gear near the dark entrance to the Kargan realm. Kelda joined Disa and Per in the small equipment-packed room. "Wear diving suits," Kelda told them. "We won't go underwater, but we'll scramble some."

"Is it that hard to get to the meeting place?" Per asked.

"No—just a crawl and one easy vertical descent. But we might go sightseeing."

Disa shucked her clothing, since excess fabric interfered with a suit's thermal exchange. The suit applied state-of-the-art space technology to the special problems of underwater work, and it would provide superb protection against rock cuts and abrasion. The diving garment's tough elastic cling brought pleasant memories of hours spent underwater with Sheppies and other beings. But it tugged too tightly at Disa's hips and strained at shoulders, chest, and toes. She had been growing.

Kelda had fitted their climbing helmets with lightweight, forward-angled lights that shone in whatever direction the wearer looked. Disa frowned, checking the lamp on her own helmet. "Has this been charged?" she asked.

"Yes, but I damped the output. You know what Kargans think of light."

Disa nodded. When she visited the synthetic cave that Circle Dawn's Kargans inhabited, she took no light at all, but then she had learned those tunnels before she could speak. She needed no light there.

Once suited, Disa thrust her feet back into the old high-topped brown boots. She tightened the soft cuffs to keep loose sand out.

"Here," Kelda said, kneepads in her hand.

The diving suit's pockets could easily have held Disa's spare light, first-aid kit, canteen, jerky bars, and the modified castanet by which she pronounced Kargan names. But Kelda warned that odd bulges might create difficulty in the cave, so Disa stuffed the gear into a soft-strapped climber's pack. "Where's Calypso?" she asked as she submitted to Kelda's double-check of her equipment.

"She'll come in underwater. Our route is difficult for her to negotiate. Let's go."

Sulman was sitting with Yvette at the cave's mouth beneath a flat limestone ledge, telling her about the groundling who had pilfered a seismic monitor twenty-five years earlier. Chasing the thief into this hole, Sulman had discovered Kargan civilization. "Remember," Sulman cautioned as Disa and her parents joined them in the chilly draft of the entryway, "radio waves don't penetrate rock —beacons won't work underground." Actually, Disa knew, the beacon that accompanied her through work, meals, play, and sleep would continue to track time and position, but she sobered at the thought of losing its help-summoning ability. "Everyone stick together. If you get lost, stay put." Disa's heart pounded as she followed Sulman into darkness.

The mud-floored passage, fifteen feet wide but low enough to make Per duck, led gently, crookedly into the limestone. Cool damp air fanned Disa's face. "These lights are useless," Yvette complained. "Couldn't we use regular ones and turn them down when we meet the Kargans?"

"This is the Kargans' home," Sulman reminded her. "Here we play by their rules. Your eyes'll adjust."

The corridor widened to a room with a ceiling twice Disa's height. Sulman stopped, waiting for the others to catch up. "Turn your lights off," he ordered, "and see what a cave's really like."

They obeyed. As her eyes adjusted to darkness, Disa saw faint illumination from the entrance. "This is the Front Porch," Sulman said. "It's as deep as light comes. Beyond this we're in elders' territory."

"I'm nervous," Yvette said with her usual bluntness.

"Ain't we all," Sulman muttered.

"I'm just glad to stand up straight," Per said.

"Enjoy it while you can!" Kelda told him. "I'll lead from here, Suli." She switched her light back on and ducked into a three-foot-high opening on the far side of the room.

Disa followed, hunching through in a duckwalk, wincing as her helmet grated on the ceiling. By the time Disa had gone fifty feet, quick-moving Kelda was nearly that far ahead of her. "We lost the rear guard," Yvette reported from just behind Disa.

Disa relayed the message to her mother, then sat down on the cool damp floor. Yvette caught up and settled herself beside Disa. Both girls looked about with intense curiosity. Odd round brown lumps, a quarter of an inch to an inch across, clustered on the tunnel's walls and ceiling. "What are those?" Yvette asked. "They look like turds."

Kelda had turned her light off. "They're called popcorn," she answered from the blackness ahead. "Made of calcium carbonate deposited by seeping water."

"I thought travertine formations were pretty," Yvette said.

"Wait till you see the lake," Kelda replied.

Per, on hands and knees, rounded the bend behind the girls. He looked thoroughly uncomfortable wedging his big frame through the low passage. "Disa, tell your mother I will make her pay for this."

Kelda giggled. "Not my fault you're overgrown."

"Have to be, to control you," Per quipped. Disa grinned. Her father wiped sweat from his face. "All right. Let's go." Everyone began crawling forward again.

Kelda waited on a ledge where the cross-tunnel opened onto thin air. "Watch your step," Sulman warned from behind. "There's a pit there."

Disa dropped to hands and knees and peered over the edge. Her light reflected on water and rock thirty feet below. Gingerly she looked upward. The cylindrical cavity extended at least another fifty feet above her. Falling water spattered her face. Something moved at the edge of her vision.

"We've got company," Per said.

Risky crouched on the far wall of the pit. Her shell

looked very like the limestone around her. "Heg," she said.

Disa answered with the Kargan equivalent. *"Daqua."*

"Where be other elders?" Kelda asked in Kargan.

"We meet Sweetwater's elders later," Risky said in English, with some difficulty. "First hear voices of *graf*."

Disa inhaled sharply. All her life, from Kelda and the Kargans themselves, she had heard stories of the *graf*— the "ancients"—and the hall they had left behind. But to get there the group had to descend that pit. Kelda had already anchored a rope and donned a climbing harness. "Belay me, Per," she said, turning on her stomach and feeling with her toes for a niche in the rock below. "Our old ladder's here, but I don't trust it."

"You want me to lead?" Sulman asked.

"Don't be silly," Kelda said. "Okay, I'm down. Send Disa next. There's a good foothold four feet down and to your right. Don't trust that rock by your hand. I think it's crumbly."

Halfway down, a heavy, fetid smell assaulted Disa. "Something's rotting," she said.

"Silkfruit," Sulman answered from above. "There's a fermentation room to your left. It was my first clue that something was going on down here."

Disa glanced sideways, spotted the side tunnel leading to the fermentation room, then returned her attention to the descent. As she reached bottom and stood aside for Yvette, Disa thought again of the mock cave that Dawn had constructed for the Kargans. Although the circle had stretched to meet the costs of constructing, transporting, and maintaining that cave, the elders considered it cramped, uninteresting, and insubstantial. Standing in the natural Kargan cave, staring at the dome vanishing into blackness above, Disa understood their frustration. Water dripped irregularly down the dome's sides, eroding them into delicate flutes. Multiple tunnels branched away at different levels. How homesick the Kargans must have been!

When all reached bottom, Risky led the team north-ward through a narrow cleft that quickly expanded to a canyon as wide as Hal's reception room and five times as high. Soon it contacted a parallel, even larger canyon containing a lake. "We call this the Meeting Hall," Kelda said.

From the ceiling hung glittering white stalactites. A stone waterfall cascaded motionlessly into the far side of the lake, twenty-five feet away. "Sso here you are," a voice from the dark water said. "My path wass much eassier."

"Does this lake connect to the river?" Disa asked.

"It openss to a sspring beneath the Meade," Calypso confirmed.

"That means be careful swimming," Kelda warned. "If the river's rising, water backing into the cave can suck you under." Disa swallowed.

"Will you join us in the Hall of Voices?" Sulman asked the Sheppie.

"I will ssee you there," she said. The lake's smooth surface broke into ripples as Calypso submerged behind her guide, Risky's cavemate Inanna.

Fifty feet beyond its interface with the lake passage, the Meeting Hall ended in a tumble of rock fallen from the ceiling. "Here," Risky said, perched atop the boulders to Disa's right. "Follow wall."

Scrambling over, around, and under sharp-edged boulders, Disa appreciated the protection of her sturdy diving suit. Twice she unslung her pack and pushed it ahead of her as she squeezed through crevices. She was tired of rock and mud and thought longingly of her jerky bars. Then she reached the other side of the rockfall and forgot discomfort.

She had emerged into a chamber 150 feet across. Once it must have had a low flat ceiling, but successive layers of rock had fallen into the center to leave a high, stepped, roughly bowl-shaped top. By the far wall a cylindrical dome, like that which Disa had just descended, pierced the roof.

Someone had removed the rubble fallen from above and polished the limestone floor to a gloss. Flowstone curtained the walls and hung in delicate rippling draperies from the ceiling. Water dripped downward through the giant dome. It struck an exquisitely tuned array of crystal pipes, in liquid harmony reminiscent of windchimes. Finally the water fell to a wide still pool in the floor.

As quietly as she could, Disa moved aside to let Yvette through.

The pond rippled as Calypso and Inanna surfaced.

No one spoke.

Kelda had said that it was all right to walk around, so long as one did not touch the flowstone on the walls. Oil from one's skin would divert the dripping water and leave the curtains marred, centuries hence. Disa walked to the edge of the pool and extended her hand. Cool water from above bounced from her fingers.

The pipes were *colored*—ruby, sapphire, emerald. Twenty years before, Calypso had found algae, frozen in flowstone on the walls, evidence of lamps set in the niches. Evidence thousands of years old.

"*Graf* worshipped here," Risky said. "Then gods came. They offered kinship, if *graf* lived in peace. But no, *graf* reached for power of gods. They used it in betrayal. Sister threatened sister. Plague broke free. The *graf* died for their quarrel. Only we remain. We keep this place for its beauty, and to warn us from *graf's* errors."

Disa stared from the chimes to blind Risky and Inanna. For how many generations, centuries, millennia, had blind Kargans scoured flowstone from this floor and cleaned the colored pipes? How long had they pondered the price of hubris?

No wonder Kargans cherished peace.

Hush reigned for several minutes. Then Sulman settled himself cross-legged on the floor behind Disa. "From dust are born the suns, the seas, and life," he chanted softly.

"Dust we are, to dust we shall return," Disa replied automatically. What a fitting place for the ancient litany!

Per's resonant voice joined Sulman's. "It swirls in hope and song, and then swirls on."

"But dust does not forget the dream that stirs it," Kelda said with Disa. Yvette remained stubbornly silent. She had not spoken the litany since her father's funeral two years ago.

Risky and Inanna echoed the chant in their own language:

From stone are hatched dry air, wet water, life;
From stone comes egg, and so in stone rests fossil.
Desire and thought shape stone, and then are gone,
But stone still shakes with steps of those who've
    walked it.

The pool's surface shivered visibly as Calypso sang the litany in the deep wavelengths of Sheppie. When all had finished, only the chimes spoke—a soft random melody akin to silence.

Long acquaintance with the ritual sent Disa into calm. She knew her people's presence threatened Kargan peace. Her people? No, she shared nothing beyond a few genes with Hal and his Frilandena. Disa's people were the humans and aliens who spoke the litany with her, who shared her conviction that the Kargans must suffer no second tragedy.

But stopping tragedy took more than mere conviction. Two years earlier, just before Uncle Jack's death, he had taken Disa and Yvette to their first diplomatic conference. "I want you to know what First-In is," he had said. Attending that conference, the girls had seen how First-In diplomacy sprang from split loyalties—loyalty to circle, loyalty to kin. They had watched Per, Kelda, and Jack stand with alien circlemates at the rough interface between species, soaking the strain into their own souls. Days later they had seen Jack pay with his life for the team's misjudgment of a human colony's sincerity.

Today, because she had been cradled by Dawn's Kargans, because she spoke their language more fluently than any of her seniors, Disa had to do more than watch. Her body tensed at the thought. She closed her eyes, breathed deep, and recited again the Litany of Dust.

For nearly an hour, they listened to the *graf*. Then Risky rose and clambered back up the rubble heap. Silent but for a few words of assistance to one another, the humans followed.

Calypso and Inanna, having returned by their underwater route, waited in the Meeting Hall. Native elders nestled in solution pockets on the walls. By itself on the floor lay some object draped in silk. Disa wondered briefly at the fabric's wild, swirling colors, then realized that the blind elders had no concern for the dye characteristics of their fermentation bacteria.

"This is it, huh?" Yvette asked, a quaver marring her nonchalance.

"Yep," Sulman said.

Disa's heart pounded. Was she really going to stand and talk to an ancient race about the death of its young? She felt Kelda's hand on her shoulder, an unexpected squeeze of reassurance. Did Kelda remember how it felt to be young and uncertain? "You'll do fine," Disa's mother told her.

Yvette, so smoothly capable in Holmstad, stood silent. Disa took a deep breath. "Dad, are you ready to record?" They would review the meeting with Risky later, to screen for misunderstandings.

"Ready."

"Sweetwater's elders wait," Risky prompted.

"Let dusst'ss dreamss guide you," Calypso advised.

Disa switched her light off, trusting to the diffuse light from her comrades' helmets. She turned toward the native Kargans. *"Daqua."*

A big elder with well-worn claws advanced toward Disa. *Snap-click* went Risky's claw, giving Disa's name in Kargan. *Buzz-click.* That must be the other elder's name.

"Daqua, snap-click," the elder said.

"Daqua, buzz-click," Disa answered, fumbling as she tried to form the unfamiliar name with her castanet. She stooped for the elder to probe her face with a scent-sensitive whisker, then went through the motions of re-ciprocation. To Disa all elders smelled like mud, but a chip on the front of Buzz-Click's shell, barely visible in the dimness, would aid later recognition.

Disa repeated the ritual with eight more elders, and each of the elders repeated it with all the humans and Ca-lypso. By the time they finished, Disa's hand cramped on her castanet.

"Daqua," Buzz-click said again when they finished. "We welcome you. Why have no gods come since *click-tap's* death?" she asked in Kargan, the only language she knew.

Disa wished the Kargans would not call humans and Sheppies gods, or that humans had chosen some other translation of the Kargan word. But since Kargan legend, like that of so many other races, saw technology as pursuit of divinity, the usage was logical. Who was Click-Tap?

"Aunt Ingrid," Kelda said, before Disa voiced the ques-tion.

Disa's palms sweated wildly as she glanced at the silk-draped form on the ground in front of her. She tried to wipe her hands, but the diving suit was nonabsorbent. She wet her lips. "How died *click-tap*?"

"Guardians."

Disa's heart pounded harder. The mythical monsters of the dreamer realm? Perhaps not so mythical.

"Where?" Kelda asked, impatient.

Kargan coordinates told Disa nothing, but she understood the statement that went with them. "She sought dreamers," she explained in Kargan, out of courtesy for the elder.

"*Click-tap* spoke dreamers?" Per asked. As linguist he had spent a career puzzling over First-In records of the dreamers.

Buzz-Click's claw grated. That meant "yes." "But then guardians took her."

"Shit," Kelda said in English, her face crumpling. Disa knew how close her mother had been to Aunt Ingrid.

"We have something for you to smell," Buzz-Click said, moving toward the covered lump.

Translation was one thing. "Smelling" was quite another. Disa looked to her circlemates for help. Nobody saw her frantic appeal. They were staring at the lump.

Buzz-Click pulled the silk aside. The lump was a dead Kargan.

"Smell," Buzz-Click ordered.

Disa knelt, trembling. The thing smelled rancid. It had no shell. A dreamer? Judging by the holos Disa had seen, a dreamer should not have air-slits, nor so much color. "What?" Disa asked, her agitation turning the Kargan word into an almost unrecognizable squeak.

"A changeling."

Disa stared at the body, while her mind raced through its knowledge of Kargan physiology. Groundlings molted yearly even after they reached adulthood. They foraged on the surface and fed "honey" to their cave-bound elders. Then one year, a groundling's elder, its mother, might feed it from her own modified honeytit. Instead of molting, the changeling's shell thickened. Its brain grew. Its eyes degenerated. It learned to breathe water. It became an elder, to replace the mother who then sought dreamerhood.

Disa knew the word "changeling" because Risky, anticipating the visit to Karg, had already initiated her groundling Enki's change.

The changeling on the floor hadn't made it.

"What happened?"

"*Gigg.*" Disa did not know the word. Neither did the mechanized translator Kelda handed her.

"Nixx," Calypso said, when Disa looked for help.

"Misbegotten," Yvette said. "A freak. A stillbirth."

"How do you know?" Kelda asked.

Yvette's voice spoke distress. "A couple months back, in the genetics lab, I tried a Calypso Twist on some testers. The pups were awful, misshapen. I tried what Disa does, went to the cave to cry. Risky asked to feel the pups. She called them *gigg.*"

Discussion confirmed Yvette's translation. The lump was not just dead but deformed; the changeling's development had gone fatally awry. "Why?" Disa asked.

"We know not," Buzz-Click answered. "We thought gods knew."

"Why?" Kelda blurted.

An hour of painstaking questioning established the facts. A few changelings, perhaps one in sixty, had always gone *gigg.* But through the years of Frilandet colony's presence, the rate had risen. It varied directly with length of exposure and proximity to the colony. In caves closest to Holmstad it now reached one in six.

"Shit," Kelda said again.

Disa thought about Enki and swallowed hard.

"If thiss cannot be sstopped, the colony musst leave," Calypso said.

Disa imagined how Leif would take that news. Yvette was right—First-In brought only heartbreak.

CHAPTER SIX

ᔕᘓᗯᔕ

TWO DECADES HADN'T CHANGED THE SET OF KELDA'S JAW when angry. Skip knew, stepping onto Hal's veranda to greet the team, that trouble lay ahead. "Heg. What's up?"

"Where's Hal?" Kelda asked.

"Waiting for you in the reception room."

Kelda stormed through the open door and stooped in the entryway to pull her boots off.

"Let me talk today," Sulman said.

Kelda kicked the right boot away and reached for the left. "He's my brother."

"That's why you should let me talk," Sulman told her.

"You are both headsstrong," Calypso said. The Sheppie increased the lift on her tank to bring it up the porch steps. "Pleasse allow me to moderate."

Kelda clenched her teeth but nodded consent. That impressed Skip even more than Calypso's credentials as bacteriologist had.

He spied Leif hovering at the top of the staircase. Yvette saw Leif, too. "Are you coming to the meeting?" she asked.

"Of course. My dad expects me to know what's going

on." Skip suppressed a smile, recalling how bitterly Leif usually complained of his father's policy.

Once again Dana led the group to the big reception hall. A table had been moved into the center. Hal waited by a big captain's chair at the far end. He nodded the First-Inners toward the armless chairs along the sides. "Bring us some tea, Dana."

Skip took a seat.

Hal turned to Kelda. "I thought I made it clear: Kargans are not welcome in this house."

"I thought I made it clear," Kelda retorted, "that they are my circlemates and as kin to me as you are. Hal, we found out what happened to Ingrid."

Hal froze. Leif bit his lip. Skip's pulse pounded in his ears.

"What?" Hal asked, ashen.

"She went down to find the dreamers. Her diving gear was missing, wasn't it?"

Hal shook his head. "I don't know. I don't remember. It was a long time before we went through her things. We'd have given the gear to Leif if it had been there." Rarely had Skip seen Hal so nonplussed. Hal's eyes sought his son's.

Leif, who had been four when his mother disappeared, shook his head. "I don't have it. I never saw it."

"She was wearing it," Kelda said. "She went to find the dreamers. A guardian got her."

Skip frowned. Hal voiced the question in both brothers' minds. "A what?"

"A guardian. Water monsters that live in the dreamer tunnels."

"A *what*?" Hal roared. "Who told you? How do you know?"

Skip saw Kelda blink, but she didn't pull back. "We asked the elders. As you should have, thirteen years ago."

His whole face distorted, Hal lifted his arm, then

dropped it without striking. "What happened to the body?"

"They put it in a garden," Kelda said. "Where they bury their own dead."

"Ingrid would have liked that," Skip said. Ingrid had shown more empathy for aliens than Kelda herself did.

Hal only laughed harshly. "A sea monster got her, and the natives buried her with honors? Don't you ever come to me with crap like that again. And don't you ever bring crabs into my house—"

"We assk your forbearancce," Calypso said. "The elderss attend becausse our disscusssion materially conccernss them. If you prefer, Sstatssminisster, Firsst-In will hosst future conssultationss." This alien has savvy, Skip thought.

Dana returned with a frosty pitcher of iced tea. She set the tray on the table by Hal and filled a glass for him. "Will that be all?"

"That'll be fine." He dismissed her with a flick of his hand. "Leif, I thought you had homework."

"I finished it last night."

"Let the boy stay," Skip said, filling the other glasses and passing them around. "You want him to know how a colony's run."

"Your wife doesn't qualify to drink tea with us?" Kelda asked as the door closed behind Dana.

Sulman glared at her. Calypso spoke up. "We have not come to quesstion domesstic arrangementss."

"You might consider gagging Kelda," Skip muttered.

Per, sitting beside Skip, pressed his lips firmly together, but the corners of his mouth quirked upward.

Hal refused to let his attention be diverted. "I take it you've decoded the crabs' complaint," he said to Kelda.

"We spent most of yesterday afternoon in the caves," Sulman replied. Skip leaned forward to catch his words. "According to the Kargans, Frilandet Colony's presence interferes with the groundlings' first change."

"Their what?" Hal asked, propping his feet on the table's undercarriage.

"First change," Sulman repeated. "The transition from groundling to elder. The changelings are malformed. They're dying."

Hal sipped at his tea, then set the glass down on its hand-carved coaster.

"Why?" Skip asked.

"We don't know," Sulman said. "That's what—"

"Then why the hell do you accuse us of causing it?" Hal grumbled.

"Shut up and we'll tell you!" Kelda snapped. She gave statistics.

"Why are they telling us this twenty years later?" Hal asked.

Kelda answered. "Because it took awhile for the problem to develop, and longer for the pattern to emerge. And because they had no way to communicate with you."

Hal crossed his arms. "It seems the Kargans' problem, and yours, not mine."

Kelda's right hand came down in a fist. "You're killing them, Hal!"

"That's only an inference."

Skip drew breath for an answer. Kelda's husband beat him to it. "The statistics are as plain to you as to us, Statsminister," Per said mildly. "Perhaps you could help us identify the toxic agents."

"On the data you've got, the problem could be anything," Hal retorted. "Crop runoff, bacteria, fumes from shuttle fuel, anything!"

"That'ss why we need your help," Calypso said.

"It's not our problem."

"If it's not solved, it will be," Kelda told her brother.

Hal's eyebrow's lifted, artfully, a hairsbreadth. "Oh?"

"Frilandet Colony's chartered under the Orion treaty. If you threaten a native—"

"You don't take that overidealistic treaty seriously."

"Your colony's chartered under that treaty!"

"A formality."

"A formality with a lot of folks sworn to uphold it—"

Per cut Kelda off. "We just want help setting up tests."

"No," Hal said. "We haven't time or money for research into matters that don't concern us. And as for threats—"

"I'll help," Skip said, wondering why he was sticking his neck out.

Hal glared. "Frilandet paid for your education. We expect you to use it in the colony interest, not on some esoteric inquiry—"

"Dammit, Hal," Kelda retorted, "it was the Kargans who paid for Skip's education! They invented the silk-processing technology, and their groundlings care for your plantations."

"My education's getting stale anyway," Skip said. "I need a good research challenge."

"What about the fiber project? People are getting tired of gray mutton hair."

"If you didn't export all the silk, they could wear that!" Skip replied, angered by Hal's presumption of control over his life.

"Silk's too delicate for everyday. You promised to find us something sturdy and comfortable."

"I did. A native flax. And the adaptation for cultivation is three-quarters done. Leif and I can do the rest in our spare time."

"I'll be monitoring," Hal warned.

"You do that. I assure you the Frilandena will still get their money's worth from me. Has it occurred to you that

I might learn something worthwhile with this Kargan project?"

"Excuse me, sir," Leif said to Hal. "I'd like to work with Uncle Skip on this."

"What the hell?"

Leif paled but stood his ground. "Miz Calypso is one of the finest bacterial geneticists in the galaxy. I could learn a lot working from her. It would be a real plus on my résumé when I apply for guild training on MacKenzie."

Hal had wanted desperately to study offworld, Skip knew, but there had been no money then. His older brother's eyes sought Skip's. Skip nodded confirmation of Leif's argument.

"All right," the father said heavily. "See that it doesn't interfere with your schoolwork." He looked at the First-In team. "Have we anything else to discuss?"

They knew they had gotten all they could get for the time being. "Not now," Per answered.

"Heg, then," Hal said. He lifted his voice. "Dana! Let's get this table moved back!"

In the entryway, Sulman turned to Skip with a wry grin. "Thanks, Master Nygren."

"Call me Skip," he answered, self-conscious and still not sure he should have volunteered. Sulman's Sheppie teammate twisted gracefully within her tank as she maneuvered it through the door and down the steps. "Will we be working with Calypso?" Skip asked.

"Of course."

Skip found his sandals amid the jumble of shoes in the entryway. "Does that mean we'll have to work—uh—underwater?"

The First-Inner laughed. "Hell, no. We outnumber Calypso, and she's amphibious anyway. She'll come up on shore with us. Why don't you come out to camp this evening? We'll feed you, show you around, and see if we can't map out an experimental protocol."

Skip smiled back. "Okay. Around five?"

"Sounds good. Bring overnight stuff in case we run late." Sulman and the other First-Inners set off down the hill.

"Heg," Skip said. What had he gotten himself into?

CHAPTER SEVEN

◈◈◈◈◈

SWEAT RAN INTO SKIP'S EYES AS HE ROWED A BORROWED skiff upriver. He was not as fit as he once was, he noted, but the First-In project promised to correct that.

Per, in a loose white cotton shirt, khaki shorts, and bare feet, but hatted against the afternoon sun, helped Skip pull the boat ashore. "Heg! I hoped that was you, breaking our perimeter."

Skip glanced over his shoulder. "You have this place under guard?"

"Remote sensors," Per said apologetically. "Warns us if a bear wanders in—or hostile townfolk."

"The caution is probably justified," Skip said wryly. He lifted a package from the bottom of the boat and handed it to Per. "Don't set it down too hard. There's a bottle in there, for you. And a couple other contributions. Where is everyone?"

"Down in the caves," Per answered, peering under the wrapping. "Spiceberry wine? And chocolate! I'm too big to fit comfortably underground, so they left me to cook dinner and meet you." He hesitated a moment, then stuck his hand out. "Let's not play games. I'm Per Sørenson and

I'm very pleased to have you as brother-in-law."

Skip stood with his mouth open. So Kelda had married into Valhalla's ruling Family! No wonder she had been silent about her husband's past. Dad would have crossed the galaxy to wring her neck, had he known. Belatedly Skip gripped the proffered hand. "I'm pleased to meet you, too—I guess—Kelda never told us where you were from or who you were—"

Per grinned crookedly. "Now you know. I understand Sørensons are unpopular here."

"It's not that, it's just—well—"

Per shrugged. "Funny. Within the circle Kel and I seem like twins—we grew up with the same language, same customs, same holidays, knowing the same history. Here that common history is supposed to make us irreconcilable enemies."

"You know what they say about family quarrels," Skip answered. "I'm sure Valhalla feels the same way about Frilandena."

Per hesitated.

"Don't they?" Skip asked.

"How many Frilandena were there?" Per countered.

"Ten thousand, nine thousand of whom emigrated—" Skip's voice faltered as he saw Per's point. Populous, prosperous Valhalla had scarcely noticed the group's departure. Anger washed over Skip as he realized that the enemy he had hated his whole life didn't bother to reciprocate. Arrogant Sørensons! Yet once Skip got beyond his stock Frilandet reaction, he liked the man's plainspokenness. They walked together to the pot of nondescript mush that Per had left simmering over a compact hydrogen stove. "One doesn't think of First-Inners marrying," Skip said.

Per stirred the mush. "Not all of us do. Somehow the circles always seem to get more men than women—although of our own children, the girls are more likely to join circles than the boys. Anyway, we have a sex-ratio problem, and it's a pretty stressful life. If a couple splits, their whole team suffers with them. So the circle won't witness pledges unless it's convinced they'll hold."

"What does everyone else do?"

"Unattached folk usually join up with established couples or each other, have someone to eat breakfast with at least. But it's not quite the real thing. Yvette's father Jack was born for a cozy hearth and half a dozen babies around his knees. He never did find the right woman. I can't tell you all the dirtside sluts that courted his discretionary pay, then kissed him off." Per sounded angry.

"And Sulman?" Skip asked cautiously, not sure how much Per knew of his wife's past.

Per shrugged. "Suli's human. He responds when the dirtside women crowd round. Not just harbor scum, either. Women with talent. Kelda's type."

"I'm surprised you turn him loose on settled planets."

"Why not? He likes it. The ladies do. Circle medics can handle social diseases. And it keeps him out of our women's hair. Not that they don't like Sulman, but sharing a frontier cabin with Suli and two or three like him can get tiresome."

"So you folks usually team with Sulman?"

"Not at all. He gave up on frontier work right after he left here. Too bad, since they say he could sort out a planet's nutrition faster and with fewer testers than anyone else around. But killing even so few testers bothered him. He's been doing diplomacy the last twenty years. We called him off another job to join us here, just because he knew the place." Per added water to the mush. "You married?"

"Not anymore," Skip said. A pretty fellow journeyman on MacKenzie had made it clear that she had no interest in out-of-the-way Frilandet. Hal had meanwhile snapped up Dana. Skip moved in briefly with someone else, but she had been too good a Frilandet wife. He tried to push the girl into standing up for herself. The harder he pushed, the lower she bowed, until they parted in bitter frustration.

The silence broke when Per handed Skip a spoon. "Think this stuff's fit to eat?"

"Tastes all right to me," Skip said, inwardly wincing. No wonder First-Inners weren't fat.

Per took a sip himself and spat. "Liar. Some sage, you think?"

"Wouldn't hurt." They doctored the porridge from awful to mediocre. "You always eat like this?" Skip asked.

"First weeks on a frontier planet we do—we're on dehydrated supplies until we see what happens to the testers, and a spice kit can do only so much." Per made a face at the mush. "Makes you sympathize with Ea and Enki—they're perpetually on rations. No wonder they keep trying to steal our food."

"It makes them sick, doesn't it?"

Per shrugged. "The protein does. But they can digest our carbohydrates with no problem. I suppose they're just eager for variety."

"Where do you get northpaw food for them?"

"From northpaw circles. Which took some arranging. First-In's no more set up for northpaw/southpaw interaction than the rest of the galaxy is."

"I'd have thought First-In would be different."

"Hardly. Worlds trade with ones like themselves. And *nobody*— present company excepted—disputes territory or asks for exploration across protein or sugar lines. There's no work for mixed circles."

"Why don't you transfer the Kargans to a northpaw circle, then?"

Per hesitated. "They're shy. Risky and Inanna wanted to stay with people they knew. And—what species were the Kargans here going to interact with? We needed a Kargan/human team standing by."

"You didn't think we'd honor our treaty?"

"Let's say we weren't sure how things would work out. You're not the first colony to attempt cohabitation and run into problems." Per dug at the mush with his big spoon. "Dust, I hate diplomacy!"

"I bet it's not Kelda's strong suit, either."

Per grinned as he covered the pot. "You're right. But her energy and earthiness are real assets on a strange planet."

"Dad was the same way."

Per moved toward a firepit farther up the beach. Skip followed, helping his brother-in-law scavenge firewood. "You sound like you spend most of your time on the frontier. Why's that?"

"Frontier's safer," the First-Inner explained. "There all you've got to fear are accidents. Get into diplomacy and danger comes looking for you. That's how we lost Yvette's father."

Leif had said as much. "What happened to him?"

Per picked up a two-inch-thick driftwood branch. "He put himself between a band of Triop refugees and a human mob, two years ago on Tapachula."

"Why?"

"Same reasons we're here now. Because he felt responsible. Because he'd approved the landing. Because he was all the safety the aliens had." Per broke the branch across his knee. "It was an ugly way to die. And bad timing with respect to Yvette."

"What about her mother?" Skip pressed.

"Contract baby. Born to a well-placed lady of the Ching Family, who declined to join First-In but thought highly enough of Jack to send him away with a daughter."

Skip chose his words carefully. "Leif somehow got a different impression."

Per frowned as he began to lay a fire with minute twigs of driftwood. "Yvette has a lively imagination. It's been a problem since Jack died."

"How long has she been with you?"

"We started teaming with Jack when Yvette was six months old. So the girls grew up with each other, us, and Jack; and usually the Kargans and Calypso. That Sheppie's superb with children."

So Yvette and Disa had grown up with three human parents—not so different from Skip's own participation in Leif's upbringing, except that the circlings had alien sponsors, as well. "It must be tough to grow up with no constancy of place."

"That's why we're careful about constancy of people. Dawn makes a point of not shifting young families from team to team. But now both girls go glitter-eyed for boys. We meant to return to Core for three or four years, let them work out their crises in a stable setting—"

"Core is the main body of your Circle?" Skip asked, handing Per an armload of fuel.

"Yeah. It travels on contract like the rest of us, but always a big enough assignment to support the administrative folk, retirees, and trainees. The rest of us come and go around the edges. Anyway, the summons from Karg changed our plans. We wondered about putting the girls in school here." He looked inquisitively at Skip.

"You'd want them in the university-track class?"

"Certainly."

Skip wet his lips. "That class is limited to those students we can afford to send offworld." Slots were assigned by merit, for the colony's need to cultivate its best talent overrode Frilandet convictions about apportionment by ability to pay.

Per's eyebrows rose. "Given Frilandet attitudes, I'm surprised you send youngsters away."

Skip, educated offworld himself and not fully committed to Frilandet isolationism, shrugged uncomfortably. "Colony's not big enough to support its own university, and we do need the advanced specialties. Anyway, there are only enough instructional units for the students with scholarships."

"No problem. Disa and Yvette have computers."

Rich bitches, Skip thought, in a reaction conditioned from childhood.

Per watched Skip closely. "A problem with that?" he asked.

Skip wiped his face with his hand. "Sorry. Here a private computer means rich parents trying to cover for kids who can't make the grade on their own."

"Our girls can make the grade. The reason they've got private instructional equipment is they've never had access to regular schools."

"It would probably work fine."

Per eyed his little pile of sticks, then stood, dusting his hands. "We'll try it, then. Did I see an overnight pack in your boat?"

Skip nodded. "Sulman said—"

"Good. Bring it up top and I'll show you the rest of the camp."

Skip followed Per up the bluff. There wasn't much to see, just a twenty-yard clearing where underbrush had been hacked away, with a handful of prefab buildings strewn across it. "Privy's over there. One-seater." Skip noted that the team had placed it downstream of the spring. "Next to the cave entrance is the equipment cache. Suli will show you round this little hut later—it holds lab stuff. Here we stash personal gear. The locks keep it from walking away with strange groundlings."

Skip peered curiously around the hut—just a big wardrobe, really, its walls lined by chests and drawers. The team's formal silks aired by a screened window on the opposite wall. Skip recognized Kelda's by its smallness.

Disa's had a bright blue sash, and Yvette's a red one; neither bore insignia. "When do the girls join your circle?"

Per hung Skip's pack from a clip on the right-hand wall. "They won't. A circle doesn't admit its own children. They have to go elsewhere, where there won't be questions about favoritism or inbreeding. Yvette wants money and security, so she'll probably leave First-In entirely." Per pulled his hat off and tucked it in a drawer. He ran fingers through his hair. "Disa loves diving and has talked of moving to Atlantis, but she'd go crazy bored without aliens. She'll have to choose a circle and win admittance the same way I did."

"Which was?" Skip asked, following Per back outside.

"Spent a season in First-In work camp. Cleaning up after a plague. Nasty. But it got me what I wanted." Per sat on a mossy rock in the long shadow of the hut. "I look for Disa to have an earring before she's nineteen."

Skip lowered himself onto another chunk of limestone and looked around. "Where do you sleep?"

Per grinned. "In the hut, if we have to. It can hold five if you face the same direction and don't eat beans. Or you can sling hammocks. Usually we sleep outside."

Skip was opening his mouth for another question when a gaggle of brown bubble-headed monsters emerged from the cave. Had the Kargan elders finally emerged to cleanse intruders from their planet? No, the monsters were too big and wrongly proportioned. The smallest took its head off—revealing Kelda, covered from nose down with dark sticky clay. Only her bright-yellow hair and her forehead, hitherto covered by the helmet, remained clean. She brushed her face with a dirty gloved hand.

A taller monster was Disa, an even plumper one Yvette, and biggest of all, Sulman, grinning broadly as he stretched and looked across the river. "What a beautiful sundown! I thought I'd never stand straight again."

"Me, too," Kelda said. "Caves depress me, but big

news down there. Heg, Skip!" She smiled hospitably. "Be with you as soon as we unsuit."

Yvette had already unsealed her suit; she had nothing on beneath it.

"Don't take it off yet," Kelda scolded. "You need to rinse it first."

"Where's Leif?" Disa asked with a shy glance at her uncle.

"His dad had chores for him," Skip said, not wanting to say that Hal saw Disa and all her teammates as bad influences.

"What's your news?" Per asked Kelda.

A grin cracked her clay-streaked face. "There's a dreamer trial coming up in about six weeks. Risky's timing couldn't have been more perfect."

"What?" Skip said.

"You know we've no dreamer on our team," Per reminded him. "Yet without one we can hardly claim to understand or represent the Kargans as a whole. So one of our elders plans to make the metamorphosis during this visit. She's already primed a groundling to take her place as elder."

"Why come here for the change?" Skip asked.

"It's not just a simple bodily change," Sulman explained. "The Kargans say it has to be initiated by a special meal from the dreamers themselves—presumably similar to the elder-honey meal that initiates a groundling's change. Then once the physical metamorphosis is done, the new dreamer needs initiation into dreamer language and tradition."

"Which is why this is so exciting," Kelda said. "Since there are more elders than dreamers, elders must compete for the right to change. The dreamers sponsor a trial only when a vacancy opens in their ranks. Risky might have waited months or years for a trial in her home warren. To have one so soon is incredible luck."

"I hope she's ready," a worried-looking Disa said.

Per squeezed her muddy shoulder. "That's for Risky to judge. Inanna's schooled her well in native tradition. And her experiences with us may give her some advantage." But he looked worried, too.

"What if she doesn't win?" Skip asked.

"She dies," Sulman said.

Skip blinked. No one said anything in response to Sulman's remark, but everyone looked somber as the group trooped down the steps toward the spring at the base of the bluff.

Kelda stopped by the bubbling spring and began to rinse her suit. Per washed mud from Disa's shoulder off his hand. Disa herself cast a longing eye toward the beach. "Can we rinse in the river?" she asked.

"Sure. Check with Calypso about currents."

"I'm rinsing in the river, too," Yvette announced. "You coming, Uncle Suli?"

He looked down at his mud-caked body. "Good idea."

"Bet I beat you in!" The girls took off at a run. Sulman shook his head and followed, with a lightfootedness rare in men his age.

Skip kept his eyes away from the water, but he heard splashing and giggling. "You leave me alone!" a deep voice protested. "Who taught you that trick?"

"Calypso," the aggressor laughed back. "You hit the water slantwise like this—" Another splash.

"Where is Calypso?" Skip asked, following Per to the kitchen.

Per handed him a stack of bowls from the module's cupboard. "Probably in the shallows there, fussing with her symbionts. She'll be out later to discuss testing procedure with you."

Skip had thought Disa shy, but there she was trotting stark naked toward them, her diving suit slung over her arm. Her ribs showed the way Leif's had the previous year, when he sprouted suddenly upward. "Smells great, Dad. Is it time to eat?"

"When you get some clothes on. We have company."

"Oh." With a startled glance at Skip, she scampered toward the cliff path.

"Modesty's not observed here?" Skip asked, a little more harshly than he intended.

"She's not a dirtside prude, if that's what you mean." Per smiled apologetically. "I grew up like you did. But go enough places with no facilities for humans, and you learn to stress courtesy rather than clothing. Clothes can't make Kel modest, and skin can't make Disa immodest. You know, I think they're so hungry they won't even notice our cooking."

"All to the good," Skip answered.

Kelda joined them, wearing low boots, shorts, and a clingy knit top. She combed damp hair with her fingers, mussing it thoroughly. "I like planets where the bugs don't like me. Is that a bottle of spiceberry wine?"

"It is—"

She rubbed her hands together.

Sulman, in an ivory coverall that accented his dark coloring, looked curiously at her. "You like wine, Kelda? I thought you fancied your spirits in purer form."

"You don't understand. This is a taste from my past."

Per grinned. "Not everyone likes Valhallan politics, but even the Frilandena appreciate its spiceberries."

"I beg your pardon," Skip said, "but this wine was not made from wimpish, overly coddled Valhallan fruit. It contains only the toughest, most competitive Frilandeter spiceberries—as developed by Frilandet's own Master Geneticist, of course."

"Really?" Kelda asked, holding the bottle up to the light.

"Got a public service medal for it, too."

"What's in the other packet?" Yvette asked as she arrived with Disa from the changing hut.

"Chocolate," Skip told her. "Compliments of Leif. Sorry he couldn't bring it himself."

"Me, too." The girls wore white blouses and garishly fringed tiered skirts that were no doubt the rage on some planet recently visited. Yvette's was a bold purple, Disa's a pale sea-green that echoed her eyes.

Per looked down at his own loose shirt. "Should I dress for dinner?"

"You're fine!" Kelda said, picking up the wine bottle. "Bring mugs when you come, girls." She walked toward the square of logs around Per's driftwood fire. Per followed with the mush kettle. Skip brought bowls, spoons, and chocolate, and Sulman carried a melon from town. The girls obediently fetched an assortment of cups.

Disa stared covertly at Skip. Yvette, seated between Disa and Kelda, whispered in the older woman's ear. Kelda smiled. "Yes, call him Uncle. Anyone I mother is niece to you, right, Skip? I don't suppose you brought a corkscrew."

He shook his head.

"Pass it here," Sulman said. He sat at right angles to Disa, facing the river. A deft maneuver with the knife he pulled from his boot, and the cork jumped free.

"Do we get some?" Yvette asked.

Kelda glanced at Per. "I think they're grown enough."

Sulman half filled the mug Disa handed him, then passed it to Skip. He continued pouring until everyone held a cup.

Per raised his mug. "To peace on Karg."

It still irritated Skip to hear Frilandet called "Karg." But he raised his mug, echoed "To peace," and drank.

Across from Skip, Disa sipped cautiously and grimaced at the tartness. Yvette, imitating Kelda, tossed the toast boldly down. She sputtered wildly. Both girls began to giggle.

Kelda looked around the square. "To old loves and new." The girls, still giggling, joined the second round.

Sulman, with his back to the looming bluff, gestured wryly. *"Constantia et integritas."*

"What's that?" Skip whispered to Per.

"Courage and integrity. Dawn's slogan. The slogan of Dawn's humans, at least." They drank to that, too.

Skip's turn. He held his glass to the skinny girl across from him and her dark-haired friend. "To the next generation—may it be pretty and headstrong as the one before."

Sulman laughed. "I'll drink to that!"

Per winked at Kelda. "I can hardly refuse, can I?"

She met his gaze with mock severity. "Not if you expect to share a bed with me tonight."

"May it be pretty as the one before, but easier to deal with," Per said, and drank.

Disa and Yvette blushed fiercely in the rosy rays of the sinking sun. A good toast, Skip thought.

They drained the wine, and Per served stew. Hungrier than he thought, Skip dug in, then stopped, embarrassed, as his companions joined hands. "May we turn this dust to dreams," Per said. The others assented in silence.

Sulman dropped Skip's hand, picked up his spoon, and took a taste of the mush. "What is this, Per? Bilge water?"

"Atlantis's best. I knew you liked imported delicacies."

"Calypso says that on Challa they really do eat bilge water," Yvette reported.

"Not exactly," Kelda told her. "They just use it for raising fishes."

"And I thought MacKenzie was bad," Skip said. "All they do is process their wool in it."

Sulman's bowl was already half-empty. "I'd like to visit MacKenzie some time. Are the dancers as fine as everyone says?"

"Better," Skip answered. "If you can stand the music. They use some really weird instruments."

Twilight dwindled to darkness by the time spoons scraped bowl bottoms. Per held an igniter to his pile of twigs. "Dessert by firelight, anyone?"

"You know what Calypso will say!" Yvette chided.

Per blew ever so gently, coaxing the tiny flame along.

"What will Calypso say?" Skip asked.

"Sheppies consider fires wasteful, unpleasant, and dangerous," Per answered, sitting back on his heels. The diminutive blaze snapped merrily as it reached for larger fuel, branches a full inch thick. Acrid smoke drifted across the empty side of the square toward the river. "But I think fire's in our genes. In a strange place, when you don't know what awaits you or don't like it if you do, nothing boosts morale like a good blaze. So we light fires every place we can, and our circlemates write it off as human perversion." He looked up into the inky blackness. "I don't see how you live with this sky. It's nothingness made visible."

So spoke the Sørenson of Valhalla. Nostalgia pricked Skip with childhood memories of that planet, in the hazy margin of a star cluster, its nights illuminated by a hundred thousand suns. Frilandet's sun drifted in the void between galactic arms, stars few and faraway veiled off by dust. The planet had no moons. To the Frilandena, seeking to live without interference for good or ill, the empty sky signaled freedom. "It's dark, all right," Skip said, unable to articulate the memories Per's comment roused. "We don't wander much at night, around here."

Darkness was not the only reason.

CHAPTER EIGHT

SKIP REMEMBERED VIVIDLY HOW, THE FIRST MORNING ON their new planet and many mornings thereafter, the Frilandena had found crates opened, supplies ransacked, and equipment missing. The groundlings' strength, dexterity, curiosity, nocturnal habits, and grotesque appearance made them nightmare creatures. Shuddering at the memory, Skip passed Leif's chocolate around. A serrated claw reached from Disa's shadow. Skip started violently. "There's—uh—someone behind you."

"That's just Enki," Disa said. "He likes to lick my bowl."

Per laid his still-wrapped chocolate on his knee. "You know, sprite, maybe you should take it away from him. Until we know what makes groundlings go *gigg*."

Wordlessly she retrieved the bowl, rose, and scraped the last bits of mush into the fire. She scraped the other bowls, as well, and set them to soak in the empty kettle. Skip wondered why she seemed so upset.

"I hope Leif can come tomorrow," Yvette said, sucking chocolate from her fingers. The candy had not fared well in the heat. "Will he come when he gets out of school?"

81

Per started to answer, but a softly hissing voice interrupted. "Ah, you are performing anccesstral ritualss
again. Perhapss I sshould not interrupt thiss barbarian
fesstival." Calypso rested on her crutches just outside the
firelight, her pink and orange a dim shadowy pattern.
"Ssomeone sshould confine you for your own ssafety."

Kelda sighed elaborately. "Someone should teach
Sheppies to respect fundamental cultural discoveries."

"We have a keen apprecciation of ssymbiont microor-
ganissmss," Calypso answered tartly. Then the well-
known scientist swept her tentacles at Skip. "Welcome,
Masster Sskip. If you have completed your repasst, I
sshould like to disscuss professsional matterss."

"I need a review of the problem," Skip said.

"Easy," Kelda answered. "We find out what's poisoning the groundlings. The colony stops it, or leaves."

He stared at her. "Haven't you got any feeling at all for
your people? You know what it costs in lives for a colony
to move!"

"You're right," Sulman agreed. "But what does it cost
the Kargans if the problem isn't solved? Already they've
got one child in six dying."

Skip thought of Borg's and Inge's emaciated bodies,
but the memory brought no sympathy for Kargans. It only
revived his fears of another move. "And you'll arbitrate.
You who have no stake in this at all." He heard bitterness
in his own voice.

"Just our lives," Sulman said.

"What's that supposed to mean?"

Sulman's finger twisted the ring in his ear. "We backed
the treaty, meaning we endorsed you and the Kargans to
each other. If they attacked you, after we counseled you
that they wouldn't, we'd block with our bodies. By the
same token, if you're killing them—" He let the sentence
trail.

"You'd die taking the aliens' side against humans?"

Skip asked, shocked even though Per had mentioned something similar about Yvette's father.

"That iss correct," Calypso said. Disa and Yvette listened, their eyes large.

Per cleared his throat. "Let's not look for trouble. The thing to do is find a solution that keeps everyone happy."

Skip blew air out through pursed lips. "Fair enough. You still haven't told me the technical aspects of the problem."

"We don't know much," Sulman explained. "Kargans are metamorphic, with three life stages. They appear to have adapted to cave living some hundreds of thousands of years ago, although the Hall of Voices—you've seen it?—suggests that at the peak of their civilization they still retained vision." Skip nodded in recollection of the colored pipes Kelda had shown him long ago. That and other relics indicated that this planet had once had an impressive civilization and technology. But the relics were all thousands of years old.

"Food's the limiting factor in a cave environment. The groundlings forage aboveground, then deliver essential nutrients to their elders in the highly concentrated form of so-called honey. Mother's milk in reverse, you might say."

Kelda grimaced. "Honey's a euphemism if I've ever heard one."

"The elderss appear to find honey exxquissitely deliciouss," Calypso countered.

"To each his own," Per said.

Frowning at the interruptions, Sulman continued. "Groundlings are the pool from which future elders rise, but Kargans do not consider them children until first change is initiated." Skip's eyes wandered to Disa. Pale and serious, she scratched the skin fold where Enki's claw arm joined his body.

Sulman looked to Disa, too, and then away. "Something's happening to groundlings near the colony, something that interferes with their metamorphoses. The relation of mortality to length and intensity of exposure indicates a cumulative effect rather than an acute toxicity. But we don't know what the agent is!"

"Haven't the Kargans investigated?' Skip asked. "Shouldn't the elders be helping plan this research?"

Kelda shook her head. "Karg's elders know the surface only from memory of their own groundling days. They don't know what to ask about activities in the colony, and if they did the groundlings couldn't answer. Also, it seems to have been biological warfare that felled classical Kargan culture. Now they consider biological research taboo."

Disa frowned.

"I suppose the dreamers are no help," Skip said.

"Let me show you what we know about dreamers," Sulman answered. He walked out of the firelight toward the bluff. Per stirred the fire into a snapping whorl of sparks, then added a thick chunk of log. Sulman returned with a projector. Battered as it was, it generated a strong three-dimensional image of Sheppies and humans in diving gear. "We got these holos twenty years ago before we left Karg. It was the only time we got anywhere near the dreamer realm."

"God, that was awful!" Kelda said as she watched the picture. "Those submerged channels had some potent currents."

"Even the Sheppies say it was dangerous," Disa commented.

Sulman glanced good-naturedly at her. "You weren't even born, pipsqueak, but you've got the story straight. Heaven knows what it's like where the dreamers live."

"I thought this was where they live," Skip said, looking again at the holo.

"No. Dreamers and elders respond very strongly, sexually, to each other's presence. So they never get together except to mate—or maybe I should say, they can't get together without mating." Suli grinned at Kelda. "Anyway, they cope with their susceptibilities by maintaining strict geographical separation—elders in passages that are dry or just below the watertable; dreamers in the very deep passages; and a neutral no-man's land between. This meeting took place in that neutral zone." From a cleft in the cavern wall scuttled a pale delicate figure, shell-less but for its claws.

"Why do you call them dreamers?" Skip asked.

"The elders suggested that," Sulman told him. "We originally translated the word as 'engineer,' because the elders used it in connection with tunnel planning and *graf* enterprises. When we got Kargan sexuality sorted out, we tried translating 'male.' But the elders use the word in question for our phenomenon of night visions." He keyed for sound.

Skip heard the faint high-pitched clicks by which Kargans "saw" in darkness, the low wails of Sheppie, and guttural noises coming from several directions. Kelda grinned wickedly as the Sulman of twenty-odd years ago ventured a question in Kargan.

Firelight played over the present Sulman's face. "Give me a break. I was just learning then." Yvette stared into glimmering coals, ignoring the playback, but Disa nodded slightly as she followed the recorded conversation.

After several minutes Per spoke up. "Hand me the projector." The scene shifted ninety degrees as Sulman complied. Per fiddled a moment with the controls. The picture dissolved, replaced by a three-dimensional multicolored display full of symbols meaningless to Skip.

"What's that?" he asked.

"A visual representation of Kargan speech," Per answered.

Kelda rolled her eyes. "I told you he was a linguist."

"Up here," Per explained, zooming until a line resolved

itself into an oscilloscope tracing, "is a raw recording of some of Risky's speech. Below's the analysis. Green marks basic vocabulary—nouns, verbs, things you'd find in a dictionary. The code letters identify standard morphemes—verbal forms, plurals, prepositional infixes, and so forth. Yellow marks terms we're not certain we've translated correctly. Blue brackets show semantic groupings—phrases, sentences. The white code letters indicate parts of speech."

Skip blinked. "This sort of work must give you eyestrain."

Per laughed, then continued his lecture. "It's a typical structure, very similar to Sheppie," he said, replacing the display with another colorful jumble, "despite the difference in sound." Skip had heard Sheppie; it sounded like malfunctioning foghorns. "Kargan, oddly, does not suit underground acoustics—another hint that the *graf* did not confine themselves to caves." Per returned to Risky's speech. "Red identifies items expressed in claw-noise, which carries well and is easier for today's elders to produce. One wonders if it's slowly replacing vocal language."

"And the dreamers?" Kelda prompted.

"These dreamers spoke briefly in the wet version of conventional Kargan, so we know they can use it, but they drifted persistently into this." Per displayed a third pattern. Skip expected something bewilderingly complex. Instead he saw a row of yellow lumps, only occasionally interrupted by white. Blue brackets, sketched in with question marks, stretched across dozens of lumps at a time.

"The vocabulary's shockingly small," Per said. "Three dozen primary terms in this sequence. Only four in this one. When we asked what the terms meant, the dreamers did this."

Per ran the recording forward. Two dreamers appeared. One was curled in the water, legs drawn to his body, claw and manipulative arms weirdly contorted. The other dreamer drifted toward him, also curled, one so-called hand extended. Taking the extended hand in his claw, the first dreamer moved the hand's "fingers." The second dreamer drifted away, rebounded from the chamber wall, returned, and got his fingers arranged to the original position. "When we didn't understand this, the dreamers left," Per said.

"Don't the elders know what it means?" Skip asked.

"No," said Per, Kelda, Sulman, Disa, and Calypso, simultaneously.

Skip frowned. "Weird for the females of a species not to understand the males."

"Human females have some trouble understanding males, too," Sulman said, with another mischievous glance at Kelda.

"I can't help it if you're irrational," she answered.

"Cut it out, you two," Per said. "Skip, linguistic labs all over the galaxy have looked at this. Fame and fortune await the Ph.D. student who cracks it for her dissertation. The elders think the dreamers are just senile. Maybe they're right."

"Guess we'll find out when Risky changes," Kelda said.

"That's your elder who wants to be a dreamer?" Skip asked. He was still working to sort out the names and identities of the First-In team members.

"Right," Sulman said. "She hung around our camp when she was still a groundling. Her first metamorphosis was our big breakthrough."

"Why does she want to be a dreamer now, if the trial's so dangerous?" Skip asked.

To Skip's surprise, Disa answered. "Legends say dreamers mediated the power of the *graf*," she explained.

"Risky thinks the dreamers still control that power, but no one knows how to unleash it."

"Should it be unleashed, given the damage it did last time?" Skip asked. The story of the *graf*'s fall haunted the geneticist. He knew what havoc biological warfare could wreak.

"Kargans have changed since the days of the *graf*," Sulman answered. "They learned a lesson. Maybe too much of one."

Sulman obviously thought the Kargans should evict the Frilandena. Again Skip wondered at his own motives for volunteering to help First-In.

"Thiss iss all very interessting," Calypso said, "but let uss disscuss the matter of the groundlingss."

Once again they reviewed the frustratingly incomplete data at hand. "If you knew anything about Kargan biochemistry," Skip said, "an autopsy of the *gigg* changeling might show you what pathways had been interfered with, and that would tell you what sort of agent to look for."

"Unfortunately," Sulman answered, "we know nearly nothing about Kargan biochemistry, although Calypso's working to remedy that. The body the elders showed us was too decomposed to tell us much. All we've got are gross findings—shell loss, stunted brain development. You realize we don't know what a normal changeling looks like under the shell."

"Then we're stuck doing exposure trials," Skip said. "But groundlings are too big and long-lived for that, besides being Kargan children. Damn, we need testers!"

"Mud nippers," Sulman said.

"Huh?"

"Mud nippers. When we took Kargans off-planet, we knew we couldn't count on getting food from here. Stuff from other northpaw planets needed toxicity screening. So we checked around. Mud nippers grow fast and are as genetically similar to the Kargans as anything else on this planet."

Skip knew what mud nippers looked like, but he knew nothing about their life cycle. "Metamorphic?" he asked.

"Juvenile to female to male, just like Kargans," Sulman answered, "and terrestrial to amphibious to aquatic, again like Kargans."

"I guess we hunt mud nippers tomorrow then," Skip said, not looking forward to it. Hidden in silty sediments, the creatures could pinch nastily. "Then what do we expose them to?"

"You are besst qualified to judge, ssince you know the colony'ss activitiess," Calypso said. "I ssuggesst making the categoriess as wide as posssible."

"We'll need a control set, of course, raised in the purest Frilandet environment we can supply," Skip said, thinking aloud. "Then raise one set in water taken from the Meade at the downstream border of Holmstad. Give another one clean water and food, but aerate the tank with smoke from the harbor district. Put another set in a clean environment except feed them southpaw food. Inoculate another set with our gut bacteria—"

"Any possibility of deliberate poisoning?" Per asked.

"What do you think we are, savages? Our folk are no different than you—they keep groundlings for chores, and eventually get to liking them." Skip hesitated. "Groundlings do tear up farmers' fields pretty badly sometimes. I'll ask around."

"Thank you," Per said quietly.

Brainstorming and subsequent winnowing of test categories went quickly. "Tomorrow we'll work on cage design," Sulman said. "We're talking a lot of nippers and we want them under controlled conditions but easily cared for."

Disa's eyes flicked anxiously from one adult to another. Skip, feeling more kinship with the shy child than with her mother, tried an encouraging smile. Disa looked away.

Sulman broke the impasse with characteristic bluntness. "What'sa matter, Dis? You look like you've been
having nightmares."

"I have," she answered in a small voice, with an uncomfortable glance at Skip.

Per's eyebrows went up. "Oh?"

"Probably smelling that damn *gigg* changeling," Kelda
said. "That'd give anybody nightmares."

"I'm afraid it will happen to Enki."

"No way to know," Kelda said. She sounded uncharacteristically defensive, Skip thought. "We can't know
Enki's exposure until we know the agent of the problem."

Disa nodded mutely, eyes brimming. Skip stared at her.
Crying over a groundling! With unwelcome force, he remembered the nanny-goat Gerda. What if Gerda had been
a lifelong companion, with parents who spoke? What if
Gerda had died on the very verge of learning to speak
herself?

Until that instant, Skip had seen the Kargan complaint
as a nuisance, a threat, at best an intellectual puzzle. But
his niece's teary eyes reflected another picture, that of an
ancient, weary people faced with new tragedy. "We'll get
it figured out, Disa."

She looked hard at him. "I'm glad you're helping,
Uncle Skip." He wasn't sure why, but that remark felt like
a victory.

Twitching visibly as she passed through a curl of
smoke, Calypso hobbled around the perimeter of firelight
and rested motherly tentacles on Disa's shoulder. "We will
do what dusst allowss, child."

Disa laid her cheek against alien flesh. "I know, Calypso. I'm sorry. I'm just worried about Enki."

"Do not apologizze for loving." Calypso let go. "My
ssymbiontss will ssuffer if they remain longer in thiss de-
tesstable ssmoke. Masster Sskip, I look forward to further

asssocciation. Kelda, treat your brother to a ssong or two before you retire. You will all feel better."

"Heg, Calypso!" Kelda answered.

"Heg!" others around the fire murmured.

"Heg," Skip said, finding the whole situation incredible. Had he really just said heg to the one of the galaxy's premier bacterial geneticists? She vanished into the river. "I thought Sheppies had no sex," he remarked.

"They don't," Kelda confirmed. "Why do you ask?"

"Calypso has a female name, and you call her 'she.'"

"Our language forces gender identification," Sulman said. "Being loquacious and rather bossy, Sheppies identify themselves as female."

"As do most aliens," Kelda added, rising to the jibe. "They find human males illogical and overaggressive."

"Sheppies do have a distinct maternal streak," Per said. "You've seen how Calypso treats the girls. Rumor says we call them Sheppies because it's like entrusting your child to a big shaggy dog."

"Hell of a smart dog," Skip remarked. They laughed. "Doesn't she get lonesome, being the only one of her kind on your team?"

"She says she doesn't mind," Per answered. "Some folk say a team should include at least three individuals of each species involved, but given alien social structures and the expense of fielding a team, that doesn't always work. Since Calypso seems happy with our arrangement—"

Kelda grinned. "On their own planets, Sheppies keep a lot of pets. I think that's how Calypso sees us."

"Whatever she thinks of us, that was a good suggestion she made," Sulman said. He rose and walked toward the bluff, carrying the holoprojector. He returned with a wooden stringed instrument, clearly old but lovingly polished. Skip wondered what a First-Inner's personal baggage allowance was and how much of it such an instrument took up. Sulman set it between his knees and plucked the top string. It rang deep and resonant. Sulman frowned and adjusted the pitch, then moved to the next string.

"Flat," Per told him.

"You're right." Sulman tightened it. When all five strings were true, he tightened the bow and began to play, a toe-tapping jig that Skip recognized from MacKenzie. Sulman followed it with a hauntingly sweet, slow, minor key melody. Per and Kelda began to sing. Their voices strengthened and diverged into harmony.

Hush, my child, the summer tide holds you,
Hush, my child, while soft wavelets play.
Hush, my child, let warm currents mold you,
Hush, my child, till the dawn of the day.

"That's beautiful," Skip said. "Where's it from?"

"Sheppie lullaby," Per answered. "In translation, of course. Calypso used to sing it to the girls."

"She still does," Yvette said ruefully.

Sulman grinned at the seventeen-year-old's expression. "You're not as old as you think you are, little lady." His fingers caressed the strings, while his eyes wandered to Kelda. "You still dance the anemone? Or have you gotten old and stiff?"

She laughed. "Bite your tongue. I dance it even better than Anna."

"That I'd have to see."

Per frowned, one eye on Skip. "You have company, Kelda."

"My reputation's beyond ruining," she said. Sulman drew the bow across his instrument. Kelda stood and kicked aside the log nearest the river. "This is a Sheppie dance," she explained. She crossed her arms and stripped her shirt off.

Skip blushed and looked away. Frilandet breasts showed only in the bedroom and in one rude bar on the far side of Holmstad.

The melody moved in an unusual rhythm, with no clear primary and secondary beats, but rather crescendos that themselves waxed and waned in strength and duration. Waves, Skip thought. Kelda listened for a moment, then planted her feet in the sand and began to sway.

Her feet scarcely shifted, but arms, head, and torso moved as fluidly as jointless tentacles washed by flowing water. The performance depended on continuity of motion, hips to headtop and fingertips. Skip had to admit it was lovely. Kelda, eyes half-closed, seemed unaware of her audience. Then Sulman shortened the swells to whitewater chop. Grinning, Kelda let herself bob in the storm.

Skip glanced involuntarily at Per. "Doesn't it bother you?" he asked, curiosity getting the better of him.

"What?" Per asked, eyes still on Kelda.

"Having your wife half-naked!"

"If it bothered me I wouldn't have married her," Per said. He watched a moment longer, then added, "Shame to let her dance alone."

He stood, shucked his own shirt, and joined Kelda on the empty side of the square. Smoothly, as if spun by current, she turned to face him. Skip wondered if one had to be good-looking to join First-In. Or was their beauty, as Kelda claimed, a function of health, training, and confidence?

Standing four feet from her, Per set his well-muscled body swaying to the current of Sulman's song. Kelda watched for a moment, then, with a sly look, sent her right arm into an impossible ripple.

The same ripple swept Per's left arm.

A cross-current tugged Kelda.

The same current hit Per, pulling at his tentacles and causing his stalk to shift slightly, as well.

Kelda nodded appreciation of his adroitness and let a passing wave carry her fingertips toward Per's chest. The same wave bent him beyond her reach, but in its back-wash his fingers brushed her hair.

Grinning, Sulman shifted rhythm again. The dancers edged closer to each other, matching move for move, ripple for ripple, playing off each other as chance acquaintances could never have done. The dance left no question about the bond between Kelda and her husband.

Disa and Yvette watched dreamy-eyed, doubtless imagining men with whom they would someday dance. Sulman wore a bittersweet smile. "Why do the best ones always marry?" he asked. Skip had no answer.

The song washed to a gentle close, leaving Per and Kelda facing each other, hands touching palm to palm. Light sweat glistened on their sleek bodies. A breeze fanned the fire, brightening the clearing. Per closed his fingers over Kelda's. She mouthed a kiss at him. Yvette tossed Kelda's shirt to her.

Per sat down a little apart from Skip and tapped the spot between them. Kelda smiled and took it.

Skip hated to ruin the moment with meaningless conversation. Silently they watched coals settle.

Kelda finally yawned and stretched. "Cave diplomacy is tiring business. Let's hit the sack."

Sulman rubbed his eyes. "Sounds good to me."

"You can wash at the spring," Kelda told Skip. "If you put your bag by the upper bluff, morning sun won't hit you in the face. The girls like sun—they swim early with the groundlings. Suli will be right next to you. Wake him if you need anything."

Kelda didn't say where she would be, and Skip didn't ask, but he listened wistfully as Per's voice greeted her from darkness.

CHAPTER NINE

❧❧❧

THE SUN HAD NOT YET BROKEN OVER THE HORIZON WHEN a cool hand tapped Disa's shoulder. Groggily she opened her eyes, considering the too-narrow, too-dark leaves above and the crisp, high-pitched squeaks of morning fliers. She had spent five weeks on ship adjusting her day to Holmstad's clock, but somebody had forgotten to compensate for seasonal variation. Disa's body remained forty-five minutes behind the sun. Waking forty-five minutes early was harder than getting up in the middle of the night. She closed her eyes and wriggled deeper into her bag.

She felt another soft tug, then heard an impatient click near her ear. She sighed and rolled halfway over. Enki's owl-eyes blinked at her. He wanted a swim before daylight.

"All right." Disa reached to the foot of her bag for clean socks. Yvette was sleeping soundly, her cheek pillowed on her hand amid a cascade of black curls. Disa frowned. Yvette did not wake gracefully, but she bitched if left behind. "I'll start tea," Disa told Enki, who liked to be talked to even if he did not understand much, "and you wake Yvette."

Disa clambered out of her bag and into her boots. Enki chittered unhappily, his feelers pointed toward Yvette. Disa grinned. "That's right. You wake her." Pulling her big camp shirt tight around her, Disa walked to the privy and then toward the bluff path, stepping cautiously around Sulman and Skip. Per and Kelda slept higher on the ridge, out of earshot.

On the beach, Disa blew the previous night's coals to life, added fuel, and set a blackened, battered camp kettle filled with spring water to heat. Everyone benefited if Kelda got her tea promptly.

Turbulence offshore betrayed Calypso's presence. Disa flipped a rock into the water. The Sheppie responded with a geyser aimed toward shore. Rising from the shallows, Calypso tossed Disa a crock of ointment. After setting her boots and socks aside, Disa began to smear the stuff on her legs.

Yvette came stumbling, grumbling, down the path. "Dust, Disa, this is only our second morning here! Don't you ever lay off?"

"It was Enki's idea," Disa said, flinching from the cold as she stripped her camp shirt off. She continued applying the grease, a Sheppie invention that repelled small and large water creatures. "You don't have to go."

Arms folded and shoulders hunched, Yvette dipped a toe in the river. "Brrr! It's freezing! We could wear suits."

Disa glanced over her shoulder at the bluff. "You can climb up and get one if you want. I'm ready to swim."

"You don't want suits 'cause you're outgrowing yours," Yvette accused. "Finally."

"I've been taller than you for a year."

"That wasn't what I meant." Yvette took the grease pot from Disa and went to work.

Enki, who knew the routine well, had broken into the

"groundling-proof" equipment cache and brought earplugs
and goggles. Disa already carried, clipped to her beacon
on a wrist strap, the synthesizer that allowed her to speak
Sheppie. She donned the additional equipment and beckoned to the dappled brown groundling. "Let's find Calypso!"

Enki scampered into the river, splashing exuberantly.
Disa trotted behind, hurling herself horizontal when the
water reached her thighs. It was warmer than the air, although noticeably colder than Disa herself. Head down,
she heard Enki's clicks and Calypso's low-pitched squeal
The Sheppie greeted Disa with a jet of water and a tentacle around the waist. Disa, knowing what to expect,
stocked her lungs with air before the tentacle dragged her
down. Silt stirred by the activity obscured vision. "Good
morning," Calypso said.

"Good morning," Disa hummed back into her synthesizer.

Released, she popped to the surface. Enki remained
below. Had his gills begun to develop? She ought to learn
to think of Enki as "her." Yvette, joined by Ea, edged into
the waves. "Come on," Disa said. "The water's fine!"

Yvette answered with an obscene gesture.

Disa hated to admit it, but Yvette was right—the river
was chilly. She raced Enki to the center and back, then
dove to admire the new net curtains of Calypso's underwater camp. Yvette stuck closer to shore, playing dive-
and-fetch with Ea. She was out and toweling dry by the
time Disa and Enki arrived.

"You didn't swim far this morning," Disa said.

"Too cold," Yvette answered. "I'm not training for
First-In. Why torture myself?"

"If you want to work with Sheppies, you better like
water," Disa retorted, wiping off as much grease as she
could. "Who says I'm training for First-In?" It irritated

her that everyone assumed that she was headed for an explorer's career.

"You did, until Leif made fun of it," Yvette said. "Look—even Enki thinks it's cold." The groundling scraped water from himself with his claws.

Disa laughed. "That or he's copying us." She sprayed on neutralizer. The remaining grease melted into a thin watery film, easy to wipe away. She gave herself a final rinse in the shallows, toweled dry, then donned her camp shirt. "I smell breakfast."

By the fire, Kelda huddled grumpily over a fragrant mug of tea. Skip was washing his face at the spring. Sulman sat to one side, trimming his mustache and making faces at the mirror. Per stirred the cereal as it came to a boil. He shook his head at the girls. "You look like you've had your dose of misery for the day. Go find some dry clothes."

"We thought we'd dress by the fire," Yvette told him.

"You'll embarrass your Uncle Skip," Per answered. "Change in the hut, and I'll have breakfast ready by the time you're back."

"You might want to wear your nice outfits," Kelda added. She took a deep draught of tea. "You've a big day ahead."

Disa gave her mother a wary look.

"Since it looks as if we may be here awhile," Kelda said, "we're going to send you to school in town."

Disa froze.

"Us?" Yvette asked, incredulous. "In a dirtside school? Why, Aunt Kelda?"

"Because it's high time you learn to get along outside the Circle."

"But Calypso was going to show me how to work up Twist applications!" Yvette protested. Calypso had also promised simulation lessons in shuttle piloting, Disa thought, but she remained silent.

"You can study with Calypso later. Now get dressed."

There was no brooking Kelda when she used that tone of voice. The girls scooted past Skip and up the cliff, donned the blouses and flounced skirts they had worn the previous night, and returned as the sun rose and Per ladled syrup over bowls of thick hot cereal. "How soon do we have to go?" Yvette asked.

"Uncle Skip will take you in to register as soon as breakfast's cleaned up," Kelda answered.

Skip, sitting beside Sulman, looked appropriately sheepish. "It's a decent school, as frontier schools go. It got me to MacKenzie. You'll be a junior, Yvette. Leif can introduce you to the class. Disa, I think you'll be a sophomore."

Disa set her bowl down.

"What's wrong?" Per asked.

She forced words past the lump in her throat. "Can't we be in the same class at least?" Enki crouched behind her, in the log's shadow.

"I thought you'd rather be with friends your own age," Skip said.

Friends? Dirtsiders? Like that awful Burr? Disa was dimly aware of a brown claw edging over the log.

"Get that groundling out of your dish!" Kelda snapped. "I expect you to eat your breakfast yourself. You need to put on some weight."

Disa retrieved the bowl from Enki. Disappointed, and troubled by the increasing light, he scuttled away toward the cave. Haunted by visions of *gigg* changelings and hostile Frilandena faces, Disa felt no hunger.

"Put you in Yvette's class? Sounds reasonable to me," Per said. "I can't imagine you'd have trouble keeping up."

Kelda shrugged. "Whatever you want."

"I don't want to do this at all," Disa said.

"The sooner you get acquainted with regular planet-dwelling people, the easier it will be." Per's strained voice said that he secretly sympathized but had made up his mind and would lose his temper if pressed.

"It would be a favor to Dawn," Sulman said.

"What?" Disa asked.

He licked the last cereal from his bowl, a habit Kelda always called uncouth. "You know what trouble we can get into by assuming a colony thinks as its leaders do." Disa knew. It had happened to Uncle Jack. "Listen to what your classmates think, and try to explain what we're about. If you don't want to do it for yourself, do it for us."

"All right," Disa said, swallowing a tasteless spoonful of cereal. She saw no escape.

School was an ugly, squat, rambling adobe structure that looked as if it had been constructed by groundlings with too little supervision. "Don't come here unless you really want an education," it seemed to say. A second building a hundred yards away reeked of fermenting silk-fruit. "That's the Weaver's Guild Hall," Skip said over the roaring clatter of mechanized looms. "They take quite a few apprentices."

The school administrator's office, a hut on the roof, caught a sea breeze free from the fumes of silk making. The administrator, a stout woman of about forty-five, looked none too happy when Skip herded Disa and Yvette into the office, but she grudgingly entered their names in her records. "How have you girls proceeded in your studies?"

I'm ready for basic astrogation, Disa thought. Or physiology of aquatic adaptation. Fat chance of getting that here!

"Put them on university track," Skip ordered. "First-In will supply equipment."

The woman frowned. "It's not just a matter of facilities. With no preparation they'll be lost."

"Don't worry about it," Skip told her, his irritation beginning to show. "Put them in the university-track class."

"Perhaps some placement diagnostics?"

Skip sighed. "Please. Put them in the class and be done with it."

The woman sighed, too. "I suppose you'll be back if it doesn't work out."

Finally she finished her forms and led the group downstairs. Skip followed. "You'll be in biochemistry this morning," he whispered. "I usually teach it, but since Leif's in the class this year I bowed out. Our druggist, Erica, took my place. She'll look out for you."

Disa and Yvette followed the administrator along a walkway under the eaves. They went the length of the building, around a corner, and halfway along the length of the next wall. Since in Holmstad's mild climate hallways were a waste of building space, each room opened to the outside only. Through one window Disa saw students questioning their teacher about a geometric display. Through the next room's open doorway she whiffed organic solvents. In yet another, two dozen youngsters sawed and planed. However varied their vocational tracks, all appeared approximately Disa's age. From building size and the number of students in the rooms she had seen so far, Disa estimated that there were around two hundred students. Certainly a colony of ten thousand had more teenagers than that! Either there was another school, or the majority of students had dispersed to apprenticeships and regular work.

In each room they passed, eyes turned. The group left a wake of whispers and sharp voices calling classes to order.

Their guide halted, waving the girls ahead of her into a room. Skip entered also. Disa, pinned by the curious eyes of her classmates-to-be, glanced at everything and registered nothing. Miz Erica's lecture stopped midsentence.

"Master Nygren's niece and her companion will attend

your class during their stay on Frilandet," the administrator said. "They have their own computers."

The students, sitting two to a table, shifted on their benches. One boy looked at Yvette and ran his tongue across his lips. A girl whispered to her neighbor, with a glance at Leif. He nodded possessively, enjoying the notoriety of relationship to the newcomers. The girl sitting nearest Disa, with a broad plain face and a single heavy blond braid down her back, smiled sympathetically. Disa tried to return the smile, but all she could manage was a quirk of her lips.

"Welcome to our class," Miz Erica said. "We are just beginning to study amino acids, which you know are of some interest on Frilandet. Kirby, Aage, please go to the storeroom and see if you can find another table and bench." The boy who had licked his lips at Yvette rose. A big young man with light-brown hair and freckles went with him.

"I think you'll be fine," Skip told Disa and Yvette. "Leif, I'll meet you and the girls at the west pier after school. You can come up to camp with us and help me lay out experimental protocols."

"Yes, sir," Leif said, his chest swelling visibly. Skip and the administrator left.

"Class, I'd like to introduce Disa Nygren and Yvette, of Circle Dawn," Erica said, surprising Disa by remembering their names.

Her dirtside relatives might arrogate to themselves the privileges of Family, but Disa herself was not used to being called a Nygren. "Just Disa, please."

"Doesn't want to own you, Leif," an anonymous voice hooted.

Leif reddened and looked accusingly at his cousin. She stared at the floor. Her quarrel wasn't with Leif! To her relief, the boys dispatched for furniture returned. Students shifted their tables to make room for the extra one.

"You sit at the new table, Valda," the teacher directed. "You and Gretchen can pair with our newcomers."

So the plain-faced friendly blonde was Gretchen. Disa started for the seat beside her, but Yvette got there first. Disa ended up at the new table with Valda, a willowy redhead. Valda gathered her skirt and shifted rightward on the bench as Disa sat to her left.

Erica picked up a wooden model made of different-sized colored balls stuck together by pegs. Disa recognized it instantly. The big black ball in the middle was supposed to be a carbon atom. Pegs stuck from it in four directions, like the corners of a triangular pyramid. On the top peg sat a big white ball with two little blue ones attached—the amino group of the amino acid. The back right peg held the acid group. On the front and rear left pegs of the original carbon hung more little blue hydrogens. "This is a model of the amino acid glycine," Erica said. "It's just like the glycine in your own bodies. Is it left-handed or right-handed?"

"Left!" Kirby said, one eye on Yvette. "All our amino acids are southpaw."

"Hands up if you agree," Erica said.

Everyone but Leif and Disa raised their hands. Disa frowned. Why was Yvette's hand up? At seventeen, Yvette was already a brilliant biochemist. Surely she knew it was a trick question!

Erica raised her eyebrows at Disa. "Care to tell me why your hands are in your pockets?"

Disa cleared her throat. "That's not a chiral molecule, ma'am. I mean it's neither right- nor left-handed. If you took its mirror image and spun it a hundred eighty degrees, it would be the same as what you have now."

Erica picked up a second model from the table, held it facing the first to show that they were mirror images, then spun it around the top peg until the bottoms of the two models matched. "I can see you'll be a fine student," Miz Erica said.

"Teacher's pet!" Kirby jeered.

"Guess Nygrens are all smart," Aage said sarcastically, looking at Leif, who had not raised his hand, either.

Yvette, her hand still in the air like everyone else's, shrugged at Disa.

"Hands down, and let's look at the next simplest amino acid." Miz Erica replaced the back left hydrogen of her glycine model with a carbon and its three attached hydrogens. "This is L-alanine, the kind we have in our own bodies."

She set up the second model as a mirror image. "This is D-alanine. Anyone think they can twist these two so they match up exactly?"

There were no takers, so Miz Erica tried it herself, without success. "These are different molecules, even though they're made of the same atoms. I have them here in solution." She displayed two beakers. "Watch what happens to a beam of polarized light shining through them." One beaker twisted the beam's polarization clockwise. The other twisted it counterclockwise. "Now," she said, holding up the model of L-alanine again, "by replacing this methyl group with other combinations of atoms, I can produce any amino acid you want. Before we go any further, let's switch on the computers and learn to call up the different amino acids and rotate them around."

Disa activated her finger-stained, scratched-up instructor and said "L-alanine" in the crisp diction acquired by every user of a voice-interactive computer. The computer obediently displayed a perspective simulation of the amino acid, with atoms coded by letter and proton/electron affinities shown in blue and red.

Everyone stared at Disa. Valda pressed her lips together and entered alanine manually on her own instructor's spotlessly clean keyboard.

Disa realized her error. In a class, one couldn't use voice-activation mode. Blushing, she disabled the function.

At last Miz Erica announced that it was time for a break. "Go outside and stretch. You'll reconvene for math in fifteen minutes." She vanished through the door. Disa wondered where the bathrooms were. But the colony students were brimming with two hours' worth of bottled-up curiosity.

"Where'd you get those skirts?" Gretchen asked.

"Yeah," Kirby said. "You look like Ephesian fire-dancers."

"Your hair looks like you stuck it under a scythe." Valda's own fiery locks were knotted high on her head in a grown woman's hairdo.

Yvette turned in a pirouette that made her skirt's fringes fly. "We got these at Regency five weeks ago. I'm sure the fashion will reach here soon." She smiled winningly at Gretchen. "I can loan you this one for a pattern."

"Do circle women really do it with all the guys?" Kirby asked.

Yvette hesitated coyly. "We don't discuss that with dirtsiders." Disa glared at her friend. Yvette made the simple courtesy of not gossiping into an intimation of mysterious orgies!

"Do you have any Hyann in your Circle?" someone else asked.

"Mmmm," Yvette said.

"Have you ever seen the moon-crossing festival?"

Yvette pushed her hair from her face with a slow caressing motion. "It was something."

"What'sa matter with you?" Kirby asked Disa. "We're not good enough to talk to?"

She kept her eyes wide open, for if she blinked tears would spill.

"I heard they gave your brother some trouble," Valda

said to Aage, the handsome boy with the light-brown hair. Disa looked at him again.

"You know Burr," he answered mildly.

"I don't blame him," Valda said. "Groundlings shouldn't be allowed in public."

Disa tried to reach Gretchen with her question, but by the time she edged her way through the press of curious classmates, Gretchen had vanished. Then a new teacher arrived to summon them inside. "Into your seats. And quiet down. I could hear you all the way around the corner."

It was noon before Disa found out where the bathrooms were.

CHAPTER TEN

{decorative divider}

SKIP APPEARED AN ANGEL OF MERCY WHEN HE ARRIVED TO escort the girls home. Disa even considered an honest answer when he asked how the day had gone, but the presence of her handsome dirtsider cousin bound her tongue. She suffered in silence through the forty-five-minute boat trip home.

Upon their arrival, Calypso summoned Skip and Leif to hunt for mud nippers. "For *what*?" Leif asked.

"Mud nipperss," Calypso repeated. "Sso far as we have been able to determine, they are the Karganss' clossesst living relativess."

Leif's half-mustached lip curled. "Do you know where those things live? Under rocks. Dark holes in muddy banks. With all sorts of other nasty scuttling things."

"I'll help," Yvette said, not above shaming someone else's squeamishness and not above leading Leif on.

"Sorry, Miz Yvette," Sulman said, stretching in the sunshine after a day underground. "You've got cook duty tonight. Why not invite your friends for dinner? Calypso will work them to sunset and a snitch beyond."

Yvette promptly extended the invitation, then flounced

toward the wardrobe hut. Sulman flashed one of his famous grins at Disa. "Smile, child! You look like you've already spent a day hunting mud nippers."

Disa wrenched the corners of her mouth upward. "It wasn't that bad."

He eyed her shrewdly. "Maybe. Why don't you go to the Porch and find Enki? He's been moping for you."

Disa left her computer in the equipment cache by the cave entrance and ducked gratefully into cool dimness.

In the small chamber Sulman had called the Front Porch, Disa's parents sat cross-legged on camp cushions with the main library console between them. Not wanting to be asked how school had gone, Disa took conversational initiative. "Where's Enki?"

"Hi, sprite," Per said. "Right by the wall there. He missed you."

Enki crouched morosely at the mouth of one of the far tunnels, toying with one of the intricate three-dimensional stone puzzles that elders sometimes carved for favored groundlings. Seeing Disa, he rose and moved toward her to rub her knee with his claw.

She crouched and hugged him. "Cut that out, Enki. I didn't bring treats. Yes, I missed you, too, but don't knock me over." She stuck a hand against the wet clay floor to brace herself.

"You shouldn't wear that outfit in the cave," Kelda scolded. "You'll get it hopelessly dirty."

"I don't care if it gets dirty! I'm not wearing it again!"

"Why not? You look lovely in it!"

"You know who else was dressed like this? Nobody! *Nobody!* They said I looked like an Ephesian firedancer. I'm growing my hair out. And I'm not going back unless I get gray clothes like everybody else wears."

"Don't be silly!" Kelda said. "You know what that stuff is? Aelollan mutton hair. It's scratchy, stiff, and doesn't breathe. Nor will it dye, which is why they all wear gray.

Any of them would kill for clothes like yours."

"I'm not wearing these to school again," Disa repeated.

"Other than that, how was your day?" Per asked.

Disa concentrated on scratching Enki's shoulder. "They called me teacher's pet. They asked is it true we sleep with all the men in the circle. My seatmate thinks I'm going to steal her things."

Per's lips twitched. "Sounds like a Monday!" Then he added more softly, "A strange school is like that for everyone. Keep your chin up and don't let them get to you. Promise?"

Disa hesitated. "I won't wear this dress."

Per looked inquiringly at Kelda. She shrugged angrily and turned away. She had bought the skirts as Midwinter presents, on Regency. "All right," Per said. "Suli's got a date in town tonight. We'll see if he can find you a colony dress. If you'll do a favor for us." He stood, reaching for Kelda's elbow and tugging her up, too. "We're searching the library for information on metamorphosis—anything we can find on its mechanisms and regulation on planets analogous to Karg. Will you continue the search? I'll send Ea for you when supper's ready."

Disa watched morosely as they walked arm in arm toward sunshine. Then she wrapped her arms around Enki's neck and cried.

Every First-Inner and circling had a small personal baggage allowance. Yvette's went to a few mementos of her father and to clothes. While Disa suffered doggedly in gray Aelollan mutton hair, which true to promise was stiff and scratchy and didn't breathe well, Yvette wore gay finery from the fashion centers of the galaxy. The same students who teased Disa unmercifully about her short-shorn hair asked Yvette where she had gotten her clothes and how they were made and whether, if one had the money, they could be ordered from the traders who serviced

Karg's orbiting station. The boys baited one another like fighting cocks for the privilege of teaming with Yvette in partner games. "Don't be such a goody-goody," Yvette told Disa when the younger girl asked the secret of such popularity.

The next day Disa joined a covert spitball battle in history class. Leif reported her to the teacher, and she sat alone in front for the rest of the day.

Enki knew that she cried herself to sleep, but Enki, of course, could not tell. Disa wondered what would happen when Enki became an elder and learned to talk. She tried not to worry about his odd new habit of scraping at himself. Perhaps the thickening shell itched.

The mud nipper experiments were going nowhere. "It must be our food poisoning the groundlings," Sulman said darkly as Kelda and Disa helped with scut work in the lab early one warm autumn morning. He waved his hand at the nipper cages. "We've raised nippers in city sewage, irrigation water, shuttle fuel fumes, and silk whey. They still metamorphose just fine."

"So why blame food?" Disa asked. "It doesn't affect nipper metamorphosis, either."

"But nippers react to it very differently than groundlings do. Nippers have enough sense to dislike L-protein, once they learn it makes them sick. Groundlings can't stay away from it."

Indeed, groundlings loved L-protein as Disa loved candy. An order to leave it alone held good only in the orderer's presence; Disa's teammates had long since learned not to leave groundlings unsupervised in the kitchen. A groundling would gorge on L-protein until its stomach filled and negative effects began to show. Disa often saw groundlings vomiting by the hedges of Frilandet fields.

"How can they like something that makes them so sick?" Sulman wondered aloud.

"Ask Martin," Kelda suggested from the lab bench where she was reading assays on nipper blood.

Disa flinched. Her family had teamed with Uncle Martin shortly before his forced retirement. Eight-year-old Disa had liked him when he was sober, but when he was under the influence of ballel his words had frightened her. "Why does he keep drinking it?" she had asked. The drug's smell still upset her.

Sulman looked up from his microscope. "Interesting analogy, Kelda. Ballel's addictive because of its similarity to natural disinhibitors. Suppose our food resembles something naturally occurring in groundlings?"

"Don't be ridiculous," she answered.

"A First-Inner should never say that," Sulman chided. "How do we know what's under a groundling shell?"

Kelda blinked. "You want to be the one to find out?"

Disa looked involuntarily at Enki, who was sniffing at the cooler she sat on. They needed to autopsy a groundling. Even Risky had surmised as much. "Take one. They are not people," she had said. But the humans and Calypso balked.

Why balk at a groundling autopsy, after the treatments given nippers? Disa looked unhappily at a juvenile nipper being force-fed through a plastic tube. Diarrhea kept the nipper's bottom perpetually sore. "Why do we have to do this to any of them?" Disa asked.

Sulman gazed somberly at her. "What does the dust say, Disa?"

She thought about dust, struggling toward beauty, swirling into dreams of nippers, groundlings, and girls. The nipper with the tube down its throat neither deserved nor understood its fate. The *gigg* changelings probably understood as little. Dust had laid the decision at Disa's feet, and any choice brought suffering. She, for better or worse, owed loyalty to groundlings. "None of this is fair," she protested against her own conclusion.

"Life's not."

Creaking oars interrupted the conversation. "There's Yvette with the specimens," Sulman said. "Help her unload while I set up cages."

Disa whistled to Enki and set off toward the beach, arriving in time to grab the prow of the dinghy and drag it onto the sand. Enki took to the water after a pair of ducklike birds that rose in flight to escape him. Disa saw a V-shaped ripple as Enki turned to rejoin his human friends. Cubical containers of water littered the boat's bottom. In them scuttled a variety of small swimming creatures caught in traps overnight. Yvette stacked the containers in carrying baskets and handed the baskets over the gunwale to Disa, who started to hand them to Enki. But he was crouched on the sand, shivering and clawing at his shell.

Disa set the baskets down in inch-deep water. "Enki! What's wrong?"

Yvette stopped working, too. "It's warm this morning. He shouldn't be shivering."

Dirtsiders thought it strange that "cold-blooded" creatures like Enki shivered at all, but Disa and Yvette had grown up with Enki and understood that he, too, was warmed by exercise and chilled by evaporation. Disa snatched a tarpaulin from the boat, dropped to her knees beside Enki, blotted the water from his sides, and hugged him close, letting her body heat warm him.

He laid his nearly blind head into her lap and shook and scratched.

Disa peeked at him in the semidarkness beneath the sailcloth. For two days she had been telling herself that she was imagining it, but she hadn't been. His shell was separating.

"Enki, can you make it back to camp?" He burrowed against her, his standard response when he recognized the voice tones of a question but had no idea what the question meant. Disa tightened the tarpaulin around him. "Yvette! Get Dad. And Suli. Something's really wrong."

Yvette paused for one question. "Risky?"

"She's below. We can't wait for her."

Per and Sulman arrived at a dead run as Calypso, with a Sheppie's sense for trouble, splashed ashore.

"What's wrong?" Per asked.

Disa did not let a tight throat interfere with critical information. "Enki's shivering and scratching something awful. I think his shell's coming loose." Sulman pulled aside the tarp. Calypso probed with a gaudy, delicate tentacle.

Sulman rocked back on his heels. "Well, pink lady?"

Uncharacteristically, Calypso hesitated. "He iss acting oddly. But we do not know what iss normal for a changeling. We sshould take him underground. Perhapss Rissky will know more."

"Kelda's summoning her to the Meeting Hall," Per said.

Sulman eyed the huddled groundling. "Can he walk?"

"I doubt it," Disa answered, sick with anxiety. "His legs are shaking too hard."

"How do you carry a groundling?"

"Sling," Per responded. "Give us that sail."

"No," Calypso said. "Hiss gillss are mature. I will take him. Find uss in the Hall of Meeting."

The Sheppie dragged Enki underwater. Per hurried with Sulman to get Yvette's specimens out of the sun. Yvette bit unhappily at her lip. "Disa?"

"Yeah?"

"I'm sorry."

"Not your fault."

"I'm still sorry. You love him."

Disa's face twisted. "He can't die!"

Yvette held her arms out. Disa, aching terribly, accepted the embrace. Tears would not come. She sniffed.

"I think Dad left the mush burning. We prob'ly ought to rescue it."

"I'll get it," Yvette said. "Go find Enki."

Disa scurried through the low oval tunnel and down the pit to the Hall of Meeting where Kelda paced. Half a minute later three other parties arrived—Per and Sulman along the route Disa had taken; Risky, with Inanna and Buzz-Click, through a small hole halfway to the ceiling; and Calypso, with Enki, from the underground river.

Kelda backed away as Per and Sulman lifted the shivering groundling out of the water. Disa listened intently to Risky and Buzz-Click's exchange. Buzz-Click probed Enki's body and spoke again. "What are they saying?" Kelda asked.

"I don't know. I think Buzz-Click is using technical terminology related to metamorphosis."

Disa saw her mother switch on a recorder. Later they would analyze the recording, review it with an elder, and ask questions about that mysterious and suddenly all-important phase of Kargan life.

When the words slowed, Disa inserted her own question. "Enki *gigg*?"

She didn't understand the answer the first time. Risky tried again.

"I think she said it's too soon to tell. Once in a while this happens with normal change," Disa said.

"That iss what I undersstood alsso," Calypso said.

"How soon know?" Disa asked in Kargan.

"Days. Two. Seven. A few."

"Ask if there's anything we can do," Kelda said.

"Watch."

Kelda straightened, wiggling her shoulders to relax them. "You had better eat, Disa. It's nearly time for school."

"I can't stay with Enki?"

"We'll call you if anything happens," Per promised.

"I should stay with him."

"Please," Kelda said. "Risky will be with him. There's nothing you can do but worry yourself sick."

No different from being at school, Disa thought, but after a lingering farewell to Enki she climbed back up to face the day.

CHAPTER ELEVEN

❧❧❧❧

RISKY NESTLED IN A CAVITY DISSOLVED IN SOFT ROCK BE-
tween two firmer beds. Water sought to refill the niche
with minerals acquired in slow seepage. Risky liked the
niche's dampness, its slippery flowstone and faintly gritty
ceiling. She felt glad to hear the gods leave. Gods, especially human ones, asked too many questions. They questioned as the *graf* had. That troubled Risky. Risky lacked
answers to their questions. That troubled her, too.

Twenty feet below her on the Meeting Hall's floor slept
her changeling. Its frantic scratching had ceased, but the
furrows raked in Risky's hopes remained. She knew, if
Buzz-Click did not, that the changeling was *gigg*.

To Buzz-Click, with a dozen sturdy groundlings and
plenty of time, that seemed no great matter. Risky had just
one groundling. She would soon be left with none.

Who would feed her? Her cavemate Inanna would lend
the services of her own groundling, but that offered only a
temporary solution.

Risky could mate.

But before the new groundlings reached usefulness, the

circle would leave. Risky would have lost her chance at change.

In her distress Risky clicked faintly. The noise glowed, to sonic eyes, reflecting from the lake in the adjacent canyon. Echoes formed vibrant patterns within the hall, hinting of variously pitched columns of air in adjacent tunnels. Diverting her thoughts from the changeling, Risky sang her song deep to feel the cavern's shape, high and strong to sense its texture. She extended her claws and snapped them at different distances, savoring null points and standing waves. How much more alive, this cave, than the sad small tunnels of the gods! How much more richly complex than the flat plain chambers they favored!

The canyon's river flowed silent and deep, from the dreamers' caverns to the waters of Beyond. Risky descended from her niche to the floor, scratched her elbows on clean sand, and lay with one claw in the water to consider further. Risky knew more of Beyond than had any elder since the *graf*'s days. Her limbs trembled at memories of the obscenely heaving ferry deck, deadly solar radiation soaking her garments, and unenclosed expanses sucking away her breath. The gods grew impatient when she crouched prudently in thick robes and said nothing. Their displeasure grieved Risky. Only their changeling, the soft-voiced fragile one, respected Risky's courage. To her, Risky was grateful.

Fleeing the hot/cold, life-overladen, radiation-washed Beyond, Risky's thoughts followed the river the other way, to the dreamers' halls. What rounded, twisting dreams amused them now? What mystic meanings lay in those disturbing shapes? A dreamer had just died, Buzz-Click said. Soon his companions would hold dreamer trial. How did an elder pass that trial?

Buzz-Click neither knew nor cared. She thought eldertime the prime of life. She had surmounted groundling silliness, yet dreams did not obsess her. She enjoyed peak strength and dexterity, without the thermal and digestive upsets of youth or the fragility of age. Only when her season came, and not before, would Buzz-Click dare the dreamer trial. Some preferred to die of age. Few chose dreamer trial before age pressed.

But Risky had never been normal. Groundling curiosity had led her to the human-gods. Petted and fed, she had grown fond of them. With affection had come frustration, aroused by nearly but not quite comprehensible demands. Throughout that time, Risky had fed her mother. For that, her mother woke her.

Risky splashed herself. What joy it had been to penetrate the riddles of speech! Her mother died in dreamer trial. Risky lived on as Inanna's cavemate. Among her own kind, she would have rested happy. Instead she lived with the gods. Like a groundling still, she perceived but did not grasp. Even changeling Disa raised questions as senseless as a dreamer's. Risky wanted to understand them.

Certain of her desire, Risky had wakened her only groundling. Richly she had anticipated the development of a daughter, an heir, a companion for her cavemate, an assurance that eldertime continued. But that was not to be.

The changeling began to scratch again. Risky took its hand in her own, seeking to calm it. She grieved for broken dreams.

She wrapped her other hand around a water-smoothed pebble to let its calmness penetrate her soul. But the very feel of the surface brought troubling images. Her people were stone, Risky thought. They were solid, firm, settled. The gods were water, ever-changing, leading rapid, ephemeral lives. But as every cave dweller knew, water shaped stone and could, in time, destroy it.

The gods, ostensibly concerned for *gigg* groundlings, asked impenetrable questions about shapes within Risky's own body. The *graf* had meddled thus. *Gigg* seemed a nightmare like that the *graf* had brought. Were the gods *graf*? Would a dreamer understand their forbidden questions? Could a dreamer judge their purpose, good or ill?

In Risky's mother's time, elders with *gigg* changelings had been barred from dreamer trial. But with tragedy rife, the dreamers had abandoned such choosiness. Despite her changeling's fate, Risky remained eligible.

Experience had aged Risky young, and more rode at stake than her own ambition. She wanted change. Second change. She would dare dreamer trial.

CHAPTER TWELVE

❧

"IT'S TOO SOON TO TELL," DISA'S TEAMMATES SAID ABOUT Enki. Intuition said "*gigg.*" For a week and a half, Disa spent her spare hours underground—reviewing lessons, refitting her diving suit, or massaging Enki's hand in darkness.

"Don't you get depressed?" Yvette asked.

"He wants me there," Disa said. Then Risky announced her intention of proceeding with dreamer trial. "Enki is dying!" Disa protested in Kargan.

Risky chittered but did not relent. "I have no time to raise new groundlings," she told Disa in English. "Trial begins. Gather silkfruit in low water." That meant, roughly, "make hay while the sun shines." "You, Disa, will be with Enki. Perhaps I will return."

Perhaps, Disa thought. Or Risky would return to find Enki dead, or Risky would not return at all. But Risky brooked no meddling with her plan.

Grief for Enki and worry for Risky's trial left Disa unhappier than ever at school. Resentment flared hottest in history class, for the history taught by Frilandena bore little resemblance to the history Disa knew. On Friday, ten days after Enki's first shivering episode and two days after Risky's departure, discussion turned to the Orion treaty.

"You all know," said the teacher, an intense young man who'd been one of Skip's classmates, "how the Sørensons squelched initiative and accomplishment on Valhalla by taxing the successful to support the lazy and incompetent."

Disa stared, her jaw open.

"You disagree, Miz Nygren?" the teacher asked.

She weighed integrity against his anger. Integrity won. "How can you say the Sørensons have squelched initiative and accomplishment? They provide opportunity for everyone, not just the rich."

"In the process," he countered, "they block selective pressure. You can't starve to death if you try. They're destroying their genetic pool. The Sørensons know it—that's why they encourage immigration."

"Valhalla's immigration rate's high because of its standard of living and excellent universities," Disa responded. "Visitors like it so much they want to stay."

"Those universities are full of students pursuing unproductive studies in the liberal and fine arts," the teacher said impatiently. "And Valhalla's cost of living is astronomical. I was born there. Believe me, it's not as rosy as they say."

If liberal studies were useless, why did Mr. Ansgar teach history? How old had he been when he last saw Valhalla? Six, if he were Skip's age. Disa had been to that planet just three years past, a guest of the Sørensons. A spitball bounced from her elbow. Whirling to see who had launched it, Disa caught Yvette's warning glare. She pressed her lips together and nodded to Mr. Ansgar—a gesture only technically deferential.

He accepted it at face value, but kept a wary eye on Disa as he continued. "This fall we've traced the destructive policies of the Sørensons back to the social democracies of Earth's prestellar age. This week we saw how clever maneuvering by pressure groups blocked healthy competition in the first star colonies."

Disa had questioned that, too. The colonies aided one another because it was that or die, she said. Earth's quarrels looked small from a distance of light-years. If a colony let *anyone* die, it might sink below critical population mass. Mr. Ansgar granted none of those points.

"Today," he said, "we'll discuss imposition of the Orion treaty. All of you memorized it in sixth grade—if you don't remember it, brush up before Monday's quiz. Under what circumstances was it signed?"

Aage Hanson raised his hand. He often seemed too pleasant to be Burr's younger brother, but at this moment he sounded very much a Hanson. "The Orion treaty was imposed upon humanity by the Carbon League with assistance from the Singh traitors. Since it was signed under duress it should not be considered binding on present or future generations."

Indira and Asoka Singh, the first humans to join First-In, *traitors*?

"Nicely put," Mr. Ansgar said. "What did the delegates sign away?"

"Their rights to free exploration and settlement," Valda answered.

"That's ridiculous," Disa blurted.

Mr. Ansgar raised his eyebrows. "Explain your outburst, Miz Nygren."

"The treaty gave access to the Carbon League registries. We could browse through planet catalogs instead of sending probes! That saved an incredible amount of time, money, and lives."

Valda snorted. "Some catalogs. They had this planet listed in the wrong protein category and with no mention of native civilization."

"The mislisting was the scout's fault, not the registry's!" Disa protested. "And in any case the registry clearly stated that the planet had not yet been surveyed for colonization. The registries aren't intended to replace First-In."

Mr. Ansgar, to Disa's surprise, spoke in partial agreement with her. "Miz Nygren is correct—Karg's mislisting was merely a stupid blunder, and under normal circumstances the registries are a great convenience. But what price do we pay for this convenience?"

"Cession of settlement rights to less competent species," Aage answered. "And surrender of sovereignty on frontier planets."

Yvette, who usually listened carefully to Aage—a means of frustrating Leif, Disa thought—frowned. "What do you mean, cession of rights to less competent species?"

"I mean that prime real estate like the Beta Centauri planets, perfectly suited to human settlement and well located with respect to Earth, had to be left undeveloped."

"They aren't undeveloped," Disa said. "The Houri are there." With beautiful leafy colonies much prettier than Holmstad.

Aage frowned. "Monkeys. If we hadn't signed that treaty, we could have established our own rights to the territory."

"What 'rights'?" Disa asked.

Leif, who normally sided against Aage because Aage was a Hanson, jumped fence. "We were stronger than the Houri, and our weapons were better."

"You can't take an established colony by arms," Disa said.

"It worked on Graycloud," Leif told her.

"That wasn't an invasion, it was a blockade," she replied. "Graycloud left itself wide open. Blockade wouldn't have worked in the Centauri system—the Houri colonies were self-sufficient. Just like a blockade can't hurt Karg."

"Frilandet," Mr. Ansgar corrected.

Disa's main point stood undisputed. The Frilandena had come to Karg for independence. The silk trade brought extra equipment and luxuries, but the Frilandena never relied on it. Aage returned to the subject of direct attack. "NovaCorp blasted that Triop colony by force of arms."

"And didn't gain a damn thing," said Yvette, whose father had died defending that colony's refugees. "Nova-Corp ruined the real estate it wanted."

No one contradicted her.

Mr. Ansgar broke the silence. "So far we've only discussed limitation of settlement rights by the Orion treaty. What about frontier sovereignty. Aage?"

"There is no such thing," the boy answered. "Even a duly registered settlement can be arbitrarily ousted by First-In." Heads nodded all over the room.

"Not arbitrarily," Disa said. "Only if there's a native civilization."

"If a planet has native civilization it should be entered in the registry that way to start with!" Aage said, flushing.

"You can't always tell by looking," Disa countered. "Often you don't find a native civilization until survey. Or what if it developed between a planet's registration and its colonization?" Actually Disa knew no instances of that. The reverse occurred more often—a planet listed with "rising technological society" would have no society at all a few centuries later. That was why First-In declared interdict on all but the most extraordinarily peaceful peoples.

"If a civilization's not advanced enough to see from space, why worry about it?" Valda asked.

"Do you have to foul up a planet to have rights to it?" Disa asked, shocked. Then, well acquainted with Frilandet attitudes, she shifted to a self-interest argument. "Besides, it pays to leave rising societies alone. A lot of them are too quarrelsome to be adaptive. Give them star drive, they'll kill you as well as themselves." Only those interdicted races that survived to develop their own stellar drive joined the galactic community.

Mr. Ansgar ignored that point. Instead he asked, "What is the flaw in granting immediate and unconditional authority to First-In when a question arises about native civilization?"

Again Aage answered. "Conflict of interest. Granting jurisdiction to a prejudiced authority."

"What do you mean, 'prejudiced'?" Disa demanded. Aage must be quoting from his father's political speeches.

"I mean First-In can hardly judge native intelligence impartially when an affirmative answer gives power to the circle."

She blinked. She had heard a lot of wild rumors about the organization of her birth, but never that one. "You think we *want* jurisdiction? You know what a hellish headache an Orion intervention is?"

Mr. Ansgar frowned, and Disa realized she sounded like Kelda. Yvette stayed carefully silent.

Careful of her phrasing, Disa pressed on. "We don't have trade interests. We don't have territorial interests, because we don't have any fixed bases. We don't have military interests, because we're restricted to defensive armament. If we're not neutral, who is? And anyway, a circle's jurisdiction under the Orion treaty is temporary, a stopgap until the situation can be decided by treaty tribunal."

Aage was unswayed. "Treaty tribunals are hardly independent authorities. They base their decision on First-In testimony. And eighty-five percent of a typical tribunal's delegates are related by blood to First-In."

Disa had never heard that before, but it might well be true, given circlings' tendency to gravitate into diplomatic professions and vice versa.

"Let's take an example," Mr. Ansgar said. "Suppose Circle Dawn is faced with a doubtful case of native civilization on Frilandet." A doubtful case? "Now, the Sørensons have an interest in seeing Frilandet colony fall flat."

Disa Nygren looked nervously around the room, wondering if anyone besides Yvette knew that she was also Disa Sørenson. She didn't want either name. She was Disa of Dawn.

Mr. Ansgar continued. "Suppose there were—"

From Disa's belt came a series of short, sharp beeps.

An emergency call! Disa yanked the beacon out and thumbed acknowledgment, her heart pounding. Once again—it seemed as if she spent her life that way—everyone stared. Mr. Ansgar impatiently pressed his lips together. Kelda's voice sounded clearly through the room. "Please come home quickly. Enki is not well."

"I'm coming," Disa said self-consciously. She jammed the beacon back on her belt, slammed the cover over her instructional console, and picked her lunch off the floor and stuffed it in her skirt's big pocket.

"Where are you going?" Mr. Ansgar asked.

She did not want to fight with him just then. "Excuse me please, sir. My groundling's dying."

"Your *groundling*?" Someone, probably Kirby, hooted.

Mr. Ansgar frowned. "Go if you must, but Monday I want an essay from you on the composition of the Graycloud Tribunal and the potential—"

Disa missed the rest of his sentence. She was already out the door.

She had both oars in the water by the time Yvette pounded onto the pier. "Disa, wait up!" Yvette threw her school pack into the boat, backed off six paces, took a flying start, and threw herself in. The boat rocked madly. Yvette rubbed her knee. "Ouch. Your mom always said flex when you land. She never said look out for specimen baskets."

"You don't have to come," Disa said, turning the boat against the current.

Yvette sighed. "Come off it, will you? I don't like their crap any better than you do. But I know better than to try to change their minds. Usually."

Disa threw her weight against the oars. Sweat beaded on her face.

"You row to the first bend," Yvette said. "I'll spell you there."

Disa nodded. It was good to have a friend.

CHAPTER THIRTEEN

࿊࿊࿊

RISKY SLID INTO THE POOL BENEATH THE CRYSTAL-PIPES.
A dreamer approached. He smelled like the one who had
sired Ea and Enki. Another time, Risky would have
burned to embrace his fragile, exposed body. Now she had
come to lose her own shell. That anxiety overrode arousal.

The dreamer began ritual questions. "How many times
has water risen on you?"

"Twenty-three."

Surprise-scent washed from him. What did others answer? Risky wondered. Most lived fifty seasons of elderhood, or sixty, before they entered dreamer water.

"You are Wanderer," he surmised. So they called her.
"Have you left your warren filled?"

"No," she said, grieving again. Worry permeated the
grief. How many centuries had passed since anyone had
answered thus? A warren might go empty when its occupant died of mischance, but no one left for dreamer trial
without waking a daughter. Would he allow her to continue?

"Why lies your warren empty?"

"I have only one groundling, and that one *gigg*. I wandered far, where no dreamer lived to fill my clutch." None had *ever* answered thus. Native elders retreated in uncomprehending horror from Risky's explanation. Would the dreamer do likewise?

He twitched provocatively as he considered the novelty. "Have you a cavemate?"

"I have. Her daughter will fill my place." An attenuated fulfillment, but better than replacement by a stranger.

"Your cavemate wandered with you?" The question was new, not from the ritual, and saner than Risky had expected from a dreamer. She grated her claw in assent. "How has she groundlings?" he asked.

"Water has risen forty times on her. She clutched thrice before we wandered, and will soon mate again."

"As dreamer you may not wander. You must remain here to dream with us and fill the clutches of elders." It was the longest and most coherent speech Risky had ever heard from a dreamer.

Never to wander with the gods again? Locked here in the caverns of stone? But there was no time for second thoughts. "I understand."

The dreamer's claw hovered before Risky's face. His pincers cradled an object four inches in diameter. "With this, you commit yourself to change. Consider carefully. Will you drink?"

Anxious, eager to know what rested in his claw, she hurled a burst of her most powerful and highest-pitched sonar at it. The echoes revealed a spiny ball and a flinching dreamer. Horrified by her own lapse of courtesy, Risky quieted, probing the ball instead with a scent whisker. It was smooth, probably hollow and liquid-filled, and odorless. "I will drink."

"May *graf*'s voices guide you." With his other claw, the dreamer snapped the tip from one of the ball's spines. Odor, strangely familiar, surrounded Risky. The dreamer thrust the broken tip toward her mouth. "Drink, Wanderer." And this time, he pronounced the name with a masculine affix.

For twenty-three seasons, nothing had entered Risky but water and honey. She poked tentatively at the ball's broken spine. It was hard, unyielding, with none of a honeytit's tough flexibility. The dreamer's presence, the male name, the tartness of the liquid in the ball, the obscenity of drinking from an inanimate object, and knowledge that the current she followed flowed but one way left Risky rigid with excitement. She sucked at the contents of the ball, choking a little.

The dreamer waited until she finished. "Your trial has begun. Return to Hall of Voices. Consider lessons of time. Consider virtues of our people. When your mind opens, we shall summon you." He continued to use masculine forms. "Go, Wanderer, He-Risky."

Risky climbed from the pool onto the Hall's polished limestone floor. If she survived, she would soon be as helpless in air as a groundling trapped underwater. Ignoring the four elders still gathered by the pool's rim, she went, as had the five before her, across the level floor to the walls and climbed until she found a niche from which she heard none of the others, but only the melody of crystal pipes. The liquid's tart taste lingered in her throat, familiar. Had she smelled such before? She rested quietly, trying to feel changes in her body. None who drank the liquid could return to elderhood. But one needed more liquid to finish change. Only the trial's winner got that. The others died.

Hours passed, water dripping on crystal. Excitement passed. Risky dozed, woke again, let her mind drift on the room's music. Mixed with crystal notes she remembered alien voices speaking of *gigg* changelings and arguing her planet's fate. Risky's claw chittered in distress. She must set those distractions aside. "May *graf*'s voices guide you," the dreamer had said.

What sort of trial awaited? Tremors of anxiety made Risky's claw click louder. She chanted the stone song to calm herself:

> From stone are hatched dry air, wet water, life;
> From stone comes egg, and so in stone rests fossil.
> Desire and thought shape stone, and then are gone,
> But stone still shakes with steps of those who've
>   walked it.

Familiar words brought calm, a clearness in which to focus on her task.

"Consider lessons of time. Consider virtues of our people." Unsettled, Risky thought about her use of the alien song. Had her travels tainted her? Could she succeed in a test of her own people's merits? What were they? A groundling merited waking by doing its task well, bringing plentiful fine honey. How did an elder merit change? Risky pondered, until a dreamer voice broke her reverie. "Follow," it said.

Risky and the nine other dreamer candidates emerged from their niches on the wall and slipped into the pool from whence the dreamer called. They swam behind him as he led down and northward, into unfamiliar channels. A stinging smell woke terror in Risky. A guardian! The creature clung to the rock ceiling of the tunnel, its body a tuft of tubular glands that secreted digestive enzymes. Below trailed sticky five-foot tentacles to shock or paralyze and ensnare any creature trespassing in the dreamers' realm.

The dreamer extended his claw with another little ball in it. Pincers closed. From the crushed ball spread a salty fluid. The guardian snatched its tentacles to itself, huddling into a small misshapen lump. The dreamer slid beneath. "Come."

The journey ended in an artificially enlarged solution pocket off a major subterranean stream. "Listen carefully," the dreamer said. "You must journey thus from here." He detailed a complex twisting route, giving directions sometimes with reference to magnetic declination and deviation from vertical, sometimes with reference to the pitch of the limestone. Risky crouched absolutely motionless, building a map in her head, sensing that her trial had already begun. She found the complex instructions surprisingly easy to remember.

"Do not expect uninterrupted passage," the dreamer warned. "Nor shall you turn back. Guardian scents your presence. He will follow."

The water's smell told Risky that she was not the only one afraid. A guardian moved slowly. An elder easily outran or outswam it. But a guardian moved inexorably, leaving no time or space for second attempts, and a guardian had many ways to kill. One took the correct path first, or not at all.

"For each of you I have special words." The dreamer spoke to each elder in turn. Risky found her instructions amended at four points by deletion and insertion. "Those who succeed will converge in final chamber, and must settle matters there. We will listen. Go now." And with that, the dreamer left.

The elders did not speak to one another. Each feared to forget her instructions or their all-important emendations. Each knew that another's success meant the guardian's sting for herself. Together they moved northward through the river, each clicking softly for bearings, none acknowledging the others.

Risky had thought star travel frightening and lonely. The present terror dwarfed it.

Soon side corridors opened from the tunnel. Four companions turned. Lost already? Risky wondered. Differing instructions? Or had she herself miscounted distance?

Spending most of her life in the woefully limited passages of Dawn's artificial cave, Risky had little experience following directions in strange surroundings. Was her estimation sloppy? No help now—the dreamer said fifty lengths north, and then forty-two degrees to the right—there! Another elder followed Risky. The final four went on.

What she followed was not a single passage but a confluence of two, one at thirty-nine degrees from the original passage, the other at forty-five. Panicky, Risky clicked, noting the position of the opening behind her and the angle of the original tunnel. Forty-two degrees would take her along the right-hand wall of the left-hand tunnel—which, she heard as she entered, soon turned rightward anyway. She must follow her instructions with absolute precision, she realized. An opening in the wall must not be cause for relaxation. The elder accompanying Risky also chose the left fork, without pausing for a corrective bearing.

Left, left, right, up two lengths and off along the bedding plane of stone. Risky's companion turned aside, but odd blips echoing through side passages told Risky that others wandered that three-dimensional maze. Down, right, angle left and up, farther left, follow a curve southeast, take the third opening, nearly hidden behind a chert boulder; up, thirty-two degrees down and right, fight the current, left, up. She smelled elderfear; someone had been that way. Around, back, through. She smelled guardian. Have I missed a turn? Sideways, angle off, left, left, go up along the rise of the rock—that was too familiar—dive, turn off. There was a waterfall somewhere in the catacomb; she could feel the stone rumble. Follow the twist, turn right . . .

Risky trembled, ran over her directions, and recalled her course. Yes, turn right. Rock blocked the turn. Knowing that she must calm herself, she cited again the star-steppers' hymn. "From stone are hatched dry air, wet water, life—"

What had her own people's representative said? "Do not expect uninterrupted passage." The disturbing undertone of falling water permeated everything. Quiet, as she had lain so many times with the star-steppers, Risky let her whiskers trail. Current flowed through the rubble to her right.

If water flowed, clear passage lay beyond. Risky began to dig.

Risky was small, having molted only eight times before her mother, bound for dreamer trial, awakened her. She was also weak. Time spent tunneling new passages and filling old in Dawn's makeshift cavern hardly equaled sixty seasons' practice at carving real stone. Risky found the blocked passage nearly impossible to clear. A boulder shifted, pinning her left claw. She could, and would, tear her arm off at the shoulder rather than fail dreamer trial. But without both claws she could not tunnel effectively. "Desire and thought shape stone," she told herself, using a tiny manipulative hand to clear gravel beneath the pinned claw. Free!

Through the submerged corridors rang the death-shriek of an elder stung by the guardian.

Risky dug.

As she cleared the crevice, water flowed through, carrying off smaller bits of sand and gravel. The undertone she had noticed earlier increased to a brain-numbing roar. Falling water. *Lots* of falling water.

Risky measured the opening a final time with her whiskers, then wedged her shell through. Straight ten lengths, leftward down a thirty-degree decline, then right and up. All the directions for that section specified distance and direction, without reference to "next opening" or "around first bend." Now Risky understood why. She was swimming in an underground lake.

The waterfall's din blinded her sonic eyes.

Risky assessed turbulence and current. She would compensate as best she could. The more decisively she moved, the less the water would carry her off course. She swam.

Straight, left, down, angle up to the right. Up, down, forward again. She wanted to protect her antennae with her hands. She needed every limb for swimming. A wall! She felt for unevenness, anchored herself. Her instructions said to go straight.

A tunnel opened a clawlength to Risky's right and down a little, within the limits of current-born error. She took it. Straight forty-five lengths, left—yes, the tunnel curved!—over, and right. Again Risky smelled elderfear. The elder who had entered the first side tunnel with Risky huddled on the floor, chittering. What lay around the bend?

Radiation. The path led Beyond, through the waters of the river by which the human-gods camped.

Risky paused in a boulder's shelter to think. The chittering behind her suggested that she had stayed on course. The other's inability to dare Beyond confirmed it as an obstacle capable of distinguishing between candidates. At last Risky's starwandering came to her advantage. She feared Beyond. She hated it. But she knew she could survive it.

Unlike the ferry deck, stone stayed still beneath her and ten lengths of muddy water shielded her from the sky. Risky probed in the silt and found two thin chips of rock to cover the sensitive patches where her eyes had once been. Cool spring water beckoned from her destination, where another cave complex opened to the river. A straight-line crossing. The dreamers had laid the course simply enough that no candidate would be lost in the Beyond.

The spring on the far side smelled of guardian, but

Risky's careful beeping revealed no tentacled body. Forward, left, forward, third right. A calm chamber. "Take
the upper exit," the dreamer had said.

A carven stone, with complex indentations, blocked
the exit. Risky probed. It did not yield.

Low-pitched, low-energy sonar revealed many small
stones and a larger one on the floor of the chamber. Risky
raised pitch to increase resolution. Those stones, too,
were carven, in twisting shapes like dreamer dance. Risky
nestled to caress the largest. "But stone still shakes with
steps of those who've walked it." This stone, composed of
many interlocked pieces, nearly matched the door's in-
dentation. If she twisted it so—Risky's whisker felt what
had to be done, but her hand was too large to do it. She
fingered the smaller pieces on the floor. That would inter-
lock with that. If she connected the other, and twisted
sideways...

Risky huddled on the floor, turning puzzle parts like a
groundling, testing her work, reshaping it. Finally she inserted the structure she had created into the larger piece
she had found. She twisted. The larger structure warped
accordingly. Risky withdrew her tool. The piece fit admir-
ably in the lock. Working faster, Risky assembled small
pieces into a trigger to swivel the keyface.

Stone swung aside. Risky swam up and through.

"Those who succeed will converge in final chamber,
and must settle matters there."

Another elder waited. Ignoring her, Risky examined
the room. Four lengths in diameter, it held water three
lengths deep, into which opened a dozen of the carven
doors, all shut again. A single passageway exited the room
abovewater; it opened from a ledge just below the ceiling
on the east side. Risky could not reach the ledge. The
room's walls were as smooth and vertical as the Hall of
Voices' floor was smooth and flat.

Another hatch opened. Risky expected an elder. Instead—a guardian!

Risky and her companion spurted away. Both scrabbled for purchase on the far wall. Both slipped back into the water. The guardian, not used to free swimming, anchored to the chamber floor and began slow motion toward the elders.

A claw clasped the rim of Risky's shell. Her fellow candidate thrust her toward the guardian.

Risky twisted and nipped the other's hand. She tumbled free, but found herself perilously near the guardian. She swam back to safety.

Until that point, the trial had shown elegance. Did it end with survivors wrestling one another into a monster's mouth? Did Risky have the strength to thrust her larger opponent to death? If not, she had the strength to drag her opponent with her. Then neither would learn to dream.

Would either learn anyway? What guarantee had they that the guardian would quit after one kill? Sometimes no one survived a dreamer trial.

The guardian came closer. "May *graf*'s voices guide you," the dreamer had said. The *graf* had destroyed themselves quarreling over a prize. Risky eyed the inaccessible ledge. With a boost, one could reach it.

In a voice made rough by fear, she said so.

Her companion cursed her for a fool. "You look to me to aid you? Your fossil time nears." Indeed, Risky's hand tingled as the guardian approached, spitting poison.

Risky's tenure had been short, as groundling and again as elder. She did not wish to die, especially when no daughter replaced her. But someone should survive. "I will lift you." With the strength of panic and despair, the bitterness of a honeytit pulled from her mouth, the grief of dreams dying, Risky boosted the other elder from the water.

The force of the lift shoved Risky downward. The

guardian's tentacles embraced her. Then current erupted, ripping her from the monster, washing her with the bitter salt of guardian-bane. "*Daqua*, He-Risky. Welcome."

Dazed and stinging, Risky felt a frail dreamer hand drag her through a door into fresh sweet water. "You learned time's lessons well. Murder is not a virtue of our people."

CHAPTER FOURTEEN

NO GENTLE LIFT ACCELERATED DISA'S BOAT AROUND THE point—Calypso must be elsewhere. Disa rowed the final yards, hiked her gray skirt, swung over the gunwale, and splashed to shore, leaving Yvette to beach the boat. "Where's Enki?"

Kelda turned from the laundry line, a wet shirt still in her hand. "Meeting Hall. Your dad and Calypso are with him. Get that skirt off, it's not good for climbing."

Disa sprinted across the beach and up the bluff to the cave's cool dimness. She snatched her helmet from the equipment cache and went on, reaching the crawlway before her eyes fully adjusted to the dark. Guided by memory and subliminal cues of sound and airflow, she ducked her way to the pit that dropped to the Hall of Meeting. Only then did she remember that she was supposed to have taken her skirt off. Hem in her teeth, she descended the ladder.

In the torchlight she could see Enki writhing on the ground between Per and Calypso. The groundling flinched from Disa's light. She turned it off, content with the diffuse illumination cast by Per's helmet on the ground a few yards away. Now that her own footsteps and heartpounding no longer filled her ears, she heard Enki chitter piteously. He thrashed viciously for a few seconds, lay rigid and trembling for the next half minute, then began thrashing again. It took Per on one side and well-muscled Calypso on the other to keep Enki from flipping himself over.

"Enki?" Disa whispered, stooping and reaching for his elbow.

"Careful he doesn't pinch," Per warned.

"He will not ssnap at Dissa," Calypso said. "He iss not angry, merely in pain."

"Careful, sprite," Per repeated.

"Is he dying?"

Calypso tipped a tentacle toward an elder hovering in shadow. "Sso ssayss Buzz-Click."

"Changeling dies?" Disa asked in Kargan.

Buzz-Click's claw grated "yes." Then she spoke a very old and formal phrase that Disa knew because Risky had spoken it when Uncle Jack lay dead. "I mourn with you."

"How lessen his pain?" Disa asked. She got no answer. The Kargans found such inquiry taboo. She looked pleadingly at Calypso. *"Hashashanallach chi-suin?"* Her synthesizer converted the phrase to the low moans of Sheppie.

Calypso, holding Enki with three tentacles, caressed Disa with the other two. "No, child. We know not enough of hiss physsiology."

Enki spasmed again, his hand's clawtips digging painfully into Disa's arm. When the convulsion passed, she spoke into his ear. "I love you, Enki."

Perhaps his warped metamorphosis had gone far enough to give him some comprehension of her language, or perhaps he merely recognized her voice. Straining against a tremor that again held his body rigid, he scanned with his scent feelers, fixed on Disa, and tried to snuggle against her.

Silently her shoulders shook.

Minutes passed slowly, like water dissolving stone.

Per's right hand kept a cautionary hold on Enki, lest the groundling hurt itself or Disa in the next round of thrashing. His left hand kneaded Disa's shoulder. Something dug uncomfortably into her right hip as she sat on the cold floor. Her lunch was still in her skirt pocket.

"Dad, can Enki have my sandwich? It's too late to hurt him now."

Per nodded. "If he wants it. But I doubt he can eat."

Disa fumbled for the sandwich, unwrapped it, and held it close to Enki's nose. The groundling convulsed, but when the fit passed he sniffed again for the alien food. Disa tucked small bits into his mouth, careful to keep her fingers clear of his teeth.

To everyone's surprise, the meal brought temporary recovery. After a few minutes of increased trembling, Enki's rigidity loosened and his breathing relaxed. Scrabbling to his feet, he edged onto Disa's lap in his old position and nuzzled at her hand to ascertain whether the treat was gone. Then he crossed his pincers and relaxed into seemingly normal sleep.

Water dripped. Disa thought, but was not sure, that she heard faint music from the Hall of Voices. Buzz-Click left. Enki's stomach rumbled comfortingly against Disa's leg, and she dared hope that his calmness was more than a respite. Perhaps a groundling accustomed to human food needed it during change, as well, and the others had died because they had no Disas to bring sandwiches in the midst of crisis. Calypso, who hadn't bothered with crutches, dragged herself to the rim of the pool. "I will remain closse by." Water closed over her.

Per's breath smoked in the coolness. He gazed meditatively into darkness. After a while, he blinked at Disa. "Want me to stay? Or you want to be alone with him?"

She looked down at Enki. "You can go. We'll be fine."

Her left leg grew numb, but she did not want to disturb
the groundling. She shifted her weight slightly and compared the cave's soft stillness to the bustle of the world
above. Did colonists truly believe that the claim of Kargan
intelligence was a First-In power play? Enki shuddered
and chittered softly, disturbing Disa's thoughts. He relaxed again. Disa replayed the history discussion, wondering how to refute Frilandet arguments. Water dripping
somewhere recalled Disa's attention to the here and now
of the cave. She stroked Enki. His body lay still, unmov-
ing. Dead.

CHAPTER FIFTEEN

꧁꧂

SKIP ROUNDED THE BEND. KELDA, DRESSED EVEN MORE trimly than usual, did a triple cartwheel along the beach, rounded off, threw herself into a back handspring, and landed neatly in Per's cupped hands. He catapulted her up and back over his head. She tucked into a double roll mid-air, landed on her feet, and, with a boost from Sulman, finished, hands thrown wide, atop his shoulders. Skip dropped his oars and clapped.

Kelda, her face flushed in the late-afternoon sunshine, trotted to meet him. Behind her, Yvette eyed the distance, took a deep breath, and began the cartwheel series. "You folks do this all the time?" Skip asked.

Kelda laughed and wiped her palms on her thighs. "Good training. I admit ninety-nine percent of our work takes no strength or dexterity at all, but when you get to the other one percent you haven't time for six months of conditioning. So we try to stay in shape. Besides," she said, winking at Skip, "Circle Diamond's throwing a jamboree just about the time we expect to leave here. They've held the tumbling championship far too long."

Yvette opted for only a single turn in midair, but otherwise completed the routine without mishap.

"Impressive," Skip said.

"She's pretty good," Kelda agreed, "although 'Vette and Disa are both a bit tall for this. They swim well. And Disa climbs better than I do—she's not lifting an extra ounce of fat anywhere, and she's got a better reach than mine."

"Where is she?"

Kelda's expression sobered. "Crying over Enki."

"He died?" Skip had guessed as much, when he heard that his niece had been called out of class.

Kelda nodded.

"I'm sorry."

"Me, too. Nothing to do about it."

The other three humans joined them. Calypso rested tentacles on the boat's gunwale, listening. "Where's Leif?" Yvette asked.

Skip frowned. "That history argument today impressed your classmates. Some of them quoted it to their parents, who came in asking for Disa's suspension. Faculty met earlier this evening. Erica spoke some pungent words about ideology and censorship, and suggested that she wasn't much interested in teaching if that was how things worked. In the end she and Disa will both stay. But Hal's decided this camp's not a salutory environment for his son." Skip wondered why he had to be the one to explain Hal's decision. Not liking the subject, he changed it. "What's so important you couldn't tell me by radio?"

Kelda looked worried. "Good news and bad."

"Give me the good."

"Risky's back."

"Really! She won?"

Per grinned and nodded. "We'll soon have a dreamer to talk to." With all the effort Per had put into deciphering dreamer language, no wonder he was excited.

"What's the bad?" Skip asked. "Enki dying?"

Sulman shook his head. "No. Guess what Risky brought back."

"An elder who *gig*ged on second change."

"Not that bad," Sulman said. "A sample of the second-change meal."

"The who?"

"Second-change meal. The stuff that triggers metamorphosis to dreamer. Guess what it is?"

Skip waited. Sulman handed him an analytic readout. Skip's eyes widened. Amino acids? An optically neutral mixture, half northpaw and half southpaw? "No!" he protested, in genuine disbelief. "This is absurd! Where would they get this?"

"Risky's descriptions are garbled, but it sounds like an inorganic synthesis, which agrees with the fact that it's racemic. I'll bet you anything southpaw acids are the active component. The candidates drink the stuff before trial and again afterward. I can't imagine it tastes good."

"Nor I," Skip agreed, wrinkling his nose. "Our food must taste like ambrosia by comparison. Is this really it?"

Suli nodded. "Now we know what's happening to the groundlings. Our food must activate part of second change in them. No wonder it fouls first change all to hell."

"And that's why our food's so attractive to the groundlings," Skip mused. "Because it *does* interact with their systems." They would have to confirm the theory, design some biochemical tests, maybe autopsy Enki's body and compare it to that of a healthy changeling, if they could find one—but Skip was already sure what they would find. "Our puzzle's solved! Why call this bad news?"

Suli, his bare shoulders glistening with sweat, looked down at the sand. "How are you going to keep groundlings away from southpaw food?"

"Oh." Skip looked down, too. Just that morning he had skirted the mess made by a pair of groundlings breaking into someone's garbage bin. Keeping groundlings from human food would be a far more complex problem than blocking exposure to some toxic pollutant.

"Let uss firsst confirm our guesss," Calypso said. "We sshould bring Enki'ss body to the lab before it decompossess ssignificantly."

"Where's it now?" Skip asked. "In the cave?"

"Yeah," Kelda said. She wiped her hand across a sweaty face. "I'm not doing anything until I wash and get dry clothes." She plunged into the river, calling, "Last one in's a purple-spotted Vargan!"

"You don't slip away from me like that!" Per answered, diving after her.

Yvette paused to shed the silk scarf tied in her hair. "Come on, Uncle Suli."

"With you in a minute." He eyed Skip. "Enki's in the Meeting Hall. Disa and Risky are with him. I'll go before dinner and ask if we can have the body. Come with me?"

Skip didn't relish the prospect, but he liked Sulman. "I guess."

Suli smiled charmingly. "Good. Now if you'll excuse me, Kelda's right. No need to dine sweaty." He spoke briefly to Calypso in Sheppie, then followed his teammates into the river.

Five minutes later they emerged and trooped toward the wardrobe hut to exchange wet clothes for dry. Skip trailed at a distance, kicking at pebbles, thinking hard. How could elders require southpaw protein for their transition to dreamer? If they secreted it, that would be odd enough. But a *manufactured* substance to initiate the change from female to male? That made no evolutionary sense at all. How had the Kargans induced change before they discovered manufacturing? Was that another aftermath of the *graf*'s fall? Just what had those ancient Kargans done to themselves?

Sulman tapped him on the shoulder. "Let's get it over with."

Skip followed him through the chamber by the cave entrance and the long low tunnel beyond. At the bottom of the pit ladder, Suli put finger to lips and nodded toward the Meeting Hall. Skip saw Risky's ghostly shape, not yet visibly changed, swaying rhythmically over Enki. In a human such motion connoted madness. Risky chirped in an ultrahigh frequency, barely audible but headache-inciting. Skip had heard that elders could damage living tissue by sonic percussion. Was it safe to share the cavern with Risky?

Disa huddled to the side, arms around her legs and chin resting on her knees, her green eyes huge in a tear-streaked face. His feet groping over the gravel, Skip moved toward her. "I'm sorry."

She looked away. "It wasn't your fault. It wasn't anybody's. Except people's. For coming here. Enki cried before he died, Uncle Skip."

Ingrid had nursed a wounded groundling once. Skip still remembered its woeful chitter. For lack of anything better, he said again, "I'm sorry."

Disa wiped her eyes, leaving a clay streak on her cheek. "Are you going to take his body now?"

"Will the elders let us?" Sulman asked her.

"Risky said yes, so long as we return it when we're done."

Skip took a deep breath. "Does Risky know it will be—mutilated?"

For all Disa's tears, she showed remarkable maturity. "It doesn't matter how many pieces it's in, so long as it's not contaminated with any chemicals. Risky will put it in the field."

"The field?"

"Her word. I think 'garden' is a better translation.

They put bodies in a special corner of the mushroom room."

"Mushrooms?" Skip asked.

"A non-photosynthetic aquatic plant the dreamers cultivate as food. It grows on decaying organic matter. Putting bodies in the garden is the Kargan way of saying dust swirls on."

"Like where you said they put Ingrid's body."

Disa nodded and lapsed silent for a moment. Then she asked, "You need a normal changeling to compare with Enki?"

"Right." Skip wished his lab manager saw implications so quickly.

"I asked the Kargans. They drummed an inquiry."

Drums? Dimly Skip recalled hearing of a low-frequency seismic communication system by which the Kargans spoke from warren to warren.

"There's a changeling about fifty miles up the coast," Disa continued, "that was killed by a flash flood after the storm last night. You can have the body if you return the parts when you're done."

"Perfect," Skip said. At that distance there would be no question of exposure to colony crops. With Hal's fast motorlaunch, they could have the body in the lab by noon the next day.

Sulman stood behind Disa, kneading the girl's bony shoulders with competent hands. "Calypso will take the body out, if you're ready."

Disa crawled forward and spoke to Risky in the harsh Kargan tongue. Risky edged aside to let Disa lay her own slim hands on Enki's lifeless body. The girl bowed her head, eyes closed. Then she swallowed and stood. "All right." She said nothing more as she climbed with Skip and Sulman to the surface, but her eyes glistened. The men's did, too.

CHAPTER SIXTEEN

❧❧❧❧

SKIP KNEW THAT FULL DISCLOSURE OF FIRST CHANGE'S biochemical pathways might take years. But by Saturday night, dual autopsies on Enki and the changeling from up the coast, combined with Calypso's physiological work, gave a preliminary answer: yes, left-handed amino acids had lodged in two of Enki's key glands, stimulating second-change developments that stalled his first change. Calypso discouraged discussion of the implications. "Let uss ssave thesse quesstionss for the Hall of Voiccess."

"What?" Skip asked.

"The Hall of Voices," Sulman said, wearily rinsing a scalpel and laying it in the sterilizer basket. "This merits a rounding of the circle. We thought the Hall an appropriate setting. Will you join us?"

Skip hesitated, thinking of the vids he had seen. "I'm really not much for ritual."

"What do you mean? You come to our daily meetings."

"But those are practical—any research group needs to communicate plans and concerns—"

"And we start with the Litany of Dust," Sulman reminded him. "A rounding is just the same writ large. If

Kelda puts up with it, you know there can't be too much mumbo jumbo. You'll come?"

"I guess. If you'll tell me what to do."

"Of course. Our circle rounds at dawn, for obvious reasons. Why don't you spend the night?"

Skip had done that often enough to grow used to sleeping in the light, firm bag, hearing coals settle in the fire, looking up to the deep, deep darkness of Karg's sky. He woke expecting the usual sounds—Disa and Yvette splashing with Calypso, Kelda swearing like a marine as she singed her finger on the teapot, bearded Per teasing clean-cheeked Sulman about his shave. But that morning Disa skipped her morning swim, perhaps because of faithful Enki's absence. Kelda sipped her tea in somber silence. Sulman and Per gazed into the dark mist over the river. Yvette, however often she had protested that First-In business held no interest for her, rose early with the rest and donned the same sort of businesslike coveralls that Disa wore.

No Kargans joined them, not even Ea. Calypso, too, kept to herself. By the time dishes were washed and put away, clouds in the east began to glow. The First-Inners' beacons beeped politely. Kelda and Sulman both reached to answer. They stopped, eyeing one another. Sulman shrugged and, with a smile, clipped his beacon back to his belt. Kelda spoke into hers with an odd hiss. *Sheefatha ssrizan?* A synthesizer converted the phrase into the low pitches of genuine Sheppie speech.

"We will meet you in the cavess," a familiar voice responded. Kelda belted her beacon. Disa picked up the last tray of sweetcakes and locked it in the kitchen unit. At the equipment cache Per distributed helmets, reserve lights, and packs. Sulman motioned to Skip and the girls to precede him into the cave.

As autumn cooled the world outside, the cave air seemed less chill, although it still felt quiet and damp.

Disa led, ducking nimbly beneath protruding knobs of chert. Yvette and Skip lagged slightly. The three adult First-Inners followed in silence, punctuated by Per's stifled curse as his helmet made unintended contact with rock.

Calypso, who like the Kargans could navigate by sonar, waited in the Hall of Voices' pool. Her garish colors scarcely showed in the dim light of the helmets. Ea sat quietly on the rubble heap through which the humans entered. Risky and Inanna crouched in niches on the left wall. Blind though they were, they wore sashes of white silk bearing starred circles. Near Risky waited a native elder.

"That's Buzz-Click," Disa whispered to Skip. Her words echoed from the polished floor. Following her example, Skip shucked his pack, pulled out a cushion, and inflated it. Calypso dipped a tentacle to her stalk in a motion that Skip recognized as checking her beacon. It must be nearly dawn. Calypso spoke, first in Kargan, then in English. "Before we turn to the problem which bringss uss here, let uss recall our common birth in dusst."

Calypso sang the litany in a deep eerie harmony. Skip found the Kargan version ugly as well as incomprehensible; still there was a fascination to its uneven rhythm. The human chant was second nature by now:

> From dust are born the suns, the seas, and life,
> Dust we are, to dust we shall return.
> It swirls in hope and song, and then swirls on,
> But dust does not forget the dream that stirs it.

Sulman spoke lingeringly; Kelda, as always, tugged for a brisker more expressive pace. Per and Disa mediated. Yvette stared at the wall, lips pressed together, blinking.

The multilingual chant mingled with bell-tones of water dripping on crystal. When voices stopped the crystal chant continued, a soothing backdrop for troubling questions. "Let uss sspeak peacce to one another," Calypso suggested.

Disa reached for Skip's elbow with her left hand. "'Peace' in Sheppie is *zhastost*, or with a synthesizer it is. In Kargan it's *blick*. Try to say that much to each one in his or her own language." Skip's suddenly-clumsy tongue was still practicing when Disa caressed Calypso's bright tentacle and spoke in fluent pseudo-Sheppie.

Calypso answered in English. "Peacce to you alsso, Dissa. I sshare your hope for dusst'ss wissdom." A second pink-and-orange tentacle found Skip's free hand. "Peacce, friend Sskip. Your pressencce pleassess uss."

Skip wet his lips. *"Zhastost."*

The Sheppie, normally punctiliously proper, had left aside Skip's title. Even the most overdrawn representations of rounding got that detail right. Dramatists loved the moment when alien generals and petty human lordlings must greet detested underlings as equals. "What do you do with hive races?" Skip had asked. Sulman had shrugged. "Wing it."

The presumption of level status resulted in Disa turning to Ea, who wandered in clear confusion. Disa smacked her tongue in the command every colonist learned, popularly translated as "sit." When Ea obeyed, Disa gravely reached for his manipulative limb with her left hand. *"Blick."* With the castanet in her right hand she gave her Kargan name, *snap-click*.

The groundling echoed *"blick"* with no apparent understanding, but when it heard Disa's name it rubbed her calf affectionately.

Disa looked over her shoulder for Skip. "Here. You need to embrace or touch him, and say *blick*. Just do your name in English." Skip obeyed, feeling like an utter idiot. Later he saw Buzz-Click engage in the same routine. How did First-In persuade elders to transgress the mores of their caste?

Eleven individuals milled about for a quarter of an hour in the round robin of greeting. "How long does this take at a major trade negotiation?" Skip whispered to Disa.

She giggled. "There are dire legends about that! Usually, though, big crowds split into working groups. The longest greeting I've been in took an hour and a half."

Skip felt inexperienced, naïve.

Finally they congregated on the far side of the room where the pool's edge lay only twenty feet from the wall. Calypso settled her brightly colored stalk in the water. Disa towed Skip to the Sheppie's right. He laid his cushion on the flat stone floor, and Disa sat beside him. Sulman sat cross-legged along the wall with the Kargans. Per, Kelda, and Yvette settled themselves across from Skip and Disa.

For twenty minutes, no one spoke. Sulman and Per closed their eyes. Kelda's lingered on the chimes. Disa watched Risky, Yvette stared into the pool, and Skip, no expert in contemplative technique, stared at them all. He looked from Calypso's shadowy tentacled form, to Risky aglow in white silk, to Disa's solemn face. Strange to think of those diverse forms living, like himself, in hope and song; struggling, as he did, with the mystery and fear of death. Enki's body still lay in the lab's cooler. Do his dreams swirl here? Skip found himself thinking.

Calypso spoke in Kargan, then in English. "We have sspoken peacce to one another, but peacce iss threatened. Ssulman, pleasse sstate our problem."

He answered first in Kargan, punctuated by the clicks of a castanet like Disa's, then, with a synthesizer's aid, in Sheppie. After a moment's silence, Risky back-translated into English. "Sulman says groundlings exposed to human-god colony go too often *gigg* when wakened. This because plants brought by human-gods trigger dreamer change before its time."

Calypso, evidently confident of her own understanding, gave no back-translation from Sheppie. Instead she asked, after a long pause, "Hass Ssulman sspoken fairly?"

In their various tongues, the conferees assented.

"Conssider then."

The tinkling pipes reminded Skip of the little bell that Gerda's kid had worn. He did not wish to think of Gerda, but he remembered Sulman's advice: "Let your mind wander by its own map." Then Sulman had quoted an ancient Earth poet. "The heart has reasons reason knows not of."

Skip wanted to cry.

Calypso shifted position, evidently a signal for discussion, because Kelda and Sulman both began to speak. Sulman inclined his head to Kelda. She continued in rapid-fire Sheppie, then in Kargan. Disa frowned. Risky said in English, "Kelda says god-warren should not come at start. If god-warren food makes *gigg*, human-gods must go."

Calypso, too, back-translated. "Kelda ssayss the colony has no right to come here in the beginning and hass no right to remain now. If their cropss are poissonouss to the groundlingss, the humanss musst leave."

"They won't go," Skip blurted, forgetting until too late that custom required pause between remarks.

"We'll make them go," Kelda said, just as careless. Sulman glared at her.

"Lissten to dusst'ss dreams," Calypso cautioned.

Kelda set her chin, but held her peace.

Half a minute later, Buzz-Click spoke. Risky translated to Sheppie and English for her. "Gods came to *graf*, testing welcoming. *Graf* welcomed not; for they fought one another. Gods, troubled by such noise, departed. Cursed, *graf* brought death upon themselves. Now human-gods test our welcoming. We will not drive them off."

Kelda began to protest the story's irrelevance, but Calypso interrupted. "Sso dreamss the dusst on thiss world. Conssider well."

Per spoke a few minutes later. Calypso continued to back-translate. "Per ssayss humanss too have legendss of divine vissitorss who tesst hosspitality and punissh ór reward according to the ressponsse. Per'ss great-grandfather Olav ccited ssuch a tale when he welcomed the Frilandena to Valhalla."

Why recall that now? Skip wondered. Had the Sørensons, in light of later friction, regretted their decision? Probably so. Even Valhalla's rulers had never adhered to ideals as these Kargans did. Did the past's shadow really loom darker over the Kargans than did Frilandet colony's continuing, fatal, presence? The pipes rang softly.

Disa spoke in Kargan. Risky answered, and the two exchanged several sentences. Clarification? Disa proceeded into Sheppie. "Dissa ssayss sshe hass been thinking of her uncle'ss goat Gerda. Gerda died as the *gigg* changelingss do, poissoned by reversse amino accidss. But Gerda alsso sshowss the ssuffering of a colony attempting to esstablissh itsself. If the colony dessiress to sstay and the Karganss dessire it to sstay, why not sseek ssolutionss that enable peopless to live together?" Disa nodded assent to Calypso's translation.

Sulman smiled at the girl.

Skip waited a decent interval. Then, knowing neither Kargan nor Sheppie, he spoke in English. "Can't you find an antidote for the poison? Or train the groundlings to stay out of our fields? There's plenty else to eat." Disa translated for him, and the aliens responded.

Kelda looked at her daughter. "If Disa couldn't train Ea and Enki to stay out of our kitchen," she said to Skip, "there's no hope of dealing with all those wild groundlings!"

"It would be easier if the colonists locked away their garbage and fenced their fields," Disa said, although Skip did not understand until the aliens reflected her words.

"Fat chance," Sulman muttered in English.

Skip nodded agreement. "It's trouble enough keeping granaries and cellars locked. And even locks don't always work." He had seen Enki fetch equipment for Disa from First-In's own "groundling-proof" cache.

Not only must groundlings be locked out, Calypso reminded them, but stray seeds must be kept in, for L-isomeric plants growing wild poisoned as surely as those in fields did.

Yvette spoke next. If groundlings could not be kept from fields, could fields be kept from groundlings, by growing food off-planet?

Skip, as second shareholder in the orbital station, knew what it took to establish habitat in space. "The colony hasn't got that kind of resources. We stretched to build the silk station, which supports just five residents. You're talking about supplying a population of ten thousand. And an off-planet food supply would leave us vulnerable to sabotage."

"We have sspent all our attention on friend Sskip'ss ssecond ssugesstion," Calypso said. "What about hiss firsst? Mere education doess not dissuade the ground-lingss. But perhapss the action of the accidss could be blocked. Or the mechanissm which renderss them sso attractive."

Elegant! Skip's mind began proposing experiments. His stomach complained that it was lunchtime.

"What other optionss have we?" Calypso asked.

"Break for lunch," Per answered, speaking in his own language for the first time since bumping his head on the ceiling. "I don't think well on an empty stomach."

Since neither humans, Kargans, nor Sheppies cherished taboos on social eating, they dined together in the

Hall of Voices, careful to leave no crumbs in the otherwise barren room. Skip found bread and nut butter in his pack. Disa handed him a jerky bar and a Frilandet apple. She looked down to see Ea poking at the other apples in her pack. She kicked his claw away. "Dammit, Ea, that'll kill you!" Her words echoed unnaturally loud in the hall with its polished floor. Ea chittered in distress. Everyone else looked around, startled.

"Please, Disa!" Kelda said.

The girl stared miserably at the floor. "I'm sorry. He was stealing again."

"We're trying to find a way to stop it," Per said gently.

After that the meal went quickly and quietly. Calypso ate fish, small ones grown from eggs in her underwater camp. She ate them raw and whole. Ea rolled over, exposing his honeytit to Inanna. Skip turned away, less comfortable with that than with a human baby nursing.

"Why human-gods must eat poison?" Inanna asked when she was full of honey and ready to think again. "When first came, human-gods ate Kargan food."

"Doesn't she know how damn sick it made us?" Skip asked, thinking again of Gerda.

"That iss not what sshe meant," Calypso said. "Sshe referss to the period in which you ate fermentation productss. That possed no threat to the Karganss."

"There's no way the colony will go back to eating gruel," Kelda stated flatly.

Skip tucked away the last of his raisin bar and nodded agreement. Given the Sheppie's own distaste for makeshift fermentation rations, Calypso ought to understand that the Frilandena would not tolerate such a regime! Yet she and Inanna spoke truly—if humans gave up their southpaw crops and ate Frilandet's own protein, groundlings would be safe.

Earlier, they had discussed tampering with Kargan physiology so that groundlings might eat southpaw protein unharmed. Inanna's comment raised another possibility. "What if you changed human digestive enzymes so we could handle Frilandet protein?" Skip asked.

The pipes chimed softly for twenty seconds, then babble began. "That would be a lot less expensive than treating a planet full of groundlings."

"Human physsiology and enzzymatic sstructure are much better known than Kargan, and we have a ready ssupply of exxperimental animalss." No more mud nippers.

"The colony would riot!"

Sulman's eyes crinkled. "It oughtn't to be that difficult," he said directly to Skip. "You'd need enzymes to slice the northpaw proteins into component amino acids. Than if you converted the isomers right there in the intestinal lumen, you could transport them into the body as L-amino acids and not have to meddle with anything further."

"But some D-amino acids would get into the system intact," Skip objected.

"That happens anyway," Sulman told him. "When you cook L-protein, some of the amino acids racemize. For that matter, a few racemize even after they're in the body. The kidney's got an enzyme that can switch them back."

"It can only handle so many, though," Skip warned.

"True. So we enhance the kidney's detoxification capacity. Somebody on a southpaw planet with anomalous D-serine already developed an appropriate enzyme and a carrier for it."

"Genetic changess often have far-reaching effectss," Calypso warned, unnecessarily.

"Wouldn't have to be genetic," Sulman said. "Could do enzymes by mouth, or gut bacteria—"

"By mouth won't fly," Kelda responded. "If the colonists' digestion depended on orally administered enzymes, can you imagine what power that would give to whoever produced the enzymes? The Frilandena would never hold still for it, even if the producer were one of their own."

Per glanced questioningly at Skip. Skip inclined his head in affirmation of Kelda's words.

"Gut bacteria would be tough, too," Sulman said, criticizing his own suggestion. "Things move right along in the upper part of the intestine where proteins are digested, and furthermore you'd have to cope with acid influx from the stomach. Tough to maintain a stable bacterial population."

That left only the option of having the body itself produce the required enzymes. Skip stirred uncomfortably. "Calypso's right," he said. "Human gene therapy is a pretty drastic move. Designing and coding the enzymes may be fairly easy. But getting them inserted in the human body—I'm impressed by what you folks can do in that tiny lab. But safety testing this procedure would take resources you just haven't got."

"You're absolutely right," Sulman concurred. "We don't have equipment or financing to complete the job. Even if we did, it's not First-In's job to supply technical salvation to treaty-breakers. But we can do exploratory studies, establish basic feasibility, then let the colony take over. With your expertise and Hal's money, it'll be easy to finish the job."

Skip wet his lips. Geneticists dreamed of managing such projects! "Maybe so. If we presented the idea with the preliminary work already done, so it didn't seem such a shot in the dark, the Frilandena might consent."

Technical details remained to be hammered out, but everyone agreed that the option merited further investigation. A few other possibilities to enable coexistence were mentioned and discarded. The gaps between comments became longer. Skip's stomach inquired about dinner.

"We have disscusssed much," Calypso concluded. "We musst do what we can to resstrict the groundlingss' ac-

cesss to colony ssuppliess and disscourage their con-
ssumption. Much work beckonss in invesstigation of
groundling physsiology and human digesstive enzzymess.
Do any of you wissh to sspeak further?"

Kelda spoke. "Kelda says," Risky translated back,
"what do we if easy answers fail?"

The pipes seemed to sing in a minor key.

"Per ssays we exxplain the ssituation to the colony and
assk them to conssider leaving."

Kelda laughed harshly. For once Skip agreed. That
Sørenson husband of hers was hopelessly idealistic. Who,
even on Valhalla, would undertake the expense and heartbreak of moving an entire colony for the sake of subhu-
man groundlings?

Yvette's reaction showed surprising sympathy to the
colony's viewpoint. "Yvette asskss will that not take all
the money the Frilandena have? And doess not a colony
ssuffer many deathss in the sstruggle to esstablissh itsself?
Frilandet colony only now beginss to recover from that
tragic period."

Disa glared at her friend. "Dissa ssayss many changelingss die now. Dissa asskss do alien livess outweigh native?"

"Kelda ssayss don't be sstupid. The Frilandena will
never move on conssciencce. The Frilandena have no
right to be here. We sshould invoke the Orion treaty'ss
ssanctionss."

Kelda had threatened that weeks before. Skip had put
it from his mind. He stared angrily at her. "Call troops
down on your own people?"

"No, Kelda," Sulman said sharply. "It's wrong!"

"What do you think a treaty's for? To stop abuses like
this!"

"Pleasse. Conssider well." Under Calypso's rebuke,
Kelda and Sulman both lapsed into silence. A minute later
Sulman's voice had softened, but he picked up his com-

ment midsentence. "Ssulman ssayss Firsst-In sshould never have ssigned the Orion treaty. We are transslatorss and mediatorss, not enforccerss. 'We come in peacce and hope it deepenss,' we ssay. That hardly convinccess when at any moment we can ssummon troopss. It iss too eassy, cosstss nothing, makess uss lazy. If we don't know that, the Frilandena do, ssayss Ssulman."

Keldá replied. "Kelda ssayss what do you care about, Firsst-In'ss reputation or the groundlingss' ssurvival?"

Sulman answered her. "Ssulman ssayss we musst look at the larger picture. Dusst hass many sswirlss."

Kelda, sitting forward on her cushion, looked Sulman in the eye. "Don't play the saint with me. What has dust got for Kargans if we leave the Frilandena here?"

He looked with wide dark eyes back at her. A sudden spatter of water set all the chimes ringing. Echoes faded. "Dust's dreams don't last forever," Sulman said, very slowly. "The *graf* died, or at any rate lost sight and civilization, because they were too belligerent. Their descendents face death by not being belligerent enough. Perhaps—" Sulman looked as if he was having difficulty forcing the words out. "Perhaps that is their choice to make."

He looked around the circle and, then, even more reluctantly, he repeated his words in Sheppie and in Kargan. Inanna's claw chittered.

"The choicce need not be made today," Calypso said after a silence. "Nor do we know what choicce we have. I ssuggesst we assk who might enforcce the treaty."

Sulman spoke. "Ssulman ssayss no, we sshould leave that boxx locked."

Buzz-Click spoke. Risky translated. "Buzz-Click says we must welcome human-gods, but we welcome also gods to protect changelings."

Calypso repeated back Per's words. "Per ssayss we sshould know our choicess. But we sshould not tell the

Frilandena of our inquiriess, lesst they think our deccission already made."

Eyes turned to Skip. He cleared his throat. "You pro-
pose to make an inquiry about the availability of enforcement troops, but withhold judgment as to whether you will
actually ask them to intervene?"

"Yes," Per said.

"You want me to keep my mouth shut."

"The choice is yours."

"God help you if the Frilandena find out you've raised
the subject. They'll go stubborn, and you'll never get co-
operation. But they won't find out from me."

"I think we should know," Disa said in a small voice.

"It's too bad you didn't decide this yesterday," Skip
told the team. "*Kotzebue* pulled away from the station last
night."

"It's still in the system," Per said. "We can relay messages to it through our ship."

Sulman rubbed his forehead with his hand. "I don't like
this. We shouldn't even think of invoking the Orion treaty.
But I defer to my circle's wisdom."

There was silence.

"I have heard the ccircle ssay we musst attempt pallia-
tive meassuress in the sshort run, that we musst invessti-
gate posssibilitiess of rendering groundlingss immune or
aversse to ssouthpaw amino accidss, and that we sshould
exxplore the posssibilitiess of adjussting the human ssys-
stem to digesst northpaw amino accidss. I hear the ccircle
ssay alsso we musst learn what enforccement can be invoked under the provissionss of the Orion treaty. Doess
anyone ssay nay?"

Could a single person's veto counteract all the discussion that had gone on today? Skip looked toward Sulman.
The nutritionist bit unhappily on his lip, but did not speak.

"Sso we have deccided. Let uss part in peacce."

CHAPTER SEVENTEEN

❧❧❧❧

"HEY, DID ANYONE MAKE SENSE OF THAT FOURTH BIO-chemistry problem?" Yvette asked.

Disa looked sharply at her circlemate. Assisting in Calypso's lab, Yvette routinely calculated mechanisms for catalyzed reductions. She couldn't possibly have had trouble with the fourth problem.

"I got it," Leif said, setting down his sandwich. During the month that he had been barred from visiting camp, he had been doubly attentive to Yvette in the classroom. He slid sideways on his bench to make room for her. "Come here and I'll show you."

"I got it, too," Aage Hanson said.

"Uncle Skip showed me a shortcut," Leif countered, tipping his console so Aage could see that the entire solution had required less than a single screen.

Aage's freckled nose wrinkled. "That's not the way Miz Erica showed us."

"I got the right answer, though," Leif told him. He reached for Yvette's wrist and tugged her down beside him. "This is how you do it."

Aage rolled his eyes. "What else does your uncle do for you?"

Yvette smiled up at Leif's rival. "When Leif's done explaining biochemistry, I have some questions about the math assignment."

"I can help you with that. I got every problem but the last," Aage boasted.

"The last one was a killer," Valda agreed. "I think it was programmed wrong. Did you get it, Leif?"

"Are you kidding?" he asked.

"I got it," Disa said with a hopeful glance at her cousin. "I'd be glad to show you."

Leif shrugged. "Miz Erica will go over it anyway, since none of us understood it."

Kirby sat down on Leif's desk. "What's in your lunch today, Yvette?"

"Scram," Leif said. Small he might be, but no one had ever seen him back down from a fight. Kirby rose and swaggered over to inspect Disa's lunch instead. "Trade you for the jerky."

"You really want jerky?" Aage asked. "There's a trader docking this evening. Shuttle will come down tomorrow, and I can bring whatever you want on Friday—if you make it worth my while."

"Now who's using family connections?" Valda asked.

Disa stared up at Kirby. She didn't like him, but she wasn't all that fond of jerky, either. The colony children considered it a rare treat. "What have you got?"

Kirby produced a plump, elongated yellow fruit. "Banana."

Valda snickered. "I bet even Disa's never eaten one of those!"

"I had a banana once," she countered. "On Mayala."

"Not like this," Kirby told her, smirking. "This is Frilandet's best."

"It's a pretty one, all right," Leif said with a grin.

Disa eyed the fruit. Jerky was a standard First-In ration. Fresh planet-grown fruit was a treat. "I didn't know you raised bananas here."

"They do very well on Frilandet. Right?" He looked around at his classmates.

They nodded, smiling.

"Deal," Disa said, wondering what everyone found so funny. Foodstuffs changed hands.

"Now wait a minute," Aage protested. "It's not fair—"

"A product is worth what the customer will exchange for it," Leif told him, quoting the history teacher, Mr. Ansgar. "You're a Hanson. You know about taking what you can get."

Disa bit into the fruit. It tasted funny, not as good as she remembered, but then it had been three years, standard, since she had eaten that last banana. Or had it been a papaya?

"You like Disa that much," Valda said to Kirby, "maybe you should back her for queen."

"Huh?" Yvette asked.

"Queen of Lights," Aage told Yvette. "For the big Midwinter dance. The whole town comes to the dance, but it's our class that gets to elect the queen."

"The boys of our class," Kirby corrected.

"Doesn't your circle celebrate Midwinter?" Aage asked.

"Circle Dawn doesn't," Yvette told him. "Our team does, because of Aunt Kelda and Uncle Per, but there's not enough of us to bother with a queen."

"Well, we have a queen," Kirby said, "so any of you girls that are interested better be nice to us." He leered at Disa. "Be nice enough, and I might even take you as my date."

"Disa's got more sense than that," Yvette said. "She'll ask someone worth going with. Aage, maybe." Aage smirked. Leif pretended not to hear.

"Not an option," Valda told Yvette. "Don't you know at Midwinter the boys have to do the asking?"

"We have the power!" Kirby crowed. Everyone laughed.

"You can have the rest of your fruit back," Disa said, tossing the banana pit at him. He ducked. The pit bounced off the wall. Mr. Ansgar walked in.

The teacher stared at the pit, to which shreds of fruit pulp still clung, then picked it up with a thumb and forefinger. "What is this, and why is it flying around this room?"

"Disa threw it," Kirby said.

Mr. Ansgar glared at her. "True, Miz Nygren?"

Hot with anger and embarrassment, she stared down at her desk.

"Anyone who resorts to such childish tricks must be desperate for attention," Mr. Ansgar said. "To satisfy your desire, you may sit in the front corner for the rest of the afternoon."

Still not looking up, Disa collected her things and moved to the "dunce seat."

"That isn't fair, sir," Kirby protested. "Why do we have to look at *her* the rest of the day?"

A soft rap on the door. "Disa? Are you okay?"

Disa sat with her forehead resting miserably on her knees. "I'm fine, Yvette."

"You've been in there half an hour."

"I'm fine!"

Yvette hauled the door open. Light flooded into the tiny outhouse. "You're not fine. What's up?"

"Frontier flu. Go away."

Yvette's forehead wrinkled. "There's no flu going around."

"There is now. Leave me alone."

"I told your mom about the banana pit."

"Great. Now I'm in trouble with the team as well as the teacher."

"She says bananas don't have pits."

Disa started to sit up straight, then groaned, pressed her arm to her belly, and doubled up again. "What I ate had a pit."

"I know. I saw it. Your mom says there's a long yellow native fruit that the Frilandena call a banana. She doesn't know whether it has a pit."

"I know," Disa said. "It does. Dust, I feel like those groundlings. The ones we see vomiting in the hedges in the morning. Suppose I'll go *gigg*?"

"Uncle Suli says you'll be okay in a couple of hours. Anything I can do for you?"

"Close the door," Disa moaned. "And kill Kirby."

The misery passed as promised. "You feel good enough for a trip underground?" Disa's father asked that evening.

"Yeah. Why?"

"I want you to see what Risky's been up to. She was asking so many questions about galactic geography that Kelda rigged a sonic display terminal for her. Risky's spent the entire afternoon projecting coordinates for star systems we've visited or talked about. She told your mom we should have taken an alternate route between Regency and Karg."

"Just for the hell of it," Kelda said, "I ran Risky's route through navigational computation."

"And?"

"Risky was right. The alternate route was more efficient."

Disa pondered. "I suppose it's natural for cave-dwelling creatures to have better three-dimensional intuition than we do."

"Of course," Per agreed. "And Risky's has always been

excellent. But this isn't good, it's phenomenal. What's happening to her?"

"Let's go see her. Maybe she can tell us."

But Risky was more interested in what was happening to Disa. "Why don't you want to go to school?" the Kargan asked.

Disa hesitated. Per, sitting in the Hall of Meeting with them, answered for her, speaking in Kargan. "Human-warren's changelings seek to drive away visitor from other warren. They welcome Disa not."

"Dawn's humans observe rules of hospitality," Risky said.

Disa's fingers grated assent on her castanet.

"Why don't Frilandena?"

"Human-gods are not all same," Per answered. "On Valhalla human-gods offered strangers welcome. But human-gods of this warren sought to differ. They came to Karg to dig warren of no-hospitality."

"Like Tapachula's humans," Risky said. It was not a question.

Disa winced. So that was what humanity looked like through alien eyes?

A hail from Sulman interrupted the conversation. His words, echoing down the dome and across the Hall of Meeting, were garbled beyond understanding—but he would not have called unless he wanted Per and Disa to come back up. "We will speak further," Per promised Risky.

"Heg, Per," she answered. "Heg, Disa."

"*Daqua*," Disa said, switching on her light.

"*Daqua*," Per echoed. He wore a thoughtful expression as he walked with Disa back toward the dome, but he did not speak again until they had climbed the ladder to the crawlway. "Disa, have you noticed how fluent Risky's gotten? Except for articles, her syntax is nearly flawless."

Disa replied with the obvious. "She's metamorphosing. Or he is."

"But if linguistic ability improves, why is dreamer language so limited?"

Disa had no answer, and the question was soon submerged in other concerns. "*Hound Dawg* just docked at the station," Sulman told them when they reached the team's new wooden cabin.

"And?"

"It relayed an answer from the Weaver's Guild on Xueyan."

"Already?"

"They'll disown guild members who stand in violation of the Orion treaty, but they disclaim responsibility for general measures."

"You know what the weavers here will care about disownment?" Kelda asked. She snapped her fingers. "That."

"We talked to *Hound Dawg*'s captain on a tight beam," Sulman added. "She said she owed Dawn a favor and she'd embargo if we asked. But no involvement that would risk her ship."

Per sighed heavily. "I guess we can't blame her. Any other word?"

"Nothing but an *Explorer's Journal of Lander Design* for Kelda. *Alouette* is due in five weeks—coming from Regency, *Hound Dawg* thought. If so, *Alouette* should carry several more answers. Maybe that news will be better."

Outside, October bark fell from the trees in long brown strips. Groundlings devoured windfallen apples and threw them up again. With Leif gone, Yvette gave her energy to the research project. Skip, Sulman, and even Calypso praised her assistance, but the group's understanding of groundling physiology grew with painful slowness. Human digestion, because better understood already, proved easier to modify. But that news was not all good, either. "Guess it'll have to be gene manipulation," Suli said without his usual grin.

"Why's that?" Kelda asked, looking up from a study guide on coolant recycling. She had run into trouble with a coolant system, two planets back, and was determined to correct that deficiency in her education.

Yvette made a face. "Bacteria just won't stay in the duodenum. Conditions are too harsh. Turnover too fast."

"Since we can't do the job with bacteria," Suli said, "we'll have to get the body to produce its own enzymes for digesting northpaw protein. Here we go sticking modified DNA into human cells!"

"Using plasmids it shouldn't be too tough," Yvette responded. "I bet we're doing tester trials in two months. You ready to leave for school, Disa?"

"Here's lunch," Per told them, handing each girl a packet. "Better eat your own today, sprite."

Disa's face flamed. "I promise, Dad. No more bananas!"

That evening Risky sidled quietly toward Disa in the Front Porch. "I came to say heg, *snap-click*."

Disa started. "What do you here?" she asked in Kargan. Seldom did Risky dare the faint daylight of the Porch, more seldom yet since her lungs had begun to atrophy in dreamer change.

Risky labored for breath to repeat her words. "I came to say heg."

Disa had come to escape the noisiness of the new cabin. She set aside her landing procedure manual. "Go we to Meeting Hall."

Risky's claw grated. "I would be more comfortable there. I thank you for your thoughtfulness."

She slid into the lake, leaving only her claws above

water. Disa sat by the edge. "Why say *daqua*?" the girl asked, agitated.

Risky wriggled. "My shell loosens. I cannot breathe well. Honey no longer satisfies me. My scent makes cavemates yearn for clutches. Among dreamers I will complete my change."

Shock swept Disa. Risky changing was one thing. But Risky gone? "Will you not return to us?"

Hearing the distress in Disa's voice, Risky rubbed her claw against the girl's leg. "Change takes time. My body must heal. My mind must grow. I will not return while waters rise. When I am settled I will summon you."

Disa swallowed. Visit the dreamer realm? "I do not breathe water!"

"You visit Calypso," Risky pointed out.

That was true enough, but cave diving was far more dangerous. "What of guardians?"

"Inanna will guide you to depths. Call my name. I will hold guardians from you." Risky hiked herself out of the pool, half into Disa's lap, and caressed the girl's face with her scent tentacles. "Heg, god-changeling."

"Don't go!"

"We will speak again. First I must change. Heg, Disa." She thrust herself backward into the water.

"Wait!" Disa nearly jumped after her, to swim with Risky as she had with Enki, but she had been warned of the currents in the Meeting Hall water. She knelt on the bank, calling "*Daqua*, Risky!"

Risky broke water on the far side of the pool, below the stone waterfall. *"Daqua, snap-click.* When next we meet, call me—" From the pool's surface echoed a word like Risky's name, and yet not. It was Risky's name stripped of its feminine ending and supplemented with a masculine ending. "He-Risky."

Forlorn, Disa saw Risky submerge a final time. Turbulence showed the Kargan's passage into a flooded tunnel.

Then the pool lay still. "*Daqua*," Disa whispered, throat aching. Where now? She could not carry her grief to the crowded, well-lit cabin. Always before she had taken it to darkness, to Enki's affection and Risky's gentle touch. They were gone. Who else would be gone, before this ended?

In November autumn rains began. "I will not return while waters rise." All wondered what Risky had become, but the dreamers sequestered their new fellow even from his former cavemate, Inanna. *Alouette* brought responses to the team's inquiry, but not the responses they had hoped for. "We enforce only where we have commercial involvement," Interstar said. "Try Newworld Outfitters."

"We're still cleaning up from the Triop affair," Newworld complained. "Somebody else's turn."

"Sulman and Calypso are the best help we can give," Dawn's Core told the team. "Embargo a possibility, but we'll need nine months' warning."

"Not our jurisdiction," Valhalla's treaty commander said. "Sorry. Lindy Sørenson sends greetings." Per glowered at that.

"Who's Lindy?" Kelda asked.

"My cousin—Morbrordatter. Tactical director of Valhalla's treaty troops. You played chess with her the day before our wedding."

"If I'd known she was a tactician I'd not have felt so bad."

"Your cousin's tactical director, and you're First-In?" Sulman shook his head. "Sørensons get around."

Per shrugged. "Talents vary. How's the enzyme project coming?"

The day before Midwinter vacation, *Burundi* entered the system and transmitted a final batch of replies. "Peace to Circle Dawn. Our troops are yours in Malagueña region, but Frilandena are Valhalla's problem. Call Sørensons."

"Shit," Kelda said.

Sulman said nothing, but he smiled.

Per loaded the wood stove, not looking around.

Kelda turned on Suli. "Go ahead! Smirk! You going to smile when we bury the last Kargan?"

He rolled his eyes. "Come off it, Kel. Big sticks don't solve problems."

"A big stick might keep the colony off the Kargans long enough for us to find a better solution."

The stove door slammed. Per stood, glowering. "Would you two quit? None of us want shooting here. The Frilandena are your people, Kelda. Why so eager to drive them out? Sulman, we need biochemistry from you, not philosophy. Why aren't you in the lab—"

Tea splashed from Sulman's mug as he set it on the table. "I was there past sundown, dammit, and again at midnight to check testers! Which, by the way, are growing fat and sassy on Kargan grain. I'll go back when Skip comes. It'd go faster if you two gave more help, instead of mooning over dreamer recordings and spaceship journals—" He stopped. "Aren't you girls supposed to be on your way to school?"

"You always ask that when things get interesting," Yvette said.

Sulman sighed and rubbed his forehead. "This isn't interesting. It's tragic. If circlemates can't be civil to each other, why do we expect better of worlds? I'm sorry, gang. I haven't had enough sleep."

"Less time in town would fix that," Kelda said.

"Stow it," Per warned in a tone he rarely used with his wife. "Suli's right. We're too close to it all; we forget what dust sees. Maybe we need to round circle."

Disa wet her lips. "Can we come?"

He shook his head. "No, sprite. You go to school and find out who's going to be Queen of Lights."

Speculation had run hot for a month about the queen's election and on who would go with whom to the festival dance. Most of the less popular students had already paired off, but Aage Hanson and Leif had yet to choose partners, and Yvette, Gretchen, and Valda had yet to be asked. No one had invited Disa, and she knew better than to expect an offer.

Yvette chattered endlessly about the matter as she and Disa trudged overland to school. "Aage's such a looker, I'd love to go with him."

"He hates First-In," Disa pointed out. "And you're too much like a Nygren for Hanson taste." She skirted a puddle. Rowing to school was shorter and faster, but as warm rain gave way to sleet and snow, the girls had abandoned their boat for the safer, muddier route.

"Besides, I think Leif's going to ask me," Yvette said. "I suppose it's silly to hold out for Aage."

Disa stared at the brambles edging her side of the road. "Up to you."

Yvette could not miss the iciness in Disa's voice. "Don't be a spoilsport. You never know who'll ask you. Kirby said something about it yesterday."

"I'll die an old maid before I go with Kirby." Those might be her options, Disa thought—if she got options at all.

Yvette gave no answer.

Leif was waiting at the bottom of the hill where the river road entered town. "You want help with your packs?"

"I'm fine," Disa answered.

"I'd love it," Yvette said, holding her arms back so he could slide the straps from her shoulders. "Has Valkyrie foaled yet?"

Leif took his own pack on his left shoulder and Yvette's on the right. Small as he was, he showed no sign of bowing beneath the double load. "Not yet, but the groom says soon." Nobody said so, but everyone knew the gray mare's foal would be Hal's coming-of-age present to Leif when Leif successfully challenged him.

The three teenagers fell into step with one another. Leif cleared his throat. "You know the big Midwinter Festival next week?"

Both girls nodded. Leif's eyes darted to Disa, and she dared a moment of hope. He reddened slightly and cleared his throat again. "I wondered if you'd—uh—go with me, Yvette."

Disa blinked in disappointment and tried to clear her aching throat. Yvette purred and leaned delightedly against Leif. The overloaded boy staggered. "I'd be delighted!" Yvette told him.

Leif caught his balance and beamed. Yvette did not forget her friend. "Have you a date for Disa?" she asked.

Leif avoided both their eyes. "I didn't know if she'd want to come—she's a year younger than us, you know— I thought she might want to celebrate Festival at home."

Disa whipped her cloak tightly around her, so that its swirling edge struck Yvette. "That's okay, Yvette, you go on to town. Your dad never spent Midwinter with the circle, either." She lengthened her pace and left the two behind. How many Midwinters had Uncle Jack spent with randy dirtsiders? Not one had cared a straw for him, either. There was no reason to taunt Yvette with it.

No reason, except that Disa hurt so badly she couldn't see the road.

That afternoon the boys would elect the queen. Tension built through the morning. Lunch passed in nervous silence. Finally, after school, the boys went into a huddle. The girls lingered outside, eyeing storm clouds billowing in from the northeast. They discussed whether they could get home before another round of sleety rain began, and they watched the schoolroom's closed door. Disa knew that the election had nothing to do with her. She tugged impatiently at Yvette. "Let's get going. The weather looks nasty."

"They'll be done in a minute," Yvette said. "I want to see who Aage's going with. He hasn't asked anyone yet."

The door opened. The boys spilled out, some looking pleased, some frustrated. They came face to face with the girls. Aage Hanson cleared his throat. "As president of the class, I'm pleased to announce that this year our Queen of Lights will be—"

A spatter of rain pelted them. No one paid attention.

"—Yvette of Circle Dawn. By prior arrangement, Leif Nygren will escort her."

"You can't elect her!" Valda exclaimed, outraged. "She's a foreigner!"

"Nothing in the rules about that," Kirby countered.

Gretchen hugged Yvette. "Congratulations!"

"Who are you taking, Aage?" Valda inquired. She sounded nearly desperate enough to defy Midwinter custom by inviting him outright.

He looked away. "I'm still thinking."

"Don't think too hard or there'll be nobody left," Gretchen warned. She didn't have a date, either.

Disa swallowed hard. "You'll be a good queen, Yvette."

"What're you gonna do, Disa?" Kirby asked. "Stay home and screw Kargans?"

Disa glared at him in dumb outrage.

Gretchen frowned. "Show some taste, Kirby."

Disa swung her pack into position for the long walk home. At least vacation was beginning. She would not have to face her tormentors again for a week and a half.

"Well, she thinks they're people, doesn't she?" Kirby said.

That shocked a response from Disa. "What do you think they are?"

"Animals, I guess."

Disa stood stock still. "You're not serious."

"Why not?" Valda asked. "Whose word do we have but yours? I've never seen their civilization. I've never even seen an elder."

Yvette stood as dumb as Disa. Only when Disa's eyes met hers in frantic appeal did the dark-haired girl speak. "You saw the elders we came ashore with."

Aage shifted his weight from one foot to the other. "We saw some things with cloth all over them. They could have been groundlings. Or machines. Or aliens from some other planet."

Yvette's eyes shifted to Leif. "You've seen them."

He bit at a fingernail, saying nothing. A sudden shift of the breeze brought the stench of the Weaver's Guild hall to them.

"You've seen the elders' silk!" Disa protested to the crowd at large.

Everyone looked at Aage. He squared his shoulders. "No, to tell the truth, I haven't. I've only seen our silk. I know First-In taught us the process after you'd huddled in the caves awhile. That doesn't tell me who invented it."

"Why would we lie? Why claim a civilization's there if it's not?"

Aage broke the silence that followed. "To destroy Frilandet colony." There was more silence. Students shifted uneasily.

"If elders exist and are so smart," Valda asked, "how come the groundlings are so dumb? And if elders can talk, why haven't they said anything to us all these years? Why do they only talk when First-In's around?"

Leif spun and paced away, shouldering his pack as he went. Distraught, Yvette glanced at Disa, then followed Leif toward town.

"What's his problem?" Kirby asked.

"His mom," Gretchen said. Everybody knew that Hal's first wife had disappeared in the caves.

Disa thought about running after Leif and Yvette. Instead, her pack thudded to the ground. She faced her classmates. "So none of you believe Kargan civilization exists?"

They glanced, startled, at one another. "Not like First-In says," Aage answered.

"Have you ever been in the caves?" Disa asked.

More hesitation.

"Well?"

Heads shook.

"You've called me a coward, a liar, and a fool," Disa said. "It's my turn now. I dare any of you to come to camp. I dare you to come down in the caves with me. I dare you to talk to a Kargan. Then see if you call the Kargans animals!"

Gretchen looked awkward and embarrassed. Kirby's eyes darted about. Kirby could be trouble in a cave, Disa thought, but he wouldn't have courage to come. Valda's jaw clenched. Aage's frank blue eyes had widened in astonishment.

Disa picked up her pack and walked away. Yvette waited at the crossroads where Leif had met them that morning. "Where's Leif?" Disa asked.

"Gone. He didn't want to talk. What held you up?"

"I got mad. Come on, let's go home."

CHAPTER EIGHTEEN

~~~~~

AN EARLY WINTER STORM RAGED FULL FORCE BY THE TIME
the girls approached camp. The Queen-of-Lights-to-be
bounced along uncaring as rain turned to sleet, then
turned to snow, but Disa's boots left dark depressions in
the slush. Her hooded cloak kept most of her dry, but
snow caked her half-grown-out bangs and ice clung even
to her lashes. Half-blind, she stumbled into Kelda. "Heg!
What are you doing here?" Disa asked.

Kelda's face was rosier than the embroidery on her
hood. "Heg yourself. Perimeter guard went off, and I
thought I'd come meet you. I hate peeling onions."

Kelda *never* cooked. "Where's everyone else?"

"Busy. Suli's working like seven demons were riding
him. Yvette, he wants you in the lab as soon as you're
changed and warmed up. Disa, your dad's down in the
Meeting Hall with Buzz-Click and company. You'd be a
help translating."

Disa frowned and brushed icy bangs from her eyes.
"What's up?"

Kelda frowned, too. "After you left this morning we
rounded circle. The elders had some things to say."

Disa's heart beat hard. "Word from Risky?"

"No. Worse."

"What do you mean?" They all walked faster, leaning against gusts of wind.

"Our food's the same as a second-change meal, right?"

Disa nodded.

"We know what that means for groundlings. We hadn't stopped to think what it meant for elders."

Disa stopped. "They don't need dreamer trial any more."

"Right," Kelda said, reaching for Disa's shoulder and tugging her forward. "The dreamers have lost control of second change. Now all an elder need do is take some of our protein."

"Isn't that better?" Yvette asked. "Why restrict change to so few? Why condemn ninety percent of the candidates to death?"

Disa shook her head. "Becoming a dreamer takes more than physical change. Risky said she had seasons of education ahead."

"I'll respect that when I hear dreamers speak with a vocabulary of more than fifty words," Kelda said.

"Besides," Disa continued, "they haven't got living space for that many dreamers."

"You're right," Kelda confirmed. "The illicit dreamers are living in the no-man's land between realms—close enough to the elders to arouse them."

"Why didn't the Kargans tell us sooner?" Yvette asked.

Kelda looked away. "They didn't have the problem. Until we told them the connection, no elder would have dreamed of tasting our food."

Disa shivered. Uncontrolled dreamer change could tumble Kargan civilization far faster than *gigg* changelings would.

"I left a kettle on for tea," Kelda said as they came in

sight of the cabin. "What happened at school today?"

Yvette glowed. Disa quickened her pace as the cabin's warmth beckoned. "Yvette's going to be Queen of Lights. Leif's taking her."

Kelda whirled to hug Yvette. Snow cascaded from Yvette's hood into Kelda's face. Kelda laughed and shook it off. "Congratulations! About time the colony kids quit being so standoffish. I was Queen of Lights once."

Disa looked up. "Really? Who'd you go with?"

Kelda grinned. "Ole Hanson. My father nearly killed me. Then next year I went with Sulman, and Dad wished I was still with Ole. At least Ole was Frilander!"

"Uncle Suli took you?" Yvette asked. "What was it like?"

"We had a good time," Kelda answered. Was that a blush on her cheeks? "But now it's your turn. However shall we dress you?"

Yvette hesitated. "I wanted to wear the pink dress, but I think I've outgrown it. The skirt from Regency, maybe, or even winter silks—"

Kelda held the door for Yvette. "Nonsense. You're queen, we have to dress you like one. What about my rounding-home gown? It's got plenty of hem. You coming, Disa, or you want to stand in the snow?"

"I'm coming." Disa brushed snow from her cloak. The rounding-home dress, the one Kelda wore when Dawn's Core welcomed its returning team? She stamped slush from her boots, not caring that she splashed her mother. She wanted that dress for herself—but why? She had no place to wear it.

Midwinter preparations provided a break from work and usual worries. Per coaxed Yvette's dark hair, lovely enough in its waywardness, into a jubilant tumble of curls. Disa grudgingly helped to let the dress out—neither Kelda nor Yvette had any knack for needlework. "I bet Aage was going to ask me," Yvette said. "Should I have waited for him?"

"Hush and hold still," Kelda answered, tweezers in hand. "Your eyebrows look like silkbrew."

"Ssilkbrew iss not unattractive." Calypso had come up to the cabin to observe what she referred to as "fasscinating ritual preparationss."

"On a girl's forehead it is," Kelda said, yanking out another hair.

"*Ow!*" Yvette squirmed away, rubbing her eyebrow, then held out an accusing finger. "You drew blood, Aunt Kelda!"

"We all suffer for beauty."

"No more till I put something on this."

"It was just a drop, for God's sake!" But Yvette disappeared into the bedroom where the medkit was shelved. "Should I use nummit?" she called.

"That'll do fine," Kelda said in disgust.

Yvette emerged, rubbing anesthetic salve on her wound. "I don't know if beauty's worth it."

"It will be," Kelda promised.

Half an hour later, she had reduced Yvette's overgrown brows to coyly pruned arches. Then she applied eyepaint and lipstick. Calypso's tentacles quivered in disapproval. "Musst you usse dye on the child? How vulgar! I maintain ssymbiont sstrainss of the proper colorss, if you will allow me to apply them—"

"Hush!" Kelda said, brandishing a cosmetic brush at the Sheppie. "Or I'll dye you."

Calypso wrapped her tentacles tightly around her stalk. "I think it iss time for me to return to my own domain. Why remain in thiss hot arid sstructure to be inssulted by barbarianss?"

"Heg, Calypso!" Yvette called.

"Heg, child," the Sheppie said from the doorway. "Merry Midwinter!"

"And the same to you," Kelda answered in Sheppie, grinning. She turned back to Yvette and surveyed her work. "You look great. Let's lace you into that gown."

The tightly fitted black bodice and full, deep red skirt, both trimmed in white, suited Yvette's dark coloring perfectly. Her figure, always eye-catching, showed to round exquisiteness. Per whistled appreciatively. "Somebody's growing up! Mind you keep the young bucks at their distance."

"Uncle Per, it's Midwinter!" A couples' festival, from beginning to end. "They won't come any closer than I ask."

Per held his tongue.

"Come have some dinner," Kelda ordered, "or you'll keel over before they crown you. You want some, Suli?"

Sulman was standing in front of the mirror, critically examining the trim of his mustache. "No thanks—I'm meeting someone in town." Since custom forbade the queen and her escort to meet before the crowning, Suli would take Yvette to town in the motorlaunch and see her to the Festival before he slipped away to meet his own date. After the ball, Yvette would spend what night remained with Gretchen.

Sulman smiled at the excited girl. "Soon as I'm dressed, we can leave. You packed?"

"My pack's in the bedroom. What do you suppose Leif will wear?"

Disa retreated into the wardrobe and shut the door. Kelda's own dress for the celebration hung waiting. Disa stroked it with longing fingers. No use trying it on—it wouldn't fit. How Yvette's creamy breasts bulged against the low-cut neck of the rounding-home gown! Disa unzipped her blouse, laid an experimental hand under her own left breast, and pressed upward. Not much there. She looked at Yvette's other dresses, and Kelda's. Tucked carelessly in a corner of Kelda's drawer lay a hand-me-down, a circlemate's gift. Kelda, whose taste ran to fairy-tale flamboyance, had never gotten around to altering the dress. Disa pulled it out. It looked as if it would fit. She put it on.

Aunt Anna, tall and slim like Disa, favored classic lines. Shimmery white, the dress fell from shoulder to toe. A diagonal green and gold sash tugged soft folds against Disa's just-blooming curves. In the wardrobe's full-length mirror, Disa assessed the effect. She liked the way the dress clung to her hips. A cold draft from the door raised goose bumps on her bare arms. Disa blushed hot when she saw Sulman.

He started to back out. "'Scuse me, Dis, I'll wait till you're—" Then he changed his mind, stepped in, and shut the door. His appraisal made Disa feel stupid and grown-up all at once. Should she turn for inspection, as Yvette would have, or laugh and cross her arms, confessing her silliness? She stood frozen.

"I didn't mean to walk in on you," he apologized. "Is that Anna's dress? You're lovely in it."

Disa blushed again and nodded.

Still admiring her, Sulman reached for his brown coat. He must be nearly ready to leave. Disa dared the outrageous. "Uncle Suli?"

He paused, coat in hand. "Yeah?"

"Will you take me to the Festival?"

She shouldn't have asked, she realized. He had a date already. But he surprised her by taking the request seriously. "I'd be honored. But you ought to save Midwinter for a boy of your own age."

"None of them wants me!"

He looked thoughtfully at her. "I know women, right, Disa?"

She looked away. "I guess so."

"You more than guess. You're no blushing fool." He stepped back a pace, hands on hips. When Disa looked at him again, he motioned for her to turn. "Come on. Let's see you."

Pretending she was Kelda, she lifted her arms and pirouetted. Sulman grinned. "*Very* nice." He sat on Per's trunk and patted the space beside him. "Sit."

Trembling, knowing neither what she expected nor what she wanted, Disa obeyed. Sulman twisted to face her, laid hands on her bare shoulders, and turned her toward him. "You are one hell of a lady."

She looked wide-eyed at his face, inches from hers.

"The boys in your class see nothing but boobs, which, by the way, you're growing. But soon they'll figure out what makes a woman is spirit, and intelligence, and caring, and courage. Until a man learns that, he doesn't deserve you."

"You think I'm not old enough for Midwinter."

"I think you should stay home and watch your parents. See what love's about." He had a funny, whimsical look. Disa guessed why Sulman, like Uncle Jack, always left the cabin on Midwinter night.

"You ready, Suli?" Kelda called from the other room. "Where the hell's Disa?"

"With you in a minute," Sulman answered. He smiled, more gently than he did at his colony admirers. "I'll take you if you want, Dis. And if I do, I'll do it right and keep you out till dawn. Or you can wait for someone less well used than Uncle Suli."

She hesitated a long moment, then smiled shyly back. "I guess I should leave you for Miz Erica."

He stood. "May the Keeper of Accounts reward me for this. It's not I didn't like your offer." He opened the door to the cabin's main room. "Found Disa, Kel. She was showing me Anna's old dress."

Yvette, already cloaked and loosely hooded, stood with Per and Kelda. Per looked inquisitively at Sulman, then at Disa. His eyes widened. Kelda's brows rose, too. "I'd forgotten all about that dress," she said. "I know who should get it! Suli, Yvette'll burst if she waits one more minute."

Sulman slid his arms into the brown coat. "Where's her pack?"

"Right here," Per answered, frowning as he hefted it. "What have you got here, 'Vette? Your entire wardrobe?"

"Just overnight things," she said with an anxious glance at Kelda's beacon. "Are we ready?"

"A kiss from the princess before I escort the queen," Sulman said. He turned to Disa.

She expected a kiss on the cheek like Uncle Jack used to give. Instead Sulman pulled her close from hip to shoulder. Disa's face flamed. She stifled the impulse to draw a hand across her mouth as he released her. Yvette's expression was wonderful. "Have a good time with Leif," Disa said.

"I will. You—uh—have a good time, too." Yvette checked herself in the mirror a final time. Sulman picked up her pack.

"Merry Midwinter!" everyone called to everyone else. Then Yvette and Sulman stepped into the night, and Disa remained with her parents by the fire.

She had never realized how outrageously they flirted with one another. Did Per always have such mischief in his eye when he spoke to Kelda? Did Kelda always swing her hips that way when she walked toward him? Conscious of herself as a deterrent, Disa retired early. "I guess we should hit the sack, too," Per said, damping down the stove. "A lot to do tomorrow."

"Midwinter night's always busy," Kelda answered from the bedroom. Per joined her, shutting the door behind him.

Disa lay in her loft over the living room. Wind whistled in the eaves.

* * *

Disa started awake when the cabin door slammed open. Icy air blasted in. She tried to orient herself. Her beacon said it was a little after four. Per appeared at the bedroom door, buttoning his plaid nightshirt. Kelda stood behind him, tousled and sleepy-eyed, wearing one of his big sweaters that fell to her thigh. "What the hell?" Kelda asked.

"I didn't expect to see you tonight," Per said to Sulman.

Sulman pulled the door shut behind him with his left hand. His right supported Yvette. She jerked free and staggered to the washbasin, doubling over it in dry heaves. Sulman slumped against the door. "Guess who I found in a rent-by-the-night room in the wrong part of town, presiding over her own fanciful version of rounding-home?"

Disa scrunched tighter under the covers. At Circle Comet's Jamboree, right after Uncle Jack was killed, Yvette had donned a bronze-and-cut-glass earring and presented herself at the rounding of a Comet frontier team. They promptly evicted her, but Yvette had embroidered the memory ever since.

Yvette, still bent over the washbasin, moaned. "Ya din't hafta drag me back. 'Speshly in the damn boat."

Sulman reached for a towel and wiped his hands. He looked worse for the evening's wear. "She was sick the whole way."

"Seasick," Yvette said. "Wafes too damn big."

Per dampened a cloth with cold water and swabbed Yvette's face. Disa's lip curled at the pungent odor in the room. Ballel! Kelda ducked into the bedroom and came out with lips in a thin angry line. "Ballel, all right. A whole medkit's worth."

Per winced. Sulman sighed. "I asked Skip to see the

rest home. Parents would've jumped to conclusions if I'd done it."

"Shit," Kelda said.

"Who was there?" Per asked.

Leif, of course, and Yvette's sweet-tempered seatmate Gretchen, escorted by one of her brother's friends. Kirby had come with a weaver's apprentice, and Sigrid with Aage's brother, Burr. The final list included all the class but Aage, whom Yvette had so wanted to attend the dance with, and Disa's nemesis Valda. Had they both stayed home, Disa wondered, or had they just skipped the dance? "I'm glad Dis' din't come," Yvette said. "She woun't ha' liked it, Uncle Per."

"Smartest move she ever made," Sulman agreed, glancing at the loft. Disa closed her eyes, feigning unawareness. Suli ran a hand distractedly through his hair. "There's more. Yvette told them we asked for treaty enforcement."

"Deep shit," Kelda said.

Yvette burst into tears. She sagged against Per's shoulder. "I din't meanta make trouble, Uncle Per! They jus' asked wha' we did in Firsht-In . . ."

He patted her shoulder, his face a study in mixed emotions. "Hush, child. You'll wake Disa."

Yvette sniffed. "I was tellin' Leif about the lab. Then 'e said a roundin'-home soundet fun. So we wen' ta haf one."

"What did you tell Leif about the lab?" Per asked.

"Jus' wha' we were tryn' ta do, tummy enzyme changes, but we din't know 'bout side effects." Per closed his eyes.

Sulman began unlacing his boots. "If we're lucky her friends were too dizzy to remember much."

"Guess we'll find out." Yvette had fallen asleep in Per's arms. He sighed. "What now?"

"Let her sleep it off," Kelda said. "It being Midwinter she was prepared for at least some eventualities."

Per eyed the loft doubtfully. "I don't trust her up there."

"Damn right," Suli said, kicking off his second boot. "She'd fall and break her fool head. Besides, Disa hates the smell of ballel. Put her in my bed. I'll sleep on the floor."

"Appreciate it," Per responded, half dragging Yvette to Sulman's bed and going to work on her dress-laces. "Kel? You got a nightshirt for her?"

"Right here," Kelda said. "Rubber sheet, too. Here, I'll finish. Take a peek at Disa before you go to bed."

Per relinquished Yvette to Kelda's brisk care. Sulman laid a bedroll by the stove. Back turned, he undressed. Per stood on the second step of the ladder to the loft. His crossed arms rested beside Disa's pillow. "Elfling?"

She breathed evenly, not sure whether to admit she was awake.

Per spoke in low voice, a murmur that would not carry to the others. "Don't play games with me, fairy-child. You're far too light a sleeper to have missed this."

She opened her eyes slightly.

He smiled at the acknowledgment. "Yvette's made some trouble. Tomorrow we'll find out how much. I'm glad you were here safe."

Disa looked at him with solemn night eyes. "Will Yvette be okay? Not like Uncle Martin?"

"Not from just one night. I hope she learned something."

"She misses Uncle Jack," Disa whispered.

Per's face twisted a little. "Hell of a way to show it. I love you, Disa."

Across the room, Yvette snored. Sulman lay in his bed-roll with a pillow clamped over his ears. Kelda paused, seemed about to come over, then turned and went to the bedroom. "I love you, too, Dad," Disa said.

He stood on tiptoes, leaned over, and kissed her forehead. Then, glancing regretfully at Yvette, he followed his wife to bed.

Hal called the next day as the pale midwinter sun reached zenith. His voice rang harshly from the com console. "Kelda, get your ass in here and tell me what's been going on. You wouldn't believe the rumors flying around this town!"

Per elbowed Kelda aside before she could respond. "You're right, we need to talk," he said. "When do you want us?"

"The sooner the better. And leave your aliens at home."

"We'll be there at three." Per cut the communications link.

Kelda had plenty more to say. "You can't let him order us around like that!"

"We do need to talk to him, and we need not to alienate him," Per reminded her. "The stakes are higher than our egos. What about Yvette?"

"I can't move." Yvette groaned. She still lay in Sulman's bed, doubled by cramps.

Suli shook his head at her. "I can believe that. Next time you want a party, tell me and I'll help you set it up. These impromptu jobs are deadly."

Yvette closed her eyes and turned her face to the wall.

"She's right, you know," Sulman said. "No way she can go to town this afternoon."

"She's done enough damage there already," Kelda answered. "Calypso can stay with her."

"That's right in the middle of her *toilette* time," Sulman warned.

Kelda flicked the objection away with a wave of her hand. "She can groom her damn algae up here."

Kelda, Per, Sulman, and Disa trudged through Holmstad under a clouding sky. Whispers and stares, harsher than usual, followed the First-Inners' passage. Disa hunched her shoulders, starting violently when a voice rang across the street. "Heg, Disa! Disa Nygren!"

She turned in surprise. Aage Hanson crossed the muddy street toward her. His lip was swollen and an ugly purple bruise circled his left eye. "Aage! What happened to you?"

He wiped one hand self-consciously across his face. "Fight with my dad."

Disa knew what that connoted for a boy Aage's age. "Congratulations?" she asked hesitantly.

He flushed. "I lost. What I wanted to tell you was—" He looked nervously at Sulman, who had dropped behind the others to wait for Disa. Suli stared politely across the street, but stayed within earshot. "I was—uh—going to ask you to the Festival."

"Me?"

Aage scuffed at a rock the way Leif did in his shyer moments. "What you said after school—about the Kargans, I mean—it impressed me. I was going to take you up on it. My dad didn't like the idea. I'm sorry I couldn't take you to the dance."

Disa felt light-headed. "What happened to Valda?"

Aage grinned briefly. "Nobody asked her. She stayed home." Disa's parents had reached the next corner. Aage turned serious and awkward again. "I better quit holding you up. Maybe we can get together another time. I just—uh—wanted you to know."

"I'd have loved to go with you," Disa said. They stared at each other. Aage stuck out a hand. Disa extended her own. They clasped hands, clung uncertainly, and let go.

"Heg!" Aage said, backing away with a wary look at the bystanders.

"Heg!" Disa answered, turning reluctantly to rejoin Sulman.

"Heg," the bachelor said with a sly smile. "I told you so."

CHAPTER NINETEEN

❧❧❧

"SHH. HERE THEY COME."

The gossipy women outside Skip's window fell silent. Sighing, he switched off his terminal and reached for a sweater. The First-Inners waited in the street. Skip nodded curtly to Kelda but held his hand out to Sulman. "Good to see you in daylight."

Sulman squeezed back. "Thanks for helping last night. I hated to roust you at that hour, but it looked like more than I could handle."

Skip shrugged. "You were right to stay low. As it was the kids were mad at us for ruining their party, and the parents were mad at me for bringing them home."

Per, like Sulman, extended a hand. "Thanks for helping."

Skip nodded acknowledgment. "I hope the rest of this is as easy to take care of. Let's get up to Hal's before a crowd gathers."

To Skip's surprise, a crowd had already gathered in Hal's yard, its attention focused on the stable where the gray mare, Valkyrie, was kept. "What's going on?" Skip asked.

Dag the smith, never fond of strangers, looked suspiciously at Skip and his companions. "Groundlings got Kyrie's foal. Knew it would happen sooner or later."

"What?" No wonder Hal was in an ugly mood! Motioning the First-Inners ahead to the house, Skip pushed past angry, muttering people toward the stable.

Valkyrie whinnied in distress. Through the open Dutch doors of her stall, Skip saw that the mare's legs were heavily bandaged. "Got cut up trying to defend the filly," someone said. Kyrie wove back and forth across the stall. Hal's groom tried in vain to calm her. "What's left of the foal is in the tackroom," Skip's informant said.

Skip slipped into the stable. In the partitioned-off area that served as tackroom he saw the body of a newborn foal, its flank ripped open, its head nearly chewed off. He heard the groom enter the room behind him. "What happened?" Skip asked.

"Happened last night," the man said angrily. "Kyrie dropped her filly by the paddock fence, and the foal rolled under, got caught on the wrong side. Bunch of groundlings pulled it down. When I got back from the dance it was too late. I killed three groundlings. One or two more got away."

Skip stared, heartsick, at the dead animal. He wasn't sure which upset him more—the loss of the young horse, or the repercussions the attack would have on the colony's attitude toward Kargans.

"Tell you what," the groom said. "I'm getting new bars on my own door. Wife and I got three kids, you know."

"Guess so," Skip muttered. He made a hasty exit and joined the First-Inners at the house.

Dana, always the concerned hostess, met them in the entryway and offered tea. "Please," Skip said, stooping to pull his boots off.

"Cream?" she asked, an extravagant offer that underscored Hal's status.

"Sounds wonderful," Per answered.

"Anything but ballel!" Sulman agreed.

"No, thank you," Kelda said. She had wiped her boots on the mat but did not take them off. That boded ill, Skip thought.

Hal and Leif waited at the big, highly polished wooden conference table. A fire crackled cheerily in the near end of the reception room. Leif's eyes searched—for Yvette, Skip guessed. Not finding her, the boy looked away and said nothing.

"Heg," Hal said to Kelda. "I hope you're proud of your group's influence on the youngsters of this colony."

"Be reasonable," Kelda answered. "This isn't the first time a high-school party's gotten out of hand."

Hal's own jaw clenched. "The rumors I've heard this morning are anything *but* reasonable."

"Let's sit down before we talk," Skip suggested, as Dana walked in with tea.

Leif and Hal sat at the head of the table. Quietly the newcomers took seats along the sides. Per made an elaborate ceremony of sweetening his tea and adding cream. When he was done, he looked at Hal. "What rumors have you heard?"

"A delegation from the Riksdag talked to me this morning. They heard you want to remove our stomachs and replace them with Kargan organs."

Skip's eyes narrowed. If that was what the Riksdag members thought, what had they proposed to do about it? Had Hal been shielding First-In from the colony council's wrath?

"That's crazy!" Disa exclaimed when she heard Hal's words. "I don't care how dizzy Yvette was, she never said that."

"Kirby's father thinks she did," Hal answered.

"I didn't hear it," Leif said. Hal glared at him. Leif squirmed and subsided into silence.

"What do you want to do, then?" Hal asked. His eyes moved to Skip. "What have you been plotting with your sister and her offworld friends?"

Skip cleared his throat. "It's not all that complicated, really. I told you the groundlings suffer warped metamorphosis because of our food. It seems impossible to keep them out of it, and we know too little of their physiology to counteract the effect. Also our crops enable elders to bypass dreamer trial and trigger second metamorphosis at will. There seems no way to save Kargan civilization but to eliminate human food crops."

Hal shifted his weight forward. "In other words, eliminate humans."

"No," Skip said, sweating violently despite the coolness of the room. "Fix humans so they can eat Kargan food." Belatedly he realized that he had picked up the First-In habit of referring to Frilandet by its native name.

Hal inhaled sharply. "It's true then? You want to put Kargan stomachs in us?"

"No!" Skip said. "Just change a few enzymes!"

"The hell you will," Hal answered. "I'm not eating Frilandeter strawberries."

"Be reasonable!" Kelda pleaded. "You're still mourning Borg and Inge. Let the dead lie, Hal. Think about the future."

Hal rose and paced to the window. Soft mist shrouded the memorial garden. A few bystanders still lingered outside the stable. "Did you hear what happened to Kyrie's foal?" he asked. "Ask me why I don't trust Kargans."

"The groundlings thought the foal was a deer," Skip argued.

"The groundlings bother your crops and livestock because they crave southpaw protein," Suli told Hal. "Learn to eat off the land and you won't have that problem."

Hal turned to study his visitors. "I don't suppose

you've gotten around to trying this procedure on anybody."

Skip waited for someone else to answer. No one did. Why wouldn't the First-Inners speak for themselves? Because he, Skip, was the one to whom Hal might listen. He took a deep breath and told himself to be calm. "Testers in the lab are eating native grain and fruit, so we know the procedure works. But we don't know what the side effects will be in a human. Our resources are too limited to evaluate the possibilities. We were going to bring our proposal to you after the holidays, ask for colony financing to finish the research."

Hal frowned. "First-In's got influence. Surely you could farm the research out."

"We can't afford to spend that kind of money on volunteer projects," Kelda answered. "We're trying to give you an alternative to leaving. It's time we got some support from Frilandet for the effort."

"Haven't we already discussed this?" Hal asked. "The answer is no."

"'No' won't do any more," Kelda said, twisting in her chair to face Hal. "Uncontrolled dreamer change could destroy a culture that's been stable for thousands of years. The dreamer gardens don't produce enough fungus to support an unlimited population of dreamers, and the illicit ones are causing mating problems. The Kargans have always been committed to peace—that's why Frilandet colony can be here at all—but if we don't get rid of L-amino acids soon, the Kargans will have just two choices: Go to war with you, or go to war with themselves." She stared at Hal a moment. "You have two choices, too. Help us test our genetic adjustment. Or have us invoke the Orion treaty."

From the corner of his eye, Skip saw Dana enter the room with a second pot of tea. Overhearing Kelda's words, Dana froze by the doorway.

Hal smiled poisonously at his sister. "Can you? I heard we were in no one's jurisdiction."

Kelda paled. "Don't you care about anyone but yourself?"

Hal gazed again toward the winter-barren paxflower bushes, dark against the white limestone of the bluff. "You're a hell of a one to ask that," he growled. "You took the easy way out. You knew if you stayed there'd be no money for school and no man who'd put up with your sass. Even Ole Hanson couldn't stomach you. So you ran. You left your parents to die of grief and me to bury them. Ingrid and I buried two children and then I lost Ingrid, while you and your merry friends flew around the galaxy. You were the one that got her interested in caves. And now you have the fucking nerve to be self-righteous! Go ahead, look down your nose at me 'cause I haven't been the places you've been. Look down your nose because I don't speak with your flawless Family accent. But don't talk to me about loyalty or sacrifice."

Kelda sat ramrod straight, her eyes fixed unblinkingly on Hal's. Per and Sulman glanced at each other, looking troubled. Disa chewed on her lip.

"We'll talk about why I left, some other time." Kelda said in a tightly controlled voice. "Right now let's talk about justice."

Hal half sat on the windowsill, facing his visitors. "Why? What's justice? A great rhetorical flourish, yes. But no one—First-In included—violates self-interest for abstract justice."

Kelda glanced at Per. "How about Valhalla? You didn't like their ways, but you have to admit the Sørensons tried to run the place for everyone's good. That's justice."

Skip shook his head. Hal's salvo must have struck deep, if he had rattled Kelda enough for her to try that argument.

Hal, like Kelda, looked at Per. "I admit no such thing.

The Sørensons made good money, tailored the economy to their own tastes, kept folk well fed enough they'd not rebel, and taxed to death anyone who might have posed a threat to the system." Per, sitting beside Skip, pressed folded hands to his mouth as Hal continued. "Valhalla's government has far more to do with Sørenson self-interest than with justice."

Disa had bitten her lip so hard that she had drawn blood. "Why argue human politics?" she asked. "Kargans have a right to live safely on their own planet!"

"What 'right'?" Hal asked. He glanced at Disa, but his real attention and enmity remained directed at her mother.

"'We hereby endorse the right of every intelligent species to pursue its own path of evolution upon its own planet, undisturbed or in commerce with the galactic community, as that species so chooses,'" Kelda quoted from the preamble of the Orion treaty.

"We were surrounded by Hyann warships when we said that, weren't we?" Hal asked. "I'd say those sentiments suited our self-interest quite nicely."

"The Hyann didn't shoot because they'd signed the same declaration," Kelda countered, her enunciation clipped and precise. "If you want the exact wording—" To Skip's irritation, she broke into the ungodly hoots and whistles of some alien language.

"Oh, shut up!" Hal said. Skip silently applauded. "Everybody says nice things when they sign a treaty," Hal continued, "but they still take each other for all they can get. Your own guidelines identify mutual advantage as the only stable basis for diplomacy."

Kelda's fists were clenched and, to Skip's surprise, she blinked rapidly. "Has it ever occurred to you," she asked, "that we might have things to gain from the Kargans?"

"No," Hal said. "What would they be?"

"That's my point," Kelda replied. "We don't know their potential."

"They're not human," Hal told her.

"That doesn't mean they're not people," Per answered mildly.

"They're not *my* people," Hal growled. "I have to look out for Leif, and Dana, because if I don't no one else will. Why do you argue so hard for the Kargans? Let them stand for their own rights!"

Kelda wet her lips. "You know they don't believe in war. At least the elders don't," she amended, glancing through the window at the stable.

"That's what First-In says. Why don't the Kargans believe in it? How've they survived so long without it? What do they do when they disagree? And how can they hang on to what they've got, if they won't defend it?"

His sister sighed impatiently. "It's their religion, like it's Valhalla's to care for the poor and yours to care for yourself." Kelda didn't understand any better than Hal, Skip thought. "It's not our place to judge their culture," Kelda continued. "What if the Sheppies judged ours?"

"That'd be the day." Hal snorted. "Crazy clowns."

Skip had come to know Calypso well. He strongly suspected that if she were present, she would undulate her tentacles and say, "I hope my difficultiess with your cusstomss do not disstresss you, ssir."

Kelda lacked the Sheppie's patience and superior indifference. Angry, she blew the cover. "Ever thought what it takes to comprehend an alien sense of humor? Can you make jokes in Sheppie?"

"You mean this alien of yours is so far beyond us she doesn't care whether she makes a fool of herself?"

"Precisely," Kelda said. "Calypso's worth ten of you."

Per's hands clamped the edge of the table. On Valhalla, Skip knew, the Sørensons had outlawed brute modes of settling family quarrels. There, a sister was her brother's equal, with the law to enforce it if she herself couldn't. On

Frilandet, power belonged to those who could take and keep it. Few women dared the insolence Kelda had displayed. Dana looked panicky.

Hal's face went red as he stepped forward to his sister's chair, locked his heavy hand around her arm, and dragged her to her feet facing him. "Like it or not, Kelda, I'm your brother. Don't you ever say that to me again."

Kelda stood with feet apart, knees slightly bent, hands curled. In one fluid motion, she jerked free of Hal's grip, reached for him, and used his own momentum to send him sprawling as he tried to regain his grip on her. Breathing heavily, Hal looked up at her, then, furtively, eyed the fireplace poker.

"Don't," Kelda advised. She stooped slightly. Her hand grazed her boot-top and came away holding the wickedly sharp dirk she used for odd jobs about camp. Skip felt as if he were suffocating.

Kelda tossed the knife onto the table. "This is man to man."

Per's knuckles showed white. Skip's own hand came down on his brother-in-law's wrist. "Stay out of it." However irregularly, Kelda had invoked challenge tradition, which forbade intervention by bystanders.

Kelda herself spared Per a glance that said in marital shorthand "Stay put."

Hal rose. Eyes locked, he and Kelda moved to the open end of the room. Dana, still holding the tea tray, stepped hastily aside.

Disa watched with wide, frightened eyes. Leif, who himself would fight Hal soon, leaned forward with parted lips.

Hal relaxed for an instant, then lunged toward Kelda to pin her against the wall.

Kelda stepped toward him. Hal hit the wall himself, staggered sideways, and bounced back swinging. Kelda, quick and well trained, avoided all the blows but one. That one resounded through the room and left an angry red streak on Kelda's cheek. She seemed momentarily dazed, but when Hal tried to press his advantage she knocked his arm aside with a lightning-swift strike. "Damn!" Hal said, stepping back and rubbing the arm. Then, evidently conscious that he had yielded psychological advantage, he closed once more.

For Skip, the fight brought turbulent memories of the day he himself had finally bested Canute, and of previous days when he had retreated battered and humiliated but determined to try again. Kelda was in peak condition, handled herself capably, and defended beautifully. Hal was stronger, with all the advantage in size and reach. The conventions of challenge ruled out eye jabs, groin kicks, and similarly damaging maneuvers. Without them, could Kelda force capitulation? Skip maintained his grip on Per's arm, not sure whether he was restraining the Valhallan or himself.

Again Kelda pulled Hal into his own swing, letting his momentum add force to her assault. As he involuntarily tried to duck her fist, she kicked his feet from beneath him. He hit the floor with a thud that drove the breath from his lungs. Sulman smiled. Hal rolled clear and lay a moment, catching his breath.

Kelda knew better than to follow him to the floor; with his advantages in weight and leverage, there was no way she could pin him. She stood back, balanced lightly on the balls of her feet, a study in contradiction. Her flaming cheeks said that she had suffered an insult requiring redress. Nervous lip-biting said that for all her bravado, she wasn't used to hitting and wondered whether her brother's bones were sturdy enough for her blows. The set of her shoulders said that she intended to keep on.

Hal got to his feet, studied his waiting opponent, then

lunged, angling his attack to block Kelda's escape. Again she twisted free, but Hal, with his longer reach, landed a second blow to the face. Blood welled from Kelda's lip as she spun to guard against her assailant.

Hal feinted, fell back, then closed with a tackle that pinned Kelda between himself and the wall, dangerously close to the fireplace. She blanched, then dropped downward, launched herself against his knees, and again hurled him off balance. He landed hard. Kelda waited grimly. "Give?" Leif licked his lips.

For answer Hal came at Kelda a final time. She met him with a vicious, high kick, numbing his right arm. She followed with an edge-handed blow to the stomach. She ducked beneath his elbow, turned, and, as he roared in frustration, gathered his arms from behind and began to twist. Hal's face contorted as he tried to recover enough breath to throw her off. She clung tight, her entire weight on him. Hal backed hard against the wall, trying to crush her. She got an arm around his throat. "Equal?"

Eyes bulging, he clawed at her elbow with hands that seemed weak and uncoordinated. He sputtered incoherently, then let his arms droop.

Kelda stamped on his foot. "Equal?" She relaxed her grip just a hairsbreadth.

Hal gulped for air. His hands remained at his sides. His voice was low and broken, difficult to hear. "Equal."

She let him go. He cradled his arms, face still pale. Skip wondered if Kelda had dislocated Hal's shoulders. She was leaning against the wall, breathing hard, cupping her hands under her chin in a vain attempt to keep blood from spattering onto Dana's polished wooden floor. She blotted the cut lip on a sleeve. "We still need help with the research, Hal."

With visible effort, he stood straight. "I'll split the inheritance with you. I'll even let you bring a stinking

Sørenson into my house. But I'll die before I help you screw Frilandet genes around. I never asked you onto this planet to start with. You've got two weeks to get off it. If you aren't gone by the fifteenth, I'll tell the Riksdag to do what it likes with you and your team."

CHAPTER TWENTY

❧❧❧❧

"YOU HUMILIATED HIM IN FRONT OF ALL OF US, HIS SON, and his wife. What did you expect him to do—throw his arms around us?" Disa flinched at the bitterness in Sulman's voice. She hoped his words had not echoed ahead to the Hall of Voices where the Kargans waited. He looked over his shoulder, past Disa to her mother. "Your temper has finally fried us, Kelda."

Kelda's fists clenched. "Why put it all on me? Why did the colony think so poorly of us to start with? You and your goddamn wenching!" Disa saw Kelda wince as too-hearty speaking pressured her cracked ribs.

Sulman stopped and half turned to face Kelda. "Think about how *you* joined First-In before you say too much."

"Quit it, both of you!" Per snapped, ducking to avoid a ripple of rock hanging from the ceiling. "We've got enough enemies without fighting each other."

From the rear of the group came Skip's voice. "Have to admit—Kelda has balls."

Skip was handling the situation with remarkable grace, Disa thought. His hours in the lab, his rescue of Yvette's dizzied companions, and his presence at Hal's discomfiture left him in poor odor with the Frilandena. Wisdom might have dictated a withdrawal from the First-Inners. But when Per had asked at the dock, "Will you round the circle with us?" the geneticist had paused only to ask "Do I need a change of clothes?" Per had squinted up at the driving rain. "We all will. I'll loan you some."

Yvette wore the same dull faraway expression she had worn since she heard the story of Kelda's fight with Hal. "Our whole lives we've heard the circle whisper that someday Karg would blow," she had confided to Disa as they donned helmets and gloves for the journey underground. "I wish we could get it over with."

"We'll work something out," Disa assured her, defying the dread in her own stomach.

They found Calypso and the Kargans in the Hall. Disa glanced toward the pool, hoping Risky might have returned, but only Inanna and the native elder Buzz-Click emerged from the water.

"We facce a difficult ssituation," the Sheppie said, unnecessarily. "We must risse above private recriminationss." Had she heard them snipe at one another after all? Disa wondered. "Dusst sseekss to dream, but only we can sstir it. Let uss recall our common birth."

Kelda, who had been heard to say that reasonable people should not resort to incantations, rolled her eyes but began the recitation. Sulman, with a final sulky glare, followed suit. Disa, too, joined in.

From dust are born the suns, the seas, and life.
Dust we are, to dust we shall return.
It swirls in hope and song, and then swirls on,
But dust does not forget the dream that stirs it.

The ancient litany echoed around the cavern in English, Sheppie, and Kargan. Yvette's lips remained firmly clamped, but Disa spotted tears on her friend's cheek.

The simple routine of speaking together restored some resonance among the angry humans. When, after silence, Calypso suggested a speaking of the problem, the glances exchanged were merely wary.

"The problem," Kelda said with quiet, reluctant precision, speaking English for Skip's benefit, "is that Frilandet crops now interfere with both Kargan metamorphoses." She repeated her evaluation in Kargan.

"No," Sulman said. "The problem is that the Frilandena don't admit there is a problem."

"More precisely," Per observed, "they won't admit it's their problem."

"And we've got two weeks to change their minds," Skip said.

In heavy silence they considered the situation. How could the Frilandena be convinced to own responsibility for the situation?

"Can't the Kargans do something?" Disa heard herself asking, in English and then in Kargan.

"If they're willing to adopt one of the plans rumor attributes to them," Sulman answered darkly. He, too, repeated his words in Kargan.

"No!" Inanna protested. She began to speak of the ancients, the duty of hospitality, and the Kargans' eagerness to maintain contact. Disa listened with rising frustration.

"Dead persons welcome no one," Sulman told Inanna and Buzz-Click in their own language. "Live now, and in other seasons you may speak with gods."

"We will not commit sin of *graf*," Buzz-Click countered.

"Why humans not eat D-amino acids?" Inanna asked. Like many aliens, she had less trouble with technical vocabulary than with grammar and everyday idiom. "Testers eat."

"Testers change before eat D-amino acids," Sulman responded. "But if human-gods change to eat D-amino acids, human-gods maybe *gigg*."

Gigg, Disa thought. An elegant translation for what they feared might happen when the enzyme genes were introduced into a human body.

Yvette, more intimately familiar with the research project than Disa was, raised her head. Because her words were for the humans, she spoke in English. "Why not try it? Tester physiology isn't that different from ours. The odds are with us. And if we prove the procedure safe, the Frilandena might come around." Disa heard Inanna, off to the side, translating for Buzz-Click.

"No," Skip said.

"It iss not ssafe," Calypso agreed.

"Inanna's and Yvette's arguments make sense to me," Per said. "Tell me again what worries you."

Slowly Skip explained. "It's a question of side effects. Tests on cultured tissue show our carrier will indeed insert in human pancreatic cells and direct production of the new enzymes. But we're not sure, for humans, that the carrier will lodge *only* in pancreatic cells. If it inserts elsewhere in the body, there'll be trouble. Imagine if your muscles started pumping out digestive enzymes. Or even if the gene didn't express, the immune system might somehow recognize the altered cells as foreign. The system is so complex we can't computer-model it. You have to test it on a tissue-by-tissue basis, which takes time, money, and equipment we don't have here."

"Or you test on a live subject," Yvette proposed. "What have we got to lose?"

Disa stared at her friend. Was Yvette serious?

"What have we got to gain?" Skip countered. "Would the Frilandena accept the procedure if we did show it successful? They don't trust First-In."

The understatement of the day, Disa thought. Kelda and Yvette both flinched.

"If they won't flex they can leave the planet," Sulman said. "As they should have in the beginning."

"I thought your enforcement inquiries fell through," Skip said.

"There are ways—" Kelda began, a dangerous glint in her eye.

Fear knotted again in Disa's gut. "Didn't Core say they could arrange an embargo?" she asked. "Why aren't we trying that?"

"That's a heck of a lot of favors for Dawn to use up on a pretty obscure situation," Suli answered.

"It would take them a year or more just to enact it," Kelda added.

"It wouldn't work anyhow," Skip said, looking genuinely regretful. "Frilandet's made sure to stay independent of imports."

"Leif's father likes his cream," Yvette countered. "Are you sure he wouldn't buckle?"

"Probably he would, eventually," Skip admitted. "But he'd hold out a few years first."

"We haven't got a few years," Kelda said. "Not with elders cheating on the trial, and not with Hal's ultimatum."

Per shook his shaggy blond head. He looked frustrated. "I can't believe the colony will murder a native race in cold blood. Maybe our mistake has been in dealing with Hal. Maybe we should appeal to the citizens at large."

Disa wondered what Kirby would do with such an appeal. "At least Uncle Hal believes Kargans exist," she said.

Per looked startled at her. "The other Frilandena don't?"

Disa related the conversation she'd had the last day of school. Per looked incredulous, but Skip nodded.

"Disa's right. And you're right, Per. The Frilandena aren't comfortable killing Kargans in cold blood. So they rationalize that the Kargans don't exist at all, or don't deserve to live if they do. Maybe it would be different if Kargans were warm and fuzzy like Houri. But they aren't; they're blind and cold and have big claws. If the colonists admit Kargan intelligence at all, they visualize it as hostile."

"That's unreasonable!"

"So's humanity," Sulman muttered.

"Invoke the treaty," Kelda said. "The colonists understand that."

"We've got no backup," Per reminded her.

"The Frilandena don't know that," Kelda said. "All they've heard are rumors."

"But they believe the rumors," Skip told her. Yvette covered her face with both hands. "You know Hal won't bluff," Skip said to Kelda.

Water dripped on the chimes.

"Why doesn't somebody just say it?" Yvette asked, her face still hidden. "We're going to take the vow."

The dread in Disa's stomach curdled and sank. Caught between a neutrality that precluded weapons and its sympathy for the oppressed of any race, First-In used the vow to pressure offenders. A team said, in essence, "over our dead bodies." The ploy generally worked, because a team included representatives of the oppressing as well as the oppressed. Groups that unwincingly slaughtered aliens often faltered at killing kin. How quiet the Tapachulan mob had become when Jack's blood spattered the refugee camp's gate! Their second thoughts, too late for him, had saved the Triop refugees.

The vow did not function on pity alone. First-In had ties in high places, both because of recruits from Families like the Sørensons, and because of circlings like Yvette, who left First-In for prestigious positions in government, business, and education. Valhalla's treaty commander might consider Karg beyond his jurisdiction, but if Per Sørenson were killed, Lindy Sørenson's ships would ask why. If the Calypso Twist's inventor disappeared on Karg, Sheppie ambassadors from Challa to Terra would press for discipline of the offenders.

Disa chewed her lip. Water continued to drip. No one wanted to speak. "Yvette hass sspoken the vission in all our eyess," Calypso said finally.

All along, Sulman had preferred the vow to Orion intervention. "Calling down troops is too easy," he had said, sounding eerily like the history teacher Mr. Ansgar. "The vow we don't take lightly, so neither do others." Now he said, slowly, "Yes."

"Don't be ridiculous," Kelda said. "What do you intend to vow?"

"That we'll protect the Kargans with our own lives—" Disa started to answer, then saw the problem.

"You can stand between a mob and a refugee camp's gate," Kelda said. "But how do you stand between a colony's cornfields and thousands of individual groundlings? We want to pressure the humans, not the Kargans!"

"The casse indeed pressentss a problem of definition," Calypso said. "How do we enact our ssolidarity?"

"What we need to do," Sulman proposed very carefully, "is create a situation in which the Frilandena can't do anything to the Kargans without doing it to us first. We could eat Kargan food every time we find a groundling eating colony food."

Disa's stomach cramped with memory of Kirby's "banana."

"A highly painful mode of making the point," Calypso warned.

"But not immediately fatal," Sulman said. "Trouble with the painless techniques is, they leave you dead. No chance for folks to change their minds."

"What the hell are you talking about?" Skip asked. "You don't mean to poison yourselves?"

"One hopes a vow need not be followed through," Per answered, "but one must take it with that willingness."

"It's pointless," Kelda said, sounding almost like Hal. "If we died of cramp at the colonists' door they'd only shake their heads at our stupidity."

"She's right," Skip agreed. "Maybe ultracivilized folk like the Sheppies, who conceptualize responsibility differently, would respond to your ploy. But Frilandena figure suicide is your own business. Even Valhallans know the difference between killing someone and letting them kill themselves. If a Frilandet mob shot you, Per, Valhalla's navy would respond. But if we tell them you killed yourself eating northpaw protein, they'll shake their heads and say First-Inners do strange things."

Per closed his eyes. "What do you want to do, then?" he asked.

"Take action ourselves," Kelda said. "Force the colony away."

Every First-In handbook, every circle charter, said that a team must not take up arms. To do so, other than in clear self-defense, would result in immediate and unconditional disownment. Offenders had the rings torn from their ears and were cast adrift, outcasts. But every First-In campfire had its stories of teams surrendering neutrality to tip the balance of otherwise unwinnable conflict. First-In could not countenance such action—but the First-In code of honor could demand it.

Disa tried to imagine herself pointing a rifle or spurt gun at Leif, Gretchen, or Aage. She could not.

Sulman stared up into the dome, his jaw tightening and loosening. "I'm afraid you're right," he said.

"No!" Per protested. "We've got no weapons."

"Throw the ship at them," Kelda said. "Crash it in the center of Holmstad; wipe out power generation, manufacturing, reference facilities, and central storage."

"And ninety percent of the population," Per said.

"Warn them first," Sulman suggested. "Or even do a demonstration strike with something smaller. The lander, say."

"Even if we threw the ship itself," Kelda argued, "people would be safe so long as they got out of Holmstad. These hills would provide plenty of shielding, and the outlying farms have enough seed stored to keep folk alive until they could take passage out on silk freighters."

"But not enough seed to feed the colony and plant next year's crops, both," Sulman said. "Especially with Holmstad's resources wiped out."

"Folk would have to sign debt contracts for passage," Skip objected.

"They have an alternative," Kelda reminded everyone. "Leave peacefully, and profits from the silk trade can pay the way."

"What happens to you?" Skip asked. "With your ship gone you couldn't leave. And the colonists would be looking for blood."

"No worse than taking the vow," Sulman said.

"It just kills more people," Per muttered.

"And protectss the Karganss," Calypso reminded him.

Disa stirred uncomfortably. "Crashing a ship on a planet; that's like a major meteor hit. What's that kind of impact going to do to the caves?"

Sulman picked at the cuff of his trousers. "A lot of damage. Especially here so close to Holmstad. But compared to what the Kargans will lose if the colony stays—"

"It's elegant," Kelda said.

"It's barbaric," Per responded. "'We come in peace and hope it deepens'—what a pack of lies!"

"We said the same to the Kargans," Sulman reminded him. "So are we any less liars if we sit on our hands?"

No one answered.

"I hear the dusst swirl to a deccission," Calypso said. "Does anyone object?" Water dripped.

"I do," Per said.

His eyes met his teammates' stares. "The Frilandena are human. They couldn't possibly behave as they're doing, if they understood the situation. Disa's said they don't believe the Kargans are people. Well, then, we've got to convince them of that." Inanna's claw snapped busily as she continued translating for Buzz-Click.

"How?" Sulman asked in a voice full of doubt and frustration.

"I think they've got to hear the Kargans speak for themselves—"

To everyone's surprise, Buzz-Click interrupted. "*Snapclick*'s father speaks truly."

"What the hell?" Kelda exclaimed.

Disa twisted to stare at the native elder as Buzz-Click continued. "My people are not guiltless. We have remained in Sweetwater Warren, mourning *click-tap*'s death and wondering when human-gods would again speak to us. But we did not go Beyond to meet them."

Everyone stayed silent, attentive. Buzz-Click spoke truly, Disa thought. She saw Sulman's head tip ever so slightly in agreement with the elder's words.

Inanna stirred. "You have said god-warren believes not we speak. I go with you, Per, and speak for them to hear."

"You will meet great danger," Sulman warned, speaking Kargan. "God-warren seeks strongly to not hear."

"The mood in town's getting ugly," Skip confirmed. "If you brought an elder in now, Per, the Frilandena might lynch both of you."

Disa stared, terrified, at her father. From the corner of her eye she saw Yvette cowering. Uncle Jack had tried to speak reason to a paranoid crowd. Not Per, too!

Kelda spoke with fierce protectiveness. "They're right,

Per. The colonists will kill you rather than hear what you're saying. Don't try it."

"We've already said that one way or another we're going to make them listen, haven't we?" Per answered his wife. "They deserve at least one last chance to hear peacefully. If they kill me then my veto will be gone and you can do it your way."

Kelda's hand half lifted as if to restrain him. "Let me talk to them!"

Calypso folded her tentacles in the Sheppie equivalent of a shaken head. "No, Kelda. To you the Frilandena will not lissten, for you do not believe they will. Only Per hass power to imposse hiss dream on dusst."

Kelda's raised hand gripped Per's. With the other hand she covered her face. The group sat in silence. Finally Kelda looked up. To Disa's amazement, her mother's face was wet. "Don't do it until we get Disa and Yvette safely off the planet," Kelda said.

Yvette raised her own head. "No. I'm almost eighteen. This mess is my fault. I'm staying."

"Don't be—" Kelda began.

"Listen to her," Sulman said. He shifted position until he sat directly facing Yvette. She stared back, big-eyed. "You may be killed by a lynch mob," he told her. "Or by a falling ship."

She paled but did not look away. "I know."

"If we have to throw the ship, and you live through it, you'll be tainted by our decision. No First-In Circle will accept you, after that."

Disa saw Yvette swallow. Even though Yvette didn't want to join First-In, she was a circling, and cared what First-In thought. "I know that, too."

Sulman paused. "I hear dust say this child is now a woman. We can tie her to her cradle. Or we can let her grow up. I think she should decide, not we."

In silence they agreed.

"I'm staying with you," Yvette declared again.

"I wish you would leave," Per said.

"I'm staying."

"Your father would be proud of you," Kelda told her.

Yvette's face crumpled. "He'd be prouder if I hadn't gotten us into this mess."

"Dusst sswirlss in sstrange wayss," Calypso said. "We welcome you."

Disa's heart pounded. Half of her wanted to follow Yvette, to stand with the team, to be part of a legend. The other half wanted to live, to have the chance to sample life and love.

"Disa's only fifteen," Per said. "I think you're right, Kelda. I don't want her mixed up in this."

The love in his voice firmed Disa's resolve. "I want to stay, too."

"No," Suli told her. "There's a circle out there that needs you. Diamond. Or Aquarius. Don't throw your life away on us."

"If we fail, ssomeone musst tell our sstory," Calypso said.

Disa imagined herself arriving at Dawn's Core, human and alien circlemates crowding around for news, Disa explaining that her family and teammates had— She blanched.

"Please," Per said softly.

Disa bit her lip. Leave her family, Yvette, Calypso? Leave without meeting the new Risky? Leave, with the strong possibility that she would see none of them again?

"*Stardust* docked at the station yesterday," Skip said. "Scheduled to pull out Friday."

"Disa goes on it," Per answered. "Dawn will take care of her. And she will speak for us."

Disa kept silent, glad for the cave's dimness. With luck, none would see her tears.

CHAPTER TWENTY-ONE

❧❧❧

"DISA? YOU'VE GOT COMPANY!"

"What? Who?"

Yvette grinned. "Come out and see."

Disa reached for her cloak. Tempers had grown as gray and threatening as the weather. Skip was in town, quenching rumors and quietly arranging Disa's transport on the silk shuttle. Sulman was gone, too, probably letting some ladyfriend soothe his anxiety. Per and Calypso huddled over team records, updating them for delivery into Disa's hands when she departed three days hence. Kelda vented frustration in a flurry of cleaning and catching-up. Yvette had retired to the lab, seeking some last-minute proof that the enzyme modification was safe.

Disa herself had cowered in the loft with her terminal, trying to lose herself in orbital attainment simulations. But her attention kept drifting from the fantasy shuttle she piloted to the one she would ride Friday. Glad of a diversion, she tightened the drawstring on her hood and followed Yvette outside.

For all the cloudy skies, the temperature hovered near fifty. Disa pushed the hood off again. An unfamiliar skiff was rocking in the river below, tied to a huge log beached by high waters earlier in the week. Voices carried cheerily from the stairway. Disa peered down the bluff. Leif—and Aage!

Disa said the first thing that came into her head. "Won't your folks kill you if they find you here?"

Leif shrugged uncomfortably. "I guess so. But that was pretty impressive, what your mother did to Dad. I wondered if you could teach me her fighting techniques, Yvette."

Disa, who hadn't thought about Leif's personal stake in that fight, remembered that he himself faced a clash with his father in the near future. Was Yvette the issue he expected to fight over?"

Yvette slipped her arm around his waist. "No problem."

Disa looked at Aage. "Do you want fighting lessons, too?"

"What? No, I—uh—what you said about seeing the caves. I wanted to take you up on it." The black eye turned his nervous smile to a leer.

"You two want to come along?" Disa asked Leif and Yvette.

"You go ahead," Yvette said primly. "Leif and I have a lot to do."

As they crossed the level blufftop on which the camp sat, Aage stared at the two-room cabin, the lab with its lean-to additions, and the equipment cache by the hillface. "I thought you lived in temporaries."

"Only when we first land. As soon as we know we're staying, we put up buildings." What would Aage say if he knew that Disa would be leaving Friday? And after that, would the Hansons have sense enough to flee the city, or would Ole linger, trying to gain political advantage? Disa twisted open the equipment cache's lock. "You'll be more comfortable if you wear a diving suit. Take my dad's—

that one there. I think it will fit you better than Uncle Suli's."

"Will we be diving?"

"No, our route's dry. Or at least not underwater. The suit's just for protection from rocks and mud."

Aage took it from its hook. "Is Suli the guy that used to be Erica's boyfriend? I didn't know he was your uncle."

"I call all Dawn's humans uncle," Disa said, unzipping her shirt and pulling it over her head. "Or aunt." Would Inanna be in her usual spot in the Hall of Meeting? Would Aage be contemptuous of the elder's broken English? If only Risky were around for him to meet! Disa kicked off her brown boots and unbuckled her belt.

Aage stood with the suit still in his hands. He wore a very odd expression. "How do I put this on?"

He was a dirtsider, she recalled. He had never gone diving or spacewalking. Disa took the suit from him and spread it open along the front seal. "For what we're doing you don't need to worry about the physiological or pressure compensation mechanisms. Just step in here, then seal it back up."

Not looking at her, he pulled his stockinged foot out of his boot and poked it into the opening.

"Not that way," Disa said, skinning out of her own pants. "Take your clothes off first."

"All of them?" he asked, his voice hoarse.

Disa froze. A blush spread over her naked body. Yes, he was a dirtsider—and on his planet, people had odd hangups about clothing. "You could—uh—leave your underwear on." Hers lay in a pile on the floor.

"Couldn't I just wear my clothes?"

"If you'd rather." Disa reached frantically for her suit. "It's just that it's awful muddy down there." She somehow got her right foot into the suit's left leg.

"That's okay," Aage said, putting Per's suit back on its hook. He couldn't seem to decide between staring at the wall and staring at Disa. "I'll tell my mom I fell in a pud-dle."

Disa got her legs sorted out and yanked the top half of the suit up to cover herself. Fingers fumbled with fasten-ings that had never given her trouble before. She wanted to turn her back on Aage, but to do so would be to admit how awkward she felt. Better to carry through matter-of-factly. By the time she had the suit sealed she was sweat-ing so hard that her demoisturer switched on. Not meeting Aage's eyes, she handed him a helmet and gloves. "These you *will* need." She showed him how the helmet light worked.

"It doesn't seem very bright," Aage said doubtfully.

"We dimmed them all in order not to offend the Kar-gans," Disa explained. "You'll be able to see okay once your eyes adjust." She led him around the corner into the Front Porch. Ea stirred grumpily. "*Taka, tikagee,*" Disa muttered.

"What was that?" Aage asked.

"I was telling him to relax," Disa said. "It's part of an old Kargan lullaby Risky used to chant to me."

It was hard to read Aage's helmet-shadowed face. "Who's Risky?"

Disa picked at her gloves. "One of our elders. The mother of the groundling that died. She did dreamer trial three months ago and beat out nine native elders for the privilege of second change. I'm going to introduce you to her cavemate."

"Do elders pair?" Aage asked. "I thought they were all female."

"They are. But they live in couples. When one leaves to be a dreamer, the other one helps educate her daugh-ter." Except that Risky had left no daughter to be edu-cated. "Anyway I used to crawl in Risky's cave when I felt dumped on as a kid. She'd sing that lullaby to me."

Aage said nothing. He probably thought it queer to go to a Kargan for comfort.

They crawled together through the long low tunnel that led to the cylindrical dome. Water dripped along all sides of the pit. Aage peered gingerly at the Meeting Hall's floor thirty feet below. "There's a ladder," Disa said, pointing. "Just be careful of your footing. It's slick in this weather."

Aage looked upward at the falling water. "Is it always this wet?"

"No. That's from all the rain we've had."

She descended, then stood to spot him as he came down the ladder. He felt his way carefully. "Hey, what's that smell?"

"Fermenting silkfruit. Don't you recognize it?"

"So the elders do make silk," Aage said thoughtfully. He wiped his forehead when he reached the bottom. "How'd you get down before you had the ladder?"

Disa shrugged. "Ropes. All those ledges make it a real easy climb. You just have to watch out for rotten rock. A lot of the limestone's nearly eaten away."

"I see," Aage said. Dampness brought an herbal scent from his clothing or body. Disa liked it better than Leif's frankly sweaty odor, although Yvette said sweat was sexy. She wondered what Leif and Yvette were doing, and what it would be like to hug Aage's tall broad frame. How hard had he looked at her while she was undressing? Had he liked what he had seen?

She led him along the canyon to the point where it intercepted the underground river. "We call this the Hall of Meeting because it has easy access for us, the Sheppies, and of course the Kargans," she said. "The water's usually not muddy, but right now it's backing in from the Meade."

Aage looked at the stone waterfall. "That's impressive. I didn't know there was anything like that down here."

"You should see where we're headed next." Disa spied

the figure she had been looking for. "First, meet Risky's sister Inanna. She's just behind you."

Aage turned and jumped. "That's an elder?"

"Risky's sister. *Daqua* is how you say heg in Kargan."

"*Daqua*," Aage said nervously.

"It's polite to sniff each other," Disa told him, demonstrating. "Sometimes the scent feelers tickle a little."

His expression unreadable, Aage knelt and submitted to the routine.

"Heg," Inanna said. "It pleases me to meet you. Few Frilandena speak to us."

"It talks!" Aage exclaimed.

"*She* talks," Disa corrected. "What did you think she did?"

"It's just—well, they haven't talked to us since—"

"Since my Aunt Ingrid died," Disa finished for him.

"My people wished to speak," Inanna answered. "You spoke not to us."

Again Aage's expression turned thoughtful. Disa, who had classed him with the worst of the reactionary Frilandena, adjusted her assessment. He had the guts to come into the caves, and the openmindedness to think about what he heard. "Do you mind crawling some more? There's a place I'd really like to show you. Inanna will come, too."

Scrambling and sliding, they burrowed through the rockpile toward the Hall of Voices. "Are you sure I can fit through there?" Aage asked, a suspicious eye on the crevice into which Disa had just vanished.

She shone her light back to guide him. "If my dad can do it, you can. Keep your head low."

He caught up with her a moment later. "Is he really a Sørenson?"

So that cat was out of the bag, too. "He is."

"And this is all a Sørenson plot?" Aage asked, scrambling after her through the next hole.

If he was that suspicious, why did he bother to ask? Disa wondered. "No. Mom's here now because she came from this planet. Dad's here because he's married to her. Come on, I want you to see this."

Aage gaped when he finally reached the Hall. "My God," he said in a hushed voice, "this is incredible! A real floor, and pipes—why isn't anything else down here colored?"

"Kargans are blind. Except the groundlings."

"Right. But those pipes—" He stared, confused, at them.

"An ancient place of worship," Inanna said. "Here *graf* gathered."

"*Graf*?" Aage asked.

"The Kargan ancients," Disa explained.

"Then came gods," Inanna said. She went on to the story of the *graf*'s quarreling and fall.

"That's why Kargans won't tell the Frilandena to go away," Disa said. "Their ancestors went blind in some horrible disaster that sounds like biological warfare. The Kargans think it was from being too quarrelsome."

Aage hesitated. "Kirby said you folks are making some kind of biological weapon—"

"Kirby was too dizzy to understand what he heard," Disa answered. "You know that colony crops make groundlings go *gigg*?"

"You said there was some problem—"

"They get malformed and die. That's what happened to—" She paused, trying for control of the lump in her throat. "—to Risky's daughter. My pet groundling. Enki. He died. Also our food prematurely changes elders into dreamers. An elder is supposed to pass a complicated test before she qualifies to be a dreamer—"

"That's the trial you talked about, that Risky took?"

"Right. Then she goes into seclusion to complete the physical change and learn all the secrets of the dreamers."

"Which are?" Aage asked.

"We don't know. They have a weird language. My dad's been working on it. We hoped Risky would be able to tell us, but now—" Disa caught herself on the verge of saying that the team would be gone by the time Risky emerged. "We haven't heard from her in a long time."

"His change done," Inanna said. "He learns secrets, forgets to summon Disa."

Disa closed her eyes. Risky had forgotten her?

Aage paced along the flat shiny floor, examining the stalactites and stalagmites that hung along the walls. "Don't touch those," Disa warned. She beckoned him to stand under the dome. "See the openings up there where other tunnels join? They say in the days of the *graf* there were lights in each of those openings. Imagine what it must have looked like!"

"*Graf* did not fear radiation," Inanna told them.

"Radiation?" Aage asked with another nervous look around.

"That's what Kargans call visible light," Disa answered.

He rested his hand on her shoulder, very lightly. "This must have been beautiful," he said. "It's a shame they destroyed themselves."

Disa tipped her face toward his, and felt his grip tighten. "I think they've been waiting all these years for somebody to talk to, to break them out of their old habits. Maybe they're right to want you to stay. If our gene modification worked you could digest local protein and stay without poisoning the Kargans—"

Aage's hand dropped. "Disa, there's no way the Frilandena will agree to your messing around with our genes. Don't you know what's happening in Holmstad?"

She stared at him, her desire submerged in fear. "What?"

"People have always hated First-In and the Kargans.

Now they're scared. That business with Kyrie's foal was the last straw. People are saying it's time to do something about—about you. And the Kargans."

A vision of Uncle Jack's bloodied body passed before Disa's eyes, only the face on the body was her father's. "What do they mean to do?"

He shrugged uncomfortably. "I don't know. It's just talk so far, rumors. But they're saying if a foal gets killed, a baby will be next. And the Frilandena won't stand for that."

"Aage, will you tell my parents what you just told me?"

He hunched his shoulders. "It's just rumors, Disa."

"You think so?"

"No—okay, I'll talk to them. What time is it?"

Disa looked at her beacon. "Three-thirty."

"We'd better go back up, then. I have to be in Holmstad before dark."

They crawled through the breakdown that choked the exit. In the Meeting Hall they bade Inanna farewell. "*Daqua*," Aage said.

"Heg," the Kargan answered. "Come again."

At the bottom of the ladder, Aage's hands closed around Disa's waist. "Let me give you a boost."

"I can climb," she said, scrambling six feet up the ladder and out of his grasp, then regretting it. What a fool she was to jerk away when a boy finally reached for her! But time refused to reverse. Disa continued upward, fretting over the incident. Had she hopelessly antagonized him? They passed through the low tunnel and crossed the Front Porch. How was she going to get her suit off? She found herself standing with Aage in the cache at the cave's mouth.

They looked nervously at each other.

"Your helmet goes back on that peg," Disa instructed.

"Oh, yeah. Of course." Aage turned to hang it up. Disa hung up her own helmet and put away her gloves.

Aage glanced over his shoulder at Disa's clothes piled on the floor. His eyes rose to her face. "Want me to wait outside?"

Her cheeks turned hot as she nodded. "I'll be with you in a minute."

The door closed behind him. She stripped off the suit and hung it up muddy—time enough later to clean it. Her body seemed very white in the dim light, her nipples very dark. What if she had told him to stay? She dressed and pulled on her cloak. "My folks are in the house," she told Aage as she stepped outside.

She led off. Aage walked beside her.

Disa reached for his hand.

He didn't pull away.

Disa walked with eyes averted. Aage's fingers played gently with hers. Disa's returned the pressure. Aage pulled her arm around his waist, tugging her against him. She started.

He frowned down at her. "For a woman of the world, you're sure spooky."

What did he mean, woman of the world? "Yvette's stories aren't all true."

"Oh?" His eyes wandered back to the equipment cache.

Disa blushed again. "I'm sorry. I didn't think twice about it. I forgot how dirtsiders do things."

"And I didn't know how circlings do things." He broke into a grin. "Don't do that again unless it's on purpose."

Disa grinned back. "I'll try to remember." She squeezed his muddy waist, then let go and opened the door. Where was Kelda? Disa wanted to see her expression when her daughter finally brought a boy home. If only Aage's news were not so bad!

Per sat at his terminal. He looked up, assessing the mud on Aage's clothes and the matching streaks on Disa, and smiled. Kelda stood behind him. "Where've you been, young lady?" she asked irritably.

"Down in the cave," Disa said. She wondered what Aage thought of girls whose mothers had black eyes. "Mom, this is Aage Hanson."

Kelda's gaze flicked over him. "Glad to meet you."

"Aage's the one who was going to ask me to Midwinter," Disa explained.

"My father said I couldn't," Aage added, pointing an explanatory finger toward his own black eye.

"Why should he object?" Kelda asked with a hint of the old mischief on her face. "He took me."

"In those days you were a political asset," Per said. He stood to meet Disa's guest. "I'm pleased to meet you, Aage. Pardon us if we're a little disrupted just now. There's been a lot going on."

"That's okay," Aage said, staring curiously around the cabin at the foldaway beds, multiple library consoles, and miscellaneous bits of exploratory equipment. "I didn't mean to interrupt your work."

"Aage says rumors in town are getting pretty hot," Disa prompted.

That got the adults' attention. "Tell us," Per said.

Looking acutely uncomfortable, Aage repeated what he had told Disa in the cave. Per's face turned bleak. "Is there any way they'd listen if I brought Inanna in to talk to them?"

"I don't think they'd give her a chance to speak," Aage answered somberly.

"Damn!" Per shook his head. "Sorry, Aage. It's not your fault. I'm glad you came out here. Want some hot chocolate?"

"I just filled the pot," Kelda said. "Probably not hot yet. Disa, would you fetch Yvette for me?"

Disa and Aage exchanged glances. "I think she's busy," Disa said.

"I need her anyway," Kelda answered. "You can get her while your water heats. Tell her I want her in the lab. Now."

Disa sighed. "All right."

"I'll go with you," Aage said. Safely outside he asked, "Is your mother always so—curt?"

"She's got a lot on her mind now," Disa said. "I guess you heard she fought Uncle Hal yesterday. She doesn't usually go around with a black eye and a fat lip. Where do you suppose Leif and Yvette went?"

"They were headed upriver when we left," Aage answered. "We should make some noise."

The searchers descended the bluff and walked west up the rain-bloated river, maintaining a strained but loud conversation about nothing in particular. Leif stood on the beach beyond the bend, hands in his pockets. Yvette sat on the sand, tucking in her shirttail. "You dirtsiders have a lot to learn about wrestling," she told him. She turned toward Disa. "What's up?"

"Mom wants you in the lab."

Yvette looked at Leif. "I'll be there in twenty minutes."

"She wants you *now.* I don't know what's eating her, but she's in a mood. If I were you, I'd go."

"What time is it?" Leif asked.

"Four."

He glanced skyward, then at Aage. "We better get going. I promised Dana I'd be home by supper."

Aage frowned, but said mildly, "I'll meet you at the boat." He tugged Disa back downstream, leaving the other couple to bid farewell. Disa half hoped Yvette would arrive at the lab late. It would be nice to have Kelda mad at someone else.

"I better tell Mom we found them," Disa said as she and Aage reached the foot of the camp bluff. "I'll be back in a second." She ascended the steps at a run.

Kelda sat alone at the main workbench. "I found her," Disa reported. "She said she's on her way."

Kelda smiled back with unaccustomed tenderness. "Thanks, Disa. Where was she?"

"Teaching Leif to fight."

Kelda's mouth quirked at the corners. "I might have known." Then she held her arms open. "Come here and hug your mother."

Wary of this unaccustomed warmth, Disa obeyed. Kelda held her tight, then spoke into Disa's hair. "You know I love you, don't you?"

Disa nodded mutely.

"Please remember it, always," Kelda said. "I love you more than I can say."

Disa's throat tightened. "I love you, too." she answered, then pulled away before the moment's intensity broke her self-control. "What did you want Yvette for?"

Kelda straightened. "Just some questions about the enzyme transfer. You wouldn't be interested," she added with an unmistakable air of dismissal.

Disa could take a hint. "Heg," she said, and backed away to rejoin Aage.

CHAPTER TWENTY-TWO

KELDA SWALLOWED HARD AS THE DOOR CLOSED. SHE loved Disa, but she found the shy, intense child difficult to deal with. Should she call her back, explain her intentions? No. Quiet, cautious, well-mannered Disa would never understand—and she was one of two people whose disapproval might shake Kelda's resolve. Kelda had said as much as she dared. If all went well, she would explain later.

Yvette slammed into the lab with flushed cheeks, shiny eyes, and a sulky expression that would pass as quickly as it had come. She was a girl Kelda understood. Kelda reached for the teapot on the stove. "Something hot?"

"Sounds good," Yvette said.

"Sit down," Kelda told her, nodding toward the conference corner with its cushioned chairs.

Yvette sat warily while Kelda scooped fragrant leaves from a jar and set them in the pot to steep. "Did Leif say anything about what's going on in town?"

A shadow crossed Yvette's face. "Some rumors. I'm scared about Uncle Per, Aunt Kelda."

"Me, too." Kelda ladled sugar into two mugs and

poured the tea. Handing one mug to Yvette, she sat across from the girl and took a sip from her own cup. The tea was far too hot for comfort. Kelda sighed and set the mug down. "You and I are Dawn's black sheep, Yvette."

Yvette's eyes dropped, but she admitted nothing.

Kelda picked up her mug again. The tea was still too hot. "I didn't call you here for a lecture, if that's what you're wondering. I remember how I acted when I was your age." She grinned in unexpected embarrassment. "You've heard the stories."

"Then what do you want?" Yvette looked worried.

Kelda paced to the cage where a pair of converted testers nibbled Kargan swampgrass seeds. "I shouldn't have let Hal goad me into that fight. Now we're caught in a black hole. One way or another it will come to blows. But Per's always said a team driven to violence must have done its job wrong. He won't give up on his crazy plan." She closed her eyes, haunted by the look on her husband's face when he heard Aage's report.

Yvette waited.

Kelda fidgeted with the latch on the tester cage. "Hal's right. I joined First-In because the men were handsome and it got me out from under my father's thumb. I never gave our philosophy much thought. When it comes right down to it I'm like Hal—I look out for my family."

Yvette leaned forward. "What do you plan to do?"

Kelda walked back to face Yvette. "If Per insists on talking to the colonists, I want him to have more on his side than truth and justice. I intend to prove the transformation's safe. Or at worst tell Skip and Calypso what they need to know to make it safe."

Yvette bit at her lip, a habit she had learned from Disa. "It's not safe, Aunt Kelda."

Kelda reached for her mug and took a long swallow. "This morning you said it was. You said the odds were with us."

Yvette's eyes strayed to the tester cage. "If it goes foul it'll probably kill you."

"So could a lot of other things."

Yvette closed her eyes. "Why are you telling me this?"

"You know enough about the treatment to administer it. I want you to give it to me."

It was Yvette's turn to pace. "Why not your brother? Or Calypso? Or Uncle Suli? They know more than I do."

"They're too cautious. They wouldn't understand. Now tell me how the thing works."

Yvette slowly returned, reached over, and activated the console on the table between their chairs. "We're using a virus to carry the DNA segments that code for the new enzymes. There are other ways of inserting—but this is least likely to give nasty surprises. The virus stays dormant except in the pancreas, where it inserts and stimulates cells to secrete the new enzyme."

"Will newborns be able to digest Kargan protein?" Kelda asked.

"No. The virus doesn't replicate in the body. It reproduces only in laboratory culture under highly controlled conditions. That way folks like the silk traders aren't at risk for infection, and you won't get immunity built up from viruses loose in the environment. Breast milk will still be southpaw, so it all works out. You won't infect children until they're ready for Kargan food."

"Couldn't someone blackmail the colony by withholding treatment from the babies?" A sad commentary on humanity, Kelda thought, that that question should occur to her.

"We thought about that," Yvette said. "We'll distribute backup supplies of the virus to everyone in the colony."

"Sounds foolproof," Kelda said.

"We tried," Yvette agreed. "The question is whether the virus will really stay dormant outside the pancreas."

"Let's find out," Kelda said, rolling up her sleeve.

Yvette gulped, glancing involuntarily at the lab incubator. "Are you sure you want to do this?"

Kelda went to the incubator herself. It wasn't hard to spot the vial of ersatz blood, marked with red trefoil and the warning TEST VIRUS—HANDLE WITH CARE. Kelda pulled a syringe from the adjacent drawer. "How much do I have to take?"

Yvette had followed her to the bench. She stared wide-eyed at the syringe. "Two mil. Let me try it, Aunt Kelda. You're too important. The team needs you."

Kelda stood on tiptoe to put her arms around Yvette. "Not true. I mostly get people in trouble. But I promised your father a long time ago that I'd take care of you. Don't ask me to go back on that."

Yvette's head drooped on Kelda's shoulder. "I'm scared."

Kelda grinned. "I'm tough. Nothing will happen to me. And if it does, it's not your fault. I've already left a message that you had no choice in the matter. If you won't inject it in me I'll do it myself." She handed Yvette the syringe. "Let's get it over with."

CHAPTER TWENTY-THREE

❧❧❧❧

COLD FINE MIST PEPPERED DISA'S FACE AS SUN AND TEM-
perature dropped. Aage waved a final time, then current
swept the boys' skiff around the bend. Disa blinked hard.
Why had Aage declared friendship just three days before
Disa left? And what would happen to her family when she
was gone? The lab's firmly closed door excluded her from
whatever secrets her mother and Yvette shared. How like
Kelda to make noises of love, then send Disa out! Too
disquieted to return to her terminal, Disa wondered where
else to go. Per and Calypso, hard at work, would not appreciate interruption. Sulman was gone, and anyway, he
was too much a stranger for the hurt she was feeling. A
swim might burn away some of Disa's tension, but even
with First-In diving equipment, she distrusted the high
turbid water of the river.

In other times and places, Disa had taken her turmoil to
the quiet darkness of the Kargans' cavern. But Enki was
dead, and Risky—

Disa licked her lips. Risky! She—no, he—ought to be
through with her—no, his—metamorphosis by now.
"Change done," Inanna had said. "He learns secrets."

234

How long to finish that indoctrination? Did it matter, when Risky stood at risk of death from colony action or a tunnel collapse when the First-In ship crashed? Inanna was not fluent enough to address an angry crowd. Disa turned for a long look at the cave mouth. If the team had ever needed Risky, it was now.

Well trained in frontier safety, the girl started toward the cabin to leave word of her plans. She stopped with her hand on the latch. Everyone seemed so determined to protect her! If she were to hint that she meant to seek Risky, even with Inanna as guide, the team would confine her to the cabin. She turned and headed directly for the cave. In the cache, she entered a time-delay message on the equipment-use log. With luck she would return before it displayed. If not, they would know where to look for her.

It was just as well that she had not bothered to clean the diving suit when she returned from the trip with Aage. Pulling it on, Disa noticed again how poorly it fit. Kelda would have to adjust it—if Kelda wasn't dead in two weeks. Disa yanked angrily at a bootstrap. Was she herself crazy? Would she kill herself there in the rock's belly? First-Inners had a penchant for self-destruction, it seemed. Yet someone had to tell Risky what was going on. The boot strap bit painfully at Disa's ankle. She refastened the strap at a more comfortable tension and warned herself to calm down.

Her climbing pack held its usual complement of fine spidersilk rope, safety belt and clips, cleats and crampons, and emergency rations. Everything was clean and functioning. Disa added knee and elbow pads, then reached for her diving mask. Soberly she checked its gas exchange and reserve oxygen, for her destination in the water-filled depths of the cave would allow no easy escape to the surface. Disa replaced the mask's bright searchlight with one of the dim beams Kelda had prepared for caving. She

tucked two spares in her pocket. She ought to bring a
visual recorder, she thought, but if she went to the cabin
for it people would ask questions. Shrugging and shouldering her pack, she entered the cave.

Inanna still lounged in the Meeting Hall. *"Daqua,"* Disa
said. "Inanna take Disa Risky."

Inanna turned a sightless head toward Disa. The girl
heard, or thought she heard, the high-pitched blip by
which Inanna distinguished one human from another. The
elder could usually smell the difference, too, but at that
moment the breeze was toward Disa. "Not Risky," Inanna
said, knowing that with Disa she need not struggle to
speak English. "He-Risky now."

Disa had unthinkingly used Risky's old, feminine name.
"Take Disa He-Risky," she amended.

"Go He-Risky forbidden. Not clutching time."

"Disa star-walk soon," the girl argued. "Speak He-
Risky first."

Inanna descended slowly from her ledge and walked to
Disa, probing with two heavy claws as if only by touch
could she judge the girl's request. Then her claw grated
assent. "He-Risky welcomes Disa. Inanna leads partway.
But Disa enters alone."

Disa tried not to wonder how far she would have to go
alone, or how accurate Inanna's directions would be.
"Come," the elder said.

Inanna led Disa to a tunnel that passed by the silkfruit
fermentation area. The passage was roomy and smooth-
floored, and nearly high enough for Disa to stand upright.
A few hundred yards beyond the stench of the vats, Disa
realized that the walls and ceiling no longer dripped. Instead, white stone petals curled from the rock like flowers
made from wood shavings. Gypsum! They must be beneath the sandstone cap of the hill. Water could reach that
place only by slow capillary action. When ground mois-
ture evaporated in the cave's dry air, dissolved minerals

formed these three-dimensional frost-flower patterns. Risky had reminisced about such flowers, complaining that her artificial cavern lacked them. Disa pulled a glove off and probed delicately at a blossom. The petal edge crumbled beneath her touch. Hastily she put her glove back on.

The tunnel ended in a breakdown pile like that which separated the Meeting Hall from the Hall of Voices. Inanna kept going, wedging her shell through an impossibly small-looking crevice between two limestone slabs. Disa held back. "Inanna!" Dust and rough rock sucked up the sound. Disa tried again. "Inanna!"

A pale claw reached back toward her. "I am here. Come."

"Disa too big!"

"Not too big. Inanna measured."

Disa recalled the feeling of Inanna's claws running over her body before the elder had consented to the trip. Had she been measuring Disa then? If so, Disa trusted her. Kargans estimated with caliper accuracy. Slipping her pack off—she would drag it by its towline—and wetting her lips, she followed Inanna into the crevice.

The grit that had powdered her face ground between her teeth. Trying to spit it out, she got another mouthful. Well, if it wouldn't go up, it might go down. Smiling grimly to herself, Disa swallowed.

She wiggled upward from the crack into what must once have been an awesome tunnel. The ceiling hung ten or twelve feet above her. Below lay forty, fifty, or sixty feet—who knew?—of tumbled limestone. Ahead, rubble rose to meet the ceiling. "Come!" Inanna said from the slab that topped Disa's part of the pile.

Disa glanced backward. Without Inanna's help, could she ever retrace her journey? She chalked an arrow marking the cleft through which she had come. Only then did she don her pack and move to follow Inanna.

The slab was five feet thick and canted at a thirty-degree angle toward Disa. She heaved herself onto it and pushed forward with her feet, her stomach against the rock to prevent slippage. Fifteen feet, twenty, and her fingertips hooked over the far edge. She pulled forward until she could see over the edge. "Oh, shit." She faced a fifteen-foot drop to an unstable-looking rubble pile below. Worse, the pile lay twelve feet below the overhang of the next large slab. Disa laid her helmet to the rock in discouragement.

"This way," Inanna announced. Disa lifted her head again. The elder was waiting in the shadows at the far left of the overhang, where a somewhat smaller block leaned almost vertically against the big one. "Tunnel," Inanna said, using the Kargan word that designated a very tight passage.

Still low to the rock, Disa scooted right. She lowered herself feet first onto a pile of three-foot chunks. Wary of loose gravel and a two-foot-wide chasm of indeterminable depth, she edged to the hole Inanna had indicated.

The opening was too narrow even for Disa's thin shoulders, so she inched through the crevice on her side. Emerging from the crack between boulders, she faced three more such openings. She paused to mark her course, then crawled doggedly on, hoping that the centuries-old rubble heap had finished settling. Finally, dragging her pack behind her, she emerged from the breakdown into a tunnel sixty feet wide and thirty high. Disa's beacon showed that an hour and a half had passed since her entry into the cave—and that she had come only a hundred yards since the end of the gypsum tunnel.

Pack comfortably on her back, Disa walked the next fifth of a mile in less than five minutes. Then Inanna stopped. The passage floor dropped in front of them.

The drop was no dramatic columnar pit, but a simple, steep-sided crack in the rock, about three feet wide where

Disa stood. The partially eroded sides of the canyon still boasted plentiful ledges and sharp edges. Its walls dropped zigzag, offering no hint of its depth. "Down," Inanna said, stepping confidently to the edge and over.

Disa eyed the rock. Were it sturdy granite, and outdoors, a risk-loving climber might descend unaided. But it was limestone; soft to begin with, it had been subjected to heavy leaching. Shards on the ledges attested how easily such rotten rock broke. A nearly unnegotiable collapse lay between Disa and safety, and she was no lover of risks. It was a safe bet that she would be badly bounced if she slipped. From her pack she pulled spidersilk line and clamps.

Indiscriminate hammering of pitons offended the Kargans, so Disa looked around for another anchor. A big round boulder, chert left behind when surrounding rock had dissolved, beckoned. Disa started to loop her line around it. She froze. There was rope already there. Not spidersilk, but good rope just the same, a sturdy synthetic of Valhallan manufacture, securely knotted. Not the sort of rope one abandoned. Whoever had left that rope had expected to come back.

Disa's eyes followed the line to the canyon's edge and down, trailing out of sight. "Inanna!" she called. "Rope bottom?"

Inanna, Disa knew, could discern her voice even within that sound-swallowing cavity, but the elder had to climb some distance before Disa understood her reply. "Bottom yes. *Click-tap*'s rope."

Disa gulped and grasped it. It held firm. She closed her eyes and prayed to dust that she, unlike Aunt Ingrid, would return to reclaim the rope. She clipped herself to it with a ratcheted catch through which only slack line could pass. If she slipped, tension on the rope would cause the ratchet to grab, stopping her fall.

She lay flat on the canyon's lip to study its walls, then

pivoted and dropped her feet, closing her eyes for a surer image of the pocket she was groping for. There! Straddling the chasm, right hand and foot on one wall, left on the other, Disa worked downward with small steps, trying always to maintain three firm anchors while she groped with the fourth limb.

The canyon's top was as dry and dusty as the gypsum tunnel, but forty feet down, Disa encountered dripping water. Traction became less certain. Tunnels led off at various depths in various directions, many only six inches or a foot wide, but two or three broad enough to admit a human. "No," Inanna said. "Down."

Disa's wedging technique failed as she emerged from the canyon into a new tunnelway at the bottom, but by then she was willing to abandon elegance, trust herself to the rope, and rappel the final four yards. Water fell around her in brisk irregular rhythm: *pa-pat, pa-pat, pa-pa-pat, pa, pa-pat.* She was standing in a gravelly, two-inch-deep pool. The rope vanished in darkness above. She pulled off a glove and caught water in her hand. Lifting her helmet and unsealing the diving suit, she bared more of her skin to a cool draft.

Her beacon's tracking system, sophisticated as it was, recorded position on a plane. It could not follow the three-dimensional meanderings of her journey. How far was it to the top? She could only guess. "Ninety feet below the dry corridor," she said into her voice recorder, adding the horizontal coordinates given by the beacon. Then she switched off her light and squatted to rest, surrounded by darkness and dripping water.

A claw tugged gently at her leg. "Come," Inanna said.

"In a moment," Disa answered, switching on her light and donning her helmet. She adjusted her packstraps, which had begun to chafe. "Now where?"

"This way," Inanna said, vanishing under a fifteen-inch-high shelf.

"What?" Disa bent down. The pool's water drained in a brisk stream through a tunnel three feet wide but little more than a foot high. "Here?"

"Yes." Inanna crabbed through sideways.

For Disa it would be a belly-crawl, in running water no less. "Shit." She resealed the front of her diving suit, took the pack back off, and slithered on her stomach under the ledge.

Wetness felt good on her hot body, but Disa hated to share critically limited crawlspace with running water. Fifteen feet in, a hand-sized pipelet poured its own tiny gush into the tunnel. Disa scanned the walls ahead. She saw another tiny tributary—and another. Her helmet scraped the roof as she lifted her head for a better look.

She piled her fists on one other for a chinrest. Water lapped midway on the higher hand and pressed her from the rear. She managed a peek behind. The tunnel was sloping downward—more water, less air. Graceful, half-inch scoops in the rock beside her said that for some considerable period of time, briskly moving water had filled the tunnel.

How much poured how fast down the sides of that canyon, when a cloudburst erupted?

"Shit," Disa said again.

"From dust are born the suns, the seas, and life..." Disa breathed deeply and considered realities. Frightened as she was to lie in a tight tunnel in a stream with the roof dropping, two facts consoled her: First, she carried the best diving equipment available; and second, she proposed to visit someone who lived underwater. Wetness was good, if it signaled an approach to the dreamer realm. With a sigh and a shake of her head, Disa hitched herself another six inches forward.

Beyond the next bend, the water situation turned critical. Flowing much more briskly than before, water filled the bottom half of a passage less than fifteen inches high.

Disa's pack bobbed against her feet. She groped for it and extracted her diving mask, making sure that the pack's tether remained attached to her belt.

The ceiling dropped again. By turning her head and pressing upward against the roof, Disa might keep her nose and mouth dry. She sighed. Why try? Her suit's gill mechanism could not exchange gas quite fast enough to support human metabolism, but with the gills' help, a little supplementary oxygen went a long way. Disa carried enough for a fifteen-hour drive. Might as well start using it. Fumbling in the tight crawlway, she sealed the mask and activated it.

After another fifteen feet, there was no air space left. Inanna waited just ahead. To the elder's right, dark turbulence indicated another tunnel full of water tumbling in.

Inanna's words, difficult to understand under normal conditions, were incomprehensible through water and the mask's sound pickup. Three times Disa shook her head regretfully, troubled by an undertone, a static, that made words difficult to hear. "Talk Sheppie," she finally suggested, glad that a synthesizer was built into her speaker. Kargans found Sheppie simpler than English, and Disa herself often used it underwater.

"Go straight, water down, Disa up," Inanna said in Sheppie.

Disa got her arms in front of her and gestured as she replied. "Go that way, go up?"

"Yes," Inanna said, plunging ahead.

Disa followed, bracing herself against the tunnel sides to avoid being swept ahead too fast. The odd undertone increased. The tunnel widened, and Disa's pack bumped by her, leaving its tether wrapped around her ankle. Pressing herself against the tunnel's side, she untangled the rope. Her pack floated a fathom ahead, tugging at its leash.

Inanna was out of sight. The noise was terrible. The

current was very fast. A silver curtain shimmered ahead—an air-water interface, but vertical! Frightened, Disa braced herself again, her back against the top of the passage, feet spread against the bottom, arms to the side. Her pack hit the silver curtain and disappeared. The tether stretched taut from her belt clip, threatening to drag her forward.

She closed her eyes. "Goddamn, fuck it to hell, shit, shit, shit." That was a waterfall up there.

"Water down, Disa up," Inanna had said. Water down, all right. What about Disa up? Just by Disa, the silver sheet of plunging water broke from the tunnel ceiling. Carefully she lifted her head until her faceplate broke the surface. The tunnel continued another four feet. Thirty feet ahead she glimpsed a vertical wall. Between the two, there was nothing but spray. No floor. No walls. No roof.

Inanna knew the caverns too well to be swept to her death by a waterfall. There had to be some exit—for a Kargan. But for a human? Disa, too close to her limits already, wasn't going to bet her life on it. She began to back up.

The first feet were hardest. The tunnel offered no protuberances to grip. She could only wedge herself, as she already had, against its cross-section. Water pushed against her body. She reeled in her pack and continued moving backward.

Retreat became easier beyond the final sweep of the water's acceleration. Still, Disa was trembling with fear and exhaustion by the time she emerged beneath the shelf in the canyon. Inanna followed. "Water down. Disa not up? Come!"

Still feeling panicky, Disa replied in English. "That was a waterfall! Were you trying to kill me? I almost got swept over the edge! How far does that water fall? No I'm *not* going that way with you any more!"

"Disa go He-Risky," Inanna said in Kargan, bending the joint of her claw-arm as elders always did when distressed. "Come." She ducked half under the shelf.

"No," Disa said, switching back to Inanna's language.

"Come!"

"No!"

"Disa no come?"

"No!"

Inanna came out and squatted on top of the shelf, on a level with Disa's thighs. "Disa go other way?"

"Where?" Disa asked.

Inanna crawled eight feet up the wall to a nearly dry opening. "Here other way He-Risky."

Disa stared at the roomy opening. "There other way He-Risky?"

"Yes."

Disa leaned her forehead against the cave's wet wall and laughed. "Other way. She asks if I want to go the other way! *Now* she asks!"

"Disa come other way He-Risky?"

Disa took her helmet off and sat on a wet rock. "Yes, Disa come other way. Disa eat first."

Inanna waited patiently. Finally, fed and rested, Disa picked up pack, helmet, and gloves. The tunnel looked easy enough to reach, but the wall's limestone ledges crumbled beneath even her slight weight, and her target was too far from the ceiling opening for the rope to be useful. Disa eyed the tunnel again. If she put her left hand *there*, and her right *there*, and used *that* little knob as a stepping-stone . . . Three minutes later she lifted her knee over the edge, glad for once that she lacked Yvette's plumpness.

Disa traveled the corridor in a stooping-sideways duck-walk, knees bent and fingertips occasionally brushing the floor for balance. Soon she heard the roar of water ahead. She paused for a moment, leaning against the wall. Her beacon's two-dimensional record showed her to be stand-ing almost precisely where she had been an hour before.

Inanna was out of sight. Some guide! Disa continued down the passage, which opened, like so many others, into a vertical face. Below, water cascaded from the last corridor she had tried.

She could not see bottom, for the pit was filled with water. In the din of the fall, it took Disa a moment to realize that Inanna was speaking. "Inanna stop. Disa go down. Far side, thirty yards above bottom, dreamer tunnel. Inanna drums that Disa comes. He-Risky welcome Disa."

"Here dreamer place?" Disa asked nervously.

"Here dreamers. Here guardians. Inanna stop. He-Risky welcome Disa."

Disa, even as she descended Ingrid's rope, had shut from her mind the elders' explanation of Ingrid's death. She avoided looking at the choppy dark water below. "Inanna will guide you to depths," Risky had said on the day of his departure. "Call my name. I will hold guardians from you." Inanna went to drum the news of Disa's coming. Disa took her boots off but did not replace them with fins; she was more likely to cling with her toes than to kick. Chewing her lip, she transferred her knife to her belt. Surely Risky would welcome her before the guardians did. There was no point to worrying.

To avoid climbing through the torrent, Disa anchored a rope, secured it to her harness, then edged sideways around the pit on a ledge. She kept careful track of her distance. Eight feet out, she was clear of the big fall, although smaller tunnels emptied their water from all sides. Disa sank a second anchor and began descending. Twenty feet passed all too swiftly. She checked seals on mask and suit one final time, then dropped into the water.

But for bubbles from the fall, things looked much as they had above—black. "Thirty yards above bottom," Inanna had directed. The bottom must be at least ninety feet below. Disa was reluctant to go so deep, but there seemed no other way to determine the proper tunnel. If she moved quickly she would be done before nitrogen accumulation in her tissue necessitated a staged ascent. Disa clung to the sides and adjusted her buoyancy, then drifted downward, paying out rope. Ten yards, twenty. She shifted sideways into the much-attenuated current from the fall. She should be directly below the point at which Inanna had said, "far side." Thirty feet farther, Disa saw bottom. She pulled her beacon and took a careful bearing. *There* should be "far side." She could not see the wall, for silt kicked up by currents made the water murky. Her fingers clutching the rope that was her guide home, Disa started across the pit.

A few yards later, some survival sense prompted Disa to look upward. Filaments trailed through the water a few feet above her head. She kicked forward and turned for another look. Above her hovered a grotesque creature, a ball of tentacles, some only inches long, many several feet. Disa had seen the sea hunters of enough worlds to guess that those tentacles would seize and digest. A guardian! "Risky!" she cried into her speaker, hoping that the guardian did not home in on sound. "He-Risky!"

The guardian rode the current's downwash toward her. Disa swam for the far wall, reached it, and began to kick her way upward. An opening, there! She ducked in, still trailing her rope. She found herself in a dead-end pocket floored in fuzzy lumpy carpeting rather than rock. She started to retreat but saw the guardian only a few feet outside.

The girl moved deeper into the pocket, nearly to the far wall, and turned so that she could examine the floor and watch the entrance all at once. The fuzzy gray lumps were plants, or fungus—a garden. A death field. Sweat matted Disa's bangs inside the mask; they dropped into her eyes. She could not reach them to brush them aside. If she got out alive, she swore, she would cut them short again.

Something of familiar color by the left wall caught her eye. A diving suit. A helmet.

Aunt Ingrid.

Flickering motion drew Disa's eyes back up to the door. A guardian.

CHAPTER TWENTY-FOUR

❧❧❧❧

"HUH?" SKIP ROLLED OVER TO SQUINT AT HIS TIMEPIECE. It was a quarter after midnight. Lightning illuminated the room. A deep roll of thunder followed. Thunder must have wakened him, he thought, burrowing back into his pillow.

No, he heard it again—an insistent pulse from the radio console, signaling an urgent call. That was the second time in three nights. As an apprentice, checking experiments every four hours around the clock, Skip had grown used to waking at odd hours. He would snap cheerfully to attention, perform his duties, and lapse as quickly into precious sleep. Over the years he had lost that skill. "What the hell?" he muttered, telling his protesting body that he had noted the intrusion and was trying to do something about it.

The pulse continued.

"Okay, okay!" He reached over and cued acceptance of the call. "What do you want?"

"Skip, we need you." Per's voice sounded as tense as Skip had ever heard it. "Can you come up to the hospital?"

Skip rubbed his eyes and looked at the rain sheeting over his window. Hal was right, First-Inners were a nuisance. "What's the matter?"

"It's Kelda. She didn't believe what you said about the transformation. She went ahead and tried it."

Skip discovered that he could snap awake, after all. "She what? Oh, the goddamn fool! What happened?"

"High fever, spitting blood, pissing blood, puffed all over. Obviously the virus lodged someplace it shouldn't."

"Sounds bad. You're at the hospital?"

"Yeah. Here in Holmstad. They sat it's a colony facility with limited resources and they won't treat an outsider without authorization." Per's voice was indescribably bitter. "Can you get up here?"

Yes, he could, but he did not want Kelda waiting that long. "Let me talk to whoever's in charge."

Minutes later the night nurse took the com. Skip reminded himself to speak reasonably. "What the hell kind of nurse are you? Look, charge it to the Nygren account. And you'll answer to the Nygrens if you don't give her the best you've got. Who's the doc on call tonight? Wake him up and get him to work! I expect Kelda in a bed and a doc by her side by the time I get there." Respectful of Skip's name, professional standing, or both, the man promised to admit Kelda.

"Good." Skip threw the disconnect switch and reached for his trousers.

A brisk walk through storm-swept streets brought him to the single-story hospital building halfway up the hill. At the reception desk, normally unstaffed that time of night, sat a middle-aged woman with light-brown hair and pale-blue eyes. She half rose as he strode through the door.

"I'm Skip Nygren," he told her. "Where's my sister?

She indicated a hallway to the right. "Bed forty-two." That was the critical care wing. Damn! The receptionist trailed him across the room, an anxious look on her face.

"Sir, that's a sterile area, you'll have to scrub and gown—"

Skip stopped at the door and took a deep breath, telling himself to be calm. "Okay. Where do I go and what do I do?"

Ten minutes later, scrubbed, gowned, and masked, Skip followed his guide to the room Kelda occupied. Skip muttered a silent prayer, opened the door, and walked in. The steamy warm room reeked of antiseptic. Kelda lay mostly immersed in a chest-high bath basin near the room's center. Tubes ran from a nearby machine into her veins. Her left eye was still badly swollen from the fight with Hal. Her right eye was open. Her cheeks burned an unhealthy scarlet. She seemed aware of her surroundings, but she submitted with uncharacteristic passivity to the ministrations of the four gowned figures around her. Skip recognized the doctor, and Per and Yvette, who were assisting with care as families always did in frontier hospitals. Per's eyes flicked toward Skip in greeting. The other man, probably the nurse Skip had spoken to earlier, beckoned Skip forward. "Master Nygren. We're preparing to put your sister in isolation. Would you hold this hose for me?"

Skip obeyed, his eyes avoiding the dark stain of the bruise across Kelda's chest where Hal had tried to crush her. Other than that there was nothing obviously wrong, just the high color, a bit of puffiness, and a subtle strangeness about Kelda's position. She was holding her joints oddly flexed, as if they hurt her. Rain pelted against the window.

The doctor looked at Skip. "I gather you designed this virus she's got, so maybe you can tell me more about it."

"Are you sure it's not catching?" the nurse asked, staying as far as possible from the patient he was working on.

"I told you it can't replicate outside the body!" Yvette snapped.

Per very gently moved Kelda's arm in order to swab

her side. She inhaled sharply and pressed her lips together, but said nothing. Kelda had never been a complainer.

"As far as we can see, this is an autoimmune reaction," the doctor continued.

"Brilliant deduction," Skip muttered.

The doctor ignored his sarcasm. "Obviously this virus of yours has gone somewhere it shouldn't have, and her body's trying to reject the infected cells as foreign. We'll have to jump hard on her immune system, try to keep her body from killing itself while we sort out the details of what's going on. She'll lose her defenses against ordinary infection, as well, so she'll need to be in a sterile environment."

Skip nodded agreement.

The doctor looked at Kelda. "I'd like to get some fluid in you. Can you drink this?" He held a straw to her lips.

Kelda sucked weakly. Her throat muscles convulsed in an attempt to swallow. Flinching, she spit out the straw. Blood tinged the liquid trailing down her chin. "I was afraid of that," the doctor muttered. "You can't swallow?"

Kelda blinked terrified acknowledgment.

"Put it through the IV, then," the doctor told the nurse. "Let's go ahead and get her in a bed. If you family members could stay out of the way for a few minutes—"

Per gripped Skip's arm and pulled him to a corner where they would not be underfoot. Yvette followed. Skip had never seen her so serious. "Suli and Calypso are already back at the lab working to figure out what happened," Per said. "You can be the most help by going back with Yvette and helping them. Our boat's at the pier. It's lightning-safed. Let me know if you need biopsies from Kelda for tissue tests; I'll get them sent out. I'm staying here with her."

"Any idea where the reaction's centered?" Skip asked.

Per closed his eyes. "Connective tissue, we think."

That was bad. Very bad. Bad because it offered too
many possibilities for which precise cell type the virus had
targeted. Bad because it meant a whole-body reaction.
And bad because the damage might be irreversible. If
Kelda's kidneys shut down, she would be in acute danger,
but at worst she could be maintained on artificial life support until new organs were cultured and implanted. But
connective tissue—there was no way to dig out and replace the tissue, interwoven through the body as it was.
Every minute the reaction continued, Kelda suffered per-
manent damage. Did *she* know that? Probably. First-
Inners rarely minced words. No wonder her expression
was so grim.

Skip walked over to his sister and took her hand in his
gloved ones. He tried not to disturb the tubes taped to her
wrists. Her sharp shallow breathing unnerved him. "Hold
tight, Kelda. We'll get it figured out."

Her hand tightened around his.

Skip turned to the doctor. "I'm going to the First-In
camp to try to figure out what the virus did and why. Call
me there if you have any questions, or any observations
that might give us clues. And if you don't give her the best
Frilandet's got—"

"It's so nice to work with a supportive family," the
doctor muttered. "All right. I'll be in touch."

Yvette bent over the other side of Kelda's bed. "I love
you."

Kelda's lips reflected the words back to her.

"Come on, Yvette," Skip said. "Let's get to work."

They hurried out of the sterile area, stripped off their
gowns, pulled on their cloaks, and stepped into the wind
and rain. Something tugged at Skip's mind, a missing person. "Where's Disa?" he asked.

Yvette choked out something unintelligible, half curse,
half sob.

"What?" Skip asked, stopping and turning to face

Yvette. Her face was a pale blob in darkness.

She tried again. "In the caves. She took off to find Risky. We found her trail but none of the rest of us can squeeze through. The elders say she's in dreamer territory. We don't know how to get to her."

Water ran in rivulets from Skip's hood and down his back. It coursed from housetops to gutters and down the hill. Dangerous weather for caving. Surely the First-Inners knew that, too. Impulsively Skip opened his arms to Yvette. "I'm sorry."

Yvette, normally so bright and confident, seemed frail and frightened. Her face crumpling, she leaned into the embrace. Skip held her a moment, then released her. "There's nothing we can do, I guess. Let's get back to the lab."

She nodded, wiping her tears, and they hurried on together toward the river.

CHAPTER TWENTY-FIVE

❦

A PAIR OF PALE ORANGE TENTACLES GROPED TOWARD
Disa. How did a guardian kill? she wondered. Ensnarement? Poison? If so, how was it distributed? Surface contact? A cloud in the water? Biological darts? What
attracted the creature? Motion? Heat? Smell? Had it vision? Dreamers moved unharmed among the guardians.
How did they avert attack?

A diver of Disa's experience could guess answers to
those questions, but Disa's best guesses suggested that
she, breathing air and guarded by the diving suit's tough
hide, should be impervious. Ingrid's body argued otherwise. Her suit showed no obvious rupture, but she had
died of something. A guardian's attack, the Kargans said.

Moving slowly, not wishing to attract further attention,
Disa drew her knife. It seemed pitifully short. If she got
close enough to use this, who knew what the guardian
might unleash? Disassembling such a creature might not
disarm it. Could she entangle it in her rope? Disa decided
that an effective ensnarement would take her closer to the
guardian than she wanted to go.

A third tentacle, greenish and thicker than the first two,

254

undulated into the garden cavity. Gripping her knife, Disa tried to think of other defenses. Soft yellow mist rose from the garden fungus where her passage disturbed it. What lay beneath the fungus? Decaying organic matter, if this room was what she thought. Might the guardian accept substitute meat? Did the fungus consume the shells of elders dying in trial? If not, one such might serve as armor.

The guardian's body clump moved within range of Disa's light. It was still outside the room, but the longest tentacles, the orange ones, reached within four feet of the girl. Other tentacles streamed toward her, as well.

Disa probed with a gloved hand in the spongy fungus mass. Yellow fog billowed around her. Spores? If the guardian had eyes, such mist might blind it. But odds were low that the monster moved by sight, while Disa herself depended on it. She withdrew her hand, tabling the dust maneuver as a last resort.

All the tentacles moved toward her. "There call my name," Risky had said. Disa did not have to worry about betraying herself—the guardian already knew her location. She switched the knife to her left hand and took the castanet in her right. "Risky! He-Risky! *Snap-click* here! Field room! Guardian!" For good measure, she tried again in Sheppie.

The guardian's body reached the door. An orange tentacle moved within a human arm's reach of Disa's face.

Her dagger sliced, left-handed.

An orange tip fell twitching. The guardian shrank away. Then more tentatively, it reached for her with muddy green tentacles. Emboldened, Disa slashed again. Pain bit. Her fingers involuntarily dropped the knife. She cradled her tingling hand. Shock! What voltage did the creature generate? If shock itself had not killed Aunt Ingrid, interference with the control circuitry of her suit might have. Disa needed to escape. Quickly.

Both eyes on the guardian, she shed her pack and shoved it at the monster. Tentacles, orange, green, brown, and white, embraced the bundle, drawing it toward the center of the guardian's body. Disa braced her feet against the room's back wall and shoved, kicking herself into a headlong dive for the door. As she passed beneath the guardian's main body mass, a second shock jolted her, but momentum carried her through the door and into the main pool. She unfouled herself from her rope and kept swimming, forcing tingling limbs to carry her away from the garden chamber.

She must not surface yet, for she had stayed at this depth long enough to be in danger of bends. She had brought it on herself, too, Disa thought ruefully. If she had kept her calm and climbed to Risky's tunnel, rather than plunging into the first available opening, she would not have been trapped by the guardian, nor would she need decompression. She turned in the water to scan for the guardian. There it was, emerging from the garden room. It moved slowly; if she kept her wits about her, she could dodge it nearly forever. A second form, pale and ghostly in the dim light of Disa's lamp, crawled downward along the wall toward the guardian. Suddenly the guardian collapsed. It dropped Disa's pack, pulled its tentacles to itself, and shrank against the wall.

The pale colorless figure kept coming. Disa stared at its frail body, exposed gill flaps, pearly thin-shelled claws, and the crazy-silk pouch strapped, incongruously, about its body. A dreamer! Relaxing its grip on the wall, it propelled itself toward Disa, landing with one claw-arm bent around her neck and a second embracing her forehead. She could see nothing; the creature blocked both lamp and faceplate. But she heard its words. *"Daqua, snap-click."*

"Risky!"

"He-Risky now," he reminded her, in Kargan. "You

tremble, changeling." With the words of an old lullaby he soothed her. *"Taka, tikagee, snap-click."*

Disa began to cry, which was uncomfortable, since her diving helmet made no provision for eye- or nose-wiping. She bit her lip to shock herself out of the unseemly display. She tasted blood.

Risky well knew the sound of Disa sniffing. "Are you sad?" he asked, showing remarkable ability to form the sounds of English underwater.

She smiled and embraced the strange delicate body. "Disa happy. Glad to see friend Risky," she said, speaking Kargan by habit.

"He-Risky," he chided. "I am glad to see you, too."

The anger of abandonment tinged Disa's gladness. "He-Risky's change complete. You said, 'We will speak again.' Why He-Risky not call Disa?"

The dreamer's claw chittered, a habit retained from elderhood. "I still learn dreamer visions. They are lovely."

Disa twisted until her lamp was free. When the beam hit Risky's vestigial eyes, he flinched. "Why not share visions Disa?" the girl asked.

His claw chittered harder. "Changelings, even elders, cannot see visions."

"Disa not Kargan," she reminded. "Disa try."

"Well enough," Risky said. "Come."

"First fetch burden," she told him, playing her light along the wall. The guardian had retreated beyond reach of her beam. Her pack lay fifteen feet below, on the bottom of the pool. She retrieved it, then paused, feeling something still missing. She had dropped her knife in the garden room. "Get knife, too," she told her companion.

He followed her into the garden room. The knife still lay atop the fungus, an orange tentacle-tip beside it. Disa glanced nervously at the door. "More guardians come?"

"Don't worry," Risky said, fumbling in his silk pouch. He drew out a fist-sized sphere. "This restrains guardians.

No elder may carry it—but you are not an elder. Here."

Gingerly Disa accepted his gift. "What do with this?" she asked. She continued to speak Kargan, although with Risky's new command of English she might as well have used her own language.

"Break it," he said. "It contains liquid that guardians hate."

Fair enough. She slipped it into a pocket, easily accessible for emergency. She belted her knife. Then she turned to Ingrid's body. The drysuit, even at that depth, was slightly distended by gas pressure; a glance at the faceplate gave sickening confirmation that the corpse had rotted. "*Click-tap* die here?" Disa asked.

"No," Risky answered. "Deep in dreamer halls. We brought body here." For all his eloquence, he still didn't understand the word "the."

Uncle Hal might want to bring the body home, but for the time being Disa needed only proof that she had found it. Rolling it half over, she wrestled its pack off and rummaged through the contents. A high-quality recorder, nearly as compact as Disa's own, caught her eye. She read the inscription easily. "To my beloved Ingrid, at the birth of our son Leif." Pressing her lips together, Disa pocketed the instrument.

"Disa unhappy," Risky said.

With her castanet she made the grating sound that meant "yes." "Let us go," she said.

Risky climbed upward to the tunnel Inanna had mentioned, thirty feet above the floor. It was smooth, clearly artificial. Now that she had Risky as guide, Disa tied her line off. It was nearly paid out anyway. They moved past one opening, then another. "I rejoice in my dreamer life," Risky said. "Visions are beautiful."

"Much stone has worn since your departure. Groundlings still *gigg*. Elders change without trial."

"Humans metamorphose?" Risky asked, remembering the research project.

Disa shook her head. *"Gigg."*

Risky rumbled sympathy.

"Human-warren angry. My father, your cavemate, speak to them. Human-gods maybe—" Disa didn't know a Kargan word for murder. "Per, Inanna maybe die."

That got Risky's attention. "Why then do Per and Inanna speak to them?"

Human and Kargan floated in the tunnel, facing one another. "Human-warren must stop raising gigg-gardens. My father and Inanna try to persuade. If human-warren refuses, circle—" She hadn't the Kargan vocabulary to describe crashing a spaceship on Holmstad, either. "Circle make human-warren die."

Risky pressed himself to the tunnel wall, both claws chittering. "No! So the ancients died!"

"Forget your ancients!" Disa said, giving up the attempt to speak in Kargan. Her suit speaker broadcast her words into the water. "We're trying to keep *you* alive!"

"Sometimes only one can live," Risky responded.

"It's your planet," Disa said. "If it's you or them, it should be you that lives."

Risky huddled silent. The pale body changed color rapidly. Disa wondered if that indicated upset. "We do not speak of trial. But you are not elder. I will tell you."

Disa knew the strength of the secrecy taboo on dreamer trial. She glanced forward and backward down the tunnel, wondering who might be listening. Risky was already speaking. "Trial begins with tests of memory and orientation . . ."

Disa listened, fascinated especially by the story of Risky navigating the waterfall pool that Disa herself had swum. The puzzle's details lost her, but she understood well enough what followed. "I lifted my companion," Risky said. "I thought to die. But dreamers averted guardian. Murder is no virtue of our people, said they."

Disa closed her eyes. "No. But some must kill to live—"

"Murder is no virtue of our people."

"But it's a virtue of my people!" Disa half yelled. "If you won't stand up for yourselves the circle will—"

"The ancients—"

"I'm sick of hearing about your ancients!"

"Care you to see their fossils?"

Disa's eyes widened. Her fingers slipped clumsily on the castanet. "Yes."

"Here."

They faced a door, perhaps the sort of door Risky had faced in dreamer trial, for he opened it with a complex instrument of interlaced stones. "Enter."

Disa pulled herself through. Her light swept six walls, showing writing, a lot of it, in no script she recognized. Its decipherment she would leave to her father. In the room's center stood a glass dome, seven feet in diameter. Disa drifted forward to examine it. Over millennia, the glass had sagged and run into a slumped, uneven mass that distorted light. Disa pressed her faceplate against a relatively smooth area.

Within the dome lay a relief map. Disa recognized the near-mountain ridge north of the Meade's delta and the river itself meandering to the sea. There was no city of Holmstad, of course, but—Disa looked again.

The delta was cultivated, and orchards grew on hillsides, tended by tiny brown groundlings, no different from Ea. One groundling carried silkfruit toward a cave entrance. Flower-strewn pavilions dotted the parklike landscape. The layout resembled that of Houri colonies, which relied on biotechnology rather than extensive heavy industry. Beside one pavilion danced a pair of graceful centaurlike creatures with strange scaly head crests. How had those beings ever become Kargans? Disa squinted for a better look.

Below her, Risky emitted high intense bursts of sound. Disa wondered how well his sonar worked through glass. He must be looking at the caves. She, too, drifted downward to peer at a cutaway view of tunnels, chambers, and canyons riddling limestone. The model showed elders working to extend a dead-end tunnel. Three more were draping silk around a creature like the ones that danced above. The silk was pure flame red, not wildly multicolored. But the elders still looked blind. Disa frowned. She had thought that the elders had been sighted in ancient times. Where were their eyes?

Dreamers, their eyes clearly degenerate, lounged in the deepest chambers. They seemed to be doing nothing, except above their heads floated weird, vaguely familiar shapes. Their visions?

The Meade had long since changed course, so Disa could not locate the camp bluff. But circling the cylinder, she spied what she sought—the Hall of Voices. There were no groundlings within. No elders. No dreamers. Only the centaurs with articulated hands and crested heads.

Disa backed away as if stung. "*Graf* worshipped here," the Kargans had said. "But *graf* died for their quarrel. Only we remain."

The First-In team, having heard similar legends on a dozen planets, had assumed that the ancients must have been Kargans. The assumption had been wrong. The Kargans of Disa's day were no decadent remnant. They were a young civilization striving upward, determined not to repeat the mistakes of fallen predecessors.

Disa looked again around the room. From amid the alien symbols, a familiar one sprang out to chill her heart —a starred circle. "Then gods came. They offered kinship, if *graf* lived in peace. But no, *graf* reached for power of gods. They used it in betrayal. Plague broke free. *Graf* died for their quarrel."

Interdict. An offer of kinship, if that crested race survived long enough to reach the stars. In reaching for what they thus learned to be possible, the *graf* had quarreled and died. Disa rubbed her forehead. First-Inners were supposed to be peacemakers. Why, everywhere she turned, did they bring war?

"Be you done?" Risky asked. He could not see the writing on the wall. "Come, see visions."

Disa didn't want to see visions. She needed to get back to the surface, tell her teammates about what she had learned. If only she had brought the visual recorder! Would Ingrid's still work? With keen disappointment, she saw that its meter registered "full." There was no room for further pictures. She could only hope that Ingrid herself had seen and recorded the room's contents.

"Come," Risky said again, eager to show her his own secrets. A few minutes to keep him happy, Disa thought. Then I'll leave. She followed him out of the room, down the corridor, and into an eighteen-inch-wide hole.

It was a worm passage, a corkscrew. Disa's heart pounded as she wriggled through. It seemed endless, but sober judgment said she squirmed only fifteen feet before emerging into a spherical room twelve feet in diameter. The walls were smooth, with a few small holes that perhaps provided water circulation. A quick sweep of Disa's light showed clutter on the floor.

"To see visions you must learn our language," Risky explained.

Disa nodded impatiently, her mind full of what she had already seen.

"*Ikava,*" Risky said.

Disa recognized the word as part of the dreamer vocabulary Per had puzzled over. "*Ikava,*" she repeated automatically.

"No, you must feel," Risky said. One of his claws closed around her wrist, drawing her hand toward the object in his other claw. *"Ikava."*

Disa blinked at the object he pressed into her hand. "Did you steal this from Erica? She will be angry..." Her voice trailed off. "Alanine," she said finally. It was not Erica's wooden model but a stone one, similarly designed, similarly demonstrating the way molecular subunits pivoted about one another. Disa pulled her wrist from Risky's claw and floated with her hands in front of her. Letting her left hand be L-alanine, the isomer in her own body, she arrayed her thumb and three fingers as the chiral carbon's amino, methyl, carboxyl, and hydrogen attachments. Using the same match of fingers to molecular components, she arrayed her right hand to match the model's structure. D-alanine, the native Kargan configuration.

"Ikava," Risky said again.

Disa snatched up another model, which she identified, by its hydroxylated benzene ring, as the amino acid tyrosine. "What's this?"

"Tik," Risky answered.

Disa tugged an -OH from the alanine's carboxyl group and a hydrogen from the tyrosine's amino group. Those went together to make H-OH, water. The loose ends on the amino acids plugged together to form a two-component protein. *"Ikava-tik!"* Risky babbled. "Good, Disa!"

Disa stared at the model in her hands. How contemptuous they had all been of the dreamers' so-called limited vocabulary, assuming that nothing could be said with four words, or forty! With how many words did dust speak matter? With how many words did matter speak organic chemistry? With how many base molecules did carbon speak life? Four for the bases of DNA, a couple or three dozen for amino acids, an odd term here and there for a sugar, a metal ion, a sulfur-sulfur bond—

At last she knew what function dreamers had performed for the ancients. Indeed they had mediated the power of *graf*, for dreamers could visualize three-dimensional protein structures and their interactions. They were living computers.

CHAPTER TWENTY-SIX

❧❧❧❧

"YOU WANT ME TO DO WHAT?" SKIP ASKED. "I CAN'T COME to town now!" For nearly twelve hours Skip and his companions had labored over beakers and medical data bases, trying to determine exactly what markers attracted the virus to connective tissue and caused it to express itself. So far they had no results, but they had to keep trying. Per ought to understand that. Per ought to know that every minute counted in the fight to save Kelda.

Per's voice sounded as if he were being torn on a rack. "Skip, Kelda will die anyway if these rumors aren't damped. And I can't do it—the Frilandena don't trust me enough. They're saying the virus is wildly contagious and we're planning to dump it in the drinking water. They're saying the Kargans are massing for an attack on the colony. They're saying we've poisoned the seed grain. If we can't put a lid on this all of us will get lynched."

Skip frowned. "That's a hell of a lot of rumors. Where are they coming from?"

"Hal thinks from Einar Hanson."

"Ah, yes. That man knows how to whisper." Einar

265

would be hoping that in the frenzy his son Ole could claim Thor's hammer.

As if to confirm Skip's thought, Hal's voice came over the com. "Please, Skip. We need you at the meeting." Hal hadn't said "please" in years.

"Why do you care?" Skip asked. "You've hardly been an enthusiastic supporter so far!"

"I haven't got a choice," Hal snapped back. "Between my sister, my brother, and my son, I can hardly disentangle myself from First-In! I stand or fall with you now."

Skip rubbed eyes reddened by lack of sleep. "All right. Where?"

"Armory," Hal said. "See you there." He paused. "Is Leif with you?"

"Here," Leif called from the bench where he sat helping Yvette process histological data.

Hal paused again. "Just wanted to know if you were okay, son. And to say—keep working." He broke the connection.

Skip looked bleakly at his companions. "I guess you heard all that."

Sulman, his face dark with exhaustion, nodded. "Get a pep pill from the medkit before you go," he suggested. "But don't take it unlesss you're willing to ssleep ssixx hourss afterward." Tiredness slurred his voice; there was a soft hiss to his esses.

Yvette looked up from the bench beside Leif. Her curls drooped. "You've been sspending too much time with Calypsso, Uncle Ssuli!"

Sulman rubbed his nose. "Not my fault. That damn hiss is catching."

"If you find my pressencce offenssive, I sshall be glad to leave," the Sheppie responded. "After all, my ssymbiontss are ssadly dehydrated." Indeed, Skip saw discolored patches on her stalk, but he knew that she would stay in the lab until Kelda was cured—or dead.

"Get a dye job," Sulman suggested.

Calypso did not answer, but she arched her tentacles indignantly as she returned to work.

Yvette's face turned serious again. "You need to take a Kargan," she told Skip.

"What?" he protested.

"She's right," Suli said. "If Per means to have a Kargan speak to the colony, this is his chance."

"There's no Kargan to take!" Skip objected. Risky had gone to dreamerland, and Inanna had vanished with Disa.

"Buzz-Click's usually in the Hall of Meeting about now," Yvette said, already reaching for her jacket.

"She doesn't speak English!"

"No, but she's all we've got," Suli answered. "And she did volunteer to go on. Per can translate for her."

Yvette was already out the door. Skip gulped down a half cup of lukewarm tea. "If the town's in the mood they say, how am I going to get a Kargan into the armory?"

Suli thought a moment. "I know. Our old wheelbarrow."

"What?"

"Our wheelbarrow. It has a cover. Save her from quite so much exposure to Beyond."

"I can't trundle an alien ambassador through Holmstad in a wheelbarrow."

"I'll get it for you. Come on."

Thus Skip found himself toiling up the streets of Holmstad, pushing a wheelbarrow holding a seventy-pound alien he couldn't talk to. Yvette and Calypso had coached Buzz-Click for the journey; Skip could only hope the elder understood what was happening. He entered the armory by the back door. Hal's security guard stared curiously at the wheelbarrow. "Heg, Master Nygren. What's in there?"

Skip's mind raced wildly. Mud nippers? Confetti? Rotted soy cheese? "Some records my brother thought he might need. Don't try to open it—there's a tamper alarm on the cover. Where is Hal? I need to tell him I've got his stuff."

The guard inclined his head toward the curtain that shielded the backstage area from the rest of the armory. "At the council table, but they haven't started yet. Go on in. Leave your barrow over there so we don't trip on it. Hell of a lot of records, isn't it?"

"If you only knew."

The spot the guard indicated was perfect, in a dark corner amid discarded decorations from the Midwinter dance. Skip wheeled the barrow over and left it, caressing it with his hand before he left. He hoped Buzz-Click would interpret the sound as a gesture of reassurance.

Pushing through a slit in the curtain, Skip saw that the armory was packed. Infants wailed. Mothers hushed babbling toddlers. Men muttered to one another. Boys Leif's age and younger ran about self-importantly, delivering messages. In front of Skip, on the raised dais where Yvette had reigned as Queen of Lights, a council table stood, supporting a podium, Thor's silver hammer, and the iron gong. At the far end of the table, in the opposition leader's position, sat Ole Hanson. Below Ole on the public benches Skip spotted Ole's wife, with Burr, Aage, nine-year-old Astrid, and Ole's father, Einar. The old man's cane leaned against the dais.

Behind the table stood Hal, talking to Erica. Per sat on the near end. His freshly trimmed beard and crisply ironed coveralls only accented the dark circles under his eyes. He sat as he did in circle, straight, hands folded in his lap, a faraway expression in his eyes. "Arrogant bastard, isn't he?" someone in the front rows muttered.

"They say his wife's dying. Looks like he's gone numb."

"Damn Sørenson thinks he can bust in and do whatever he wants to us."

"Funny company the Statsminister keeps these days. Heard his son was sticking it to the gypsy."

"Kelda's girl?"

"No, the pretty one. The queen."

"Heard everybody was."

Skip took a deep breath and walked over to his brother-in-law. "Per, I've got Buzz-Click with me. I left her in back, just behind that curtain. Nobody knows she's here."

Hope died in Per's eyes. "No word from Disa then."

Skip shook his head. He knew that Disa's diving equipment was good only for fifteen hours. She had been gone more than twenty. Per's eyes dropped. Skip handed him the castanet Suli had sent. "You'll need this if you're going to talk to Buzz-Click."

Per's hand closed on the instrument, which he tucked in a breast pocket. "Thanks. I guess Buzz-Click's our last resort. An elder who can't speak English won't be very convincing."

Erica walked over. "Heg, Skip. You won't believe what they're saying. Germ warfare in the water. A Sørenson plot to kill silk production. Kargans burrowing the foundations from beneath Holmstad's buildings."

"That's bullshit."

Her gaze wandered across the crowd. "Convince them of that."

Skip set his jaw. "We'll try." He walked with Erica to a vacant spot on one of the rough benches near the front. A sturdy farming couple stared hard, whispered together, and crowded rightward, leaving a space between themselves and Skip. He remembered leaving Disa in the schoolroom. Had she been treated like that? How had *she* felt?

He didn't want to think about Disa.

Hal strode to the podium at the table's center, raised the silver hammer, and struck the gong with it. The gong's thunder brought an end to pandemonium. Closing their conversations with hasty whispers, people clambered over other people's knees to seats or stationed themselves along side and back walls. Old Einar leaned forward. Riksdag members settled around the council table. Per's jaw tightened as he surveyed the room.

Hal lifted the hammer, the symbol of his authority as Statsminister, two-handedly in pledge to Thor, then laid it in its display rack. "In accordance with the colony charter, I convene the Riksdag of Frilandet."

The crowd waited.

"Shortly after our arrival on Frilandet, we of the colony commissioned a professional survey." Hal glanced sideways at Einar, who had failed to commission the survey sooner. Einar did not flick an eyebrow. "The surveyors claimed Frilandet harbored a native species and civilization, tucked away in lightless caverns that we of Frilandet never entered." Hal found it convenient to forget Ingrid for the moment.

"We were told," Hal continued, "that under normal circumstances the colony would have been evicted under the terms of the Orion treaty. But the native civilization registered no objection to our presence, and there existed no foreseeable conflict. We accepted their offer of tenure in perpetuity, and signed a treaty accordingly."

"I didn't sign any treaty," muttered the farmer next to Skip, but nobody publicly challenged Hal's statement.

"Enough ancient history," Ole Hanson said. "Come to the point."

Hal's fierce blue glare reduced the room to silence. "We've been accused of violating that treaty," he stated. "I leave explanation to First-In's spokesman." Skip's hopes that Hal would give active support to the team's cause evaporated. Despite his earlier statements to Skip, Hal placed himself within the colonial circle of "we" and his brother-in-law with the outsiders, the accusers.

Per stood, straight-shouldered, the circle's gemmed earring glittering barbarously in his ear. Somebody hissed. Per eyed the crowd as if taking their measure. Then he lifted his chin.

"You all know I'm a Sørenson. And you all know I married Kelda Nygren. You think that by joining First-In and marrying me, she betrayed you."

Shocked by his bluntness, people stayed quiet. "Consider," Per said, "that as Kelda left Frilandet and married a Sørenson, so I left Valhalla and married a Nygren."

He moved smoothly to the next issue. "You know you share Frilandet with another species. The young of that species are less than fully intelligent, by our standards and those of their own people. But the groundlings' willing aid has brought Frilandet Colony the security, prosperity, and prospects it has today.

"What you may not know," Per continued as people nodded grudging agreement, "is that your crops are killing groundlings. So long as they remain groundlings, no signs show. But when the best and brightest are chosen for transition to full intelligence, the ones who've eaten Frilandet's food die."

"Not so," the history teacher, Ansgar, said. "Your daughter said it was only a statistical correlation. A possibility."

"Let's talk about those statistics," Per said. "One in sixty groundlings used to die in change. Of those who've worked in the colony, one in six. It's like Juleskaggen."

Older folk nodded, remembering when a Valhallan company's allegedly innocuous by-product had resulted in miscarriages and monster births a decade later.

"Furthermore," Per told them, "by eating southpaw amino acids, an elder can change into a dreamer without approval, without undergoing dreamer trial. As if boys married and seized inheritance without first succeeding in challenge." He paused a moment for that thought to settle.

"Finally," the First-Inner explained, "groundlings from beyond the Holmstad area migrate here to feast on your crops. You experience it as nuisance damage to your fields. But those of you whose children stayed on Valhalla, or who fear your children will leave Frilandet, think what this means to those groundlings' mothers—"

"Why do we let them eat our food?" Aage's nine-year-old sister asked. Her grandfather frowned at her.

Per smiled. "If we could make them stop, it would solve everything. But it's like keeping little ones from Midwinter gifts."

Per speaks well, Skip thought. He puts an alien species' tragedy in terms that touch Frilandet hearts.

Einar's cronies recognized Per's effectiveness, too. Dag the smith rose to his feet. "How do you know so much about all this? Kargans never said anything to us about it."

"I went to their cave. They showed me one of the deformed bodies. Have you ever been in the caves?"

"No, but—"

"You might try it, since you share a planet with them."

"It's dangerous down there!" Dag's wife objected.

"Crabs don't like us!" someone else said.

"You know what happened to Hal's wife."

Per closed his eyes. Skip wondered again what had become of Disa.

"What about your wife?" Ole Hanson asked.

"Yeah, what did you do to her?"

"Is it true she's going blind like the Kargans?" Clearly, everyone had heard rumors, and they were hungry for news of Per's scandalous, good-looking mate.

"I didn't do anything to Kelda," Per said, anger surging into his voice, "and if I'd known what she planned I'd have stopped her, because she means a damn sight more to me than your stiff-necked, bickering colony!" He paused, visibly reining his temper. "Skip, I think you better tell what happened to Kelda. I can't talk calmly about it."

Skip rose reluctantly, clambered over two benches and onto the dais, and made his way around the edge of the table, past Per's empty chair, toward the microphone. Per retreated quietly. Three thousand people stared at Skip.

Wordlessly Hal handed him a glass of water.

Skip sipped. He brushed clinging drops from his mouth with a shirt cuff.

Everything was so quiet.

Skip looked at Ole's daughter, Astrid, who had asked why food could not be kept from the groundlings. "Do you have a groundling at your house?" Skip inquired.

Wide-eyed, she nodded.

Skip smiled reassuringly. "What's its name?"

She spoke so softly that it was hard to hear her answer. "We have three. My favorite one is Balder."

"Do you give Balder treats?" Skip asked.

She nodded affirmatively. Skip hoped his listeners could imagine her responses.

"Does Balder ever find treats for himself?"

Her nose wrinkled in distaste. "He likes to go through the garbage."

Skip pressed on. "If you didn't give Balder treats he would still find those other things, wouldn't he?"

The small blond head bobbed up and down.

"Can you think of any way to keep Balder from finding his own treats?" Skip asked.

Slowly she shook her head back and forth.

Skip straightened. "Astrid can't keep Balder from stealing 'treats.' Neither can the First-In team. But don't leave it to them. If you can protect crops from groundlings and vice versa, please speak now."

He genuinely hoped someone would answer. He heard whispered arguments. No one stood to speak.

"You know the Orion treaty," Skip said. "If you were First-In, what would you do?"

The farmer whom Skip had sat beside rose to his feet, face flushed. "Damn monster lovers can't take me off my land!"

"They don't want to," Skip answered. "There's another solution." Could he explain gene adjustment to this volatile mob? "Our presence is not the problem. Our crops and livestock are the problem. If we could eat Kargan food—"

"You can't make us into Kargans!" a woman screamed.

"You eat it first, mister!"

"Go to my kids' graves and say that!"

"Is *that* what happened to your sister?"

Skip hammered on the podium for attention. "It can be done! But doing it safely will take help from you—"

"Was Kelda supposed to prove it was safe?"

"What does First-In care if it's safe?"

"Shut up!" Skip bellowed. "Listen. A southpaw system *can* digest northpaw amino acids. We've done it with testers. But we didn't have the resources to know if it would be safe on humans. Rather than ask you to leave, Kelda tried the procedure on herself—"

With backing from the Frilandena, and what they had learned from Kelda, Skip wanted to say, the procedure *could* be made safe, though maybe not in time to save his sister. But the crowd didn't wait to hear. "You doing that to *us*?"

"Think again!"

Ole Hanson pounded the table. "The Nygrens have gone too far!" People cheered.

Per stood, tumbling his chair to the floor. "Enough!" he said in a voice that rang across the room. "If you won't believe this from us, you can hear it from the Kargans!"

The crowd went quiet.

Per jerked his chin toward the curtain. "Get Buzz-Click, Skip."

With sweating palms, Skip obeyed. He pushed the wheelbarrow through the slit in the curtain, brought it to a stop beside his brother-in-law. Per had been telling the crowd about the Kargans' admission that they, too, had been at fault in allowing communication to fail. Per unlatched the barrow's cover, cracked the lid, and stooped for a quiet word with Buzz-Click. The Valhallan glanced up at Skip. "Can we dim the lights any?"

Skip nodded and went behind the curtain where the building control panel was located. Hush reigned as the room went nearly dark. As Skip reemerged, Per opened the wheelbarrow's cover and lifted Buzz-Click onto the council table. She wore a hastily assembled cloak of multicolored native silk to protect her eye-patches and the exposed skin of her legs and arms from light, but her crab-like shell shone ghostly white in the dim hall, and her powerful main claws protruded from beneath the silk. Chairs scraped as Riksdag members edged away from the alien.

Buzz-Click spoke in the grating Kargan tongue, punctuating with her claw. "Buzz-Click says she greets you on behalf of Sweetwater Warren and her people," Per translated. "Sweetwater Warren is the cave complex just northwest of Holmstad," he added when he saw the confusion on people's faces.

Buzz-Click spoke again. "She thanks you for the opportunity to address your council, and apologizes that water has risen so many times since her people last spoke with yours."

Benches creaked as people shifted uneasily.

"If they wanted to talk to us, why didn't they come and find us?" Hal asked. Per began translating the question into Kargan.

"You don't think that creature's really talking?" Ole Hanson asked, his eyes on Hal.

Per, too, looked across the table at Hal. "Buzz-Click says all people have their fears. Her people fear light, which they perceive as deadly radiation. Your people fear the Kargans."

Einar Hanson stood, swinging his cane. "I'm not afraid of crabs!"

Voices rang out in agreement.

Buzz-Click tried to speak.

A half-rotten apple arched across the room and splattered against Per's fallen chair. Another flew from somewhere to Skip's left. Horrified, Skip saw Dag the smith heft a more dangerous missile—the pedestal from a flagstand. Per flung himself across the table to shield Buzz-Click. The heavy metal pedestal hit Per in the side of the head, knocking him backward toward the elder, gouging an ugly cut in his forehead. The wound bled profusely. Buzz-Click's claw began a rapid, rhythmic clacking quite unlike the elder-speech Skip had become accustomed to.

"Get that crab out of our hall!" Ole Hanson ordered.

His son Burr jumped onto the dais and ran toward Buzz-Click.

"Stay away!" Skip yelled, suddenly recognizing Buzz-Click's clacking as a threat display.

Per took more direct action. He scrambled toward Burr, tackling him and knocking him to the floor before the boy came in range of Buzz-Click's deadly claws.

People in the crowd shouted. Ole's face reddened as he saw his son wriggling in Per's hold. The opposition leader called to his supporters, "Get him!"

Six brawny farmers closed on Per.

Buzz-Click, still clacking fiercely, moved across the table toward Per. Skip dove for her, grabbed her chipped shell and hauled her back, praying that in her agitation she would still recognize him as friend.

Burr rolled free. Per sent two farmers staggering before the other four subdued him.

"You've no authority for arrests!" Hal bellowed at Ole.

"No?" Ole asked. "I think this colony needs a change of power."

CHAPTER TWENTY-SEVEN

❧❧❧❧❧

THE VISIT WITH RISKY HAD BEEN A LONG ONE. IT WOULD have been longer, but Disa's dive meter called with gentle insistence, warning that her gas supply was running low. From this depth she could not simply rise to surface even if the tunnelways allowed. She would have to pause during her ascent or risk nitrogen bubbles in her body. To have oxygen for it all, she must leave immediately. "*Daqua*, He-Risky. I will return."

Risky, as excited by their conversation as Disa had been, grumbled but agreed to escort Disa out. "I will watch for guardians. When Per goes to speak with colony, summon me."

"I will. I thank you." Checking to be sure she still had the D-alanine model Risky had given her, Disa slipped into the corkscrew tunnel that led out of Risky's room.

The tunnel's twists seemed tighter than before. Disa told herself that the main passage lay only a few feet away. There she found new trouble. The water, reasonably clear when first she passed, had turned turbulent and muddy. Disa's light penetrated only a few feet. Bracing with feet and left hand against the current, she reached back with her right hand for Risky. "I cannot 'see'!" The Kargan word she used designated the processing of sonar feedback into spatial information, and they used it for human vision just as humans spoke of Kargans "seeing" by sonar. The Kargans used an entirely different word for aural perception of language.

"Why not?" Risky, Disa knew, perceived the cloud of fine particles only as a smell, or perhaps a texture. Silt posed no problem for his blunt-range sonar.

Disa tried not to panic. "Disa see radiation," she reminded Risky. "Radiation not cross mud water."

She felt Risky's claw snap softly as he considered this. "I will lead you."

Slowly they proceeded upward, the current growing stronger. Risky's body, well suited for his own travel, lacked the strength to assist a clumsy human-god. The one advantage of their slow ascent was that Disa did not have to concern herself with decompression stops. She tried not to wonder whether her oxygen would last long enough to get her out.

She came within twenty yards, vertically, of air. But at the tunnel that led to the waterfall pit and safety, the current defeated her. Muddy water poured from the pit through the tunnel in a swirling torrent. Disa held herself from being swept away but made no headway. She couldn't see where she was going. She couldn't see her hand six inches from her face. Risky tugged, but that did not help.

Disa's limbs trembled with exhaustion. Much more of such effort, and she would be swept backward. She edged into a relatively quiet pocket and reached from long habit for her beacon. No. She could summon no one from her present location. She closed her eyes and tried to think. Where had the water come from? A major storm must have blown in. Where was the water going? A flow that heavy must have some outlet. She asked Risky.

"Water goes Beyond, to Meade River," the dreamer answered.

Disa cursed herself for a fool. Of course the dreamer realm had underwater exits that elders knew nothing of. Why hadn't she asked sooner? "How far?"

"Half mile."

"How deep?"

"Thirty feet."

"Small tunnels?" Probably not, she thought, if such floods came every winter. "Disa fit?"

"Tunnels big. Disa fits."

Disa stuck her hand a final time into the current and felt the water's strength. She had fifteen minutes of air. If she did not have to work through any squeezes, if the route did not dip low enough to require further decompression, if she was not injured by being slammed against rocks, she would make it.

If not, she would be dead—as she would be if she stayed where she was. "Lead me."

Her heart pounded in terror as the current swept her through flooded corridors, but the journey went quickly. Toward the end the water slowed again, as tunnels widened into majestic halls, and the surface drainage carrying Disa met the Meade's frigid backflow. Risky guided Disa into a pocket. "Beyond is just ahead."

Laughing with relief, Disa hugged her companion. "*Daqua*, He-Risky. I will return."

Risky's feeler probed Disa's mask. "*Daqua*. I must speak to dreamer council of our finds. We didn't know gods dreamed."

Gods don't dream, Disa thought. Even a Sheppie could not visualize molecular structures as the dreamers did. But gods did know something that dreamers had never suspected: the significance of those structures. Interesting discussions lay ahead. "I will speak to circle. Calypso will come."

Risky swam with Disa to the very edge of the spring. The water, previously black in every direction, glowed reddish brown. "Heg, Disa."

"*Daqua*, He-Risky." Disa kicked upward toward the light.

She reached camp to hear Yvette exploding with her own news. "I did it! I found it! I know what caused the reaction!"

"What reaction?" Disa asked, still wet-haired but swathed in blankets and downing a huge mug of sugared tea. Everyone looked stricken. Reluctantly Sulman explained to Disa what Kelda had done and where Per was.

There was no time to summon Risky. Suli, Leif, and Calypso stayed in the lab to work out the application of Yvette's discovery. Yvette and Disa headed for town. The budding geneticist went to the hospital to encourage Kelda. Disa, dry-clothed and wearing white dress boots because her brown ones still lay by the waterfall pit, went to the armory to inform Per and Skip of discoveries that brought hope for warrens, circle, and colony alike. When she arrived, she stood, appalled, by the door. The room was nearly dark. Blood streamed down her father's cheek as Burr and a half-dozen other toughs bound his arms. Skip clung desperately to an angry Buzz-Click. Hal and Ole stood nose to nose on the platform. "I know your ambitions," Hal spat at his old opponent, "but this is still a government by law."

Ole laughed. "Haven't seen much evidence of that recently. How much did First-In pay you to keep quiet about their tricks? Why haven't you acceded to the Riksdag's requests?" He beckoned to Per's captors. "Bring him here. We need some questions answered."

The crowd, nearly all on their feet by then, yielded mixed reactions. Some stood with mouths half-open in protest. Others, friends of the Nygrens, looked about as if fearful for their own safety. Mothers herded small children toward the exits. The rougher Frilandena laughed. "Let's see how tough a First-Inner is!"

Other snatches of conversation washed across Disa. "...get out of town before it blows..." "...no good, the whole area's contaminated..." "...all a trick to put us off guard..." "...told you at the beginning we should leave the groundlings alone..." "...kill the Kargans before they attack..." "...warned the Sørensons about interfering with us..." "...clean out the camp while we're at it."

It sounded like the crowd on Tapachula, the frightened, rumor-mad mob that had killed Uncle Jack. If Disa intended to move, she must do it before things got any uglier. She fought her way forward through frightened mothers and talk of Kargan killing and camp cleaning. Most people in the aisle, intent on their own escape, ignored her. A few stared and pointed.

Erica plunged downstream to meet her. "Get out of here!" the druggist snapped from twenty feet away. "This is no place for circlings!"

Disa kept going. Erica grabbed her elbow. "Did you hear me? What's wrong with you?"

Disa blinked at her teacher. "I got trapped in the cave. Risky got me out. Yvette's figured out the virus reaction and she's at the hospital telling Mom."

That got Erica's attention. "She sorted it out! Thank God! But the mood this crowd is in—"

"I've got to talk to Dad," Disa said. "I found out about the dreamers. And the ancients."

Erica's face twisted. "Disa, you can't—"

Behind Erica, on the dais, somebody asked Per something. Not liking his answer, the vigilante struck Per across the face. "Try again, Sørenson!"

The hall was emptying. Soon only the most disaffected Frilandena would remain. Disa saw Per's eyes on her.

"Get out!" he ordered. "Erica, get her away—" As in stage fright's worst fantasy, people turned to stare and mutter.

Erica's hold on Disa tightened. The druggist was not circle, Disa thought. Erica did not understand that safety lay only in resolving the conflict. Disa saw Thor's hammer on the table, and the iron gong behind it. She gathered her strength and lunged past Erica.

Burr jumped to intercept her as she reached the dais. His hands closed on her, but he let go as she kicked his kneecap. She scrambled onto the platform, seized the heavy silver hammer, and struck the gong a ringing two-handed blow.

Conversation ceased. Movement stopped. Everyone in the hall turned to see who had rung the gong and why.

Disa stared back at the sea of eyes. They all expected her to say something. She raised the hammer in salute, then laid it in its rack. Buzz-Click, agitated by the noise, was struggling to break Skip's hold. "Rest quiet," Disa called to the elder in Kargan. "Please rest quiet. I will speak." Buzz-Click subsided.

Disa stepped to the podium.

Each second seemed an eternity, but she did not have many of them. She must get the crowd on her side before Ole's supporters reasserted themselves. She glanced longingly at her father, but there was nothing he could do to help her.

Should she talk about Kelda? The newly reopened possibility of enzyme modification? Threats against the Kargans? "Truth iss our protection," Calypso loved to say. "Peacce built on decception will not lasst." Truth had brought a lot of suffering recently, Disa thought. She feared that by using it she would betray her Kargan friends. But it was the only weapon she knew. She cleared her throat. "We have to talk."

People looked at each other, then back at Disa. "I just came out of the caves," she said.

Someone said something in a low voice, and someone else sniggered. Disa ignored it. "I went down to the dreamers. I found out what happened to Ingrid Nygren."

"That's of no concern now—" Ole Hanson started to say.

"Shut up and let the girl speak!" Hal snapped, so viciously that Ole subsided.

Disa slipped her pack off, terribly aware of how the starred circle flashed on its fabric. She tugged at mud-gritted fastenings. Her fumbling fingers found what they sought. "It wasn't a Kargan that killed her. She got caught by a guardian, a sort of jellyfish that lives in the deep passages. The Kargans buried her in one of their own tomb chambers. I left the body there. But I did bring this." She held up the recorder.

"Oh, God," Hal said.

"How do you know it's hers?" Ole asked.

Disa held it out so the rival leaders, standing next to each other, could read the inscription. Hal rubbed his face with his hands. Ole swallowed. "Okay, it's Ingrid's. That doesn't change the situation now."

"Let me show you what she found," Disa said, thanking dust that Ingrid had recorded what she did and praying that she herself had not somehow erased the recording when she and Yvette had reviewed it in the boat.

The scene formed over the council table, shadowy since Ingrid had used only a dim helmet light. "In this room," said the voice of a woman long dead, "the dreamers preserve relics of the *graf*, whom we call the ancients. Kargans themselves draw a sharp distinction between themselves and the ancients." The camera centered upon the dome in the center of the room. "This replica of the Holmstad area shows why. The *graf* were a distinct species from the Kargans."

Ingrid must have been an accomplished photographer, for she managed a tolerable focus through water and warped glass. "Here are a pair of *graf* dancing. Other scenes show them eating, assembled for ritual, trying on clothes, and supervising various procedures. If I read this evidence correctly, *graf* used groundlings for manual labor, as we do today. Elders appear to have performed more sophisticated tasks such as mining, tunneling, and manufacturing. The model shows dreamers interacting with the *graf*, but I do not understand their function."

Hal sank into a chair, his face white. He must have loved Ingrid very much, Disa thought, for her recorded message to hit so hard.

Disa switched off the machine. "Ingrid found her dreamer contact, an elder called Namtar who'd recently passed dreamer trial, playing with small rock 'puzzles.' Ingrid didn't recognize them because she'd had no organic chemistry. But I brought one back with me."

She held up the model Risky had given her. Most stared blankly, but Erica's jaw dropped. "Alanine," the druggist said.

Disa gestured desperately for her to stand. Erica climbed onto a bench and faced the crowd. "That's a model of an amino acid," she said. "We use them in class all the time."

"So what?" a farmer asked impatiently. "What sort of civilization did those *grafs* have? Is there treasure in the caves?"

Burr snorted. "It doesn't look like much of a civilization to me. Where are their buildings and machines?"

"Their buildings were underground," Disa answered, trying to relax her voice so it would carry. "They didn't have very many machines. They had a biological technology, like the Houri. They saved the surface for agriculture and parks."

"I'm still waiting to hear what's in this for us," Ole growled. Hal still sat stupefied.

"There's treasure in the caves," Disa said, "but you can only get it by befriending the Kargans." She held up the alanine model again, twisting the molecules around their bonds. "See how complicated this is? See how its shape changes? Can you imagine precisely what a dozen or a hundred of these together would look like?"

She let the silence stretch for only a moment. "A dreamer can imagine. In his *head*. A dreamer's a biochemical computer more powerful than anything we or even the Sheppies have." Disa stared around the room, trying to meet every person's gaze. "With the dreamer's help, you could make this planet a galaxy center for genetic design. But only with the dreamers' help. And only if you get rid of the crops that are poisoning the Kargans."

The mood went sour. "Oh no, you don't! We saw what happened to Kelda."

"My mother will be fine!" Disa shouted, hoping that what she said was true. She brought her voice under control. "An hour and a half ago our lab team got the problem diagnosed. From there a cure is fairly easy. If we can't work it out, the dreamers will. Do you understand what Mom risked herself to offer you? By changing your digestion, you can eat from the land here. By learning to work with dreamer partners, you can get rich."

Einar pounded his cane on the floor. "You're not putting a Kargan stomach in me!"

"Don't be stupid!" Skip answered. Buzz-Click lay quiet, allowing Skip to release his hold. "Frilandena know the difference between truth and rumor," the geneticist told Einar. Disa wondered if her uncle was being sarcastic. Skip shifted his attention to the crowd. "Friends, don't decide now. Help us for three or four months while we work out final adjustments on the genetic change. The next human subject will be me. You watch then. Watch me eat Frilandeter strawberries. Then you decide."

"Why didn't we hear about any of this before?" Ole

asked. "About dreamers and biochemistry and all?"

Disa wet her lips. "Nobody knew. Even the dreamers. So far as I can tell, the *graf* taught the dreamers biochemistry as a pure art form. Maybe they were afraid of what the dreamers could do. Anyway they never told them the practical significance. The dreamers didn't know until I went there today." Again she wondered if truth was always best. What would the dreamers make of their new knowledge?

"This is all too neat," Ole protested. He fell back on old arguments. "Who knows what the Kargans plan? Why should I believe they'd welcome us? How do I know this isn't all some First-In trick?"

"You've got a Kargan right here!" Per said, his arms still pinned behind his back. "Why don't you ask?"

Ole made a gesture of dismissal. "With only you to translate? Why didn't you bring a Kargan who speaks English?"

"He didn't have one," Disa answered. "They were both down in the cave with me. But there are Frilandena who *have* talked to Kargans." She took a deep breath. Skip could not serve as witness—he was identified too closely with the team. Leif might have done, but he was back at camp. Aage Hanson sat just in front of Disa to her left. His frightened sister, Astrid, clung to his hand. "Ask your son," Disa told Ole. "He's talked to them."

Anger flamed across Ole's face. "What are you talking about?" He spun to face his son. "Have you been in the caves?"

Aage went pale, but he stood and answered clearly. "Yes, sir." Then he stepped onto the dais and turned to face the crowd. "I haven't talked to a dreamer. But I did talk to an elder. She told legends about the *graf*, and how they destroyed themselves because they were too competitive and couldn't cooperate. She and her people are determined not to repeat that mistake. They do want to cooperate with us. But I'm afraid we're like the *graf*. We're so knotted up in our arguments we can't perceive our own best interest."

"I think we can change," Skip said. "Who's willing to give this three months, spend some time looking into it?"

Around the room, heads began to nod. Disa sat down. Her part was done. Minutes later Per joined her, his hands freed but blood still oozing slowly from his temple. "Let's get you back to the hospital and fix that," Erica suggested.

Per shook his head. "I want to hear the rest of this."

"Well, at least let me clean it up." Somebody handed Erica a first-aid kit. She began applying a temporary bandage to Per's head. Up at the council table, Ole Hanson agreed to a six-month cooling-off before colony elections. Disa leaned against Per, grateful for his warm familiar smell. Discussion went on, but Disa, who had been awake for thirty-two hours that encompassed the most exhausting adventures of her life, heard no more. She had fallen asleep on her father's shoulder.

CHAPTER TWENTY-EIGHT

❧❧❧❧

"WHILE WATER ROSE TWENTY THOUSAND TIMES, WE dreamed, and took joy in dreaming. Our visions have beauty. Why taint them by contact with Beyond?" the deepest dreamer asked.

"From beyond came our dreams in time of *graf*," Risky argued. "But *graf* held from us their meaning. Water has risen twenty thousand times since then, but we have been as dry stone: sterile, unchanging. Gods are water, dissolving old ways but depositing new. Let us open our minds to their visions."

"Human-warren holds not gods but *graf*," grumbled another dreamer deeper than Risky. They were all deeper than Risky, for he, as youngest, occupied the high chamber nearest the elders' realm. "They cause *gigg*. They seek to enslave. They bring not peace but conflict."

Risky stirred uncomfortably, having had such thoughts himself. But crystal had more than one face. "Gods of legend were circle-warren, as I have wandered with. Their trial is not like dreamer trial. Dreamer trial tests virtues of our people. Gods' trial tests weakness. *Graf's* virtue was conflict. Gods tested peace. Our virtue is dreaming. Gods-

289

test waking. Will we fail as *graf* did, by our virtue?"

"Let us be as stone which does not bend," the deepest dreamer answered.

"Water, by taking what shape it can, defeats stone," Risky countered. "Let us be as water."

"If your gods are those as came to *graf*," the second-shallowest dreamer asked, "why did they not speak thus to us sooner?"

"*Snap-click* spoke of this. Our memories are stone, but theirs are water. To remember, gods must feel fossils." Actually they looked at strange patterns of radiation, but Risky had given up trying to explain reading to his peers, who operated upon oral and tactile tradition. "A foolish human-god called *ikava echo-ikava*." Indeed, Risky thought, if that human-god had not mistaken *ikava* for its echo image, the colony would not have come at all. "So gods sought our fossils in *echo-ikava* bed." That bed, the "southpaw registry," Disa called it, had borne no record of First-In's contact with the *graf*, because that long-ago First-In team had entered its contact, quite properly, in the northpaw registry. Why human-gods had not searched the registries again after discovering Karg's misidentification was a question Disa had not been able to answer.

"Deepest dreamer speaks well," the second deepest said. "We of stone have no words for those of water. Stone did not give birth to us for us to wander Beyond."

"Stone did not give birth to us at all!" Risky said, claw chittering. Had they not understood even that much? "Stone gave birth to *graf*, to many beings, but *graf* themselves shaped our eggs. By visions like our own they shaped us!"

Risky recalled the star-steppers' hymn: "Desire and thought shape stone, and then are gone, but stone still shakes with steps of those who've walked it." *Graf* desire and thought had shaped Kargans from a race much like blind mud-nippers into one capable of tunneling and visions. Those same *graf*, to keep control of slaves, implanted the need for L-protein. Risky, after observing the virtues of many other races, suspected that *graf* had also tampered with Kargan competitive survival instincts. "*Graf* desire and thought shaped us. But now we have desire and thought. Let us shape not only visions. Let us shape ourselves. To do thus, we need water."

"Dry visions cut no caverns," the second-deepest dreamer said, "but also they destroy none. If we listen to Beyond, might not we fall as *graf* did?"

Risky did not answer.

"Elder realm has no beauty," the second-shallowest dreamer said. "Beyond has less. It is groundling space. Why think of it when one might spend time dreaming?"

"We will not cease to dream," Risky answered for what seemed the thousandth time. "We will find new dreams Beyond." He pulled out his painstakingly carved models of echo-amino acids. "See, these visions lie in bodies of gods."

"Let me feel," demanded deepest dreamer, who had never before imagined echo-visions. "In what ways move these dreams?"

Without realizing that they had acceded to Risky's request, the dreamers began visioning Dawn's problem of constructing L-proteins to digest D-protein.

CHAPTER TWENTY-NINE

꧁꧂

THREE DOZEN PAIRS OF EYES FOLLOWED A PARTRIDGELIKE creature's drumstick from Skip's plate to his mouth. He bit off the last hunk of flesh and chewed ostentatiously. Suli said that in time, Skip's nose would come to recognize the meat's vaguely plastic smell as delicious. Skip returned the bone to an otherwise empty plate, which Dana whisked away. Then Skip reached for dessert—a slice of strawberry pie. He had practiced until he could eat without gagging, without the pale faces of Ingrid's twins haunting him. With that memory conquered, the berries tasted fine, much better than the meat.

Skip took a final sip of juice, swallowed, and wiped his mouth with Dana's white napkin. "That's it, folks. Delicious."

The First-Inners, sitting together toward the back of the room, clapped lightly. Conspicuous by her absence was Kelda. She hated to appear in public anymore, and while no one was cruel enough to say so, they were just as happy for her to keep a low profile. Kelda was unlikely to be a positive influence on the colony's decision.

"How soon will your procedure be available on a general basis?" Erica asked.

Ole Hanson frowned. "Let's not rush things. I want to see how Master Nygren feels next week."

"Nobody's rushing," Hal said. "We'll watch and see how Skip does. We need more D-protein supplies, too, before we start converting. Another month at least, before we give the treatment to anyone else."

Skip saw doubtful looks on Riksdag faces. He swiveled in his chair. "Dana? Is there any more of that pie?"

She brought it with a wry smile. "No one but you seems to like it."

"That's my luck!" he proclaimed, patting his stomach.

Leif and Aage Hanson sat together toward the front of the room. Like most rivals, they had always had much in common. Now that both had spoken publicly for the Kargans, and both dated circlings, they had formed a cautious alliance. The boys glanced at each other, then Leif cleared his throat. "Aage and I volunteer for the first round of treatments."

Skip's heart sank. What he proposed for the colony, even for himself, was more than he cared to ask of this favorite nephew. "Leif, I don't think you should—"

"Why not?" Ole Hanson asked.

Skip looked desperately at Sulman. Almost imperceptibly, Sulman nodded. The issue raised by Leif's request must be discussed.

"The problem," Skip said, "is that once Leif takes the treatment, it will be awfully difficult for him to apprentice with the genetics guild on MacKenzie."

Hal, who had been briefed on the subject, sat silent.

"Why?" Ole asked.

Skip wet his lips. "It has to do with the enzyme design. The new enzymes that digest northpaw protein are themselves composed of southpaw protein—the kind we eat and digest right now."

"If you left the old enzymes around," Leif said, "they'd digest the new ones before the new ones could do their work." Leif understood what rode at stake, Skip knew.

Dana frowned. "Why don't the enzymes we have now digest themselves?"

"They do," Skip told her. "But it takes awhile. Digestive enzymes break proteins apart at certain specific points. For instance, trypsin cleaves amino acid chains where they contain arginine or lysine. Chymotrypsin cleaves adjacent to tyrosine or phenylalanine. Normal digestive enzymes fold to keep susceptible bonds hidden inside the molecule. But in the new enzymes we had to leave some of those bonds hanging out—"

"I didn't come here for a biochemistry lecture," Ole said. "What's the bottom line?"

"We sliced out the old enzymes and put the new ones in their places," Leif answered.

Ole stared at him, working out the implications.

"The dreamers showed us how," Sulman explained. "It's got real elegance. As it stands our bodies have exquisitely balanced feedback systems that control production and release of digestive enzymes. We'll leave those systems intact to control production of the new enzymes."

"Once you have the treatment, you can't digest regular food any more," Ole said.

"That's right," Skip confirmed. "But it's not a problem since there's more than enough very nutritious, very delicious food here on Karg. You'll like the oysters."

"It's only a problem if you want to go off-planet," Ole said.

Skip nodded, reluctantly.

Ole's eyes swung to his old rival. "Well, Statsminister? You going to chain your son to Frilandet?" Ole knew where to twist the knife.

"It won't be impossible to leave," Yvette protested. "Leif could take his own food with him to MacKenzie. Or eat gruel." Importing food would be extravagantly expensive. The expressions on the faces of the older Frilandena in the room showed that they remembered how gruel tasted. Skip's own face puckered.

"There are other places to study genetics besides MacKenzie," Sulman said softly. "There are plenty of DNA-based northpaw planets, and their peoples have institutes, too."

Leif, with whom this possibility had already been discussed, looked down. Custom had driven the separations between northpaw and southpaw so deep that few even of the First-In circles combined humans and northpaw aliens. Leif could go to a northpaw planet—but he would be alone among the aliens and trying to learn their language from scratch. Maybe later, he had said.

Hal, conspicuous by his silence throughout the conversation, buckled to fatherly concern. "You're almost old enough to leave for MacKenzie, Leif. Why not take the treatment when you return?"

Leif tipped his chin up. "Because I'm a Nygren. Leaders are supposed to go first, not last. You never went off-planet to school."

Skip clenched his hands, telling himself to stay out of the discussion. He wished he was sure that the boys had thought it all through for themselves, that they were not just trying to impress Disa and Yvette.

"I never had the chance," Hal answered.

"I can apprentice with Uncle Skip," Leif said. "And I've already worked with a finer geneticist than any of MacKenzie's. Calypso, I mean," he clarified for listeners unfamiliar with the team. "The pink Sheppie."

Words slipped out of Skip against his will. "I'm proud of my work, Leif, but I'm not the sort of—"

"You're excellent," his nephew said. "Even Calypso says so. And I have one resource neither MacKenzie nor the Challa Institute have."

"What's that?" demanded Yvette, who had ambitions of her own in genetics.

"The dreamers."

Hal, ill positioned to weigh those arguments, glanced at Skip. Skip swallowed and nodded. "On that he's right."

Sulman stood, an unhappy look on his face. "Wait. Let's be blunt about what you're getting into. Everything you've heard about the dreamers, and about the more general potential of Kargans, is true. But they're a free people who make their own decisions. Don't assume they'll teach you all they know."

Skip bit his lip, admiring and regretting Sulman's honesty. Yes, cards should be on the table, but what if the colonists changed their minds?

"The Kargans's decision will depend on what they hear from us, won't it?" Aage asked.

"That's certainly a factor," Sulman admitted.

"Then some of us had better start talking to them," Aage said. "To do that we need to be on Frilandet. And to be on Frilandet we need to take the treatment."

"You can't talk to Kargans," Ansgar said scornfully.

"My mother learned their language," Leif answered. "So will I."

"High time some of us did," Aage agreed.

Ole looked at his son with as much dismay as Hal had looked at Leif. "You're throwing away your future!"

"You always said Frilandet was my future."

"But—to cut yourself off—from the rest of humanity—" Ole stammered.

"Wasn't that what we came here for?" Aage asked.

Ole and Hal looked at one another. One reaps what one sows, Skip thought. "You have a month to decide," Skip reminded them. "As for me, I've committed myself, and I'm looking forward to strawberries with breakfast."

CHAPTER THIRTY

ᨏᨏᨏᨏ

"You look very nicce today."

Kelda wished Calypso would not say that. It brought too many memories, too fresh, of a time when it had been true. But Kelda could no longer face a mirror, even to comb her slowly regrowing hair or straighten her collar. Her birdlike, gnarled hands were bad enough, with their dreadfully thin fingers and thick joints that screamed with pain. It was bad enough to have to sit in an airchair, needing groundlings' aid for things as simple as bathing. But it hurt worst of all to see her own gray eyes in the wrinkled face of a hag.

Calypso planted herself on the grass by Kelda's feet. The Sheppie extended her tentacles toward the sun. "Ssummer approachess."

Kelda dipped her chin in assent. Maybe she should drool, she thought, and complete the picture of an incontinent old relic. She supposed she should be grateful for Calypso's company. Hal avoided her. Perhaps he felt guilty for her plight, or maybe she just reminded him of his own eventual aging. Skip and Suli were too busy for pleasantries, for, having determined which native foods were

safe, they must now settle the nuances of balanced diet.
Per spent what time he could with Kelda, but he also had
to translate *graf* writings and attend to the girls. When he
joined her, Kelda wondered what revulsion he suppressed. When he left, she lapsed into self-pity and if-only.
If only Kelda's immune reaction had confined itself to
vital but replaceable organs like liver and heart, rather
than attacking the tissues that held her body together! If
only Yvette and Disa had taken a few hours longer to
make their discoveries! Then Kelda could have been dead,
heroically dead, remembered with grateful affection and
admiration. Instead she lingered, a crippled burden to herself and everyone else.

"Ole Hansson hass agreed to take the treatment," Calypso said.

"How many does that make?" Kelda asked wearily.

"About a hundred. But the number rissess exxponen-
tially as people ssee no harm to thosse who've gone before."

No harm. No harm to anyone but Kelda, and she had
brought it on herself. A tear trickled down the side of her
nose.

Calypso noticed, of course. "You take no pride in having enabled thiss?" the Sheppie asked.

Angry, Kelda wiped away the tear. "Disa found the
dreamers and the ancients. Yvette found the complicating
antigen. Those things made the real difference."

"Yvette'ss disscovery and the dreamerss' conclus-
sionss required clinical data. You provided that," Calypso
said.

Kelda wanted to believe that her life's ruin had accomplished something. She wanted to believe so badly that
she felt compelled to argue. "The dreamers could have
figured it out."

"Neither they nor we knew enough of human physsiology," the Sheppie countered. "Biological mechanissmss

are eassier to exxplain than to predict. The ssituation required a human ssubject."

That was some solace, if not much, for one who had gone from beauty to witch. Kelda suspected that Calypso had more on her mind than emotional support. "How is Ea's change coming?"

"Very niccely. Sshe hass grown gillss and beginss to attempt sspeech. By ssummer sshe sshould be ready to travel." Calypso wrapped warm tentacles around Kelda. "Are you fit to round the ccircle? Deccissionss musst be made before the sship liftss."

Kelda clenched her gnarled hand until the misshapen joints screamed. She had known this was coming. She would *not* bawl like a baby!

Kelda could not reach the Hall of Voices at all, and she refused to be carried like meat to the Hall of Meeting. Instead the group gathered in a small damp chamber accessible from the river by boat. Kelda slumped in her airchair on a sand spit along the west wall. Per sat on the sand by Kelda. The girls and Sulman perched on a ledge along the opposite wall.

Risky remained submerged in the stream, staying as close as possible to Disa and as far as possible from Buzz-Click, Inanna, and Ea. Kelda hoped that the small room allowed enough distance to forestall sexual stimulation.

Calypso planted herself in shallow water near Kelda. The litany began. "From dust were born the suns, the seas, and life. Dust we are, to dust we shall return..." Kelda dissolved in broken sobs. Per's arm encircled her in the dark. Sulman's tenor, and Disa's and Yvette's soft feminine voices, carried the chant to its finish.

The ensuing silence was broken by Yvette. As always, Calypso back-translated for clarity. "Yvette ssayss on thiss planet sshe hass learned why her father defended the Triopss. Ssometimess dusst'ss demandss transsscend our livess.

"Per ssayss give thankss the pricce wass not sso high here."

Speak for yourself, Kelda thought. But Per was right, she admitted as she looked around the circle. Disa still had parents, even if they had become sadly mismatched.

"I feel," Calypso said slowly, "thiss tassk iss done."

Sulman expressed reservations, with which Kelda agreed. The situation contained grave potential for abuse. Already Burr had remarked that Kargans, bred as slaves, must need new masters. Kargans themselves debated the question. Their civilization could flower, some said, only under outside direction. Others said that twenty centuries had dissolved the chains. Kargans had learned to make their own decisions. Some even spoke of their own re-shaping, modifying the genes implanted by *graf* so long ago. Who would guard the Kargans, in the interim, from human cupidity?

"Some Dawn-gods should remain," Inanna said.

There was an affirmative silence.

Kelda closed her eyes. What had she to look forward to in the Circle, crippled as she was? Retirement to Core, playing backgammon with old Martin while Per traveled the frontier with younger folk? Yes, Dawn needed an ob-server. Kelda knew who it had to be. Dust had swirled her back to Karg and marooned her there. With difficulty, she cleared her throat. "I'll stay," she said in Sheppie and in Kargan, following the custom of the circle she thus tore herself from. She felt as if she were pronouncing her own death sentence.

She was not the only one whose body had changed. Risky spoke. "In dreamer trial I pledged I would not wander. I will stay." In the dimness Kelda saw circlemates gesture assent. Risky's new body was frail, and he had much to learn on Karg.

"I will stay, with Ea," Inanna announced. "She must learn our ways before she travels." Inanna did not want another cavemate as untraditional as Risky, Kelda thought, amused.

"Circle-gods need Kargans," Buzz-Click announced in painfully acquired English. "I go with. My cavemate follows."

"We welcome you," Calypso said in fluent Kargan.

"I'll stay," Per said.

There was one thing in the universe harder for Kelda to say than "I'll stay." She gathered her courage and said it. "You don't need to. Your soul's wrapped in the circle. Go with Dawn, Per."

Kelda saw Disa's huge troubled eyes on them.

Per's hand tightened on Kelda's. "My soul's wrapped up in you, too."

He was being a Sørenson, noble and unrealistic. Her heart breaking, Kelda tried again to set him free. "Your cock's wrapped up in me." Or used to be. "Your soul just came for the ride."

"Don't be cute with me," he chided. "I'll stay. I don't need a scout ship to be First-In."

"Without you, Kelda," Suli said softly, "we'd all be disinherited now. Per's right. The two of you are Dawn's —even if you're here."

A nice sentiment, but nothing like the excitement of exploration, probing virgin planets, wandering the starways between assignments . . .

"Per, Kelda, Inanna, Ea, and Rissky will sstay," Calypso confirmed. "What of Dissa and Yvette?"

Yvette twisted her hands together. Certainly she, like all of them, had seen this coming. Kelda wondered what the girl had decided. Even a new understanding of her father's decision was unlikely to turn Yvette toward First-In. What about her ambitions for the Sheppie genetics institute on Challa? Her work on Karg surely qualified her. But starved as Yvette was for affection and security, Leif posed a hefty temptation.

Yvette wet her lips. "I—I love you all. But I'm not noble enough to be a First-Inner. I want money and a home that doesn't wander, and no responsibility for the fate of planets. Leif and I talked—"

Oh, no, Kelda thought. Yvette was right, she didn't fit First-In, but this god-forsaken backwater was no improvement!

"If I stay now, I'll be tied to Karg forever. It seems better to get my training first." Yvette blinked. Kelda remembered how young love felt to those in its sway. "I don't know what happens then." The tears broke loose. "Aunt Kelda, Uncle Per, I don't want to leave!"

Per waded across the shallow stream to her. "We love you and we'll always welcome you. But you're right, the institute's where you should be. Someday maybe—" He dropped his sentence there. First-Inners didn't say "We'll meet again."

"I will transsmit your application to Challa, with my recommendation," Calypso said. "Until you begin sstudiess there, you will travel with uss."

Yvette sniffed, wiped her face on her sleeve, and dredged up a smile. "Thank you."

Eyes slowly shifted to Disa. Barefoot, she trailed her toes in the water and watched the ripples. Kelda swallowed hard and let Per speak the words in their minds. "You're only sixteen now, Disa, but you've shown yourself a woman. This decision is yours."

He might have gone on, telling Disa that they loved her dearly and would miss her desperately, but that as Jack had entrusted Yvette to Per and Kelda, they would trust Disa to Dawn. Per might have told Disa that she would be truest to them by leaving—but she knew all that.

The girl sat silent for long seconds—perhaps deciding but more probably trying to get control of her voice. It squeaked when she finally spoke. Kelda heard the decision with pride, pain, and no surprise. "Aage talked to me about staying. But I don't want to be a farm wife on Karg. I've got two more years with Dawn. Then I'm applying to Diamond or Aquarius." She sought understanding in her parents' eyes.

Tears streamed down Kelda's cheeks. She wanted to do as Per had, to wade the stream and take Disa in her arms. Instead she sat, a prisoner in the airchair.

Disa reached toward the dark water. Kelda's Kargan was barely good enough to follow her daughter's words. "I'm sorry, He-Risky. I leave, but I will dream of you."

Summer deepened. Kargan rice grass rippled in the fields that the previous year had grown corn and wheat. In Sweetwater Warren and again in the Holmstad armory Karg's residents, native and human, bade their visitors farewell. Finally, under a slowly brightening sky, the departing team boarded ferry. Risky had already said his good-byes, but Inanna and Ea, Per, and Kelda accompanied their circlemates all the way to the lander. Kelda looked ruefully at her body. She didn't fill the silk uniform as she once had. She remembered the elegance and serenity of Dawn's senior stateswoman Li. "I'd like to look like that some day," Kelda had said. The time had come sooner than she had expected or wanted.

Skip rode the ferry, of course. Hal came, too. Still uncomfortable among Kelda's circlemates, her adoptive family, he said little but blinked often. Leif accompanied the team less as Hal's son than as Yvette's beau. The young couple stood apart from the others, their heads close. Suli had invited Erica, in quiet acknowledgment of her public support and many long evenings in private. Beside her stood the girls' schoolmate Gretchen, who had been kind when no one else was.

Aage came, too. Kelda shook her head slightly at the sturdy young figure. He had known Disa how long? Nine months? Three of which he had spoken nothing but slander? He and Disa knew that this was the end for them, but still the girl clung to his hand. Why wasn't she with Kelda and Per?

How Kelda's own parents must have resented Sulman's presence when Kelda herself left Karg, twenty years before! Saying good-bye to a child was hard enough, without that child's attention held by newer, younger, loves. At least Kelda, unlike Canute and Brynhild, approved of her daughter's departure.

They reached the lander unbearably soon. Over the last two weeks the team had scrubbed and safety-checked it to shining perfection. By unspoken tradition, the easiest farewells were said first. Gretchen and Erica murmured final words. While Disa and Yvette bid their young men goodbye, Kelda asked Per to lift her from the chair. She braced herself on crutches, a modified version of Calypso's. Thank dust the sea was calm, so Kelda could stand to see her team away. She exchanged final peace with Buzz-Click, her cavemate, and their groundlings. Eager to escape the open, the Kargans disappeared into the hatch.

Loneliness filled Skip's eyes as Suli shook hands with him. "Sure you won't lift off with us?" the First-Inner asked. "How can I run a lab without you?"

Skip forced a smile. "I'd starve," he joked. "I can't eat ordinary rations anymore, thanks to you." Firm as he might be in his loyalty to Karg, Skip stared wistfully at the space-bound vessel. Kelda shared his feeling.

Warm tentacles diverted her attention from Skip. "I will misss you," Calypso said. "We are grateful for your ssacrificce." She didn't say which sacrifice, the human tester act or staying on Karg. "I and our ccirclematess will do the besst we can for your daughterss."

Kelda squeezed wordlessly back.

Suli turned from final words with Inanna to embrace Per. "If everyone in this universe were Sørenson, we wouldn't need First-In."

Per cuffed him back with poignant playfulness. "So long as you're loose there's no danger of the universe being populated only by Sørensons. Don't get shot by a jealous lover, friend."

"Me?" Suli asked. "I know better than that." Releasing Per, he turned to Kelda, lifting her in an embrace that left her crutches dangling. Automatically she turned her face up for the kiss that had made Suli a legend on so many planets. Tears blurred her vision. It was Suli who had told her, so many years ago, that First-Inners must assume that good-byes were final.

"Kelda," he whispered, "you're as fine a wench as ever was."

Tears came harder when she remembered how wrinkled her face had become.

"I'd have you again today if you'd let me," he said. She felt through the thin silk of their uniforms that he meant it.

She pressed back. "Thanks for everything, Suli." He set her carefully down onto her crutches. "You keep away from my daughter," Kelda warned.

He gave a leer too blatant to be serious. "Isn't she old enough to make her own decisions?" Then, to Kelda's surprise, his expression softened. "And if anyone doesn't respect her decisions, they'll answer to me." He turned to follow Calypso into the hatch.

Kelda wept again.

She wept harder when she embraced her daughter. Disa pressed quivering lips together and smiled. "I'll be careful, Mom. It's you I'm worried about. Please don't do any more experiments."

Kelda laughed a little hysterically. "I've had my fill of it. Let us know when you're initiated. Maybe we can meet at a jamboree."

"I'll let you know," Disa promised.

Kelda knew there would be no more jamborees for her. But final good-byes or no, she needed the fiction.

As Disa wrapped her arms around Per's neck, Kelda found herself face to face with Yvette. The girl was crying even harder than Kelda was. "I don't know what to say, Aunt Kelda." She sobbed. "I love you."

"I love you, too." Kelda snuggled Yvette close. "We all have to grow up. I'm as proud of you as your dad would be."

Then the hatch shut behind the team, and the ferry backed away to give the lander room. Kelda sank back into her seat, remembering the day less than a year earlier when she had piloted that lander down. She had never dreamed then that she would never leave . . .

The lander engines started. The ferry rocked in the wake of the moving ship. Kelda hastily killed all lift on her airchair. Per stood behind her, his hands on her shoulders.

Dawn broke over the horizon.

The lander accelerated, breaking free of the waves as it picked up speed. Ea and Inanna retreated to the ferry's pilothouse. The colonists stood along the railings, leaving Per and Kelda alone in the center of the deck. The departing ship banked for a farewell pass, rosy sun glinting off the starred circle on its side. Still at subsonic speed, it waggled its fins—so awkwardly that it nearly stalled.

"Calypso's getting clumsy," Kelda said in a voice that cracked.

Per's fingers sank into her shoulders. "That wasn't Calypso." Less experienced hands had helmed that dip.

High above, the lander broke the sound barrier. In a thin flare of light, it vanished skyward.

CODA

SUNLIGHT FLASHED IN DISA'S EYES AS SHE GUIDED DAWN Three's lander across the terminator and into Karg's atmosphere. From below, she knew, the ship appeared to be a plunging ball of fire. It trembled as Disa dropped it lower, braking off hundreds of miles per hour against the atmosphere's friction. As her ship slowed to subsonic speed, Disa circled and followed the coastline to Meade Sound. She saw the delta clearly, and the barrier island offshore. "Where's the camp?" she asked her copilot in Sheppie.

"Ssomewhere in thosse cliffss," Calypso answered, flashing an arrow on the visual-integration screen that coordinated the window view with map data from the navigation banks.

At that speed, Disa had little time to stare. She turned the lander upwind for final descent, sighted the welcome ferry, and tipped her ship in an exuberant bob.

"I ssee you have learned to ssignal without sstalling," Calypso remarked.

"Practice makes perfect," Disa retorted in English, because the proverb did not translate well into Sheppie. "May I splash down?"

"As you pleasse," Calypso answered.

Disa took the lander lower, skipped it once against the water to confirm altitude and dump speed and, she had to confess, because she liked the splash. Finally she dropped the ship to a halt. Steam outside obscured vision through the pilot's window.

"Niccely done," Calypso said.

Disa pursed her lips for a long exhalation. Much as she enjoyed piloting, she still felt relief at each safe landing. Miscalculated velocity or hidden reefs killed quickly. She didn't bother to scan approaching small craft for weaponry. That, at least, Karg had grown beyond. *"Aya tasish,"* she said, which meant "thank you" in Sheppie. Then she unharnessed and swam through the water-filled cockpit toward the upper exit.

In the small lock behind the hatch, Yvette, two Sheppie scientists, and Disa pressed back against the wall, while Dawn's team gathered into a circle. "Since my people stand neutral in this negotiation, and I am eldest of them present, I shall serve as speaker," rumbled Gris, a handsome, well-groomed Elysian. "Do you consent?"

The humans, Li, Chan, and Phillippe, nodded assent, as did Gris's fellow Elysians. He repeated the question in Kargan and Sheppie. Buzz-Click and her cavemate rasped agreement. Calypso said "yes," too. When young, Disa had thought it a silly ritual. Everyone agreed on who would speak for them before they started! But she had since come to understand the uncertainties that lay beyond the hatch, and thus the need for confirmation.

Gris returned to English. "Do any wish to withdraw?"

Phillippe, tall, black-haired, and black-skinned, shook his head. He had joined the circle since Disa's departure, and she did not know him well, but she thought him good-looking and so did Yvette. Leif had better be glad the voyage hadn't been any longer than it was.

Sturdy, white-thatched Chan slid an arm around Li's

waist. She smiled up at him, and then at Gris. "We'll do what we came for." Disa wondered how long it had been since Chan and Li's last field assignment. As Circle Dawn's human coordinators, they normally moved only with Core itself.

Gris repeated his question in Kargan and Sheppie and received assent. "May we recall our place in dust," he said, signaling for recitation of the litany.

Disa felt oddly choked as Dawn's team swore in without her. She tossed her head. Her newly acquired earring swung reassuringly against her cheek. Dawn wore ruby and topaz. Disa's hoop sparkled in sapphire, emerald, and diamond. She had a lifetime of swearings-in ahead, she reminded herself.

The team finished its litany and dropped hands, tentacles, and claws. Gris nodded at Disa.

Leaving her spot by the wall, she braced both legs, wrenched the latch open, and let the hatch down. Blinking in morning sunshine, she stepped out on the low balcony formed by the hatch door. The air, as always after weeks in space, smelled strong and spicy. Scents she had not known she remembered nearly overwhelmed her.

People waved from the ferry deck. "Disa! Heg, Disa!"

Legs planted apart against sea-motion, Disa raised both hands in greeting.

Hal's honor band must have practiced nonstop since Dawn's first communique had arrived, for they never missed a note. Before Phillippe could fetch the ladder, Per, in circle white, stepped forward to swing Disa down. Leif, grown taller and broader, reached for Yvette with eyes full of questions and hope. Disa grinned. Wait until he learned that with Yvette came representatives of the galaxy's most prestigious DNA-genetics institute!

Disa felt a moment of hesitation when she saw Aage Hanson behind Leif. How could she explain her new horizons to steady, lovable Aage? Worry vanished as she saw

Gretchen, markedly pregnant, by Aage's side. They would do well together.

"Disa!" Kelda still rode an airchair, and her face still carried twenty years more than it should have, but her eyes were bright as she rose to hug her daughter. Half laughing, half crying, she traced the circle on Disa's shirt, then reached to touch her earring. "Aquarius?" she asked.

"Aquarius," Disa confirmed. How could Kelda have any doubt about the oxygen-double-hydrogen logo of First-In's oldest terrestrial-exploration circle? "I just finished Grand Tour. I can stay here about three months. Then I take passage to Tripoli to start my general studies sequence."

"Dissa iss very eager to reach universsity," Calypso said. "At leasst one of her Aquarian teammatess will join her there . . ."

Kelda arched her eyebrows inquisitively.

Disa blushed. "I was going to bring him here, but the last stop on Tour was his home planet and he wanted to talk to his folks before he went to Tripoli, but I know you'll like him, Mom, he's taller than Dad and speaks twelve languages and swims like fish and we were thinking maybe if I specialize in aquatic adaptation and he does some work in—" She paused for breath and realized that out of all that her parents had absorbed only the one most pertinent detail. "Anyway you'll like him."

Kelda and Per grinned at each other.

Disa, much as she wanted to tell her parents what was going on in her life, moved respectfully aside as Phillippe helped Aunt Li and Uncle Chan down the ladder. Li, six inches taller than Kelda, held the younger woman in the light, respectful embrace of the elderly and kissed her forehead. "Peace, Kelda. I regret the price you paid, but you can be proud of your gift to this planet." Li had to stand on tiptoe to kiss Per. "Your cousin Hulda passed our

camp on Trin with honors and just started training at
Core. She sends your Family's greetings."

Per's eyes wrinkled in amusement. "Lindy's daughter?
That's poetic justice! But I thought she was still a kid."
His eyes unfocused as he tallied years. "She was a year
younger than Disa, so she'd be nineteen now, give or take
a little lag—I'm getting old, Li. Losing track of time."

"Don't get too lazy, Per Sørenson, because you're on
active assignment again."

He blinked in shock. Clearly he had thought his First-
In career at an end. Kelda reached anxiously, possessively, for his arm.

"You, too, Kelda Nygren," Li announced. "Think we'd
let one pert as you away?"

Skip tried to say something to Disa. She smiled, put her
finger to her lips, and gestured with her eyes that he
should listen.

"Don't tease me, Li," Kelda said. "I'm stuck on this
backwater planet."

Phillippe, beside Skip, cleared his throat. "Excuse me,
but the Statsminister desires a formal greeting."

Li gestured imperiously. "Tell him we need five minutes
first."

"You tell him," Phillippe muttered, but like everyone
he obeyed her.

"This backwater planet," Li said, "will soon be seeing
interplanetary traffic on the surface, and not just up there
at the station."

"Why?" Kelda asked.

Leif interrupted. "Uncle Skip!" He gestured at the dirtside Sheppies who waited patiently by the railing. "Yvette
says the Challa Institute wants to open a branch here!"

"Huh?" Skip asked. "What?"

Li nodded. "Calypso's folk want to talk to the
dreamers. Since Kargans aren't much for travel, the
Sheppies decided to come here."

Disa had worried since she heard this plan. How would a colony that restricted access to its own orbital station tolerate a steady stream of alien visitors? "Will the Frilandena agree?" she asked her mother.

"Ask the Frilandena," Kelda said. "But be warned they've changed a lot since you were here. Conversation with Kargans has been an exciting experience for them, and they want to know more about the galaxy. Yet travel to human planets is very difficult, and they're still a bit shy of visiting alien worlds. To have the galaxy come here would be a blessing—"

"I hate to be a pessimist," Per said, "but how will all these southpaw visitors fit into Kargan ecology? I don't want to live our crisis over again."

Li rubbed her fingers together in the gesture that meant money. "For what the Sheppies will pay, they can grow food in orbit or ship it in. But not everyone who comes will pose that problem."

"Huh?" Kelda said.

"Kelda, you better give up your temper and learn diplomacy. In six weeks a team comes in from Circle Helix."

"Helix?" Kelda asked. "What does Helix want with us? They're northpaw—oh."

"Right. After your application of Calypso's Twist, a lot of peoples are rethinking the terran-type planets' split into independent stereochemical communities. We're realizing just how accessible our planets are to northpaws, and theirs to us. With maneuvers very similar to what you did here, the split between right- and left-sugared worlds could be bridged, as well. That means major First-In contracts and restructuring the circles themselves. Helix will meet us here with at least one of their senior coordinators, to dicker a conjugation with Dawn." She paused, bright black eyes on Kelda. "You ready to work like a First-Inner again?"

Disa lost track of the conversation at that point, for Aage had approached guiding a large opaque tank. "Here's somebody that wants to talk to you."

"Risky!" Disa scrambled to unzip the tank's collapsible light-lock. "He-Risky!"

"Welcome, changeling. I have many dreams to tell you."

It seemed no time at all before Gris interrupted their conversation. "You may visit later. Right now, kinswoman from Aquarius, we ask you to speak peace for us."

Dawn's representatives gathered, arm in arm, in the traditional half-circle, including even tank-bound Risky, Ea, and Inanna. Kelda and Per took places, too. Disa had never seen Kelda's face happier.

The visiting Sheppies attached themselves to the right end of the semicircle, with Yvette beside them. Next to her, Leif began an arc of Frilandena. That was how the greeting formation was supposed to work, Disa thought: circlemates in solidarity with one another but also continuous with ordinary society, gathering multiple species into fellowship. Gris gestured Disa to the left end of the half-circle, by Buzz-Click. Skip reached for Disa's free hand, closing the gap between Circle and colony on both sides.

Hal, in full statsministerial regalia, cleared his throat. "On behalf of Frilandet Colony, I greet your circle. May peace attend you on KetKarga."

Disa sucked in her breath. They had resolved the old quarrel over worldnaming! The planet still bore the name the humans gave it: "world of freedom." But it bore it in the native Kargan language.

The other First-Inners looked expectantly at Disa. She squared her shoulders and lifted her voice. "Circles Dawn and Aquarius give thanks for your welcome. My friends, we come in peace, and hope it deepens."

About the Author

Marti Steussy is a Renaissance Woman. An ordained minister and Ph.D. candidate in Hebrew Bible, she has also done graduate work in human nutrition and written maintenance manuals for line haul tractors. She based her first science fiction novel, *Forest of the Night*, on logging experience in the woods of northern Minnesota. *Dreams of Dawn* she researched in the caves of central Tennessee and southern Kentucky. "I haven't decided what to try for the next book. Mountain climbing? Scuba? Origami?"

Marti's husband, Nic, a family practitioner, assists her writing by making coffee, brainstorming, and occasionally taking the kids out of town. Cally and Dave, three and five when this book was completed, think writing looks fun—Dave's hard at work on his own dinosaur novel.

Family, writing, academics, and ministry make Marti's life a busy one. Her formula for coping hasn't changed: "Marry a saint, and ignore the dust on the baseboards."